Ultrazone

"The ghosts who shadow the living through the alleys of Tangier are not only intimately alive, they are as vivid as Joyce's ruminating Dubliners in a tale as rich as anything by Poe. What's more, *Ultrazone*'s mix of fact and fiction gives it the authority of a well-researched document nested within an exotic, fully imagined world."

—JAN HERMAN

"Reading *Ultrazone* is like watching a trippy ghost movie full of your favorite beat icons. All inhabited Tangier during the hedonistic Interzone period, and here they haunt the mysterious underbelly of this magical and sinister city. Fun and riveting!"

—SARA DRIVER

Ultrazone is equally a serious book—the writers tapping into that particular world of beliefs in spirits, devils, curses, witchcraft that is so unlike the West—and funny, in a light-touch way. Ghosts gather in well-tended cemeteries, discuss their plans of action. And, yes, there are Mugwumps . . . This life after death opens up so many possibilities. We return to the unfolding days of an as yet unpublished *Naked Lunch*. The book has taken me by surprise, and it's a delight to read.

—KEVIN RING, *Beat Scene*

MARK TERRILL
FRANCIS POOLE

Ultrazone

VERSE CHORUS PRESS

Published by Verse Chorus Press LLC, Portland, Oregon, USA
Issued under license from The Visible Spectrum

Cover design by Mike Reddy
Interior photographs © Francis Poole
Interior design: Steve Connell | *steveconnell.net*

ISBN 978-1-959163-11-4

Library of Congress Control Number: 2025932254

You never know what's hidden in the sleeve of the qaftan.
—Paul Bowles

Prelude

Tangier is a strange and mysterious place. The city itself dates back at least two and a half thousand years, but archeological evidence, including fossilized humanoid bones, shows that the land it sits on has been inhabited for perhaps as long as two hundred thousand years. The oldest historical relics in Tangier—besides the aged dowagers and queens who live in faded luxury in the Marshan—include a necropolis with Phoenician tombs. Legend says that Tangier was founded by Antaeus, a Libyan giant who compelled visitors to wrestle with him and after killing them, built a house from their skulls.

The city lies on the northwestern tip of Africa, at the edge of the ancient world. Just to the east the Pillars of Hercules—Jebel Tarik (Tarik's Mountain, which the English call Gibraltar) and Jebel Moussa—guard the entrance to the Mediterranean which separates Spain and Christendom from Muslim North Africa.

Tangier is part of Morocco these days, but from 1924 to 1956 it was the Tangier International Zone, jointly administered by several European powers. In those "Interzone" years, it developed a reputation as an inexpensive and permissive place for artists, writers, and adventurers to live and be left alone to follow their various artistic and sexual pursuits. The American expatriate writers Paul and Jane Bowles are the figures most closely associated with Tangier, but many others came and went, such as Francis Bacon, Truman Capote, Tennessee Williams, and Alfred Chester. The artist and experimental writer Brion Gysin became obsessed with the Sufi trance music of the Master Musicians of Joujouka from the mountains south of Tangier, and introduced them to the Rolling Stones in the 1960s. William Burroughs moved to Tangier in 1954 and tried to kick a drug habit while writing the "routines" which were eventually edited into what became his infamous novel *Naked Lunch*; for him, as for many, Tangier was "a sanctuary of noninterference."

Though its clear skies, Mediterranean vistas, and exotic mixture of cultures beckon, Tangier's charms only slightly veil the underlying currents of an impenetrable native consciousness, in which belief in animism and the casting of magically induced spells continues to this day. The city attracts more than its share of neurotics, smugglers, drifters, hustlers, poseurs, and lost souls. They come from America and all over Europe, drawn like insects to a black-light bug zapper, often congregating in the cafés and restaurants of the medina around the Petit Socco, referred to by locals and long-time expats by its old Spanish name, the Zoco Chico.

The English have had an interest in Tangier since the mid-seventeenth century, when it was acquired from Portugal as part of the dowry given to Charles II on his marriage to the infanta Catherine of Braganza. Their occupying forces were subject to ceaseless attack by local tribes, however, and in 1684 they abandoned the city after first destroying it. But since it is in their nature to believe they have the right to feel at home anywhere, the British found it difficult to keep away, and over the next two centuries they gradually filtered back in. In August 1883, Sir John Hay Drummond Hay, Her Britannic Majesty's Minister to Tangier, made a request to the Sultan of Morocco for land on which to build an "English Church" for the expatriate community.

In October of that year a message from the Sultan, delivered by the Khalifa, the Sultan's representative in Tangier, declared that His Majesty was pleased to grant the infidels a parcel of land for the purpose of erecting a place of worship. The site granted by the Sultan was on the western edge of the main bazaar, the Grand Socco, wedged between two Muslim cemeteries and a coal market, and bounded on one side by a foul stream. In late 1884, a prefabricated iron church was purchased from a company in London and erected in twenty-eight days. This temporary church served the parishioners of Tangier until a permanent church was completed in 1897. Constructed in the Moorish style by builders and craftsmen from Fez, it was named for St. Andrew the Apostle. The Church of St. Andrew—St. Andrew's, as it would be called—was an example of the finest design and artistic standards in the Andalusian tradition.

The cemetery of St. Andrew's Church was not established until 1906, following the drawing up of burial regulations by the church wardens. Initially only British subjects had the right to be buried there. A church committee had to approve the design of proposed tombstones; there would be no guardian angels perched forlornly on broken urns, no mournful madonnas, no plump cherubs cavorting across headstones. The first person to be buried in the churchyard was Edward Joseph Taylor, a typhoid victim laid to rest on April 9, 1906. Not long after, a plan for the proper layout of the cemetery was drawn up, complete with landscaping and plantings by a trained gardener and horticulturist.

The establishment of the St. Andrew's Church cemetery came as a relief to the Anglo-Christian community, given the careless way burials had been performed at the Tangier cemetery where the English had previously been interred. Graves were often too shallow and haphazardly dug, leading to the subsequent opening of vaults and other abuses. Many coffins and their contents had to be exhumed for reburial. In short, it was difficult for the dead to find the eternal repose they deserved before St. Andrew's opened its welcoming gates. But was the peace and quiet to last?

Batterie Nâam

EL GUENAOUA

KASBA

Pal. du Sultan

Pal. du Gouvern.

DJENAN EL CAPTAN

Prison

Ancien Trésor

Tribunal

DAR EL BAROUD

Rue de AMEIRAH

BELAI

Kasba

Douane

Batterie des Salves

Porte de la Mer

Batterie du Port

Télégr. anglais

Collège Israëlite

Marchan

Télégraphe Anglais

GUESNAIA

SKALAYED

R. des Chrétiens

Rue de la Marine

Poste angl.

c

C

Grande Mosquée

PETIT SOCCO

Poste espag.

R. de la Leg.

Poste et Télégr. français

Ancien cimet. chrétien

Anc.ne Légation d'Allemagne

ère nan

Montagne

ulman

Francisco

Rue Ez Ziaguine

Eglise Catholique

Marché couv.

BENI IDER

Rue de la Dguane

Boulevard

Cimetière protestant

GRAND SOCCO

Postes Tél. chérifiens

Collège Espagnolte

Rue

Rue de la

Cimetière Juif

Légation d'Angleterre

Légation des

suselité bel

Légation de France

a

Cimet.re Israël

Théâtre espagnol

de la Plage

Rue du

Résidence

Rue du

1

It was that time of day when the length of a man's shadow is the same as his height, and in the cemetery of the Anglican Church of St. Andrew in Tangier, there is one shadow that always falls in the wrong direction. It's the shadow of Walter Harris, usually wearing one of the many Riffian tribal disguises he had worn when alive. Harris had lived in Tangier for many years as a correspondent for *The Times* and a member of the British secret service. In many ways Harris was the ur-Tangerino: a world traveler, an arms dealer, a colorful, gay expatriate author shrouded in mystery and intrigue—a veritable prototype for the many eccentric characters who would populate Tangier in the years to come.

When Harris died suddenly in 1933 at the age of 66, he had been living in Malta, but his body was returned to Tangier and buried in St. Andrew's cemetery, in accordance with what his surviving relatives assumed he would have wanted. Given his long residence in Morocco, his many legendary exploits and highly placed friends, it was a memorable funeral. The *Tangier Gazette* reported that an immense crowd followed his cortège from the port up through the medina. Among the chief mourners were the distinguished Moroccans, Sir Mehdi Menebhi and Sidi Kacem Duckali. A simple and elegant headstone in the form of a miniature Moorish façade sheltered by a projecting roof of green tiles was later erected over his grave. Since then his ghost had reportedly been seen many times at night, moving through the churchyard in the leafy shadows cast by the full moon, and sometimes even in broad daylight. His ghost was apparently a restless one.

Moustapha, the cemetery watchman, although relatively well versed in Moroccan black magic, didn't know the appropriate spell for getting rid of the ghost of the Englishman. Having been brought up as a Muslim, he'd been taught that ghosts as such did not exist, in fact—there were only djinns, supernatural creatures who inhabit an unseen world, a dimension beyond the visible universe of humans. Like human beings, djinns can be good, evil, or neutrally benevolent, and hence have free will, like humans and unlike angels. But after many years working in the cemetery, Moustapha had come to believe that ghosts existed as well, and often haunted a particular locale, thus becoming a source of continual annoyance, like the ghost of Walter Harris. There was a café on the other side of the medina where an old sorcerer with a lazy eye could usually be found smoking kif. On several occasions Moustapha had seen him in the cemetery picking datura flowers and other strange plants. Perhaps it was time to pay him a visit.

Zora, the queen of the cemetery cats, rubbed herself against Moustapha's leg and gave him one of her looks. Zora's looks always meant something; he wondered what it was this time. Then he noticed a shadow moving behind a large tombstone. He grabbed his staff and walked slowly toward it, his footsteps on the dry leaves the only sound in the otherwise silent cemetery. Suddenly he heard the metallic twang of a sitar and immediately knew whose shadow he'd seen. It was Ravi Kahn, the expatriate Indian, come to play a devotional raga at the grave of his wife, the painter Brunhilde Reinhart. Ravi's brother Tarik owned a small bakkal in the Zoco Chico and Moustapha owed him five hundred dirhams. So there was no need for a confrontation with Ravi Khan.

Moustapha turned slowly and walked back to his post near the cemetery gate. Maybe I can ask the sorcerer for a spell that will make Tarik forget what I owe him, he thought, scratching his chin while watching a lizard doing slow-motion push-ups in the sun. And, Allah be praised, I would also like to silence that cursed sitar. But most of all I would like to get rid of the bothersome ghost of that Englishman.

All that together would be a lot to ask, though, and the sorcerer would want to be reimbursed commensurately. A sheep or a goat might cover the bill, but Moustapha had neither. The only thing he had of any real value was a dusty old fedora Moustapha's mother had given him, a relic from the days when she worked as a maid in the Hotel El Muniria, which had passed into local legend as the place where William S. Burroughs wrote *Naked Lunch*, and other members of the Beat Generation such as Jack Kerouac, Gregory Corso, Allen Ginsberg, and Peter Orlovsky also stayed. Moustapha's mother didn't know for sure whose hat it was, although she thought its previous owner had been Paul Lund, a former smuggler and jailbird who later ran a bar in the Rue Moussa Ben Noussair. But his mother was dead and there was no one to challenge him if Moustapha were to claim the hat had in fact belonged to Burroughs, who after all was hardly ever seen without a fedora. That would make it a much more valuable item, perhaps something he could sell to a collector or even some unsuspecting tourist.

From the tinny-sounding loudspeakers mounted on the minaret of a nearby mosque came the low-fi sound of the muezzin's pre-recorded call to Asr, the afternoon prayer. *Allahu akbar, Allahu akbar* wavered out across the sun-drenched rooftops where rows of laundry flapped and snapped in the afternoon breeze coming off the Strait of Gibraltar. Moustapha took advantage of the timing and slipped out of the cemetery. He walked over to his sister Laila's house, where he often ate and slept, and where he kept a few possessions stored in an old trunk. Laila asked if he would like something to eat but Moustapha said he only wanted to get something from his trunk to sell in the market. After retrieving the fedora, Moustapha left and went to his regular café on the Boulevard Pasteur. It was filled with a noisy late afternoon crowd who were drinking tea and smoking. He sat nervously fingering the hat brim as the waiter approached. "Salaam," said the waiter, an old friend. "That hat looks like it belonged to a Nasrani. Did you steal it?"

If there was one thing Moustapha could not abide, it was being falsely accused of wrongdoing. "No!" he replied adamantly. "My mother gave it to me. She used to work at El Muniria, where many foreign writers used to live. One of them left his hat there when he couldn't pay his bill. Later he became famous and now I hope to sell the hat."

"What famous writer?" asked the waiter.

"William Burroughs. He died a few years ago."

"Never heard of him." The waiter took Moustapha's order and walked away.

Moustapha looked across the street and caught a glimpse of Aicha, the ancient prostitute and part-time sorceress, in her totally out-of-date cat-eye sunglasses, bouffant hairdo, and blood-red djellaba. Some people said she'd been around when Picasso painted *Guernica*. These days she was just a walking monument to times gone by, her once striking features now faded by age, her supernatural powers a mere echo of their former potency.

During her years as a prostitute Aicha had known many famous men and women, and was said to have learned magic at the hands of a Riffian woman. It was rumored that Aicha put spells on wealthy expatriates, including the heiress Barbara Hutton, so that she received large sums of money from them, enough to live in comfort in her small villa on the Old Mountain. Aicha's sister, Cherifa, had a long, troubled liaison with the writer Jane Bowles, and was said to be partly responsible for Jane's ill-health and eventual death—some even speculated Cherifa had put a spell on her.

It occurred to Moustapha that Aicha might be able to solve his problems for him. In exchange he could offer her, not the hat, but cuttings from plants that grew in St. Andrew's cemetery. It was believed that *materia magica* from Nasrani graves held great powers when used in sorcery. The more Moustapha thought about the idea the more he liked it. He could also offer her fragments of old tombstones, something else of value to sorcerers. As he finished his glass of tea, Aicha disappeared among the crowds.

Moustapha paid for his tea and hurried down the boulevard until he had almost caught up to her, then followed her from a distance. At one point she turned around 180 degrees and continued walking, but now facing backward. Moustapha had seen her do that before; it was one of her many eccentricities, allegedly the result of her dealings with magic and drugs. A minute later she swiveled around again without breaking stride. Moustapha continued to follow her as she turned down a side street and entered the door of Le New York Bar. Small, windowless, smoky, and usually filled with drunk Moroccans and a few adventurous tourists, it was the sort of place Moustapha would normally never go into, but he went in after Aicha.

It took a few moments for his eyes to adjust to the gloom. The bar ran along the right-hand wall; Aicha was seated alone at one of the tables to his left. On the walls hung paintings in garish Day-Glo colors on black velvet depicting Janis Joplin, Clint Eastwood, Bruce Lee, and other celebrities. The jukebox was playing a song by Creedence Clearwater Revival.

Moustapha went over and sat down at Aicha's table just as the waiter approached. He gestured toward her; she ordered a cognac and he ordered a bottle of Stork beer, both of which he paid for.

"To what do I owe this pleasure?" Aicha asked, one of her painted-on eyebrows rising above the rim of her sunglasses.

"I need your help. And maybe you could use mine," Moustapha said, placing the fedora on the chair next to him.

Moustapha told her about the paranormal goings-on in St. Andrew's cemetery and expressed his hope that she might be able to resolve them, in exchange for datura and other plants that grew there, plus some pieces of old tombstones. He also mentioned the fedora, thinking it might somehow be of use.

Aicha removed her sunglasses and placed them on the table, then took a sip of her cognac, considering Moustapha's offer. Her eyes were a cold aqua blue that reminded Moustapha of the snowpack he'd once seen high in the Atlas Mountains.

"And you say that hat belonged to William Burroughs?" she said thoughtfully.

"With absolute certainty," Moustapha replied, picking up the hat for her to see.

Aicha eyed the fedora critically and shook a Dunhill from its package, then offered one to Moustapha, which he refused with a silent wave of his hand. She lit her cigarette with a tarnished brass lighter and exhaled a cloud of blue smoke that quickly merged with the haze that lingered overhead.

"Well, starting with your first problem, the best way to fight ghosts is with another ghost. With that hat, I can try to conjure up the ghost of William Burroughs and use him to chase the other ghosts from the cemetery. There's no guarantee, but it's worth a try. Tonight we have a full moon, which is perfect. We should meet at midnight at the cemetery. I'll bring most of what we'll need; the rest I can get there."

Surprised, Moustapha nodded and said, "Yes, fine."

Aicha finished her cognac, stubbed out her cigarette, and without saying anything more, got up and walked out of the bar. Moustapha looked at the hat which was on his lap and thought, Hey hat, you are going to bring magic and good luck. He drank the last of his beer and left.

As he walked back toward the boulevard, Moustapha had another idea. He would stop by the El Muniria where Burroughs had stayed, in case Burroughs's ghost was lingering there. If the hat had indeed belonged to Burroughs, it might take on some of Burroughs's mojo and acquire more power; power that Aicha could use. Moustapha knew the woman who managed the hotel and for a few dirhams he was sure she would let him in. When he knocked on the door, a maid opened it holding a bucket of bleach water in one hand. He asked if the manager was there and was told she was at the market. Moustapha asked if he could come in and the maid said no, unless he wanted to rent a room. He offered her fifty dirhams if she would let him see the room that William Burroughs had stayed in. The maid seemed annoyed but shrugged and took the money.

Moustapha followed her down a flight of stairs and along a short hallway which led to the garden. She stopped in front of a dark blue door with the number 9 on it. "This is the Burroughs room. I was about to clean the floors, but you can have a quick look and then you must leave." She opened the door and Moustapha felt a cold blast of air on his face and neck. He tried to step inside but the maid, who was rather stout, blocked his path.

He could see that the room was simply furnished with a bed, a chair, a small table with a lamp, and a few pieces of Moroccan folk art on the walls. Above the bed was a framed photo of William Burroughs wearing a fedora. It looked identical to the hat in Moustapha's hand. Burroughs's deadpan yet piercing gaze seemed to be looking directly into Moustapha's soul. The hairs on the back of his neck stood up, and he backed away. His hands were trembling as he surreptitiously rubbed the hat against the door. "Now get out before someone sees you," said the maid, moving toward him with her bulk. She closed the door again and locked it.

When he stepped outside into the Rue Magellan the hat actually felt warmer, and Moustapha smiled to himself. Perhaps it had indeed picked up some of Burroughs's ghostly power. It was now close to five o'clock and time to lock the gate to the cemetery, so Moustapha hurried back to St. Andrew's. He had left his young nephew Yousef to watch over things while he was gone.

As Moustapha passed the café where he had been earlier, the waiter came out and called after him. "There were two American tourists here after you left, young kids with long hair and rucksacks. They were asking about Paul Bowles and Mohammed Mrabet and that writer you mentioned, Burroughs. I told them I knew someone who wanted to sell his hat and they were very interested. I sent them up to the cemetery to find you."

"It's not for sale anymore." Moustapha could feel the hat getting warmer still in his hands as he spoke.

"How could I know that? I only wanted to help you."

"Never mind," Moustapha said, turning and starting toward the cemetery, aware of the hat getting warmer and warmer as he walked.

When he arrived at the gate he couldn't see Yousef anywhere. He walked into the cemetery and called his nephew's name, but there was no sign of him. Zora the cat emerged from behind a tombstone and looked up at Moustapha with what he interpreted to be a concerned expression. She seemed to be looking at something behind him, but before Moustapha could turn around he heard their voices.

"Hey, there's the dude with Burroughs's hat."

Moustapha turned around and saw two kids, late teens or early twenties, one with long curly brown hair and brown eyes, the other with long blonde hair and blue eyes. They were wearing T-shirts, shorts, and sandals, and had large rucksacks on their backs. The one with the brown hair approached Moustapha. "Hey, is that the hat you want to sell, the one that used to belong to William Burroughs?"

Moustapha looked down at the hat, hesitated a moment, then looked back up at the two kids. "It's no longer for sale. I still need it."

"What do you mean, you still need it? I'll give you fifty dollars for it, right now." The kid produced a fifty-dollar bill and waved it in the air.

Moustapha could feel the hat getting really hot now. "No," he said, "I still need the hat. Maybe later."

"Ah, come on man, I'll make it a hundred." The kid produced another fifty-dollar bill and waved them both at Moustapha.

"I'm sorry. Perhaps tomorrow or the next day." By now the hat was almost too hot to hold.

"Okay, dude, we'll come back tomorrow. But can I just see it for a moment? Maybe try it on?"

Moustapha could anyway barely hold the hat anymore. He tossed it to the kid, who grabbed it and put it on his head.

"Perfect fit! But hey, what the hell? It's *hot*, like *way fucking hot*. What's that all about? Shit, man, it's—"

Before the kid could finish, the hat burst into flames. He knocked it off his head and it landed on the ground between the three of them, where it flared up in an blaze of blue, red, green, and gold flames, with showers of sparks and acrid white smoke.

"What the fuck, man," said the blonde kid, stepping back from the flames. "This is some kind of wacky Moroccan voodoo or something."

"Let's get the hell out of here," said the brown-haired kid, and the two of them turned and ran out of the cemetery.

Moustapha tried to stomp out the flames as best he could, but by the time the fire was out there remained only a pile of flaky black ashes. He went into the tiny watchman's shack next to the gate and grabbed a sheet of old newspaper, then scooped the ashes into the newspaper and folded it into a small packet which he put into the pocket of his djellaba. He called out again for Yousef but there was still no sign of him. As he locked the gate of the cemetery, something inside caught his eye. Amid the long shadows cast by the tombstones in the early evening light, one shadow was definitely leaning the wrong way. Moustapha spat on the ground and turned toward his sister's house, where hopefully dinner would be waiting for him.

2

When the taxi let Aicha off at her villa on the Old Mountain, Mohammed, her watchman, was standing by to open the large gate. At the same moment the old fedora burst into flames in the cemetery, Aicha had felt a burning pain at the back of her neck. I must find the source of this pain, she thought. She went straight to the salon, removed her embroidered slippers, and stretched out on the banquette. Pressing her fingers to her temples, she was gradually able to visualize the scene with the young Americans and Moustapha. When she saw the burning hat, she realized that Burroughs's ghost, or whatever djinn had been inhabiting the hat, was now free. All Moustapha had was a pile of useless ashes.

But why had the hat gone up in flames—and, if it was indeed Burroughs's ghost, where had it gone? Aicha considered the possibilities. The ghost must still be in the cemetery, she decided, perhaps searching for something new to inhabit. This will be more difficult than I thought, and Moustapha (whom Aicha had concluded was something of a fool) will have to give me more than a few plant cuttings and pieces of Nasrani tombs.

It was almost ten o'clock, and a full moon had risen over the Bay of Tangier. Aicha went to her bedroom and opened an old inlaid wooden box. Inside were various dried herbs and other objects: vials of water from magic springs in the Rif, monkey teeth, horned viper skin, tiger whiskers, falcon claws, dried lizard feet, as well as her fingernail clippings and pubic hair. She selected several items and placed them in a black velvet pouch with gold-braid drawstrings, which she put in the pocket of her djellaba. The burning pain in her neck suddenly vanished. She still needed one item that was not in the box—dried snail slime. She closed the lid and went out the kitchen door and down the stairs into the expansive garden.

Clouds were scudding past overhead, propelled by the stiff breeze blowing through the strait. One minute the full moon was shining down with bright metallic intensity, the next a wall of passing clouds plunged the night into murky darkness. Across the strait could be seen the twinkling lights of the coast of Spain. Aicha made her way through the garden toward the fishpond which lay behind a large bamboo grove. The wind rustled the leaves of the bamboo in erratic raspy crescendos. In a flash of moonlight Aicha saw the goldfish and koi circling slowly in the depths of the pond, their bodies glowing iridescently. Across the stones surrounding the fishpond was a shimmering trail. With a paring knife she'd taken from the kitchen she scraped a small amount of the snail slime onto a piece of paper, which she carefully folded and added to the other items in the velvet pouch.

From a nearby villa came the sound of amplified music, somewhat distorted by the rise and fall of the wind. At first she thought it was an electric guitar, but then recognized it as an electric oud. That strange musician from New York, Tony Mahoney, had a recording studio in his villa and liked to practice with all the doors and windows open, which Aicha sometimes found quite irritating. From the other direction, further up on the Old Mountain, she heard a low roar, followed by deep growls and screeches. That would be from the villa of Mr. Garland, the eccentric English millionaire with a menagerie of exotic animals, including lions, tigers, and Barbary macaques.

While Aicha was listening to the rustling of the bamboo, the wavering electric oud music, and the distant roars of the lions and tigers, something caught her attention. She looked down at the pond where the fish were circling and saw them suddenly stop, as though frozen in the water. Together, the goldfish and the koi formed the features of a man's face, looking up from the depths of the pond. It was a gaunt, bony face, peering out from under the brim of a fedora. A face she had not seen for years but recognized well: it was William Burroughs. The goldfish and the koi began to swim in lazy circles again, breaking up the apparition as quickly as it had formed. Aicha shuddered, realizing she might be getting involved in something that exceeded her own powers and knowledge. Quickly and silently she recited the Verse of the Throne and the last three chapters of the Qur'an, then started back toward the house. She had thought of a plan that would require the assistance of someone in the expatriate community; she would call Mr. Everly Tweed.

Moustapha sat sullenly in the salon of his sister Laila's house. The meal spread out on the low table before him was his favorite, chicken tagine, but he was so upset about the burned-up fedora that he could barely eat. How would he explain the handful of ashes to Aicha? And without the hat how would she be able to conjure up the ghost of William Burroughs to chase the bothersome ghosts from the cemetery? He walked into the kitchen. His sister usually kept a small jar of majoun for the maids and he needed some. He found the jar on a shelf behind some other cans and jars and, taking a small teaspoon, scooped up a little of the dark jam and quickly put it in his mouth. He swallowed with difficulty, then rinsed the spoon and put it in the sink before his sister returned.

When he left the kitchen he heard Laila's husband talking in the salon. Ahmed, who worked as a fireman, always seemed annoyed whenever Moustapha came by the house to eat or to spend the night. As he entered the salon, Ahmed said, "You look lost. What's the matter? Don't you like the tagine?"

Moustapha replied that he wasn't feeling well and was only thirsty. Laila poured him a glass of water which he hurriedly drank to wash down the majoun. "I have to go back to the mesquita now. Some strange young Nasranis were there today asking questions and I want to make sure the gate is locked. Those hippies will steal anything."

"Next time you come for dinner, bring your hunger," Ahmed said in the schoolmasterly tone that always annoyed Moustapha.

Moustapha said nothing as he let himself out and stepped into the street. It will take the spirit of the majoun a while to reveal itself to me, he thought, and headed up to the Café Hafa.

Not only was Moustapha's sister a wonderful cook, she was an excellent maker of majoun. She used nothing but the best dates, nuts, and honey, along with kif from the biggest, strongest buds from the town of Chefchaouen that she could afford. Even before Moustapha reached the Café Hafa, the streets began to look stranger and stranger. The wind made weird rustling noises in the trees and the branches under the streetlights cast flickering shadows across the ground and the whitewashed walls of the buildings as he walked along. A cat dashed across the street in front of him, then stopped and looked up at him. Moustapha could have sworn the cat had a human face. He shut his eyes and shook his head. When he opened his eyes again the cat had disappeared.

Moustapha went through the café and out into the garden, which was a series of tiered terraces perched at the edge of the cliff overlooking the strait. Illumination was provided by lights strung through the trees, and in the distance the coast of Spain faded in and out of view as the clouds passed in front of the full moon. Moustapha sat at his usual table on the uppermost terrace, ordered a mint tea, and looked around at the other tables. This was a strange place, he thought. So many famous writers and artists and musicians had hung out here over the decades; the Beatles had been here, the Rolling Stones, Jean Genet, Paul Bowles, and many of the Beat writers, including William Burroughs. In a way the Café Hafa was like a cemetery, he thought. Probably plenty of ghosts wandering around here as well.

The familiar clicking of a backgammon game interrupted Moustapha's reverie. He looked down and saw Mr. Garland at a table on the terrace just below, his tame ocelot with its jewel-studded collar and leash lying on the ground next to him. Mr. Garland was playing backgammon with a lady who wore a fancy evening dress with a mink stole, too much make-up, and a ridiculous blonde wig which only made her look even older than she was. Moustapha shook his head and smiled a spiteful smile. Some day he would be pulling the weeds and watering the flowers on their graves in the St. Andrew's cemetery.

The ocelot slowly turned its head and looked up at Moustapha; the animal's face looked even more human than those of Mr. Garland and his female companion. It was moving its lips as though trying to say something. Moustapha quickly turned his head and took a sip of his tea. At another table further below, near the wall to the west, there sat a group of young foreign tourists, talking and laughing. They were speaking English, but few of them were American or English; most spoke heavily accented Euro-English. One of the group, a young woman, tattooed and pierced, and dressed in a sleeveless black t-shirt, black shorts, and black leather boots, wore a slightly beat-up fedora tipped back on her head.

Moustapha sipped at his tea and watched the tourists. Something at the edge of his vision caught his eye and he looked down and saw a small lizard on the top of the low wall next to his table. Moustapha almost choked on his tea when he saw that the lizard's face was a human one, with a pained, anguished expression, looking up at him as though it was about to cry. He quickly looked away.

The wind blew through the garden in occasional strong gusts, which seemed to be intensifying. Maybe the wind would blow the lady's wig off, Moustapha thought to himself and laughed. He noticed his friend Driss sitting at a table further down with some other men Moustapha didn't know. They were all smoking kif. Driss was always smoking kif. He ran a small bazaar near the Hotel Minzah that was primarily for tourists. He also dealt kif on the side, both to tourists and natives. He always had the best quality kif available. Moustapha waved and caught his attention and motioned for Driss to join him. They exchanged greetings and Moustapha told Driss about the troubles at the cemetery, the flaming fedora that had allegedly belonged to William Burroughs, and his imminent appointment with Aicha.

Driss loaded his pipe and passed it to Moustapha. "Here, my friend, this may not solve your problems but it may make them appear somewhat smaller."

Moustapha was already feeling the effects of the majoun in such a way that he didn't need any kif, but he didn't want to appear impolite, as he was considering asking Driss a favor.

"You see the hat that girl in black is wearing at that table down there?"

Driss looked and nodded.

"I need a hat like that. Tonight. Right now. Do you have any hats like that in your bazaar?"

Driss leaned back and stroked his chin thoughtfully. "No, my friend, I'm afraid not."

Driss began to load his pipe again. Suddenly there was a scream; they both looked down and saw the girl in black reaching up for her fedora, which had been caught by a strong gust of wind and was now sailing over the low wall of the garden. The girl and some others at the table ran over to the wall where the hat had disappeared into the darkness below. Be it Allah's doing or whatever, Moustapha saw a window of opportunity opening before him.

He finished his tea, bade farewell to Driss, and descended the steps to where the foreign tourists were. He stood next to the girl in black and looked over the waist-high wall where the others were staring down into the adjacent empty lot, totally overgrown with weeds and brambles, which stretched all the way down to the beach below.

"Does anyone see it?" The girl was asking the others.

"No, it's too dark," said a tall blonde guy.

"I see it," Moustapha said. "It's stuck in the limbs of that tree over there."

"Oh shit," said the girl. "How will I ever get it back?"

"I can get it for you," said Moustapha.

"Really? You think so? That would be great. I absolutely *have* to get it back."

Moustapha went down to the lowest terrace, climbed over the wall, and let himself down into the brush and brambles below. Slowly he worked his way back up on the other side of the wall. It was tough going. The thorns were ripping holes in his djellaba and scratching his hands and arms. Moustapha got to where the tourists were leaning over the wall and then looked up at the hat in the tree, wondering how he could get it down. The majoun had made him feel like he was floating on a cloud, on the verge of falling asleep. But the kif he'd smoked with Driss was now working in his head. He felt as strong as a hundred donkeys about to plow the fields. He shimmied up the tree and grabbed the hat.

"I've got it!" Moustapha yelled up to the tourists.

"Oh, great!" the girl shrieked.

As Moustapha was shimmying back down the tree, a branch broke and he lost his footing. He fell onto some springy bushes from where he bounced further down the hill. He was unable to brake his momentum, and the branches he grabbed broke off in his hand as he tumbled further and further down the hillside toward the beach below. Finally he landed with a thud on the sand, just a few yards from the breaking surf. Still clutching the battered fedora, Moustapha got to his feet and looked down at his ripped djellaba and the bloody cuts and scrapes on his arms and legs. Nothing was broken, thankfully; the brush and shrubs had cushioned his fall on the way down the hillside. His years as a member of his family's acrobatic troupe had served him well.

Moustapha looked back up the steep moonlit hillside toward the Café Hafa, now out of sight behind the tops of the trees. The only sounds were the rustling of the wind in the branches and the waves breaking on the beach behind him. He looked down at his watch, its glass now scratched and cracked. It was twenty minutes before twelve. If he hurried, he could just make the cemetery by midnight, where Aicha would hopefully be waiting for him. With the crumpled fedora under his arm, Moustapha set off for the Church of St. Andrew.

3

Seated in the back of the petit taxi coming down from the Old Mountain, Aicha clutched the velvet pouch containing the magical items she had selected to use in place of the burned-up Burroughs hat. She pulled back the sleeve of her djellaba to look at her watch, an antique gold one that Jane Bowles had given her before she left Tangier to die in the Catholic convent in Málaga. The tiny hands showed a quarter to twelve. As the taxi rattled down the Old Mountain road, a disheveled figure suddenly stumbled out of the darkness and into the headlights' glare.

Aicha shouted *Stop!* to the driver and he pulled over to the side of the road. The man approached them limping. Aicha had thought he looked like Moustapha and as he got closer, she realized it was indeed him. The driver opened the front passenger door and Moustapha peered inside, looking at the driver and then at the passenger in the back seat. He immediately recognized Aicha, even with the hood of her djellaba pulled over her head. She still wore her cat-eye sunglasses, although the sun had long since set. Did she think she was in Hollywood? The driver looked at Moustapha, then glanced in the rear-view mirror. Aicha nodded, Moustapha slid into the seat beside him, and they continued down toward the town.

The driver noticed Moustapha was holding a crumpled man's hat and wondered if he might have attacked and robbed one of the Europeans who lived high up on the Old Mountain. That might explain the fresh cuts and scratches on his hands and face. Not wanting to know what this apparent madman might be involved in, he drove in silence until they reached their destination, the Church of St. Andrew. Aicha paid the fare and let herself out. Moustapha then opened his door and falteringly made it to his feet.

Without looking back, Moustapha walked slowly over to the cemetery gate and unlocked it with the clunky, old-fashioned key he kept

on a braided leather lanyard around his neck. The effects of the majoun, then more kif at the café, followed by his fall down the hillside
had left him feeling woozy and unfocused. Aicha looked at him and
said, "You are m'hashish, no?"

"I ate some majoun and smoked a little kif at the café," Moustapha
admitted. "I thought it would calm my nerves."

As he entered the grounds he heard footsteps behind him,
turned—and stopped dead with shock. A few meters away stood the
gaunt figure of William Burroughs, wearing his usual horn-rimmed
glasses and a somber suit and tie, but for once hatless.

"Well, well, if it isn't old Moustapha," said the apparition in that
unmistakable nasal drone, as flat and dry as the Missouri prairies.
"Friend to every Nasrani corpse in Tangier. How about handing over
my fedora, then we'll discuss the situation. You see, I am keenly aware
of your, uh, problems, and maybe we can be of use to each other."

His mouth hanging open in disbelief, Moustapha turned toward
Aicha, who was just now stepping out of the shadows into the pool of
light cast by the single lamp at the cemetery gate.

"Aha," said the ghost of William Burroughs, "Look what the cat
dragged in. It's the Wicked Witch of the Rif."

Aicha removed her sunglasses and slipped them into a pocket in
her djellaba. A cool blue light seemed to emanate from her eyes. She
stood clutching the black velvet bag in one hand, her other hand on
her hip, slowly shaking her head while looking at Moustapha.

"What kind of fool do you take me for, Moustapha? First you
come here with the intention of giving me that phony hat which never
belonged to William Burroughs, to cover the loss of that *other* hat
which actually belonged to Paul Lund, and now you have this . . . this
imposter in tow, pretending to be Burroughs's ghost."

Moustapha's head was spinning. "What do you mean?"

"That is *not* the ghost of William Burroughs," Aicha spat. "Do you
really think he would just show up here on his own accord, as if he had
nothing better to do than help out some hapless hashhead cemetery
watchman?"

"But . . . if it's not the ghost of Burroughs, then who is it?"

"Don't listen to that old whore, Moustapha. Of course it's me. I
remember you from when your mother worked at the Muniria."

Moustapha scratched his head and took a step backward.

"Nonsense," Aicha said to Moustapha. "It's just a djinn who has assumed the form of Burroughs, working with your subconscious and your will, both of which are under the spell of all that majoun and kif you've had. And you know as well as I do that a djinn can be more dangerous than any ghost."

"And what makes you say this is not Burroughs's hat?" Moustapha asked, holding up the fedora, his mind swimming in a sea of confusion.

"I know everything I need to know and what I don't know I find out."

"Ah, a *clairvoyant* whore to boot," said the mystery figure.

"Come, Moustapha, we have work to do if we want to get the *real* ghost of Burroughs to appear. Get me a mijmah and make a fire."

Moustapha looked at the djinn, shrugged his shoulders and went into his shack by the gate to fetch the brazier and some charcoal. When he came back, the djinn had vanished. Aicha told Moustapha to go to the grave of Walter Harris, which lay further back in the cemetery. "Place the mijmah at the head of the tomb and light the charcoal."

While Moustapha readied the mijmah, Aicha slipped into the darkness where the Burroughs djinn waited, out of earshot of Moustapha as he knelt to fan the coals, and handed it a two-hundred-dirham note. The djinn was in reality Mr. Everly Tweed, an elderly alcoholic Irishman who lived in a small apartment in the medina near the Café de los Navigantes. Tall and gaunt, with black horn-rimmed glasses, and always willing to do anything for the price of a few drinks, he made the perfect Burroughs stand-in.

Aicha pulled her veil down and said, "When Moustapha has the mijmah ready, I will do my magic and convince him that you are the *real* ghost of Burroughs. You must threaten him so he will be afraid. Then he will be completely in my power."

"That sounds delightfully devious," said the Irishman. "Perhaps you could see your way to easing me another two hundred dirhams? I worked quite hard on perfecting that Midwestern drawl."

Aicha hated to be chiseled by men, especially Nasrani men, but there was no time to bicker. With a disparaging look she slipped Tweed another two-hundred-dirham note, then turned and made her way to Walter Harris's grave, where the coals in the mijmah were now glowing bright orange. Good, she thought. Soon he will be my goat.

Moustapha was startled by Aicha's appearance and jumped to his feet.

"Now Moustapha," she said. "You must do as I say, or things may go badly for you—and perhaps for others also."

"What do you mean, *others*?"

"Your sister Laila kept the Nasrani hat hidden in her house for you. A hat inhabited by strange powers. Isn't that true?"

Moustapha nodded sullenly.

"Now walk over to that marble gravestone, the one with the Egyptian Ankh carving."

Moustapha did as he was told. Aicha went on; "I want you to lie down on the gravestone and close your eyes. I will then summon the true ghost of William Burroughs."

Moustapha walked unsteadily to the grave that Aicha had pointed out.

"Moustapha, you forgot the mijmah. Go back and get it, and place it at the foot of the grave. And hurry. I only have so much time for this. Soon the moon will be waning."

Still very high from the kif, Moustapha stumbled backwards, turned and picked up the mijmah, spilling some coals and trailing sparks as he carried it to the grave. Then he lay down on the cool, flat stone and closed his eyes. In seconds he began to feel at peace, as though he were a bird flying up through blue and white clouds to where the sky was clear. In the distance he heard Aicha's voice repeating strange words, then he heard a hissing sound and smelled a scent that he remembered from his childhood; the dizzyingly sweet smell of datura blossoms.

"Moustapha, open your eyes." Aicha commanded him.

There at his feet, in the white smoke rising from the mijmah, stood the figure of William Burroughs. To Moustapha, it didn't look any different than the djinn, although apparently Aicha's magic had conjured up the real ghost. But how could he know for sure?

The figure spoke: "Moustapha, tell me the truth. Is the hat you brought with you tonight really my hat?"

Moustapha turned his head to look at Aicha, who had her arms crossed across her chest. He looked back at the figure and said, "I told you, ghost or djinn or whatever you are, the hat belonged to that *hombre invisible*, Burroughs!"

Aicha bit her lip and the Burroughs apparition reached inside its coat and pulled out a small, curved dagger. It then picked up a vase of slightly wilted roses that stood by the grave and addressed Moustapha. "Each one of these flowers represents one of your relatives. Every time

I cut one with this dagger, a member of your family will fall ill or die."

At this Moustapha stood up and said, "Aicha, I thought your magic was strong. And I thought this ghost was going to help us. Min fadlik, make it disappear!"

"You cannot lie to a ghost," she said. "You must tell it the truth or it will haunt the cemetery forever and cause harm to you and your family. There is a turtle in this cemetery that hears and sees everything. It told me the hat originally belonged to Paul Lund and is anyway now only ashes."

Terrified, Moustapha shouted, "I lied. I *lied*. Take the damned hat!" and tossed it at the feet of the figure. "Aicha, now do your magic and send this ghost to hell!"

Burroughs's ghost snatched up the hat as if it had just found a ten-pound note and placed it on its head.

"What are you prepared to do for me in return?" Aicha asked.

"Anything! Anything you wish!"

"You'll let me take as many datura plants as I want?"

"Yes!"

"You'll let me take the tombstone of my choice?"

"Yes!"

Aicha put two fingers to her lips and whistled loudly. The taxi driver appeared out of the shadows with a spade and some burlap sacks. Aicha told him which datura plants she wanted, and he began to dig them up and put them in the burlap sacks.

She then pointed out a weathered granite tombstone lying nearby, which had long since cracked into two pieces. It was the tombstone of Joseph Dean, former proprietor of Dean's Bar, and was inscribed with the words, "DEAN. MISSED BY ALL AND SUNDRY. DIED FEBRUARY 1963."

"No!" Moustapha said pleadingly, "Not *that* one! Everyone who comes here wants to see Dean's grave. How will I ever explain its absence? I will lose my job for sure!"

Burroughs's ghost held up the flowers in one hand and the dagger in the other, slowly bringing them together, the blade just touching the stem of one of the flowers.

The driver produced a tire iron and pried up the two halves of the broken tombstone, which he then lifted into the trunk of his taxi, placing the sacks of datura flowers on top of it.

From her perch atop a nearby obelisk, where she had observed the proceedings with increasing alarm, Zora leaped through the air like a bolt of furry lightning and landed squarely on the ghost's shoulders.

"What the bloody hell?" it roared in a thick Irish brogue. Zora bit into its neck and it screamed, dropped the dagger and the flowers and, clasping the hat firmly to its head, ran toward the cemetery gate, Zora's teeth still locked into its flesh.

Aicha and Moustapha looked at each other in stunned silence.

Then Moustapha spoke; "Since when is a ghost afraid of a cat?"

Aicha frowned. "That wasn't a cat, that was another djinn, fighting for control of the ghost of Burroughs. This is getting very complicated. We are dealing with very strong forces here."

Very complicated indeed, Moustapha thought. He was about to explain that the cat was Zora and not a djinn, then decided against it. There was something strange about Aicha's particular brand of magic, and something *very* strange about the ghost of William Burroughs. And Moustapha suspected that it couldn't all be explained by the majoun and the kif he'd consumed.

"There's nothing more we can do now," Aicha said. "The djinn broke the spell and scared the ghost away. We will have to wait until the next full moon and try again."

Aicha turned and followed the taxi driver out through the gate. Moustapha heard the doors slam shut and the taxi drove off into the night.

As Moustapha stood in the ensuing silence, pondering all that had just happened, he felt something rubbing against his leg. He looked down and saw it was Zora. This time it was a cat with a cat's face, not a human one, but Zora was smiling, nonetheless.

Moustapha put out the fire in the mijmah, locked the shack and the cemetery gate, and started walking toward the medina. Although it was already late, he knew he would still find the lazy-eyed sorcerer in his usual place in the Café Triangle.

4

The Café Triangle was located high up in the Kasbah, jutting out of a wall on a winding street. By the time Moustapha got there, he was out of breath and he stopped, put his hands on his knees, and looked out over the lights of the harbor. His ears were ringing with the blood pulsing through his head. The effects of the majoun and kif were wearing off, and his legs felt wobbly.

A couple of men sat playing dominoes at one of the outside tables. The main room was painted blue and got darker the further back you went. Several small square tables and a banquette ran along one side, and on the opposite wall a TV perched high up in a corner. Several men were sitting on the banquette smoking kif and staring up at the fútbol game flickering on the screen. Moustapha looked around at the tables and saw Kazim. He had a short, neatly trimmed white beard and wore a shiny green pinstripe djellaba and a maroon turban. Well into his nineties, he still radiated a dynamic youthfulness, despite the sleepy look in his sparkling blue eyes. Moustapha approached the table and Kazim looked up at him with one eye while the other eye remained fixed on the game.

"Peace be upon you," said Kazim.

"And you also," Moustapha replied.

"Sit and have a coffee with me."

"Shukran," said Moustapha and took a chair.

Kazim motioned for the waiter and ordered two coffees.

"You have the look of a frightened hen," said Kazim. Taking in Moustapha's disheveled appearance he added, "who's been attacked by a jackal."

"Since this afternoon I have felt the hot breath of Satan himself on my neck."

Kazim had known Moustapha ever since he moved back to Tangier after being dismissed from his family's acrobatic troupe. He remembered when Moustapha was hired by the rector of the Church of St. Andrew. Kazim had known the previous caretaker, too, who had gone mad after only two years on the job. The man would still appear in the Zoco Chico occasionally, shoeless, in ragged clothing, and talking to himself as he went from café to café. He would sometimes run up to a group of Europeans and begin yelling and waving his arms hysterically. The waiters would chase him off while the Europeans looked at each other in shock.

"Are those Nasrani ghosts becoming a big problem?" asked Kazim.

"I have more than ghost problems. I am being haunted by that Riffian witch, Aicha. I feel as if I am sliding down the well of Abdiel in Sidi Bennour."

Kazim smiled. Both men took long sips from their glasses of coffee. Then Kazim spoke. "I am not sure why you are telling me this. Aicha is someone who can be dealt with. But you know that sometimes ghosts and djinns can drive a man mad, leaving only part of his soul on earth while the rest wanders lost in the clouds. If you know who your enemy is, you have a choice—be a peg and endure the knocking, or be a hammer and strike."

Moustapha took another sip of coffee and sat back in his chair, pondering Kazim's words. In the darkness at the back of the café, a mirror ball began to scatter splinters of light in mesmerizing patterns which shot through the clouds of blue-gray smoke that perpetually hung in the Café Triangle.

From the folds of his djellaba Kazim produced a pipe and a bag of kif, and the two of them smoked several pipes while watching the fútbol game on the TV. Moustapha explained his predicament to Kazim, who seemed to be only half listening. He was hoping that Kazim would perhaps offer to help without being asked directly. If he were to ask outright for Kazim's assistance, what could he offer him in return? If he lost his job as watchman, he would no longer have access to the datura plants or the tombstones.

Out of the corner of his eye Moustapha saw someone approaching from the direction of the bar. It was Just-Call-Me-Ishmael, a little unsteady on his feet as usual at this late hour, but still walking with the rolling gait of a former seaman. Just-Call-Me-Ishmael was an American merchant seaman who had jumped ship in Tangier decades ago and never left. In the first bar he'd stepped into in the harbor, the Moroccan bartender had asked him his name, and he had replied in jest, "Just call me Ishmael." The bartender had never read *Moby Dick*, so the joke was over his head, but the name stuck. Back in the old days, Just-Call-Me-Ishmael had made a good living from smuggling and other less-than-legal capers. These days he seemed to survive mainly on the charity and good will of others, although allegedly he had a nest egg stashed away somewhere from his smuggling days.

"Who's winning?" asked Just-Call-Me-Ishmael.

"Benfica," replied Kazim. "As I predicted."

"Ah, cut the shit, Kazim. You don't predict, you look into the future. That's almost like cheating."

"Almost, except that the future is there for everyone to see, at least for those who have eyes for it."

"So maybe you can look into the future and tell me who's going to buy me my next drink."

Kazim smiled and motioned for the waiter.

After his second glass of coffee Moustapha got up to go to the toilet. He walked to the back of the café into the narrow hallway at the rear of the room. A doorway on the left led to the tiny kitchen, another into a storeroom, and a third, even smaller doorway opened into one of those rudimentary Moroccan toilets that was no more than a hole in the cement floor.

Having relieved himself, Moustapha stepped back into the hallway and was about to return to Kazim's table when he heard strange music coming from behind him. Moustapha peered back into the gloom at the far end of the hallway and saw a crack of colored light issuing from under a closed door. He'd been in the Café Triangle many times, but he'd never noticed that door before. He couldn't understand how there could even be a door there, since the café butted up against one of the thick stone walls of the Kasbah.

Moustapha walked back toward the door, stood in the darkness, and listened. The music came from behind the door. It was somehow familiar but at the same time very peculiar. He cautiously pushed open the door and was startled to see a huge room with low tables and cushions on the floor, lit only by candles in lanterns of metal and colored glass, which sat on the tables and hung from the walls. The room was thick with smoke from incense and kif and was filled with people, what looked like a mixed crowd of locals and tourists, all watching a group of musicians on a low stage that ran along one side of the room. Against the back wall was a bar, where several dark figures were seated on stools.

Moustapha slipped inside and stood against the wall, letting his eyes adjust to the subdued lighting. On stage he recognized Ravi Kahn, as well as Tony Mahoney, the crazy New York musician who lived in a villa up on the Old Mountain. Ravi was playing his sitar and Tony was playing an electric oud, along with an ensemble of Gnawa musicians who were generating hypnotic rhythms on their hand drums, castanets, and gimbri. Moustapha felt the rhythms penetrating his being and was already starting to move in time with the music, a cycling, pulsing, telegraphic tempo he was powerless to resist.

His head rolled slowly from side to side in time with the back-and-forth rocking of the Gnawa drummers. The colored light from the lanterns flickered like so many eyelids opening and closing, and he began to sink into the lassitude of someone who has just received a deep muscle massage after a hard workout. Then he suddenly stiffened, as if a piece of red-hot charcoal had been pressed into his stomach. Seated at the feet of the oud player was the supposed ghost of Williams Burroughs, wearing the fedora Moustapha had thrown to him in the cemetery.

The Burroughs impersonator slowly rose to his feet and with a sweeping gesture of his right hand, led the musicians into a Gnawa version of the Beatles' "I Am the Walrus." The rhythm slowed as the violinists and the electric oud player formed the dirge-like notes of the song. As soon as the group was playing in sync, the imposter began to clap his hands—soon all the audience joined in, keeping perfect time. Then he started to intone, "I am he, as you are he, as you are me, and we are all together." He repeated the same line several times then on the third chorus paused with "as you are me," and the guests sang out in unison, "and we are all together!" This rhythmic call-and-response continued, growing stronger and louder with each repetition.

A breeze blew across the back of Moustapha's neck, and he felt cold fingers on his arm. He looked to his left but there was no one there. He looked to his right—also no one. A chill ran down his spine.

"I am the Walrus" ended in a roar of applause. The Burroughs imposter doffed his hat, bowed, and sat down on a pile of cushions near the low stage. Immediately the musicians started into a version of Led Zeppelin's "When the Levee Breaks." Tony Mahoney was playing his electric oud through an array of effect pedals, creating all kinds of weird feedback, distortion, and echoing loops. The beat was kept like clockwork by the many drummers, now playing almost as loud as John Bonham himself. The song seemed to grow and take on a shape of its own, gradually filling the entire room. More and more people had gotten to their feet and were dancing to the music.

Again Moustapha felt that frigid breeze blowing in out of nowhere, or perhaps some other realm, and again he felt the cold fingers on his arm. But when he looked there was no one there. This time the chill made him shudder.

Meanwhile the castanet players had quadrupled the beat and the tempo of the song increased, creating an overwhelming sonic vortex into which Moustapha felt himself being pulled. He was so drawn into the music that he started dancing too, slowly moving toward the stage where other dancers were writhing and wheeling about. One of them fell on the floor and started thrashing about like an epileptic. People from behind the bar came and carried the downed dancer off through a doorway into yet another back room.

The music grew louder and faster, and the rhythms were now pulsing through Moustapha's entire body. He was losing control, but it no longer seemed important whether he was in control or not. The music was just too strong. He was whipping himself around in circles now, a kif-crazed whirling dervish, jerking and twitching in time with the music. In his mind's eye he saw a succession of images flying by— the fedora bursting into flames in the cemetery, the ocelot with the human face trying to speak to him, the lizard with the human face that looked like it was on the verge of tears, Aicha and the Burroughs impersonator in the cemetery, Dean's tombstone and the sacks of datura plants disappearing into the trunk of the taxi, the taxi driving off into the night . . . Moustapha felt his legs go out from under him and his body fall toward the floor, although in his mind he was rising up, up to a place higher than the highest cloud, higher than the sun itself, where all was bright and the light was completely blinding.

5

On the dead is bestowed the privilege of an all-pervasive awareness that permits them to know far more than the living, and Walter Harris, now dead for more than half a century, knew it all. He knew about Moustapha's situation and his current dilemmas, about the fiery fate of Paul Lund's fedora which Moustapha had been trying to pass off as belonging to William Burroughs, about the quirk of circumstance by which Moustapha had come by a second hat, about the deceit practiced on him by Aicha and Everly Tweed—and he knew that Moustapha was now bound to lose his job at the cemetery.

As Harris drifted down to the harbor through the twisting streets of the medina for his late-night constitutional, dressed in his Riffian turban and burnoose, it occurred to him that he might be in a position to help Moustapha—and Moustapha might be able to help him. It was, after all, Harris's own ghost that Moustapha wanted to see banished from the cemetery. If Moustapha were able to exhume his remains and get them shipped back to Malta, so that he could be buried in the Addolorata Cemetery next to his beloved Pierre, then life—or rather, the afterlife—could return to normal.

When he reached the harbor, Harris followed the train tracks running alongside the beach, sat down under a palm tree, and looked out across the Bay of Tangier, sparkling in the moonlight. He listened to the sound of the waves breaking on the beach and thought about how best to proceed, how he might enhance the intrinsic interdependence that connected all beings, living and dead.

Moustapha lay on the floor unnoticed for some minutes before two women wearing red sequin-covered scarves and heavy silver bracelets stopped dancing and knelt at his side. One of them lifted his head. With all the noise and commotion it was hard to tell if he was breathing. She tried to pry his mouth open, but his jaws were clenched shut. She pinched his nostrils together, and after a few seconds he began coughing and gasping. His eyes opened wide and he said, "Allah be praised. At last I am free of the cursed demons and devils." The two women helped him sit up and someone brought a glass of strong black tea which he drank thirstily.

Moustapha felt a hand on his shoulder again, and was set to ignore it when he realized that this time the hand was warm. He turned and saw Kazim, who helped him to his feet and guided him to a banquette on the opposite side of the room from the stage.

"I wouldn't count my blessings too soon," Kazim said. "A brief journey into the other world does not necessarily purge someone of their demons. For every demon or spirit that departs a human being there is usually another waiting to take its place. But not all of these demons and spirits are evil in nature. Sometimes they can be good and provide assistance in troubled times. Everyone is possessed by something; the trick is to find out what."

Moustapha sipped at a second glass of tea that one of the women had brought him and pondered Kazim's words. "What 'other world' are you talking about?"

Kazim leaned back against the cushions and looked out across the crowd of people, who were now mostly sitting down again as the musicians worked their way into an acoustic version of Brian Eno's "Spirits Drifting," which served as a signal that the evening's musical performance was coming to an end. "Think of it like this, Moustapha," Kazim said, one eye on the musicians, the other roaming the room.

"There is this world and there is that world, much like the two different worlds the kif smoker and the alcohol drinker inhabit—they both get high, but in very different ways. These two worlds are in many ways complementary, interdependent, and coexistent. But this duality is a very primitive model, hardly sufficient to account for all the mysteries and nuances and ironies of existence. What most people do not realize is that beyond this world and that world there is *another* world. In this other world there is no duality, because all is one. It's like when you are at the beach or out in the desert or up in the mountains, among nature and the animals and with no humans around—you soon see that nature knows nothing of either good or evil, of reward or punishment, there are only consequences, a never-ending chain of cause and effect. Only when human beings enter the picture do the concepts of good and evil arise. And so it is in the other world, which is so large and all-encompassing that this world and that world can both exist inside of it simultaneously. But you can't access the other world without first passing through either this world or that world. So in order to master the demons, the magic, and the so-called good and evil that are present in this world and in that world, you need to learn how to recognize where the one world starts and the other ends, so you can navigate all three worlds."

"Ya latif!" Moustapha exclaimed. "That's too many worlds for me. I'm having enough trouble in this world right here."

"Maybe a more concrete example will help you understand what I'm talking about. You see those two figures at the end of the bar?"

Moustapha peered into the furthermost corner of the room, where two hulking figures sat on stools, drinking brightly colored translucent liquids through alabaster straws. They were neither human nor reptile, but something in between. Protruding from fleshy purple-blue lips were razor-sharp beaks of black bone. Their flesh was blackish-pink and along their spines ran a fan of green cartilage covered with erectile hairs. Occasionally a ripple of motion would run up and down the fan, like the dorsal fin of a fish languishing in shallow water. Moustapha recoiled in horror. What kind of creatures were these?

"Those are Mugwumps," Kazim said, as though he had been reading Moustapha's mind. "The same Mugwumps Burroughs described in *Naked Lunch*. As you see, he didn't make them up—they're as real as you and me. One only has to learn to access the other world in order to experience the full spectrum of existence, both material and immaterial. I taught Burroughs how to navigate these three worlds, and in much of *Naked Lunch* he was merely describing what he found there.

"When Burroughs was writing the work he called 'Interzone,' I would sometimes visit him in his room in El Muniria. He was suffering from various addictions—to kif, majoun, morphine, codeinetta, Eukodol—and was still depressed over the fatal shooting of his wife Joan. There was also the pain of his love addiction for his friend Allen Ginsberg. I would ask him, 'Mr. William; does it hurt?' And he would reply, 'Only always.' 'Mr. William,' I told him, 'You must make your skull an open eye, an eye that can look through the walls of the medina, across oceans, into the haunted jungles of your subconscious. Take all you know and combine it with what you see and hear in the interzone of your mind.'

"He would sit on the edge of his bed while I made him tea. Bits of food, dead insects, syringes, and morphine ampoules were scattered among the typewritten pages that littered the floor. Once when he could not write for weeks, I visited him and said, 'Mr. William, open your mouth. There, just behind your tongue is a ragged hole in your throat through which I can see satyrs, Arab women, Javanese dancers, Aztec priests, bums, junkies, drug pushers, drunks, pimps, poets, prostitutes, and philosophers. Listen to their voices and they will tell you the story of your interzone. You see, Mr. William, everyone experiences a different interzone. This one will be uniquely yours—an "Ultrazone" if you wish, which will serve you well for the rest of your writing life.' Burroughs sat silent for a moment, staring down at his folded hands. 'Does it still hurt, Mr. William?' I asked. 'Only always,' he replied. 'You must try to write the hurt away,' I told him. 'Begin anywhere . . . The rest is easy . . . and hard.'"

While Kazim was talking to Moustapha, on the other side of the room Everly Tweed was leading the musicians in a slow descent and outro from "Spirits Drifting," the pulsing rhythms giving way to a soothing drone which eventually disappeared altogether, like a wisp of smoke rising and then dissipating in the room. Tweed reached into his pocket and pulled out a miniature monkey skull on a leather cord. The skull gave off a bluish glow, as if lit by a black light. He swung the monkey skull back and forth in front of the crowd like a pendulum. Then he began to chant over and over, "Your power is high among us." Soon those gathered together in the sweaty, smoky room echoed his words and repeated, "Your power is high among us." This continued for some time, until he reached up and grasped the glowing skull with his other hand, extinguishing the glow. For a few moments a vast silence reigned throughout the room. I think I have regained my hypnotic skills at last, Tweed thought to himself and smiled.

Unknown to his acquaintances in Tangier, including the Riffian witch Aicha, Everly Tweed had been a successful hypnotist in England before succumbing to drink and laudanum. He had reportedly cured many forms of neurosis, as well as helping people find items they had lost—and had often been rewarded handsomely if the item in question was valuable. Tweed had also delved into the occult and through self-hypnosis had practiced telepathy and telekinesis. On occasion he had even made contact with departed spirits. After being institutionalized for a time because of his addictions, he had been forced by creditors to flee and ultimately washed ashore in Tangier to join the other lost souls and expatriates of dubious origin who occupied the so-called Port of Saints.

As Tweed walked slowly toward the low doorway which led out of the room, Moustapha glared after him and asked Kazim if he knew who that man was.

"That is Mr. Everly Tweed, a highly gifted man who squandered his talents. He too once knew his way among the three worlds, but now has trouble finding his way home at night."

As Walter Harris listened intently to the soft sound of the waves breaking on the Tangier beach, he had heard Everly Tweed's voice as if it were carried ashore on the crest of the foaming waves. He heard the chants of the audience in the Café Triangle growing louder and more insistent, "Your power is high among us." But not as high as mine, Harris thought in the disembodied, ethereal, spacey-ness of ghost-thought. If I could harness Tweed's powers as a hypnotist and exert them on the gullible and superstitious Moustapha, I might find the peace I seek far away from the city of Antaeus.

Harris left the beach and moved along the darkened Avenue d'Espagne towards the ancient, crumbling gateway to the walled city. On up the Rue Dar Baroud he glided past the Hotel Continental overlook to the Rue Mohamed Bergach, where he waited for Everly

Tweed to return home. Once Tweed was alone behind the thick walls of his flat, Harris would have his chance. In theory he could control Moustapha directly, without any outside help, but after all his years living in Morocco Harris knew well the workings of the Moroccan mind and its oblique relationship to logic and rationality, which made Moroccans almost impervious to anything even remotely related to Western, "Nazarene" thinking. It would take a powerful hypnotic spell to make Moustapha overcome his fears and dig up the corpse of Walter Harris, and Everly Tweed was looking like the right man for the job.

While he waited, Harris drifted over the twisting streets which wound through the connected houses in the medina, over the rug merchants' shops, the metal-smiths and leather workshops, until he reached the Café Triangle. There he hovered above Moustapha, who sat alone at an outside table, sipping at a glass of tea and slowly recovering from the episode in the back room. Then he floated up the Rue Siaghine to the Grand Socco and on to St. Andrew's cemetery. He saw Zora the cat lying on his tomb, fast asleep. When he sensed Tweed was nearing his flat, Harris transported himself back to the Rue Mohamed Bergach in an instant. A tired-looking Everly Tweed shambled up the street and entered a small apartment building sandwiched between two larger ones. From the loudspeakers mounted on the minaret of a nearby mosque came the sound of the muezzin's call to Fajr, the dawn prayer. *Allahu akbar, Allahu akbar . . .*

By the time Tweed had climbed the stairs to the second floor and entered his flat, he was so exhausted he just dropped his clothes in a pile and climbed into bed. Soon he was sinking into the deepest sleep he had known in months. Then, once he had reached the blackout depths of oblivion, he began to drift to the surface and into a dazed, semi-conscious state. His eyes opened and in the doorway he saw the glowing figure of Walter Harris, outlined by a red aura. Slowly Tweed slipped back into a deep sleep, at which point Harris entered the keyhole of his dreams and went to work, strengthening Tweed's hypnotic powers and embedding his plan to turn Moustapha into the tool of his search for permanent repose.

In her villa up on the Old Mountain, Aicha was tossing and turning, unable to sleep. The bright moonlight shone through a narrow gap in the drawn curtains and threw a luminous band of light across the bed. Aicha got up, drew back the curtains, and opened the window.

The wind was still rustling the leaves of the bamboo grove, but other than that it was quiet. She stared down into the moonlit garden and focused on what the problem was, why she couldn't sleep. It was as if some kind of negative energy lurked nearby, perhaps even within the villa.

The story of how Aicha came to own the villa had become part of Tangier legend. It began in Kenya in the late forties, where a certain Major Rumey-Hill bought a vast estate and commissioned a house in the grand style. The native-built luxury home was dubbed "Moonlight Mile," and Major Rumey-Hill became known for staging lavish parties there, inviting friends from all over Europe to visit and play. But after a year or so, the Major became bored with guests who began drinking immediately after breakfast. He left Kenya for Hollywood to become an actor, selling the estate to an old friend and frequent visitor, Sir Michael Woodstonecraft.

Sir Michael's wife, Lady Ofelia Woodstonecraft, was a lithesome beauty with an adventurous nature and erratic willpower and, not long after moving into Moonlight Mile, she began an affair in Nairobi with the dashing Gilford Colville. Six months later, Colville was found dead in the front seat of his 1935 SS Jaguar saloon, shot in the head. The murder remained unsolved. Lady Ofelia soon divorced Sir Michael and left Nairobi for Marrakech. After a few months, she surfaced at the Hotel Continental in Tangier, nearly broke. It took some time before the money from her divorce settlement reached her in Tangier, and by this time she had begun an affair with Aicha, at that time an infamous prostitute. Flush with cash from the settlement, Lady Ofelia bought a villa overlooking the strait on the Old Mountain and moved Aicha in with her. There they lived together behind a stone wall and tall iron gate. Aicha hired a watchman and his family to live on the property. The watchman had grown up in the country and he and his wife gardened and raised rabbits and chickens.

Lady Ofelia had always had a drinking problem and occasionally she and Aicha would have it out. Aicha tried to get her to smoke kif or try majoun instead, but nothing would get Lady Ofelia to abstain from drink. Aicha grew increasingly impatient with her frequent binges and their relationship soured. When they argued, Lady Ofelia would threaten to make Aicha move out. Such a threat from an alcoholic Nasrani did not sit well with Aicha.

After a particularly nasty fight over her boozing, Lady Ofelia decided to drive to Chefchaouen, where there was a nice hotel for foreigners, telling Aicha she planned to spend a few days there until tempers cooled. But as she drove along the twisting mountain road near Zinat, she somehow lost control of her car, which tumbled down a rocky hillside into a shallow riverbed, killing her immediately. Was alcohol to blame, as gossip suggested, or did the brakes mysteriously fail? The authorities attributed the cause of the accident to "Allah's will" and left it at that. After a protracted legal dispute, Aicha inherited the villa. But there was little money left and most of that went to the Moroccan lawyers.

As Aicha stared at the sparkling lights of Spain across the strait, she heard a loud crash. She put her hands to her temples and shut her eyes to envision what had caused the noise, but there seemed to be some kind of interference; no image came into her mind. She heard the crashing noise again—it seemed to be coming from inside the villa, maybe from the garage. Perhaps someone was trying to break in. Aicha's collection of art and jewelry, amassed in earlier years, was both very impressive and very well known. It wouldn't be the first time that burglars had tried their luck. But where was her watchman, and why were no lights on downstairs?

Aicha took a pearl-handled derringer and a flashlight out of the nightstand drawer and went down the stairs, through the kitchen, down another flight of stairs to the garage. Outside the closed door that led into the garage she listened for a few moments but heard nothing. Slowly she opened the door, the beam of her flashlight stabbing the musty darkness. Then she reached in and flicked the light switch. There was no one there and the garage door was shut. Her vintage pistachio-green Mercedes 290 SL hardtop convertible sat untouched in the middle of the garage under a thick layer of dust.

But then something unusual caught Aicha's eye, and she walked over to the large workbench that ran along the back wall of the garage. She remembered distinctly that the taxi driver and her watchman had placed both halves of Joseph Dean's tombstone on the workbench, but now one half lay on the concrete floor, the upper half bearing his name. Setting down the derringer and the flashlight, she tried to pick it up and put it back on the workbench, but it was too heavy.

Where was that useless watchman of hers? She called out his name but there was no answer, no sounds. She considered going out to Mohammed's cottage by the gate but decided against it. She would give him a scolding in the morning. Aicha picked up the derringer and the flashlight and went back to bed.

A few minutes later, she heard another crash. She jumped up and went back down to the garage. At first she didn't notice anything different, but when she went over to the workbench she saw it was the lower half of the tombstone that was now on the floor while the upper half lay on the workbench. Had she mistaken the two halves of the tombstone in her initial shock and confusion? She knew that was very unlikely. And that did not bode well.

She checked the garage door again, then went back upstairs. Just as she had shut her eyes in a concentrated effort to finally fall asleep, she heard yet another crash. Again she went down to the garage, where she now found both halves of the tombstone lying on the cement floor. On the one hand, she was relieved that it wasn't her mind that was playing tricks on her. On the other hand, she wondered who was.

6

Everly Tweed woke up at the rooster's third call. The faint gray of morning appeared as a weak glow behind the curtains. Although he hadn't slept for very long at all, he was strangely invigorated and leapt out of bed as if he'd just had a shot of vitamin B12 and speed. His first thought was that he had something important to do, without being conscious of what it was. He felt a sense of drive and purpose the likes of which he had not known in years. An image of Moustapha holding a shovel and standing over an empty grave came to mind. Tweed recalled the previous evening, the charade at St. Andrew's cemetery and the bungled attempt to convince Moustapha that he was Burroughs's ghost. The ensuing wild night at the Café Triangle was like a layer of gauze wrapped around his head. He was surprised at himself for getting caught up in the frenzied dancing and his grandstanding effort at mass hypnosis.

As he prepared his breakfast of day-old croissant, yogurt, and tea, Tweed had an odd feeling, as though he were living very slightly in the future, perhaps only a half-second ahead of the present time. Somewhat troublingly, though, the experience of being slightly ahead in time coexisted in his mind with a sense that there were pieces missing from reality. Though he was fully awake, the reality he perceived had blind spots, as though certain things had been erased. As Tweed drank his tea he examined the way he was experiencing the present, which seemed to be a sequence of brief flashbacks, each flashback accompanied by an exhilarating burst of psychic energy.

I have to try and get used to this, Tweed thought. It's like no drug I've ever had. Could I have inadvertently hypnotized myself? Or perhaps someone spiked my drink at the Café Triangle.

He finished his breakfast and went to wash. Standing in the tiny bathroom, he looked at his face in the mirror and saw his features change before his eyes, as if an image of someone else's face were being superimposed onto his own. The face reflected in the mirror was that of a handsome, middle-aged man with a short, well-groomed mustache and beard. The eyes were intelligent and piercing. Tweed's heart began to palpitate as a rather high-pitched voice with an odd British accent began speaking in his mind's ear. Finally, when the voice went silent, Tweed's own face reappeared in the glass like an image emerging on photographic paper in a developing tray. What the voice had told him was now as firmly part of Tweed's being as his own name. The message had become part of his psychic DNA and was clear in its intent: Place Moustapha under your power through hypnosis and instruct him to exhume the body of Walter Harris so that it may be transported to its final resting place on Malta.

As Tweed got dressed to go out, he noticed the fedora that Moustapha had given him the night before, lying on a chair where he'd tossed it before he'd fallen into bed. He placed it on his head; it fit perfectly. When he looked at his reflection in the mirror on the old armoire, he looked more like Burroughs than Burroughs himself. He took off the hat and inspected it closely, turning it around slowly in his hands, flipping it over. On the inside of the hatband was a monogram stamped in silver letters: *WSB*. That's strange, Tweed thought. Didn't Aicha say the real fedora had been destroyed and Moustapha had been trying to pass off a phony one? If it was a counterfeit, then someone had gone to a lot of trouble. Or maybe there had been some kind of mix-up and this was in fact the genuine article. Either way, it could be sold off for a tidy sum to the right person.

Tweed left his apartment, double locking the door, and headed back to the Café Triangle. Kazim would probably not be there but one of the waiters or doormen might be. A plan was forming in his mind. If he could hypnotize Moustapha and control him long enough to have him exhume the body at St. Andrews, he would still need to have a means of transporting the body out of the cemetery and beyond. Something like an old carpet that the body could be hidden in. Then, even if Moustapha came out of the hypnotic trance at some point, Tweed would be able to blackmail him into helping ship the body to Malta. Moustapha knew the law regarding grave robbing and the severe penalty if he were ever caught, but Tweed would have him where he wanted. The strange voice in the back of his mind seemed to approve of his plan and urge him on.

Despite his lack of sleep and a serious kif hangover, Moustapha was up early, eating a meager breakfast of baguette, marmalade, and coffee in his sister's kitchen. When Laila had first seen him in the morning, covered in cuts and bruises from his fall down the hillside, she gasped and, eyes wide, asked what had happened to him. Moustapha explained about the tourists at the Café Hafa and the girl with the hat and how he tried to rescue it from the tree. The way Laila looked at him, he knew she didn't believe him, even though he was telling the truth. He continued eating his breakfast in silence, preoccupied with his thoughts, while Laila busied herself in the kitchen. When she offered him another coffee he politely declined and got up to go. He didn't want to be there when her husband came in and have to explain what happened all over again. Ahmed wouldn't believe him either.

Moustapha left the house and started walking toward the Church of St. Andrew. As he walked, his mind was spinning. How would he explain the missing tombstone to the rector? Would he lose his job? Could he possibly get the tombstone back before the rector noticed it was missing?

As Moustapha turned into the street that led to the church, he passed a small workshop where they made papier-mâché masks and figures for festivals and parades. It gave him an idea. He asked the owner how fast they could make something. The owner said they might be able to have it ready the same day, depending on how involved the project was. Moustapha asked for a piece of paper and drew a fairly good picture of Dean's tombstone, in two pieces, with the lettering and with the approximate dimensions. The owner looked at the drawing and glanced up with a frown, but said they could have it ready that afternoon and deliver it to the cemetery as soon as it had dried.

Moustapha explained that he wouldn't be able to pay until he received his paycheck at the end of the month. The owner frowned again, but he knew Moustapha was the watchman at the church and decided to trust him. Moustapha thanked him and left.

The key squeaked and scraped in the rusty lock, then Moustapha opened the cemetery gate and stepped inside. He went straight to the tool shed and selected a sharp sickle, then walked to the very back of the cemetery where several wooden wheelbarrows were parked next to the large compost heap of dead flowers, plants, and weeds. Behind the compost heap was a large cane grove. Moustapha cut several armloads of cane and piled them on one of the wheelbarrows, then threw some old flowers on top. He wheeled the load back through the cemetery and deposited it on the plot where Dean's tombstone had lain. Hopefully the absence of the tombstone would remain undiscovered until the papier-mâché replica arrived. Meanwhile he had to figure out how to get the real tombstone back, or he would surely lose his job.

Aicha lay in bed and thought back on the night. Had she dreamed all that about the tombstone, or had it really happened? A look in the garage would tell her. She got slowly out of bed, parted the curtains, swung open the double panes, and looked out across the garden at the deep blue waters of the strait. This was definitely one of the drawbacks of getting old, Aicha thought. It used to be that she could clearly tell the difference between dreams and reality, even when she was envisioning that reality remotely, by way of her psychic powers. Nowadays she found herself often taking her dreams for reality, and believing reality to be her dreams. That could prove dangerous. Fading powers, fading beauty; the ageing process was not for weaklings. Sometimes she even caught herself looking forward to the time when she was no longer a part of the physical world, with all its material exigencies.

Standing at the open window, looking down now into the garden, Aicha recalled a dream she'd had during the night. She had never been to St. Louis, or anywhere in America, but in her dream she knew she was clearly seeing Bellefontaine Cemetery, where William Burroughs was buried. It was like a gigantic park, with meticulous lawns, many trees, and elaborate mausoleums and obelisks stretching as far as she could see. A number of cats were carousing between the trees and graves and tombstones. Others were sitting, conversing among themselves, and Aicha understood what they were saying. They talked about the weather, about other cats, and a newly hired gardener who seemed to have a soft spot for cats. Although it was forbidden by the management, the new gardener was surreptitiously feeding the many feral cats whose home was the cemetery.

A smaller group had gathered around Burroughs's grave, where a sturdy tabby was addressing the headstone. "Hey, Bill," she said, "our pal Zora in St. Andrew's cemetery in Tangier sent us a message along the feline grapevine. She said there's some weird shit going down there, and your old nemesis, Aicha, seems to be behind it. Moustapha, the watchman, had been trying to pawn off an old hat of Paul Lund's as one of yours, and then the hat went up in flames. Some kind of crazy spontaneous combustion. By means of someone impersonating you, plus some kind of psychic extortion, Aicha then made off with Joseph Dean's tombstone. As you can imagine, Dean's ghost is none too happy."

"Yes, I'm aware of all that," said the ghost of William Burroughs in his Midwestern drawl. "I've been trying to ignore it, hoping it would take care of itself, although I did send a burst of telekinetic energy through the ether to blast that damned hat into oblivion, where it belongs. Imagine someone trying to sell Paul Lund's hat as my own. What kind of fraudulent bullshit is that? And what would Aicha want with Dean's tombstone?"

"Maybe you better get on over there and check out the scene, before something really bad goes down and you get all the blame," suggested the tabby.

"So much for resting in peace. Actually, a trip back to Tangier might not be such a bad thing. Haven't been there in eons. Probably won't even recognize the place. Maybe I can connect with Kiki's ghost and relive some of them good old days long gone. Nothing like a little romance to liven up the afterlife. Or maybe I can rustle up the ghost of my old pal Brion Gysin. Sounds like Aicha's scheming could stand a few real-life cut-ups."

Burroughs's ghost rose up out of the grave and hovered above the family plot.

"We'll keep an eye on things here and keep our paws crossed that all goes well," said the tabby. The other cats each raised a paw in a gesture of farewell.

"Adios, amigos," said Burroughs's ghost and whooshed off into the firmament.

A bank of dense gray clouds moved in from the Atlantic and slipped in front of the sun, casting a broad shadow across the sprawling city of Tangier. Aicha stepped back from the window and put her hand to her mouth. It was not a dream. That was reality, she was certain. Burroughs himself had set Paul Lund's hat on fire, and now the real ghost was here in Tangier, and sooner or later Aicha would have to deal with it. But what about the other hat? Where did Moustapha get it and who did it belong to?

The clouds were slowly increasing. It looked like it might rain later in the day. Several of the more psychic mountain women from the Rif who were selling eggs, goat cheese, and vegetables in the market noticed a particularly odd cloud formation moving in from the west. Twin sisters Saeeda and Salima looked at each other and simultaneously pulled at the long white hairs that grew from their tattooed and wrinkled chins. "By Saint Ali el Goumi," said Salima, "That cloud is from the dark world."

"Yes," said Saeeda, "Tangier is no place for an innocent when sorcery is afoot. We should sell what we can quickly and ride back to our village on Amine's truck."

"And keep our doors and windows locked tonight," said Salima.

Burroughs's ghost arrived first at the door of what had been Brion Gysin's famed restaurant, the 1001 Nights, in the Dar Menebhi Palace. He did not enter the building, which was perched high up in the Marshan overlooking the strait, but merely lingered a few minutes to reflect on what had been a deep friendship. Burroughs and Gysin had been great collaborators and had often crossed the frontier of the Third Mind in pursuit of creative energy and fresh ideas. Some of Gysin's animus still hovered about the place and Burroughs's ghost felt it as a sign of welcome. It was good to be back in Tangier.

His ghost next moved down through the medina past the Café Triangle, the Hotel Continental, on to the Zoco Chico. There outside the Café Central, he surveyed the patrons sipping their mint teas al fresco. The usual mix of pushers, pedophiles, and Eurotrash, he thought to himself. And here's a couple of retro American hippies just off the boat, stoned, wide-eyed, and lost.

Already a few hustlers had begun moving in, circling around where the pair was sitting, waiting for them to leave the refuge of the café. Just for fun, Burroughs moved in between the pair and, trying his hand at a bit of telekinesis, dislodged the hippie girl's colorful cloth bag from the back of her chair. It landed with a thud, spilling its contents onto the dirty pavement. Her partner laughed nervously as he helped her pick up her things. Burroughs smiled mischievously and thought to himself, Welcome to Tangier, kids—the den of iniquity, as Paul Bowles used to call it.

Burroughs stayed long enough to peek around the corner at the first hotel he had lived in when he arrived in Tangier. Then he floated up the steep street to the Grand Socco, which held a chaotic mass of buyers, sellers, strolling families, petit taxis, arriving and departing buses, and the odd group of Spanish tourists being led through the main food market. As he hovered above the scene, Burroughs recalled the times he had walked through the crowds on his way to the farmacia to refill his various prescriptions for codeinetta, morphine, and Eukodol. Back then, dressed like a door-to-door encyclopedia salesman in a gray suit and tie, glasses, and a dark fedora, Burroughs caused barely a ripple of notice. His changeless expression of weary bemusement and his measured, methodical gait were a kind of camouflage amid the sea of Moroccans in djellabas, qaftans, and mix-and-match western clothes. So nondescript was his appearance that the street urchins began to call him *El Hombre Invisible*. These days, that moniker carried a different sort of weight.

Further up the street, past the Rif Cinema, Burroughs felt the presence of the ghost of Joseph Dean, the mysterious owner of the fabled Dean's Bar. There was a definite psychic disturbance coming from the Rue Amérique du Sud. He slipped around the corner and there outside the entrance to Dean's was the ghost of Joseph Dean himself, and Burroughs sensed that he was very upset. Dean recognized him immediately.

"Ah, Monsieur Burroughs. We have not seen you in Tangier in many years. You look as gaunt and dissolute as ever. Did your old habits finally catch up with you?"

"Well, well, if it isn't the old saloon-keeper. The last time I was in your dive, you refused to serve me a vodka tonic because you thought I was a dope fiend. Which I was, of course, just not the pernicious nasty kind. Merely a bad habit. And hey, look who kicked the bucket from OD'ing on cheap coke cut with paregoric. Looks like you've still got the shakes. So how's business been?"

"I'm not hanging around here to count bottle caps, Bill. I've been resting peacefully in St. Andrew's churchyard since 1963, in some very distinguished company. In fact I was starting to romance a lovely Canadian artist named Henrietta who died of cholera in 1938. And then along comes this inept and superstitious groundskeeper, Moustapha. Apparently he was tricked into handing over my tombstone to some hag witch named Aicha. Since then I've been passing back and forth between the two worlds. The loss of my tombstone has left me feeling naked."

"You always were the kind of guy who would wear a tie without a shirt, Dean. As for me, I was happily at rest with the Burroughs clan in St. Louis when I got wind of some devilment going on involving the sale of what was supposed to be an old fedora of mine which actually belonged to that sniveling, good-for-nothing petty criminal Paul Lund. And now your tombstone has gone AWOL."

"Why don't we proceed to St. Andrew's, Monsieur Bill? Perhaps we can join forces and solve the mystery of my missing tombstone and the fraudulent fedora."

"Not a bad idea, Dean. I haven't been to St. Andrew's cemetery since Jay Haselwood's funeral in 1965, or was it 1966? Dean, this could be the start of a beautiful—"

"Don't say it, Bill, you old prankster! Bogart himself came to my bar in 1943 on some kind of USO tour and we toasted the Allies with champagne just like in the movie. And at no point did he say, 'Here's looking at you, Dean.'"

7

Everly Tweed was an intelligent man with prodigious mental abilities, but his moral fiber was about as robust as cotton candy. Self-discipline, determination, and perseverance were almost totally absent from his psychic make-up. Given the choice between working purposefully towards a fixed goal or capriciously following the whim of the moment, Tweed invariably took the latter course, especially if it brought immediate gratification. As he was walking to the Café Triangle through the streets of the medina, filled now with the sounds of early-morning activity and the smells of garbage, urine, and the salty whiff of the bay, it occurred to him that if he combined the four hundred dirhams he'd received from Aicha with the payment he'd received for the article on "Belief Perseverance" he'd sold to the *Journal of Experimental Psychology*, plus what he'd gotten for hocking his typewriter, he could afford a small bag of heroin, a luxury he had not been able to allow himself in many months. The money was right there in his wallet. This idea pleased him greatly. So much so that he turned on his heel and started walking toward the Café Central in the Zoco Chico, where his favorite dealer, the Blue Messiah, could usually be found.

As Tweed approached the Zoco Chico, although totally unaware of their presence, he passed the ghosts of Burroughs and Dean travelling in the opposite direction on their way to the Church of St. Andrew.

"I'll be goddamned," Burroughs said as he saw Tweed coming down the street. "That guy's a dead ringer for me, right down to the damn fedora."

"He may be a ringer but it's you that's dead," Dean replied.

"Very funny."

Tweed entered the Café Central and looked around until he saw the Blue Messiah at a table in the corner, dressed in his blue silk turban and matching blue djellaba. He went over and sat down at his table.

"Be greeted, Señor Tweed. Long time no see. You are well?"

"Well enough. But I could be better."

The Blue Messiah grinned, displaying a mouthful of pearly white teeth which contrasted with his ebony complexion. "Very good. How much would you like?"

While Tweed and the Blue Messiah were taking care of business in the Café Central, Aicha dressed and went into her kitchen, where Zodelia, the watchman's wife, was preparing breakfast.

"Where's Mohammed?" Aicha asked.

"Feeding the rabbits and the chickens. Would you like breakfast in the dining room or out in the garden?"

"The garden. Unless it starts to rain."

Aicha went down to the garage. The two pieces of Dean's tombstone were lying on the floor next to the workbench. So that was not a dream either. As she looked down at them, wondering what black magic or spiritual hocus-pocus had been at work, she glimpsed something dark and shiny emerging from a crack that ran along the broken edge of the lower half of the tombstone. It looked like a centipede, but it was no ordinary centipede. As it wriggled out of the crack and onto the floor, it was already the size of a fat viper, and it continued to emerge from the crack, while the part of its body that was already on the floor moved in Aicha's direction. She screamed and jumped back, bumping against the Mercedes with a hefty thud.

Mohammed came running down the stairs and into the garage. He saw Aicha, paralyzed with fear, pointing down at the gigantic centipede, which was still wriggling free of the tombstone. He grabbed a shovel and began hacking at it, chopping it into chunks as big as sausage links. As fast as he did so, each piece began to grow into another centipede, and the floor was soon almost black with the squirming, slithering giant creatures. Mohammed threw down the shovel and grabbed Aicha by the arm, and the two of them ran out of the garage. Mohammed slammed the door shut and locked it behind them.

Panting heavily, they looked at each other with expressions of disbelief. "What in the name of Bou Jeloud is *that* about?" gasped Mohammed.

Zodelia peered around the doorway at the top of the stairs and looked down at the two of them. "What happened?" she asked.

"Nothing," Aicha said. "Just a centipede."

Mohammed was about to speak, but Aicha turned to him and put her finger to her lips. Zodelia went back into the kitchen.

"No need for everyone to get hysterical," Aicha said. "I will find out what evil lies at the root of this and deal with it accordingly."

"You never should have brought that Nasrani tombstone here. It will bring us nothing but wickedness."

"You take care of your business, Mohammed, and I'll take care of mine."

From behind the door of the garage they could hear thousands of wriggling feet scratching on the cement floor.

Mohammed looked back at Aicha with an expression of grave doubt.

Everly Tweed stepped out of the Café Central with the subtlest of smiles on his gaunt face. Should he continue to the Café Triangle and follow through with the project that had been in his mind since he'd woken that morning? Or should he first swing by his house, find that syringe and needle he'd long since stashed away, and enjoy a little taste of the Blue Messiah's finest wares?

Before he could come to a decision, Tweed heard a shrill voice yelling "Look, there's my hat! That guy's wearing my hat!"

He glanced over to the other side of the street and saw a young woman in a black T-shirt and shorts pointing at him. Next to her stood a tall blonde-haired man. The two started across the street towards him. Tweed quickly glanced around, turned to his right, and started running. As far as he was concerned, the hat belonged to him now.

Before he ducked into one of the many tiny streets of the medina, Tweed glanced back and saw the couple running after him. He figured he had two things going for him: in his youth he'd been a track star at Trinity College in Dublin, and after many years in Tangier he knew the medina like the inside of his vest pocket, where a little packet of heroin wrapped in blue foil was currently deposited.

He ran up a few steps and into a huge market hall, now bustling with early morning activity, then between the various stalls, where pyramids of fragrant spices towered next to cages of chirping birds, crates of fruit and vegetables were displayed in impressive cascades, and buyers and sellers haggled over prices. Tweed zigzagged back and forth between the rows of stalls until he reached the other end of the hall, where another door and some steps led down into a narrow alley. He misjudged his last move and grazed a tall pyramid of cartons of eggs; he heard it crash to the ground behind him and the owner's curses as he shot through the door and down the stairs.

Tweed cut right and followed the alley into a courtyard where rows of laundry hung from lines stretched between the buildings. Several women were busy with their washing at a complex of cement basins and water spigots. Seeing Tweed they cursed and hissed at him, their ruckus echoing loudly between the walls of the buildings. Tweed ran on, turning left into an even narrower alley that sloped down toward the harbor. At the bottom of the alley, where it opened into a small street, a melon vendor had set up his wares across the steps. Tweed's momentum was such that he could no longer stop or even slow down. He leaped over the seated melon vendor and his piles of bright yellow fruit, but his trailing foot caught one of them, causing an avalanche of melons to go bouncing and rolling out of the alley and into the street.

Ignoring the mayhem and anger he'd unleashed, Tweed cut left and headed up the street. Glancing behind him, he was relieved to find that the girl and her friend were nowhere to be seen. He cut right down another dark alley that snaked along, curving left and then right, with other, even narrower passages forking off it, most of which Tweed knew were dead ends. Eventually he emerged into another street, turned left, and followed it up the hill. Completely winded by now, he slowed down to a trot. He passed a group of boys hanging around outside a hole-in-the-wall internet café, one of whom called out to him, "Hey meester, you want see Kasbah? It's not that way, it's this way."

"Piss off," muttered Tweed.

"You want to ride camel? Come this way . . ."

"I said, piss off!"

Tweed continued up the street, leaping out of the way as a petit taxi careened around the corner and almost ran him over. Five minutes later he was inside his flat, where he collapsed in a panting heap on his bed, the fingers of his right hand gently stroking the blue foil packet in his vest pocket.

After several minutes, when he had caught his breath, Tweed got up slowly and walked into the sitting room. The light from a multi-paned colored skylight fell in odd-shaped shards across the banquette, the faded Berber carpet, and along the walls. Tweed stood mesmerized, still clutching the foil packet between his thin, kif-stained fingers. He looked down at the fedora on the floor in the corner, where he had flung it on entering the flat.

Enough of wearing that goddamned stupid hat, he thought. This whole Burroughs business and that witch Aicha have only complicated things. What I need is a small vacation. There was enough heroin in the packet for two or three good highs. Always frugal to the point of being a tightwad, Tweed got a small glass bottle and a rectangular mirror from his medicine cabinet. He gently emptied the packet onto the mirror and, using the long, manicured nail of his index finger, divided the heroin into three piles. He scooped up two of them with a sheet of paper and tapped the powder into the bottle, which he closed with a rubber stopper, then looked down at what was left on the mirror.

"The hell with shooting this shit," he muttered. "I'll just snort it."

It took Tweed two hits, one in each nostril, to inhale the Blue Messiah's junk. After putting the mirror back in the cabinet, he picked up the empty blue foil wrapper and noticed a strange symbol stamped on the inside. It was the figure of a creature that was half-man, half-goat, its legs spread to show an erect cock. Its eyes were wide open and hollow-looking, and its face bore a wide-mouthed, toothy grin. Tweed tossed the wrapper on the table and leaned back in his chair. The effect of the heroin was beginning to soften the light in the room, and Tweed felt like lying on the banquette, where he could stare up at the skylight and dream. First he went into his small kitchen and poured a shot of green absinthe flavored with cannabis. He sipped it slowly, savoring the woody flavors. Then he walked over to the banquette, spread a silk and camel-hair coverlet over it and stretched out.

Soon all the stress of being chased through the medina had left him. His muscles seemed to melt until his whole body felt like it was liquefying—as if he were becoming part of some ocean of idleness, free to flow in a half-dream state through fragrant gardens where gentle music played. The music he heard was not hallucinatory, though. It came from the young boy who lived in the building next door, who would often sit on the roof next to Tweed's skylight and play his flute.

Tweed's eyelids closed and he visualized a red velvet-covered door with a blue handle. As he reached for the handle he saw a plaque hanging on the door on which the same man-goat figure was etched in gold. Tweed, or what could be considered the Tweed consciousness, entered a long hall lit with colored Christmas lights. As he took hesitant steps down the corridor, he heard voices coming from behind the walls.

First a woman's voice: "How can you afford to give me such expensive gifts and so often?"

Then a man's voice: "It comes in small packets and it will be good for you. Trust me."

Then he heard his own voice: "It's all in the relaxation and the giving up of your will to me. You will not remember my words. Only the feeling your thoughts have been turned inside out."

Then a different woman: "It's me, Mildred. The frog-lipped whore you tried to rob."

Another man's voice: "You plainclothes guys better be on your toes or you'll be back in uniform."

Then a radio advert: "Rock band hooked on junk, needs a full-time roadie slash embalmer. No experience needed."

Tweed's voice again: "I'm looking for a new disguise. Something involving a green nylon aviator's jacket, one of those Peruvian wool earflap hats, tight black leather pants, and silver Doc Martens."

A young woman's voice: "I wasn't chasing you to get my hat back. My boyfriend and I just want to fuck you. Ha, ha, ha . . ."

Then a voice with a clipped British accent: "I took you into my confidence, gave you a gift in exchange for delivering me from Tangier, and you would rather squander your time with the Blue Messiah's junk. You've behaved abominably and in a most unceremonious fashion. And, I might add, you know nothing of the affairs of the church."

Next came Moustapha's trembling voice: "Please don't let Aicha steal my soul. That witch is a djinn from hell. She has already caused my member to shrink to half its normal size."

Then Aicha's deep and somber voice: "Hello my darling Señor Tweed. Underneath my qaftan I have a surprise for you."

Tweed groaned in horror at the thought of Aicha's "surprise" and attempted to roll onto his side, only to find he couldn't move, as if the junk in his veins had turned to lead. He was virtually paralyzed, rendered immobile by the Blue Messiah. But it was a pleasant kind of paralysis, a sort of womb-like suspension, not a cause for alarm. With a Herculean effort Tweed managed to open one eye, then the other. Staring up at the colored skylight he heard the flute music suddenly stop. The silence that followed was occasionally punctuated by distant traffic noise or a blast from a ship's horn somewhere in the harbor.

Now a shadow loomed over the skylight. Tweed heard a metallic scratching noise as the skylight was pried open. It creaked open just wide enough for the boy with the flute to stick his head in and look down at Tweed lying on the banquette. Then another, smaller head appeared next to the boy's. It was a monkey. The boy spoke to him, but Tweed didn't understand Arabic. He couldn't move or speak in his present state. The boy pushed open the skylight a little wider and lowered the monkey on a long leash. The monkey scampered about the room as though looking for something, stopping briefly to look at Tweed with eyes that glowed yellow with mischief.

The monkey carefully surveyed the contents of Tweed's flat. Seeing the tall bookcase, it clambered up to the top shelf and took out a book. It looked at the front cover as though reading the title, then tossed the book over its shoulder to the floor, where it landed with a thud. It picked out another book, did another mock-read of the cover, and tossed it as well; soon the entire contents of the bookshelf lay strewn across the floor. The monkey then opened the old wooden armoire that contained Tweed's clothes and quickly emptied its contents onto the floor, item by item. It looked over at Tweed again and seemed to grin with satisfaction.

Spying the hat lying in the corner, the monkey grabbed it and leaped up onto the table. It then caught sight of the small glass bottle with the rubber stopper and grabbed that as well, before shimmying up the leash and out through the skylight, which slammed shut behind him. The two shadows hovered there for a moment, then disappeared.

Tweed groaned and his eyes slowly closed, like two flowers folding their petals in response to the encroaching darkness of night.

8

The pile of cane cuttings and dead flowers on Joseph Dean's grave concealed the absence of the tombstone, at least for the time being. As Moustapha stepped back to survey his work, Zora emerged from behind a cracked obelisk. She gave him a look he knew well, and he turned to see who was approaching before he heard their footsteps. It was the rector of St. Andrew's, Augustus Bridgetower McLean, bald and portly, waddling along in his black robe with its red sash.

Although a man of the cloth, McLean lived in the shadow of a dubious reputation that had followed him from Edinburgh to Tangier. There were rumors that a penchant for young boys had gotten him in trouble in the past, but that the affair had been swept under the carpet; in any case this was of only minor significance in anything-goes Tangier. Nevertheless, it got in the way of Moustapha's attempts to cultivate any sort of respect for the clergyman.

"A most pleasant good morning to you, Moustapha."

Behind McLean's treacly pleasantries there usually lay some ulterior motive, and this always put Moustapha on guard.

"Good morning, Señor McLean."

Looking up at the gathering clouds, his thick-lensed, nickel-rimmed glasses sliding down his bulbous nose, McLean rubbed his hands together in a gesture of anxious anticipation. "Looks like we might have a little rain finally. The flowers will be most grateful, don't you think?"

Moustapha glanced at the dark clouds above, which seemed more ominous than promising, and nodded, waiting for him to get to whatever issue it was he actually wished to address.

"By the way, Moustapha . . ."

Here it comes, he thought.

"I spoke briefly this morning with Mrs. Walcott, who lives just over there behind the cemetery. I'm sure you've seen her at the Sunday services. A most charming woman indeed. And she's proved so resolute since the death of Mr. Walcott, the poor soul. Anyway, she told me she heard a strange commotion coming from the cemetery last night. She saw lights and smelled smoke, as though someone was burning something. Have you any idea what might have been going on?"

Moustapha furrowed his brow in what he hoped would be interpreted as serious consideration, then shook his head. "I have no idea, Señor McLean. When I arrived this morning and unlocked the gate, everything was as it should be. Perhaps she is mistaken."

"I hold Mrs. Walcott in the highest esteem; she is an astute woman of the most upright character. The sort of person whose word I would never doubt or question. But alas, even God's most honest children are allowed the occasional error."

"Yes, Señor McLean, we Moroccans see it that way as well."

"Ah, yes, of course," McLean said dismissively, obviously bristling at the very thought of the hedonistic natives having any concept whatsoever of God. "Well then, I'll let you get back to your work. Tourists will be visiting, and we have a funeral coming up this week, so I'd like to see the cemetery in pristine condition."

"Certainly, Señor McLean. As always."

"You can begin by carting off that rubbish," McLean said, pointing at Dean's grave. "It belongs on the compost heap at the back and not here in the middle of the cemetery."

"Of course, Señor McLean," Moustapha said. Looking back at him out of one half-closed eye was Zora, who had curled into a ball directly on top of the pile of cuttings and flowers. Moustapha smiled to himself. "As soon as Zora is finished with her nap, I will take care of it."

"Oh, by all means do not disturb Zora."

McLean turned and shuffled off, while Moustapha continued to smile and absentmindedly scratched his chin.

From behind nearby tombstones the ghosts of Burroughs and Dean had been watching the proceedings, not without a certain amusement.

"You know, Dean," Burroughs said, "If we had a nickel for every subterfuge that was perpetrated and every lie someone told in Tangier, we could buy out Fort Knox, the whole kit and caboodle."

From a little further off, behind his very own tombstone, Walter Harris observed Burroughs and Dean. Could they be of assistance in his plan to get back to Malta, or would they too just create more complications, as Moustapha, Aicha, and Tweed seemed to be doing?

Harris had seen a lot of strange goings-on during his life in Morocco and even more since his death in 1933. The second son of one of the wealthy owners of the Harris-Dixon shipping line, he had sailed around the world before his 18th birthday. He recalled arriving in Gibraltar from Brussels and having to wait onboard for the British health officer—scarlet fever was rampant in Belgium at the time and strict health regulations were in force. The health officer pulled up alongside their ship in a rowboat, from where he advised the captain that they would have to move to the quarantine ground and remain at anchor there for up to forty days. During that time boats would come and go bringing supplies and delivering messages to the ship. To prevent the spread of disease in case of infection aboard ship, all currency or bills of payment had to be taken by long wooden tongs and then dipped in vinegar to disinfect them. Finally, after a few days and much grumbling by the ship's wealthy passengers, the health officer inspected everyone on board and, finding no evidence of infection, gave clearance for the vessel to proceed to Tangier.

Once in Tangier, Harris's wealth gained him entrée to the close-knit circle that made up Tangier's high society. He also spent many hours in the Zoco Chico at Sotiry's, a cave of a bar named after Antonio Sotiry, the fat Cypriot who ran it. The bar had an old upright piano and a clientele of Europeans who gathered there to drink red wine, smoke hashish, and gossip. In its day, Sotiry's was probably the most bohemian bar in Morocco; the place reeked of drunkenness, illicit sex, and other debauchery. Sotiry's is long gone, its location now occupied by the Café Central, a focal point these days for tourists, the pseudo-hip, and day-trippers from Spain, along with the usual mix of drug dealers, black marketers, and hustlers.

As Harris mused over his Tangier past, he watched the ghosts of Burroughs and Dean hovering near Dean's grave and listened to their conversation.

"Look, Monsieur Bill, I may not know where my tombstone is, but whoever has it is in for quite a surprise," Dean was saying. "Not long after my funeral, some thieves tried to carry it off but were stopped by the watchman at the time, a Spaniard named José Losa. They ran off, dropping the tombstone, and it broke into two pieces."

"Not a good way to begin your final repose."

"Exactement, Bill. So I visited a Moroccan magician in a dream and had him infuse my tombstone with a unique security device."

"Don't tell me you placed a curse on your tombstone?"

"Mais bien sûr. I got the idea from you—the black centipedes. It was one of my favorite parts in *Naked Lunch*."

"You went for the old centipede fix? That was a leftover from when I worked as an exterminator in Chicago. God, I hated those loathsome creatures. On one of my jungle expeditions in South America I discovered how truly revolting they can be. The Peruvian centipede is the world's largest, fast and very aggressive, like all the scolopendra. Its bite can be compared to a viper's, and its venom is a neurotoxin that is secreted through its powerful jaws. The victim is paralyzed and eventually succumbs to a slow, horrible death by suffocation.

"I passed through a village of a particularly hostile Indian tribe where a giant centipede had just bitten a young girl. The damned thing was over a foot long and had actually wrapped its body around the girl's leg. Its fanglike jaws were buried deep in her foot. She was barely alive. After one of the natives had chopped off the bugger's head and removed it, the village witchdoctor tied some colored cloth around her leg and started chanting. I managed to convince him to let me use the cloth as a hot compress over the wounds, which drew out some of the venom, and the girl's breathing improved. I had brought a couple of vials of penicillin with me on the trip, and I managed to give her a shot to fight off infection. Then I beat it out of there.

"I was scared shitless—more of the centipede than the natives. In Chicago I had seen some huge buggers that were immune to pyrethrum powder. A few times I had to use a baseball bat to kill 'em. Bullets were no use—they would just pass through their segments leaving globs of yellow ooze on the floors and walls."

"Now I understand why you included them in *Naked Lunch*," said Dean.

"Indeed, Dean. But how did you manage to conjure centipedes to safeguard your tombstone?"

"The magician was also an herbalist and amateur chemist. For several nights I worked on his subconscious and suggested the centipede curse. He resisted my hauntings at first but eventually gave in and came up with the fix. I'm afraid I gave him a few scares when I had him dream of centipedes crawling up his ass."

"And just how did he devise the curse?"

"He caught a number of centipedes that are easily found in Tangier and made a mash with their bodies. Then he combined that with various fungi. The result was a compound which would act as a theft deterrent. The spores are not deadly, but contact with them would have troubling consequences. If my tombstone was disturbed, spores would be released that induce hallucinations of giant black centipedes in the culprit. Unfortunately, the spores are not easily controlled—they can be passed from person to person."

"Like a virus then, eh?"

"Sort of. The effects could last for minutes, hours, even days, and come and go without warning, I was assured. The hallucinations would sometimes seem so real that you'd believe the centipedes were crawling on your flesh."

"Wonderful," said Burroughs.

"Very effective, at any rate. I know this because the magician experienced the effects himself before he applied the solution to my tombstone. I could feel his panic via supernatural empathy. It was terrifying."

"Any antidote?"

"Fortunately, yes. Once the tombstone is returned the spores that had been released will die and the centipede curse, too—until the next time someone tries to steal it."

"I would certainly like to meet your magician. It sounds like he developed a psychoactive pharmaceutical with medical and commercial potential. Kind of reminds me of yagé. I believe the ancient Egyptians might have been working on such a concoction to scare off tomb robbers."

"Like a pharaoh's curse?"

"Well, *something* definitely knocked off that Tutankhamun grave robber, Lord Carnarvon. Sir Arthur Conan Doyle believed that his death was caused by 'elementals' created by royal priests to guard the royal tomb."

"Very interesting, Bill. Maybe if we linger here awhile we will see if the black centipedes are doing their job."

Burroughs chuckled with obvious enjoyment. "The curse of Dean's tombstone . . ."

Up on the Old Mountain, Mr. Garland stood on his balcony drinking his morning tea while watching the groundskeeper and his assistant feed the animals. The lions, tigers, and ocelots paced back and forth in their enclosures, growling and snarling, while the macaques hooted and chattered. Occasionally one of the peacocks let out a loud scream. The horses, donkeys, and goats, the chickens and geese were all restless as well, contributing to the overall tension. Eventually all the animals had received their food and the mood began to settle back to normal.

Mr. Garland called the number for the petit taxi and asked to be collected at the usual time, preferably by Farid, the driver who catered to most of those who lived on the Old Mountain. Farid was running a little late this morning. He had overslept after his exertions ferrying Aicha back and forth from the cemetery and carrying her plants and the tombstone. He neither liked nor trusted Aicha, but she was a regular customer, and she had tipped exceedingly well last night, in return for a vow of silence concerning everything he had witnessed.

It was Mr. Garland's morning ritual to take an outside table at the Café de Paris on the Boulevard Pasteur and read the *International Herald Tribune* while drinking an espresso accompanied by a glass of avocado juice, ignoring the entreaties of countless shoeshine boys and assorted hucksters, beggars, and scam artists. When Farid pulled up to the curb in front of the Café de Paris, Mr. Garland asked him if he had a business card with his name and phone number, as he wanted to recommend Farid to a new neighbor on the Old Mountain. Farid reached over and opened the glove compartment and immediately let out a blood-curdling scream. He wrenched open the door of the taxi, leaped out and ran down the street, screaming the whole way until he disappeared into the winding streets of the medina.

As Mr. Garland climbed out of the back of the taxi, looking with bewilderment after him, a policeman approached and asked what had happened. Mr. Garland told him about asking for a business card, Farid's opening of the glove compartment, and his sudden screaming exit: "He was shouting something about giant centipedes."

The policeman looked inside the petit taxi but saw nothing unusual or out of order. He pulled a small notebook and a pen from his shirt pocket and began to make some notes.

9

Mr. Garland picked up a copy of the *Herald Tribune* and a pack of Gauloises at a tabac next door to the Café de Paris and found an empty table outside commanding a view of the Place de France, now swarming with the usual traffic and pedestrians. A waiter appeared and he placed his order. That was odd, he thought. I'm sure if there had been a large centipede in the glove box it could not have escaped that quickly. And I would have seen it too, unless it had wings. Perhaps Farid had been dipping into the majoun jar.

Mr. Garland took a sip of espresso, followed by a sip of the avocado juice, unfolded his newspaper and started reading. It was his habit to read the entire paper front to back; if he was in the mood, he would also do the crossword puzzle. He was only on page two when he registered a shape moving into his peripheral vision. An important element of Mr. Garland's paper-reading ritual was the total blocking out of anyone who approached him or wanted something from him. The idea was to read the entire paper undisturbed and uninterrupted. But the shape was drawing closer and closer, and he heard a familiar voice with a trace of a Spanish accent: "Good day, Mr. Garland. May I join you?"

With a slight air of annoyance, Mr. Garland looked up into the round face of Dr. Microbio, with his drooping black moustache and his round glasses. Tipped back on his head was a somewhat threadbare black Homburg, exposing a few strands of greasy black hair plastered against his brow with a film of sweat. Under one arm he clutched a disorderly bundle of books and papers.

"Good day, Doctor. By all means, have a seat."

Dr. Microbio sat down, grunting. He was always a little short of breath. Mr. Garland didn't know the doctor's real name, it seemed no one did. Dr. Microbio was a nickname he'd picked up, and it had stuck for all the years he had lived in Tangier, ever since he came over from Spain as a teacher of sex education, before he was embroiled in a scandal that almost resulted in his expulsion by the authorities.

Some whispered that he was actually a Gibraltarian, descended from British and Spanish stock. Fluent in Spanish, he spoke perfect English with a slight accent. Once the scandal had died down (the rumors involved sex abuse and human trafficking), Dr. Microbio began to practice medicine. After bribing the appropriate officials, he was able to rent a small office on the ground floor of his apartment building in the Rue de la Liberté and put up a brass sign on the door. Dressed in his white physician's smock, with a fake M.D. diploma hanging on the wall, he saw a steady stream of Moroccan and expatriate patients. Though he was not a real doctor, he had served as a corporal in the Spanish Army Medical Corps—mostly treating blisters, ingrown toenails, sprains, cuts and bruises, dysentery, the clap, and common colds. On occasion he had also assisted a real surgeon in performing appendectomies. In Tangier he was soon cutting open the bellies of appendicitis sufferers himself and snipping out the offending organ. He performed his surgeries in a back room on an old billiard table that had belonged to the British Legation, and always required payment in advance—cash from the well-off, a service or item for barter from those short on funds. In this way he had carved out a comfortable niche for himself.

Over the years he had removed hundreds of appendixes, regardless of whether they were the cause of the patient's complaint. His hands were often unsteady after a night of heavy drinking or the consumption of various drugs, and a slip of the scalpel had occasionally resulted in the patient's death from sepsis or a perforated intestine. But since autopsies were rarely performed in Morocco, the cause of death was never attributed to malpractice on Dr. Microbio's part. The deaths were ascribed to "Allah's will" and, in accordance with custom, the bodies were buried before sundown.

Dr. Microbio remained a somewhat dubious figure on the Tangier scene, part of the detritus that had washed up on the tides of fate. He moonlighted as a veterinarian on the side and volunteered at the English Society for the Protection of Animals, in the hope of rehabilitating his uncertain standing. But the scandal in his past, his unknown origins, and his reemergence as a man of medicine gave him what was perhaps most coveted and respected among the expatriate community: the status of a bona fide Tangerino.

The doctor ordered a café au lait and a glass of water. It was with a sense of almost gleeful anticipation that Mr. Garland waited to see what would happen next, even though he knew precisely what to expect. Dr. Microbio took a sip of the coffee and set it down, then picked up the glass of water, held it up to the light, and squinted at it through his glasses. "Muchos microbios," he said, shaking his head disdainfully. "Muchos microbios."

Mr. Garland smiled and went back to reading his paper. But not for long.

"What's new in the world, Mr. Garland?"

"Not much," said Mr. Garland without looking up. "The usual cavalcade of horrors and absurdities, a new virus with pandemic potential, rupturing silicone breast implants . . ."

"Would you say that there was more evil or more good at play?"

"Judging by what I've read so far, I'd say it was about fifty-fifty."

"Ah, that's good to hear."

"Why's that?" Mr. Garland said, looking up from the paper. "Wouldn't it be nice if for once there wasn't any bad news?"

"Oh no, that would be alarming, a sure sign that something was terribly wrong."

"How do you come up with that?"

"The harmony of the world rests on an equilibrium between good and evil. You can't have one without the other."

"I see," said Mr. Garland, returning his attention to the paper. It was too early in the day for such philosophical musings. But Dr. Microbio was just getting warmed up, it seemed.

"I just finished reading *Lord of the Flies*," he said, leaning back in his chair. "I hadn't read it in years and thought I'd see how it held up."

"I haven't read it since I was a teenager. A solid piece of writing, if I remember correctly. Perhaps the symbolism was a bit heavy-handed."

"Exactly. Jack as the Id, Ralph as the Ego, and Piggy as the Superego; it's just too easy, too black and white. And anyway, why should Ralph be seen as the embodiment of good, when all he wants to do is get everyone rescued from the island and returned to society, the same society that made them into helpless robots in the first place?"

"Given the choice between remaining on the island living like savages and returning to society, I think Ralph's efforts can be seen in a positive light."

"That's the problem right there. Most people's interpretation of good and evil is far too simplistic, too shallow. Look at the bullfight, for example."

Mr. Garland had no desire to think about bullfights, he just wanted to read his newspaper in peace, but he didn't want to be impolite. Begrudgingly he put down the paper and took a sip of his espresso, then looked up at Dr. Microbio, who continued, "For some the bullfight might appear to be some kind of allegory of good versus evil. But which of the participants are good and which are evil? Is the bull good or evil? Is the matador good or evil? And what about the audience?"

The doctor's unanswered question hung ominously in the air. Mr. Garland waited patiently for the imminent answer.

"It's the *audience* that is the embodiment of true evil, creating the need for such a bloody barbarian spectacle, goading the other participants, and condoning the bloodshed and murder. The bull and the matador are just pawns in the game, the greater game of manipulation that society is constantly playing."

Mr. Garland glanced down at the *Herald Tribune*, wishing he could continue reading. Clearly it was not to be. He looked back up at the doctor and saw that the damp film on his forehead had been replaced by beads of sweat. Suddenly he felt hungry. The smell of kebabs grilling down the street was making his stomach growl. A hamburger! I'd like a hamburger, he realized. He finished the espresso and the avocado juice and folded his paper. "Well, Doctor," he said, getting to his feet. "This particular pawn is about to make a move." He threw down some dirham notes on the table, saying, "It's on me."

"No, no," Doctor Microbio protested feebly.

"I insist. Our conversation has been most thought-provoking. Good day."

The only purveyor of authentic hamburgers in Tangier was Eric's. Tucked into an arcade-like side street off the boulevard and open 24 hours a day, Eric's Hamburger Shop had a pair of open-air counters, each with a half-dozen bar stools. Mr. Garland's favorite was the Lamb Burger, smothered in onions, served on a roll and covered with french fries.

As he walked, he looked over his shoulder and saw Farid sitting on the curb. Two policemen stood nearby among a small crowd of onlookers. One of them he recognized as Kazim, the old sorcerer from the Café Triangle. Kazim had his hand on Farid's shoulder and seemed to be speaking to him. As Mr. Garland observed them, Kazim looked up and fixed him with a penetrating look. Since he was half a block away by then, the eye contact startled him, and he felt a slight shiver. Mr. Garland was well aware of the native belief in the "evil eye" and consciously made the mano fica as a gesture of protection. He quickly turned away and began to walk faster.

The grill cook with the jauntily placed sailor's cap greeted him and Mr. Garland hastily placed his order and sat down. He was panting and perspiring, and still somewhat puzzled by the scene with Farid back at the café, as well as his conversation with Dr. Microbio.

A young tourist couple at the other counter was being pestered by a particularly persistent street urchin. The boy was barely into his teens, with close-cropped hair and a dribble of snot under his nose, wearing a faded black T-shirt and greasy jeans from which two dirt-encrusted bare feet protruded. The T-shirt had a cartoon graphic of two vultures looking at each other, with the caption, "If I don't eat soon, I'm going to kill something." The kid was silent but kept gesturing with his open hand and an expression of irreconcilable pathos. The couple was trying to ignore him, but the kid moved in closer and tugged gently at the sleeve of the man's shirt. The cook said something harsh in Arabic, but the kid ignored him.

The two tourists had both ordered Eggburgers, an Eric's specialty, and watched as the cook cracked eggs into a pair of metal rings on the grill which formed them into two perfectly round hamburger-sized fried eggs which he deftly flipped onto two sizzling hamburger patties with a flick of his spatula. Again the cook said something to the beggar boy and again he was ignored. He picked up an egg and raised his arm, but the kid was already running down the street, so the hurled egg cracked and spattered on the pavement, and he turned to laugh before disappearing around the corner.

The ground lamb and onions were sizzling on the grill when Mr. Garland felt a presence behind him. He turned and there stood Just-Call-Me-Ishmael.

"Good morning, Mr. Garland."

"Good morning, Just-Call-Me-Ishmael."

"'A lamb burger for breakfast gives a man the strength of a hundred camels in the courtyard,' if I may misappropriate the Nchaioui proverb once used by Paul Bowles."

"Yes, I was quite hungry, and one of those fluffy air-filled Moroccan croissants would not have done the job. And you?"

"Just passing by to see if there might be a familiar face here. I'm a bit short on funds and was wondering if perhaps you could spot me fifty dirhams or so until I'm flush again."

Without further comment, Mr. Garland produced his wallet, fished out a green fifty-dirham note, and handed it over.

"Much obliged. How's the menagerie?"

"All fit and frisky."

"Wonderful. Well, I must be moving along. You should stop by the Café Triangle again someday; we can play a few hands of poker."

"My animals keep me pretty busy, but perhaps one of these days."

"Great. Have a good day. And thanks again."

Mr. Garland smiled and nodded and watched Just-Call-Me-Ishmael walk back down toward the boulevard. When he turned back to the counter his burger was sitting on a sheet of waxed paper in a plastic basket in front of him. He picked it up, hesitated, then placed it back in the basket. A cold current coursed up his spine and he felt a sudden anxiety. Should he go back to check on Farid and see if he would be able to drive him home later? The thought of asking him about the centipedes was not appealing. And right now he was ravenous. He looked down at his burger and grabbed it with both hands, taking a huge bite. As he chewed the meat juices ran down his chin and dripped onto his khaki blazer. Bloody hell, he muttered, and picked up the counter table-wipe to dab at the juice stains.

Mr. Garland paid and headed for the American Bar a few blocks away. He was glad to escape the raucous clamor of the Tangier streets and enter the quiet velvety darkness. As his eyes adjusted he saw there were only a couple of Moroccans in the place, seated on stools at the bar, drinking beer and eating tapas. Mr. Garland took a table in a far corner and asked the waiter for a bottle of gin and a glass. He needed a drink to calm his nerves and his worries, not just about Farid and the cold eye he'd received from Kazim, but even more about the continued well-being of his animals. Several neighbors had complained recently about the noise and the smell. One of them was Aicha, and the stories he had heard about her made him concerned for himself as well as for the safety of his menagerie.

Farid had been taken by the police to the mental hospital at Beni Makada for observation. He continued to insist there were large black centipedes crawling around inside his taxi and refused to go near it. Though skeptical, the police were superstitious by nature and called another taxi driver to remove the car. He carefully examined the car, looking under the seats, in the trunk, even under the hood. Finding nothing, he got in and drove Farid's taxi to a vacant lot near the port and parked it.

The ghosts of Burroughs and Dean were now sitting on a tipped-over tombstone surrounded by thick green foliage, watching Moustapha as he went about his work, which currently consisted of repairing the damage caused by the uprooting of several datura plants the night before. The ghost of Walter Harris was still observing from a distance, seated on his own tombstone with a few cemetery cats. As Burroughs and Dean watched Moustapha, they reminisced about the good old days of Tangier's legendary splendor, when it was an International Zone alive with intrigue, trickery, and gossip, peopled with colorful characters more eccentric than any writer could imagine. They re-called notorious parties and enumerated the bars the expatriate community used to frequent: Jay Haselwood's Parade Bar, Brion Gysin's 1001 Nights, the Atlas Hotel Bar, Scott's, the Viking Bar, the Gospel Disco, Guitta's, and the Ranch Bar, not to mention Dean's. Other cats had gathered at their feet and listened with awe to the tales of outland-ish and just plain ridiculous human behavior.

As Burroughs and Dean were talking they became aware of another ghostly presence and turned to see Brunhilde Reinhart, the German neo-Fauvist painter who had lived and worked and died in Tangier, approaching from the direction of her own grave. Born in Berlin at the end of the Second World War, Brunhilde had grown up determined to escape the confines of East Germany and to live as a painter. At eighteen she fell in with a group of people planning to escape to West Berlin via a tunnel under the newly built wall. She carried only a suitcase with some clothes and personal belongings, and a portfolio of her best work. But when it was her turn to enter the tunnel, she was told she could only take one item. She threw aside the suitcase, clutched the portfolio to her chest, and descended the wooden ladder into the dank depths.

After a few weeks at her uncle's in West Berlin, she started hitch-hiking south to put as much distance as possible between her and cold, gray Germany. Tangier was her destination, where she imagined endless Mediterranean vistas and vivid North African colors under an intense sun. Once in Tangier, Brunhilde found a job as personal assistant to an aging Austrian writer who lived alone in a sprawling villa on the Old Mountain. She turned his empty stables into a studio and used every spare moment of her time to paint.

A complete autodidact, her first paintings were filled with arresting compositions, bright colors, and distorted perspectives, and heavily derivative of Matisse, Derain, and Dufy, but she rapidly developed her own idiosyncratic style. Her first exhibition was in the Gallimard Agency bookshop on the Boulevard Pasteur with other local artists, including Ahmed Yacoubi. Through him, Brunhilde met Paul and Jane Bowles and her contacts among the expatriate community of artists, writers, and intellectuals multiplied. Solo shows followed in Tangier, then in Spain and France and beyond. She quit her job and moved into a villa of her own. After she fell in love with Ravi Kahn, the Indian sitar virtuoso, they lived happily together for many years until one evening, while Ravi was away on tour, someone broke into their villa and murdered Brunhilde, stealing several paintings as well as the black Moleskine notebooks in which she'd kept a journal since the day she emerged from the tunnel. The crime remained unsolved, one of the many grisly mysteries in Tangier lore.

Brunhilde came walking through the graves and tombstones decked out in one of her typical long dresses and flamboyant floppy-brimmed hats, wearing lots of cheap jewelry.

"That's fantastic!" she said. "I heard you two waxing nostalgic about the old Tangier, and I thought, My God, but that sounds like William Burroughs and Joseph Dean. And lo and behold, it is! What a wonderful surprise!"

"Likewise," said Dean. "It's been ages. But you still look positively radiant."

"Oh Dean, you old charmer."

"Ah, Brunhilde," said Burroughs. "What an unexpected pleasure. You were always one of my favorite painters, and an important influence as well. You and Brion. After I settled in Lawrence, Kansas, I got into painting again, and I often thought about the work of yours I'd seen and admired in Tangier. From what I heard, you became quite successful. I remember some of your paintings going for hundreds of thousands of dollars at Christie's not long after your death."

"Like most artists, dying was the best thing I ever did for my career. Too bad I wasn't around to enjoy the material benefits."

Dean raised his arms in a gesture of dismissal. "But what good would material wealth do us now? Our greatest capital is the fact that we don't need any."

From the direction of the front gate of the cemetery came the sound of a car pulling up. The three of them saw a young man in paint-spattered overalls climbing out of a small Renault van. He opened the back and lifted out a large object wrapped in newspaper. Moustapha met him at the gate, took the parcel from him and signed a receipt. The young man left, and Moustapha walked over to Dean's grave and propped the parcel against a neighboring tombstone. Zora jumped down from the pile of cuttings and dead flowers, so that Moustapha could load all the refuse into a wheelbarrow and Dean's grave was completely exposed again. He unwrapped the parcel and the ghosts saw the papier-mâché replicas of Dean's two-piece tombstone.

"What the fuck?" Burroughs said.

Moustapha placed the two halves of the papier-mâché tombstone in the slightly sunken space where the original pieces of granite had lain. They fit perfectly. He then adjusted the surrounding grass and dirt, so that for the uninitiated it appeared as if the tombstone had been lying there untouched for years.

"Well I'll be—" said Burroughs.

"Does he really think he'll get away with that?" asked Dean.

"What a marvelous idea!" exclaimed Brunhilde.

Moustapha got to his feet and looked down at his work admiringly. He breathed a long sigh of relief, while Zora wove between his legs in an infinite figure eight, purring loudly.

10

Everly Tweed awoke to the sound of rain drumming on the skylight. He seemed to be coming back from somewhere very far away. Had he dreamed that stuff with the crazy voices? The kid and the monkey? He propped himself up on his elbows and looked around the room. The fedora was gone, the heroin too. Now it was all painfully real, along with the grim awareness that the gnawing ache at the center of his being was the first sign of the return of his junk sickness, the insatiable need for another fix, which he naively thought he'd left behind him. There was also some unfinished business involving Moustapha and a plan to exhume the body of Walter Harris. These thoughts pushed past the junk sickness into the forefront of his consciousness. I must get that body out of Tangier, Tweed thought.

He knew the story of Harris and his lover Pierre Rambeaux. It was a Tangier legend. The two had been separated in death by a thousand miles of water. As Tweed became more awake, the grip of Harris's spell grew stronger, comparable to the obsession certain people have with trying to swim the English Channel or jump the Snake River on a motorcycle. In Tweed's muddled consciousness, reason held no sway. The body of Harris must be moved, and it is I who will move it. With Moustapha's participation, of course, willing or not. Hypnotism is all I will need to get Moustapha to start digging, he thought. The more difficult task will be getting the body out of Tangier.

Tweed picked at some fuzz on his tongue and smacked his lips. The heroin and ensuing sleep had left him with a dry throat and mouth. He stumbled through the strewn books and clothes into his tiny kitchen and took a long drink from a bottle of mineral water. I just have to find a quick fix to stabilize myself and then I can get started, he thought. Wouldn't want to cramp up or get the shakes.

Scoring more heroin from the Blue Messiah was out; Tweed knew he would be on his way to Casablanca by now. But there was an old smuggler at the top of the Kasbah who might have what he needed. Tweed put on his black wool cape over a light jacket, donned a beret, and stepped out into the street. Several boys were using long sticks to roll metal hoops noisily up and down the street, ignoring the falling rain. Or perhaps that was part of the fun. One of them looked over at Tweed as he passed and said, "Hey, Dracula, where you going?" Tweed gave him the finger; the boys laughed and continued to chase their clattering hoops.

It took him a few minutes to get his bearings as he climbed the slippery steps leading to the houses on the high cliff. He reached the street that ran beside a low wall overlooking the strait and tried to remember which house was Abdul's. Finally he stopped in front of a large wooden door covered with metal studs. It had a brass door-knocker in the shape of a hand. Tweed struck it three times and an old woman leaned out of an upstairs window and stared down at him with a frown. The rain dripped in his face. There was a rustling sound from within and the huge door creaked open slightly. A single yellow eye peered out from the pitch blackness within.

"Abdul, is that you?"

After a pause he heard a deep, raspy voice say, "Ah yes, my friend, come in."

Tweed entered the larger of two rooms which were separated by a Moroccan blanket that served as a door. Lit by a single candle in a filigreed brass lamp, the room he stood in was bare except for piles of cushions along all four walls. The floor was covered with old, damp-smelling carpets that overlapped one another. Short and stocky with a scraggly salt and pepper beard, Abdul wore a dark burnoose and a black stocking cap.

"Please come and sit, my friend. I have just now got up. Ow wow wow. What a deep sleep I had. Would you like some tea?"

"Yes, thank you."

Tweed hadn't seen Abdul in quite some time, but his welcoming manner and gentle hospitality were unchanged. He sat down near the lamp and Abdul went to fuss with a small gas camp stove. The shadows from the lamp danced on the walls and ceiling, creating a fascinating light show.

Abdul had been in and out of jail several times, both here and in Germany, where he had established an extensive network of trafficking connections over the years. "I have just returned from Frankfurt," he said when he reappeared with the tray of tea glasses. "Ow wow wow. Is crazy to do business in this time. Everybody steal from everybody. The customs take my passport, put me in airport jail and not let me in the country for two days. But now I am back in Tangier, Allah be praised. Business finished."

As they sat having tea Tweed brought up the matter of needing to score a quick fix.

"I just need a little, a few days' worth to get me by."

"Yes, my friend. I understand. If you have honey you don't need money. Abdul have something for you. You will like very much, inshallah."

Abdul walked into the other room and soon returned with a cat under one arm and carrying a pocket-sized brass oil lamp. It looked like a miniature Aladdin's lamp, decorated with several precious stones.

"Here is what you need. No ordinary honey. This is huile du djinn, oil of the djinn. One drop on your tongue and ow wow wow. Here, I put a drop in your tea." Abdul filled Tweed's tea glass and added a drop from the spout of the lamp. Tweed took several noisy sips and leaned back on the cushions.

After about five minutes he suddenly jumped to his feet with excitement. The heroin itch had vanished and he felt curiously energized. As he stood gazing at the lamplight, the room seemed to float on a slow undulating wave. He was warm now and took off his cape.

Abdul's yellow eyes stared back at him inquisitively. Tweed felt as if he'd had an atom bomb, hashish mixed with heroin, only this was much mellower.

"I feel really high, Abdul. It's weird, though. Like stepping off a cliff without falling."

"Ah, that is the oil of the djinn. You like?"

"*Like*? What is the meaning of *like*? Rather, what is the meaning of *meaning*?"

Tweed slowly sat down and let the waves wash over him and through him. Two hours passed while he lay on cushions gazing at candlelight visions of paradise dancing across the ceiling and walls. Visions of smiling faces and Buddha-like figures that radiated a sense of peace and well-being. Meanwhile Abdul, who had taken two drops of the djinn oil in his own tea, went about feeding his cat, tidying up the other room, and doing other domestic chores, all the while humming a Farid el Atrash tune.

When he was finished with his chores Abdul sat down on a cushion at Tweed's head and softly stroked the cat which had promptly curled up in a ball on his lap. Tweed tilted his head, looked at Abdul's upside-down visage and sighed deeply.

"Abdul, I don't believe I can stand up."

"Oh, my friend Tweed, you can stand up any time you want. No problem. The oil of the djinn, she will help you do anything. If you do not offend her."

"How could I offend her?"

"By having evil thoughts while you are in her embrace."

"Thanks for the warning, but I think I'll just lie here. Do you mind if I talk?"

"You are my guest. Do as you like. My cat will also listen."

"Abdul, I was on my way to buy a carpet when I stopped by your house. I need a carpet to use in transporting some, uh, contraband."

"What kind of contraband?"

"Let's just say it's an old and rather large Moroccan artifact. I need to get it out of Tangier and safely delivered to Malta without any hassles."

Abdul looked puzzled. "How would a carpet help?"

"Well, I planned to wrap the artifact in the carpet and then—"

Abdul cut him off. "That won't work. The customs officials know all those tricks. Smuggling things by putting them in Moroccan goods like a tourist is no good. The dogs would find it, or their djinn-like machine which can see through anything. But if you had a special carpet, that might work. I have one such carpet that might do what you need."

"May I see it?"

"Of course. It is one of the carpets in this room. But I have forgotten which one. I bought it some years ago at a village market in Toubkal. Perhaps if the carpet is willing I can lend it to you. Wait here and I will show you."

Abdul disappeared into the adjoining room. Tweed slumped back against the cushions wondering if it might be a good idea to leave. The dosing of his tea had made him regard Abdul with some suspicion and a little fear. But realizing those were possibly evil thoughts, he focused again on the patterns of light on the walls.

Abdul returned a few minutes later carrying a red velvet bag with green drawstrings. He pulled from it a flat stone disc engraved with some strange writing. Then he spoke several words in a language Tweed did not recognize. There followed a silence so total you could hear the cat breathing. Then one of the carpets began to rise. It was an ancient-looking maroon flat-weave with golden abstract bird figures around the edges. Abdul's cat growled deeply then jumped up and ran out of the room. The carpet continued to rise until it hovered a good three feet off the floor. Tweed gasped with surprise and his heart began to palpitate.

"What is this?" he cried out.

Abdul held out his hands, turned his head slowly towards Tweed and responded mellifluously, "C'est un tapis magique!"

A few streets away, Just-Call-Me-Ishmael was preparing to leave his small apartment and walk over the hill to do his afternoon shopping at the Fez Market. First he needed to replenish the cash in his wallet, but when he opened the small wall safe in his bedroom, hidden behind a framed ink drawing by Mohammed Mrabet, he realized he was running low on funds again. It was time to sell another piece of art from his secret depot in the old villa he'd bought on the Old Mountain many years earlier. The villa itself was uninhabited but was guarded by an electronic security system and a well-armed groundskeeper with a couple of Doberman pinschers, who lived in a caretaker's cottage on the property, behind high stone walls topped with shards of glass.

That Just-Call-Me-Ishmael lived in a modest apartment in the medina rather than in the luxurious villa he owned was part of an arduously constructed wall of deception he'd built around himself since his arrival in Tangier. His shabby appearance, his constant mooching for drinks in local bars and cafés, his frequent borrowing of money (which he rarely repaid), his complaints about living in near-poverty—these were all part of a complicated ruse. Securely locked away in his villa was a huge collection of paintings and drawings, carefully stored in hermetically sealed cabinets—mostly works by the foremost Impressionist and Expressionist artists, but also by other leading exponents of modern art and a few old masters.

Whenever Just-Call-Me-Ishmael needed money, he would select a painting by Monet or Chagall, or a print by Beckmann or Kirchner, and arrange for its sale at a discreet auction house in Switzerland that specialized in selling works of dubious provenance to private collectors. These works of art had been accumulated by the Nazis, either confiscated from museums as "degenerate art" or extorted at knockdown prices from Jews desperate to raise enough money to flee. By 1939, when the Nazis were struggling to finance their ravenous war machine, they decided to sell off much of this art in Europe and America. Deals were made via middlemen with galleries and collectors, and the works were secretly shipped out of Germany in exchange for much needed cash or gold.

One of these middlemen, chosen by the Führer himself, was Dr. Konrad Gassenhauer, an art historian, gallery owner, and collector whose less than one hundred percent Aryan background Hitler was willing to overlook in light of Dr. Gassenhauer's contacts and expertise, especially concerning French Impressionist and German Expressionist art. Having put together an impressive collection of confiscated art, as well as works originally intended for the *Führermuseum*, Dr. Gassenhauer was given the task of transporting some fifteen hundred of these to Lisbon, from where they would be shipped to America and sold.

Dr. Gassenhauer supervised the packing and crating of the art (the crates were listed as "agricultural machinery") and accompanied them on the train journey from Berlin to Lisbon. There he hired a tramp freighter, the *Rio Tejo*, oversaw the loading of the valuable cargo (only he knew the true contents), and sailed out of Lisbon on a rainy moonless night, destined for Boston, where a small group of dealers and collectors were waiting with keen anticipation. They waited and waited, but the *Rio Tejo* never arrived. It was never heard from again.

Two days out of Lisbon, Dr. Gassenhauer slipped unnoticed into the ship's galley and put a newly developed delayed-onset poison into the food that had been prepared for the evening meal. Within a few hours, the entire crew was dead. By pre-arrangement, a fishing trawler based in the nearby Azores then came alongside the *Rio Tejo,* and the crates of "agricultural machinery" were transferred to the smaller vessel, which set course for Lisbon, once Dr. Gassenhauer's hired help had opened the seacocks of the *Rio Tejo* and sent it to the bottom of the Atlantic with its deceased crew. Back in Lisbon, he had the crates transferred to a warehouse and paid off the crew of the trawler. On their way back to the Azores that night, a huge explosion ripped the trawler apart, killing all on board and sinking the vessel without a trace.

Dr. Gassenhauer took a room in the Hotel Bragança, just off the Cais do Sodré, and found the perfect hiding place for his treasure in a former automotive workshop located in a quiet side street near the harbor, only a twenty-minute walk from the hotel. The premises, which he bought under a fake name and paid for in cash, were only accessible via a roll-down steel door. He was able to move the artworks there in total secrecy and hang his favorite paintings on the walls.

Absolute confidentiality was essential for his survival, and Dr. Gassenhauer stayed on in the Hotel Bragança under another fake name, living an anonymous life while spending many happy hours in his own private museum. By the time the war ended, he had become so enamored of Lisbon and his new life that he continued to live in the Hotel Bragança and occupied his time making undercover deals with galleries and collectors in Lisbon and elsewhere, selling the least valuable paintings from his secret collection and buying new works to expand it.

None of his family had survived the war; in the following decades Dr. Gassenhauer lived quietly but comfortably, an eccentric recluse and a lover of the arts who warded off his bouts of loneliness by engaging ladies of the night who worked the seaman's bars and brothels just below the windows of his hotel in the Rua de S. Paulo.

Shortly after the Carnation Revolution of 1974, Just-Call-Me-Ishmael arrived in Lisbon for the first time, working as an oiler on a ship delivering wheat from the USA. The grain ship was a rusty old hulk that should have been scrapped years ago. It needed extensive boiler repairs and was laid up for more than six weeks in Lisbon, during which time the crew was put ashore in local hotels. Just-Call-Me-Ishmael had no desire to be with the same drunken idiots he'd been cooped up with onboard for the last few months and found a different hotel. He chose the Bragança for its proximity to the harbor, the red-light district, and the train station at Cais do Sodré.

Every morning at breakfast, Just-Call-Me-Ishmael saw an old man, well into his eighties, eating alone at a table in the hotel dining room. He spoke English, but with a strong German accent. One evening, he saw the old man in the Texas Bar, around the corner from the Hotel Bragança, and started up a conversation. Dr. Gassenhauer, who introduced himself merely as Konrad, was cool and distanced at first, but warmed up as the night wore on and the alcohol continued to flow. In the weeks that followed, they met often and sometimes had dinner or went to a Fado bar to enjoy a night of wine, tapas, and music. They took the train out to Estoril to visit the casino, and further out to Cascais, where they walked along the beach and dined at one of the many seafood restaurants near the harbor. Just-Call-Me-Ishmael was the son of an artist and had a good working knowledge of art, which became the common denominator of their conversations.

One typically rainy Lisbon winter night, shortly before the crew of the grain ship was to move back on board in preparation for the return trip to the USA, Just-Call-Me-Ishmael and Dr. Gassenhauer were walking down the Rua do Alecrim on their way back to the Bragança when a taxi came down the hill too fast. It lost control on the wet streetcar tracks and flew up over the curb and onto the sidewalk. Just-Call-Me-Ishmael could jump out of the way, but the taxi caught Dr. Gassenhauer and slammed him against the wall.

The driver lay unconscious over his steering wheel, but Just-Call-Me-Ishmael managed to drag Dr. Gassenhauer out from under the taxi and laid him on the sidewalk. Someone called the police and an ambulance and while they waited, Dr. Gassenhauer whispered a brief version of how the Nazi art plunder had come into his hands, and where it was now. With a last dying effort, he took a key from his pocket and pressed it into Just-Call-Me-Ishmael's hand. "It's yours now," he said, "Do with it what you like. Sell it and live like a king, give it to a museum so others can enjoy it, or keep it for yourself and marvel at the sheer beauty of so much great art." With those last words, Dr. Gassenhauer was gone.

Just-Call-Me-Ishmael told the police only that he knew the old man as Konrad, a fellow guest in the Hotel Bragança. The next morning, he located the auto workshop, unlocked the steel door, and quickly rolled it shut behind him. He gaped at the paintings hanging inside, then spent the day going through the crates, increasingly overwhelmed by the magnitude and quality of what he saw. The collection was obviously worth a fortune. And now it was his, as long as he kept his head. He would never have to work on a ship again. He would never have to work again at all.

When the grain ship sailed out of Lisbon, Just-Call-Me-Ishmael was not on board. He'd never even gone back to the ship to get any of his meager belongings or to explain his absence. By way of some shady characters he met in the Texas Bar, Just-Call-Me-Ishmael found a buyer for a Beckmann landscape, who paid in cash, enabling him to finance his plan. Through a shipping agency in Lisbon he arranged for the crates of "agricultural machinery" to be shipped to Tangier, and went on board the small coastal freighter to accompany his new property on the voyage. In Tangier, he greased the officials' palms and paid the requisite baksheesh to get his crates through customs and safely stored in a warehouse without anyone even questioning, let alone examining the contents. He bought the villa on the Old Mountain, and having installed the armed groundskeeper and a security system, he moved the crates there and began his new life. To cover his tracks, he invented the story about how he got his name, spread a few rumors about a dubious past, and over time became another member of the colorful cast of characters that made up the expatriate population of Tangier, albeit one with a very valuable secret.

Now Just-Call-Me-Ishmael called a taxi to take him up to the villa, and while he waited, he tried to decide which painting or drawing he could most easily bear to part with. Over the years, he had developed almost personal emotional relationships with every one of them.

When Moustapha woke from his siesta, the rain was pattering on the tin roof of the watchman's shack. As he stepped outside and looked up into the dark gray sky, he heard a large vehicle pull up to the gate. He turned and saw a group of tourists descending from a bus, some with umbrellas, others decked out in waxed cotton jackets and waterproof hats. Even before he could hear them talking, he realized they were English. Only English tourists would take a guided tour of a cemetery in the rain.

Moustapha sighed and went back inside to exchange his straw hat for a red fez and prepare to slip into his role as official tour guide. It wasn't something he particularly enjoyed, but Mr. McLean expected it of him, and sometimes tourists would tip him well. Not the English, though—they were terrible tippers, not as bad as the Russians, but stingy compared to Americans or even the Japanese.

Moustapha welcomed the tourists, gave them his usual thumb-nail history of St. Andrew's church and cemetery, and led them inside the church to the memorial plaque for Emily Keene, the first thing the English usually wanted to see. Born in 1849, the British humanitarian married the Sharif of Wazzan, a local religious leader, and is said to have introduced the cholera vaccine to Morocco. Moustapha then took them to the grave of Sir Harry Aubry de Vere Maclean (no relation to Rector McLean), born in Scotland in 1849, whose illustrious military career included a stint in Canada fight-ing the Fenians. Later, in Morocco, he gained the confidence of the Sultan of Morocco and eventually became a commander in his army, fighting against local warring tribes. Moustapha's tour continued on to the resting place of Commander Roy Howell RN and his wife, the Alexandria-born socialite Claire de Menasce, whose daughter from her first marriage, Claude-Marie Vincendon, was the third wife of Lawrence Durrell.

The rain was still coming down and, despite their hearty demeanor, Moustapha sensed a diminishing of interest among the English tour-ists as he showed them the graves of Paul Lund and Walter Harris. He was bringing the tour to an end when someone asked about the grave of Joseph Dean, former proprietor of the quasi-legendary Dean's Bar.

The ghosts of Burroughs, Dean, and Brunhilde Reinhart had all been watching the tour with somewhat bemused interest as it pro-ceeded through the cemetery. The rain fell right through them with-out effect, so they felt no discomfort. As Moustapha and the tourists approached the grave of Walter Harris, the others noticed his ghost sitting on the grave, and saw how it got up and hid behind a nearby tombstone.

"Isn't that Walter Harris's ghost?" Burroughs asked.

"It certainly is," said Dean.

"So what's he hiding from if he's a ghost? No one can see us, right?"

"Well, yes and no. I have rather more experience than you in this respect, Bill. If your spiritual account is settled and you have no unfinished business or any reason to haunt anyone, then sure, your ghost will be invisible. But, if there are unresolved issues—of revenge, or jealousy, injustice, or even some sort of unhappiness with your ghostly situation—then you will sometimes be visible. That's one of the ways the dead communicate with the living. The thing is, you don't always have control over when your ghost is visible or not."

"Sort of like in Scientology, when you're a 'Clear' or you're not," Burroughs said.

"The *other* thing," Dean continued, "which makes it all even more complicated, is that some people are able to see ghosts but others cannot. That appears to depend entirely on the psychic constitution of the person concerned."

Burroughs and Brunhilde looked at each other with baffled expressions. "Wow," said Brunhilde. "So we're probably both visible as well sometimes, considering our past lives."

"You mean because of Joan's death?"

"Yes, and since I never even saw whoever murdered me, because they came at me from behind, we're talking about some *really* unresolved issues."

"Hmm," said Burroughs, pushing his glasses back up his nose and scratching his left ear thoughtfully. "So *El Hombre Invisible* isn't always as invisible as he thought."

Moustapha and the tourists were approaching Joseph Dean's grave, not far from where the three ghosts were sitting.

"You two better hide behind that tombstone, just in case," said Dean.

Burroughs and Brunhilde ducked behind a large marble tombstone and watched as Moustapha stopped in front of Dean's grave, turned and began to tell the story of Dean and his bar's role in the history of Tangier. He didn't have all his facts straight, and Dean was about to correct him, but thought better of it.

As Moustapha was talking he noticed some of the tourists looking past him with a strange look on their faces. He turned and looked down and saw that the rain had dissolved the paint on the replacement tombstone and was starting to melt the papier-mâché. Glistening fragments of *El País* and *Le Soir Échos* could be clearly seen as the papier-mâché forms began to disintegrate into a soup-like mess in the hollows where the two halves of Joseph Dean's granite tombstone formerly lay.

"Holy shit," Burroughs said. "Old Moustapha's in trouble now."

"I guess that wasn't such a smart idea after all," said Brunhilde.

Dean shook his head and smiled.

"I have an idea," Burroughs said. "Let's head up to the Old Mountain and pay Aicha a little unexpected visit, maybe rattle her cage a bit. We need to get this tombstone business straightened out before poor Moustapha gets canned."

11

Everly Tweed watched intently as the carpet floated toward the door then stopped and moved left toward the wall. The light was dim, but he could see that there were no wires holding up the carpet. Abdul held out his hands and repeated a few more strange words, at which the carpet floated towards him and descended until it was again lying on top of the other carpets on the floor. The effects of the djinn oil were wearing off, and Tweed got up and walked over to stand on the carpet. "If this is a real magic carpet, am I supposed to sit on it and fly off like Sabu in *The Thief of Baghdad*?"

"Señor Tweed, the carpet is not from this time. C'est très vieux. Today no one would believe a carpet can fly through the air like a bird." Abdul chuckled softly and called to his cat, "Sophia!" She peeked around a corner of the blanket separating the two rooms and surveyed the scene carefully before slowly tiptoeing toward Abdul.

"Then how will the carpet be useful for my purpose?" asked Tweed.

"Oh, I will need some time to understand its magic completely," said Abdul. "But I believe this is the best way for you to move the . . . what was it you wanted to move?"

Tweed felt perhaps the best way to ensure Abdul's further help was to tell him the truth.

"It's a body. A body buried long ago in the cemetery of St. Andrew's."

The mischievous smile disappeared from Abdul's face.

"Ah, St. Andrew's. Then it must be the body of a Nasrani. It is forbidden to disturb a Muslim grave—but a Nasrani, that is a different matter. It is not unusual for Europeans to send their dead home so they can find peace. Tangier is sometimes as difficult for dead Nasranis as it is for live ones. But, ow wow wow, moving a body is not easy and much baksheesh must be paid to many people. It is better what my carpet can do."

"How exactly will that work?" asked Tweed.

"You dig up the body, you place it on the carpet, say the invocation, and voilà, it disappear from Tangier. But I must have time to bring full magical power to the carpet. An unridden carpet is like an unplayed oud, which is like an unloved woman. You must be gentle. It requires a delicate touch and much patience."

Tweed thought over what he had just witnessed. Could Abdul have pulled some magic show trick on me while I was stoned? Or perhaps such carpets do exist, or used to? He put on his cape and beret and prepared to leave.

"More tea, Señor Tweed?"

"No thank you, Abdul. I have to go now. When do you think the carpet might be ready for me to use?"

"That is hard to say. I need to review the various spells. Maybe two days? Then you come back and I will show you, and we will discuss payment."

"And the djinn oil? I would definitely like to buy some."

"No problem," said Abdul, reaching into his djellaba. "Here is a small vial you can have. Enough for three, maybe four days. You pay me when you return."

"Shukran bezzef, Abdul. I will see you then."

"Inshallah, amigo Tweed."

Abdul opened the door, looked up and down the narrow street, and nodded. Tweed shook his hand and stepped out into the gray afternoon. It was still raining and the rivulets of water running down the Rue du Kasbah made a gurgling sound. As Tweed walked he began to speculate.

During his time as a practicing hypnotist in London, Tweed had on occasion performed in variety shows, and from stage magicians he'd learned the secrets behind some of their more difficult tricks. Like the Box of Death, in which a comely magician's assistant would be sawed in half, or the Indian Rope Trick. Then there was the Floating Body, where a woman lying on a table would be covered by a silk cloth, and then rise and float in mid-air. After walking around the floating form and passing a cane above and below it, the magician would pull the cloth away revealing that the woman had vanished. Most of these tricks were accomplished with mirrors and diversion.

Tweed had never seen a flying carpet until today, and he was still skeptical. Maybe Abdul and the djinn oil had combined to trick him. But why? Well, at least he had gotten a few days' worth of the djinn oil, which would hopefully last until the Blue Messiah returned from Casablanca. I wonder what Kazim knows about smuggling or magic carpets, Tweed thought. Even if he had only heard about them through folk tales, it might be good to talk to him. He may have other advice that could help me fulfil my mission.

The Café Triangle was not far out of his way, so he headed there hoping to find Kazim. When he arrived, the café door was closed and locked. Very unusual, Tweed thought, even during the lazy mid-afternoon. Typically there would be several men inside smoking kif, drinking tea, watching TV. Tweed was about to turn away when he heard "Pssst, pssst." He looked around and saw a young street urchin approaching. The boy was wearing a black t-shirt with a graphic of two vultures on it. "Café is closed. What you want, mister? You want hotel? You want kif, whores?"

"I don't want anything. I live here."

"You not live in this place. This is Triangle Café."

"No, I live in the medina and I am looking for someone."

"Oh, you want Paul Bowles. No problem. I take you to his house."

"I happen to know that Paul Bowles is dead, so if I were looking for Paul Bowles I would be looking for a ghost!" said Tweed, half shouting.

The door to the Café Triangle opened and there stood Kazim. He glanced sternly at the boy and said, "Imshi, Imshi," and the boy ran off down the street toward the port.

"Salaam alaikum. Good afternoon, Señor Tweed. How are you? Please come in."

Tweed entered the café and Kazim closed the door behind him. Then he led Tweed to a table. The place was empty except for three waiters who were washing glasses, cleaning the floor, and straightening up.

"A crazy night," said Kazim. "The café will open soon. Would you like some tea?"

"Thank you," said Tweed. "I don't think I have had such a wild night in years. The musicians were fantastic."

"I saw you, Señor Tweed. You made everyone go so wild. It was like a moussem. All people dancing and shouting."

"I hardly remember what happened, Kazim. I got a little carried away. I came by the café today because I wanted to speak to you about an urgent matter I am dealing with. I need to get something out of Tangier, but I can't ship it through the post or by the other usual methods. And customs would be a problem."

Kazim sat back in his chair, as if recalling a pleasant memory. "When I was young and lived in the Rif near Ketama, smuggling was an art. We used camels in those days to take hashish down to the coast near Sebta. The thick camel hair would be cut away and packages of hashish were glued to the animal's sides. The camel fur was then replaced to hide the drugs. Once the camels reached the coast the packages would be placed in water-tight bags and moved onto boats for the crossing to Spain. The bags were weighed down with blocks of salt. If we were challenged during the crossing, we would toss the bags overboard. In a couple of days the salt would dissolve and the bags would rise to the surface, where they could be picked up. Those were good times. Plenty of hashish, plenty of money . . . Alhamdulillah!"

"That's a great story, Kazim, but I'm not planning to smuggle drugs. I need to move a rather large artifact from Tangier to Malta without it being discovered. Tell me, have you ever heard stories about magic carpets in Morocco? Someone told me they existed, and that a magic carpet would be the safest way for me to transport contraband out of Tangier."

"Hah," said Kazim. "There were tapis magiques, it's true, but that was long ago. They were brought from Baghdad and Cairo across the deserts to Timbuktu and then to Marrakech. Sultans and sorcerers used them to fly from city to city. But all that is past. No magic carpets have been seen in almost a hundred years, since before the French Protectorate."

"But it is possible that they still exist," said Tweed.

"There is an old saying here: 'In Morocco never be surprised. If you see a donkey flying, just say Allah is capable of anything.'"

A waiter appeared with a tray of tea glasses and some gazelle-horn pastries.

"Come to my house after we have tea. My maid is cooking a fine couscous for dinner. We will discuss your problem and perhaps Kazim can help you find a solution."

Up in her bedroom, Aicha was cleaning and reloading her derringer while listening to the rain rasp against the window. The gun wouldn't protect her from ghosts or djinns or giant centipedes, but it made her feel a little more secure. Her thoughts were interrupted by the sound of a car stopping in the street. She looked out and saw a taxi parked at the front gate of the villa next door, the empty one with the guard and the watchdogs. She saw Just-Call-Me-Ishmael ring the buzzer at the front gate, which was opened by the guard. He was admitted, spoke briefly with the guard, and went up the stairs of the villa. After typing a code into the keypad by the door, he stepped inside.

Aicha had seen Just-Call-Me-Ishmael coming and going from the empty villa for years now, without ever being able to discern what business he had there. Now and again he would leave with a flat package under his arm, and sometimes he arrived with a similar one, but she had never seen anyone else in the grounds except for the guard and the dogs. She had often tried to use her powers to see inside the villa, but either the walls were too thick or the security system thwarted her efforts. She put her fingers to her temples and closed her eyes, trying once more to obtain some sort of image of the interior of the villa, but it was like changing channels on a TV with bad reception—all she got was snowy, grainy nothingness.

She wondered if her powers were beginning to fail her in her old age. Sometimes they were there, sometimes not, but she could no longer rely on them. When Aicha opened her eyes again, her attention was caught by something in her garden. Standing in a circle around the fishpond, looking down and talking, were three ghosts—William Burroughs, Joseph Dean, and Brunhilde Reinhart.

A gasp escaped from her dry lips, and she stepped back from the window. She quickly recited the Verse of the Throne and the last three chapters of the Qur'an. Three djinns, or ghosts, or whatever they were—visible in the middle of the day. What strange powers were at work here? And what were they doing in her garden? Aicha went over to the table, picked up the derringer and weighed it in her hand. Then she shook her head, laughed at her own stupidity, and put it down again. She opened the inlaid wooden box sitting next to it on the table and quickly put together a concoction of various dried herbs, a tiger claw, a piece of dried bat wing, a falcon beak, a tooth stolen from the tomb of El Aroussi, the dried stinger of an albino scorpion, and a pinch of her own pubic hair, as well as a clump of dried menstrual blood. She put this powerful anti-djinn cocktail in a small leather pouch and hung it around her neck.

When Aicha looked down into the garden again, the three ghosts were gone. She was wondering if she had actually seen them when she felt a presence in the hallway. The door opened, and in they glided.

"Surprise, surprise," drawled Burroughs. "You didn't know you were expecting company, eh? But here we are."

Aicha clutched the pouch around her neck and took a few steps backward.

"If you think that little bag of toad dicks, ear wax, belly-button lint, and monkey shit is going to save your sorry ass, then you've got another think coming," Burroughs said. "I can't vouch as to your abilities as a whore, fortunately, but I know for a fact that as a witch you never made it out of Little League."

"What do you want from me?" Aicha cried.

"Scheisse," Brunhilde exclaimed, pointing at a large painting of Marseilles hanging over the bed. "That's one of my paintings that was stolen from my villa after I was murdered."

"The plot thickens," said Dean.

"So where did *you* get that painting?" Brunhilde asked Aicha.

"I inherited it from Lady Ofelia, like everything else you see here."

"You're lying. Lady Ofelia died two years before I was murdered. That painting was still hanging in my studio then."

"And what about my tombstone?" Dean asked. "Did you inherit that as well?"

"That was given to me by Moustapha, the watchman."

"Don't try to put the blame on poor Moustapha. He's in enough trouble as it is. In fact, if you don't get my tombstone back where it belongs very soon, Moustapha will lose his job."

"That's none of my concern," Aicha said defiantly.

"Well, you might wish to reconsider that point of view," said Burroughs, moving over to the table where the derringer and the box of bullets were lying next to a rag and a bottle of gun oil. "Would you look at that," he said, picking up the derringer. "I used to have a little number like this when I lived in Mexico City. Had to sell it to help finance my first trip to South America looking for yagé. A worthless toy, basically. You'd be lucky to hit a barn door at twenty paces. But maybe this one is different. Dean, would you see if there's a glass in the bathroom, please?"

Dean went into the bathroom and came back with a water glass. "What should I do with it?" he asked.

Burroughs motioned toward Aicha with the gun. "See if you can balance it on her head."

Dean and Brunhilde exchanged a quick knowing look.

Dean nestled the glass in Aicha's bouffant and took a few steps back.

"So, Aicha," Burroughs said, sighting along the tiny barrel of the pearl-handled derringer. "I assume you're familiar with the story of William Tell?"

12

The rain had stopped, the clouds were parting, and the afternoon light cast crooked shadows through the alleys of the medina as Kazim and Tweed made their way to Kazim's house. The shadows reminded Tweed of Arabic calligraphy, which he had taught himself during his years in Tangier. But if there was a message in the shadow-writing, Tweed couldn't make it out. When they reached his front door, Kazim turned to Tweed and pointed up the street: "Paul and Jane Bowles used to live in that little house. With rats. The rats lived in the sewers and came up through the squatter hole. Brion Gysin also lived there with Paul for a time, and I think he got rid of the rats. Gysin was un gran amigo. He gave me one of his Dreamachines. Maybe I will show you it."

Kazim pulled out a large, ornately designed key and unlocked the massive front door, which was heavily studded and intricately carved. He invited Tweed to step inside, then closed the door behind them. Tweed found they were standing in a small dark entryway that was closed off by another door. Kazim pressed a buzzer and a woman's voice could be heard from the other side. There was a click and the second door swung open. They entered a small enclosed garden with a fountain in the middle. The garden walk was set with mosaic tiles and adorned with various plants: hibiscus, dwarf palms, pots of geraniums, even a small banana tree. Kazim's maid and cook, Habiba, came to greet them, wearing an embroidered qaftan, a red hijab, and with a gleam in her green eyes, then disappeared into the house.

"She is making a special couscous this evening," said Kazim. "With tofu, lamb, cabbage, and golden hashish powder." Tweed could already smell the rich aroma of spices and he was getting hungry.

"Let's go into the salon, Señor Tweed, and be comfortable. You can remove your shoes here in the garden." Tweed saw a basket containing several pairs of worn Moroccan slippers by the door to the salon and put on a pair before going inside.

The salon was large for a medina house and had a hand-carved Moorish-style plaster ceiling. The room was painted red with a metal-flake finish that sparkled in the dim light. One wall was covered by a Bedouin tapestry with a Moorish keyhole arch design. On another wall hung several framed Van Gogh prints, including one of his sunflower series. In the center was a large velvet painting of Jimi Hendrix seated on a Mehara camel, his Fender Strat slung over his shoulder. At the far end of the room was a floor-to-ceiling bookcase filled with books. The salon was furnished with a bamboo and leather papasan chair, several ottomans, and a long banquette covered in plush lambskins. On a round wooden table with geometric inlays in front of the banquette was a marble, cubist-style sculpture of a man's head and a turquoise ceramic vase filled with narcissus. A T. Rex album was playing through small speakers set into the walls.

Tweed walked over to the bookcase and saw there were many antique leather-bound volumes in Arabic, by Ibn Batouta, the great Moroccan explorer, and other Arabic scholars, philosophers, astronomers, and mathematicians. He recognized the *Sharh al-Nuqayah* and also *Sargudhasht-i Sayyidnā*, the biography of Hassan i Sabbah, founder of the Hashashin sect known to Westerners as the Assassins.

"This is an incredible collection, Kazim. Where did you find these books?"

"I can only say that they are here now but may disappear tomorrow," said Kazim. "There is much wisdom, and even magic, in these books, but I am still learning from them."

On other shelves Tweed saw works by Jane Bowles and Paul Bowles, William Burroughs, Brion Gysin, Mohammed Choukri, and Mohammed Mrabet. There was a copy of *Morocco That Was* by Walter Harris, as well as Francis Poole's *Everybody Comes to Dean's* and Mark Terrill's *Here to Learn: Remembering Paul Bowles*, rounding out Kazim's collection of Tangier lore. There were also several titles by Aleister Crowley.

"I see you have *The Book of Lies* and *The Book of Thoth*."

"Señor Crowley sent me those. He was here in Tangier many years ago with that donkey of his, Victor Neuburg. They were on their way to the Algerian desert, I think to practice his sex magic with some djinns. *The Book of Thoth* can be useful for reading Egyptian tarot cards."

"Yes, I have seen many discarded tarot cards in the streets," said Tweed.

Tweed had known someone in England who had been part of Crowley's harem when he lived in the Abbey of Thelema in Sicily. The man had told Tweed he was lucky to get out of there alive.

"Please sit, Señor Tweed, Habiba is bringing tea. We should discuss your problem."

After Habiba served the tea and left the salon, the two men leaned back against the plush cushions and drank their tea in silence until Kazim spoke again.

"First, you will need to find a magic carpet," he said. "And then comes the hardest part—using its magical powers in a way that will not bring harm to you or others. I could ask one of the old rug merchants if they knew how to find one."

Get it on, bang a gong, get it on . . . played in the background.

There was a loud pounding at the outer door. Tweed looked at Kazim, and Kazim slowly rose from the banquette and walked into an adjacent room. He came back a few moments later carrying a long, gleaming Japanese katana sword. The pounding increased and was joined by Habiba's shouts. Both men made their way to the front door, Kazim holding the sword at his side.

As they stepped into the entryway they heard a man's voice. Kazim opened the large door to reveal Abdul and the grubby urchin he had seen earlier outside the Café Triangle. A donkey stood beside the boy, a rolled-up carpet tied across its back. Tweed recognized the carpet he had seen at Abdul's.

"Salaam alaikum, Kazim. Labas, Señor Tweed."

"Who is the boy with the donkey? I remember him from the Café Triangle."

"That is Steetoo, my nephew," said Abdul. "He is a good boy. No problem."

Kazim motioned for Abdul to step inside and closed the door, leaving the boy and the donkey outside. The three men shook hands and kissed cheeks. Abdul looked at the nervous Tweed and said, "Maybe you not believe Abdul will give you what you need, so you come to ask Kazim?"

Not for the first time Tweed was aware of a kind of telepathic consciousness among Moroccans which seemed to enable them to read one another's thoughts. "Oh, no," he said. "I just stopped by for a visit. We were having tea and talking."

"No problem, my friend. Kazim is like my brother. He did not know I had such a carpet. I came because we must hurry to St. Andrew's. After you left I found some other talismans which were very strong, and some notes with the proper spells. The owner's manual! The carpet, it is come alive! Quickly, we must take it to the cemetery to make the magic work. I know Moustapha locks the gate soon, so let us go now! Inshallah, its magic will be great."

Kazim nodded in agreement. "If you are moving the body of a Nasrani, Señor Tweed, that is your business. Abdul can help you more than I could. You should go with him. I am tired and must stay here. Habiba promised me a special treat after I eat her delicious tagine." There was a twinkle in his eye.

A few houses up the street from Aicha's villa on the Old Mountain, Tony Mahoney and Ravi Kahn were comfortably installed in Tony's recording studio. The lights were low, the colored blobs in multiple lava lamps were glowing and morphing from one shape to another, and the soundproofed double-glass doors were open to the terrace, letting in the fragrance of eucalyptus trees and the rain, which had now stopped but still dripped from the trees. Behind the vintage Fairlight mixing console along the back wall of the studio were mounted a series of identically framed photographs of producers who—in Tony's estimation—had made major contributions to the world of music: Phil Spector, Jack Nitzsche, Jimmy Miller, Bob Johnston, Mickie Most, Jack Clement, Andrew Loog Oldham, Martin Hannett, Tom Wilson, Lou Adler, Tony Visconti, Giorgio Moroder, Paul Rothchild, Bill Laswell, and more. Curled up on the long black leather couch below the framed portraits were Tony's two black cats, Fear and Trembling.

Ravi touched the flame of a Bic lighter to the chunk of hashish in the bowl of a large and extravagantly painted glass water pipe, the hand-embroidered tube of which was tipped with a hand-carved wooden mouthpiece that was placed firmly between Tony's pursed lips. The smoke bubbled up through the water with a cozy gurgling sound, and Tony filled his lungs with the savory water-cooled smoke. Glancing at the computer screen without exhaling, he clicked the mouse and a sample of Led Zeppelin's "Stairway to Heaven" boomed through the speakers on each side of the console. He clicked the mouse again and there immediately followed a sample of AC/DC's "Highway to Hell."

"That's it!" Ravi cried. "'Stairway to Hell'! Wait till the ravers in Barcelona hear that!"

"Yeah, it could be good. We just gotta work out the tempo thing and figure out the parts for the Gnawa guys, then we'll be rocking."

Ravi and Tony high-fived each other and leaned forward in their chairs to better get on with their work. This newest collaboration was a last-minute project ahead of their upcoming tour as the Apostles of Pandemonium, during which they would be accompanied by the ensemble of Gnawa musicians they'd played with last night in the Café Triangle, at what was a sort of live rehearsal. The tour would start across the strait in Gibraltar and pass through Algeciras, Seville, Lisbon, Porto, Valladolid, Madrid, Zaragoza, Barcelona, Ibiza, Montpellier, Marseilles, Genoa, Florence, Rome and finally Malta, before returning to Tangier for a grand finale. Tony, Ravi, and the road crew would ride in one tour bus with the equipment in back, while the Gnawa musicians would follow in their own passenger bus.

The idea for "Stairway to Hell" had originally been just one more late-night kif-inspired whim in the Café Triangle, but one morning on first entering his studio Tony started cuing up various samples and playing them back and quickly realized it could actually work. Played live with the Gnawa ensemble, without the aid of the samples, it would become an autonomous and highly incendiary piece of music, potentially the cornerstone and crowning glory of their tour repertoire. And if it caught on with club DJs and was picked up by radio, who knew, it could become a mega-hit.

Zodelia the maid stood in Aicha's kitchen wondering what to do. Mohammed had given her strict instructions not to enter the garage under any circumstances, but Zodelia's curiosity was getting the better of her. Under the pretense of fetching a sack of potatoes in order to prepare dinner, she went down the stairs to the garage and unlocked the door, switched on the light, and looked around. Seeing and hearing nothing unusual, she walked toward the small pantry room on the other side of the garage, where the potatoes and onions, bags of couscous and flour, dried fruit, garlic, and other staples were stored. As she passed by the workbench along the back wall, she noticed the two halves of the granite tombstone lying on the floor. The strange Nasrani inscription carved into the cracked, mossy stones caught her attention. She kneeled down and, as though in a trance, reached out her hands and began to trace the strange letters with her fingers.

Two floors up, a shot rang out, followed by the sound of breaking glass.

13

Abdul and Tweed said goodbye to Kazim, and he closed the main door behind them. Steetoo was struggling to hold the rope attached to the donkey's halter. The animal was obviously agitated and trying to pull itself free. Its shrill braying had attracted several neighborhood kids who were laughing and teasing Steetoo. He responded with a stream of curses in Darija dialect. Abdul saw that the ropes securing the carpet to the donkey's back had loosened and the carpet had slipped. He calmed the donkey with a few softly spoken words and adjusted the load, then the four of them, Abdul, Tweed, Steetoo, and the donkey, started for St. Andrew's. The rain had stopped and the late afternoon clouds were coming apart like shreds of wet tissue, so that streaks of dark blue and pink shone through. From the minaret of a nearby mosque came the muezzin's call to evening prayer, *Allahu akbar, Allahu akbar . . .*

Abdul decided to avoid the busy streets and noisy cafés of the Zoco Chico and took a less trafficked path that wound its way through the medina toward the run-down Cine Alcazar, through the Jardin de la Mendoubia, and on to the Rue San Francisco. Tweed was beginning to regret going to Abdul's. Now I'm about to become involved in a farce more ridiculous than Aicha's crack-brained plan to disguise me as William Burroughs, he thought. I could probably have handled this whole caper on my own if I'd had a chance to get Moustapha alone so I could hypnotize him and get him digging. Once Harris's remains had been exhumed, I could probably have hired a smuggler to move them to Malta. But fuck it, now I'll just have to play along and see what happens.

The evening markets were coming alive. The donkey halted a few times to sniff at the tempting piles of vegetables and other produce that lined the way, at which Steetoo shouted "Yallah, yallah" at the animal and jerked his head back with the rope. Once, though, the donkey managed to snatch a head of lettuce and hastily chomped it down. The vendor yelled in protest, so Tweed fished out a few dirhams and tossed them at the man. Soon they reached the perimeter of the Grand Socco. Abdul told Steetoo to keep the donkey to the far-right edge of the busy traffic circle. Once they had passed the hodge-podge of basket shops, tiny restaurants, and clothing stalls, they halted, and Tweed walked on ahead to the cemetery. The gate was open, which meant Moustapha must still be around. Tweed went over to the shack where Moustapha could often be found resting on an old sway-back chair, but he wasn't there. He looked around the cemetery but didn't see anyone. Perhaps Moustapha is inside the church, he thought.

Tweed went back to Abdul, Steetoo, and the donkey and motioned for them to follow him. In the waning light, the party of four made its way toward the rear of the cemetery and Harris's grave, with its imposing tombstone, where they were quite hidden from the rest of the church grounds. Steetoo tied the donkey's rope to the handle of a heavy amphora that sat in front of a nearby grave, and Tweed and Steetoo held the carpet as Abdul untied the ropes. Then the three of them placed the carpet on the ground next to the grave.

"Now where did I put the talismans with the magic writing," said Abdul, searching under his djellaba. He reached into the right side and then the left but found nothing. He stopped and with a nervous laugh lifted his wool cap and removed from it three pieces of aged-looking yellow paper.

"Should I read them?" asked Tweed.

"No, no. The carpet only knows me. It is like one of my cats. Now which is the grave, Señor Tweed?"

"This one with the tall headstone. The grave of Walter Harris."

"Ah, Walter Harris. Everyone knows about Sherif Harris. He lived like a Moroccan. Very strong and brave man, alhamdulillah."

"Can we hurry up?" prompted Tweed. "It's getting late and I'm afraid Moustapha will see us. Or lock the gate while we're still inside."

The ghost of Walter Harris observed the whole scene from his perch on the tombstone of the Reverend Cyril Clay, the only rector of St. Andrew's ever to have committed suicide. At the time of his death, it was rumored locally that he had been driven mad by malevolent spirits. Harris looked on with amusement and curiosity. Why had he bothered giving that bumbling junkie Tweed enhanced hypnotic powers? It would have been much easier to engage a donkey, an old man, and a street urchin from the start.

Harris's ghost was invisible except to Steetoo, who was gifted with a form of second sight. And he was unafraid—he had heard many stories about ghosts and spirits from his uncle Abdul, and more than once had himself seen ghostly figures slip around corners and pass through walls in the medina.

Harris was becoming excited as his hopes rose for the liberation of his remains and a reunion with his lover. He sat perfectly still so as not to disrupt the proceedings, whatever they turned out to be.

"Where exactly do you want the body of Sherif Harris to be sent?" asked Abdul.

"To the Addolorata Cemetery in Malta, where he can be reburied next to his companion, Pierre Rambeaux. Only then will Walter Harris find peace. That is my mission. But doesn't the body have to be exhumed first?"

"Yes, uh, maybe, I'm not sure. Let me consult my notes."

Tweed glanced around nervously while Abdul shuffled the yellowed pieces of paper.

"No exhumation necessary," said Abdul. "But I do not know the full power of the carpet and what it can do. The carpet must be near the object and open itself up to the magic woven into it by the ancient weavers. If it does not connect, then it will be just another carpet. Let us place the carpet over the grave."

The two men unrolled the carpet so that it completely covered the area where Harris's remains were buried. As soon as they had finished, iridescent flames of red and purple began to flicker around its edges. Abdul smiled and his eyes grew wider. The carpet seemed to be drawn tightly to the grave as if embracing it, pulled earthward by an invisible vacuum pump. Steetoo kept glancing over at Harris's ghost and saw its eyes begin to glow ever brighter until they were like two blazing coals.

Standing at the foot of Harris's grave and facing the headstone, Abdul fumbled with the talismans until he found the one he wanted and read the magic words, ending with the destination of Harris's remains. Tweed felt the ground tremble beneath his feet. The donkey jerked its head and stepped backwards wrenching the vase to which it was tethered loose from its mounting. A high-pitched sound like a woman's scream rose from the grave and an explosion of light brighter than a welder's arc momentarily blinded everyone. As their sight slowly returned Abdul and Tweed stood transfixed, staring down at Harris's grave. Where moments before there had been a carpet, there was now only a rectangle of pulsing blue light which quickly faded. The carpet had vanished. Steetoo's heart was racing. As he looked back, the figure of Walter Harris turned luminescent, flickered like a defective light bulb, then disappeared.

Inside St. Andrew's Church, Moustapha had been checking that everything was locked for the night when he heard a shriek and saw a flash of light through the windows. He immediately thought of Dean's tombstone and what he had done. What sort of evil was now at work?

In the warmth of the late afternoon sun that shone down through the tattered fragments of cloud into Aicha's garden, Dean and Brunhilde stood beside Burroughs, who was seated on an old iron chair next to the fishpond, his body convulsed with deep sobs. Dean and Brunhilde each had a hand on his shoulders, trying to comfort him.

"What a fool I am," he said between sobs. "With that same stupid William Tell trick I killed the woman I loved, the mother of my son. A fatal mistake. It was Joan's death that maneuvered me into a lifelong struggle with the Ugly Spirit, in which I had no choice except to write my way out. And I came pretty damn close, you know? And now I manage to shoot the damn glass off the head of some penny-ante fake-witch whore who would anyway be better off dead. Jesus fucking Christ. Is that what you call grim irony, or what?"

The rhetorical question went unanswered in the quiet of the garden, where the last drops of rain could be heard dripping from the leaves. There was a sudden flash of reflected light and the three looked up toward Aicha's bedroom window, which she had flung open. She stood in the open window and glared down at the three ghosts with a look of cold, calculated defiance. A trickle of blood oozed from a cut on her forehead. Suddenly the garden seemed ten degrees cooler.

"And it didn't even phase her," Burroughs said.

"I think we need some stronger medicine," Dean said.

"Yes," Brunhilde said. "Fight fire with fire."

As his sobbing eased up, Burroughs continued to stare up at Aicha. "Hmm, I wonder if my old friend Kazim is still around. I'm sure he could help us out."

From further up on the Old Mountain came a sudden blast of loud music, a weird sonic mish-mash of electric guitars and sitars, bass, drums, and soaring vocals. "What the fuck is that?" Burroughs asked. "It sounds like—"

"Led Zeppelin and AC/DC," said Brunhilde.

"Yeah, but at the same time?"

The three ghosts looked at each other with puzzled expressions.

"That sounds like Ravi's electric sitar," Brunhilde said, a beatific smile spreading across her face. "He must be jamming with his friend Tony. Something crazy always happens when those two get together."

Burroughs suddenly stood up and looked into the distance toward town. "I feel a very weird vibe coming from St. Andrew's."

"What do you mean?" said Dean.

"Well, it was like an echo of a high-pitched shriek. It even cut through the Armageddon of noise coming from the Old Mountain. How about we head back into Tangier *ville* to see what's happening."

"Good idea," said Brunhilde. "You two go. I'll stay here and see if I can conjure some mischief to keep Aicha jumping. At least distract her."

At that Burroughs and Dean swiftly rose into the air and zoomed toward the center of town.

Moustapha was reaching out to make sure the door of the rectory office was locked, when it opened and Rector McLean stood in the doorway.

"Ah, Moustapha. How convenient. I was just coming to look for you. Do come in, won't you?"

There was something in McLean's voice that Moustapha did not like. There was always something in McLean's voice that Moustapha didn't like, but this time it seemed different, more ominous.

"Please, have a seat," McLean said, motioning toward the wooden chair facing his large oak desk. The rector sat down in his old-fashioned swivel chair, leaned back, and clasped his hands. "Moustapha, you don't need to tell me what happened to Joseph Dean's tombstone, because frankly, I doubt your explanation would make sense even if you did tell the truth. However, I suspect it went missing because of some native heathen hocus-pocus. What I *do* know is that you must have been involved, that the tombstone is gone, and that you attempted to fool me with your papier-mâché substitute—a trick which backfired, unfortunately for you."

"It was Aicha, that witch, and her black magic!"

McLean held up his hands. "Spare me your talk of witches and black magic, Moustapha. I have no choice but to relieve you of your duties as watchman, gardener, and guide. That sort of behavior can simply not be tolerated in the Anglican Church of St. Andrew." McLean glanced up at a painting of St. Andrew hanging on the office wall as though seeking confirmation, and then looked back at Moustapha. "I will—out of the generosity of my heart, and taking into account your many years of service to St. Andrew's—attach a condition to your dismissal. If you see to it that Joseph Dean's tombstone is returned within a week, I will let you have your job back. In the meantime, your nephew Yousef will take over your duties."

"But, but I—"

"No buts, Moustapha. My decision is final." McLean held out his hand and Moustapha timidly handed over the ring of clanking keys, as well as the gate key on the lanyard.

"Thank you, Mr. McLean," Moustapha said begrudgingly, more out of decorum than any sense of gratitude. As he turned toward the door, he glanced up at the painting of St. Andrew, who, despite his golden halo, elaborate robes, and patriarchal beard, seemed to be wearing a very smug expression on his face.

On a rooftop in the medina, Sayyad, the flute-playing boy, sat with Cheikh, his pet monkey—who was no run-of-the-mill monkey, but a Barbary macaque—as they inspected Cheikh's recent haul. It wasn't much: a small glass vial with some white powder, and an old hat. The hat had sweat marks around the band, and the felt was faded and stained. Inscribed on the inside of the hatband were three Nasrani letters that Sayyad could not decipher. The first looked like an upside-down mountain. The second one was like a snake. And the third one resembled two beehives tipped over on their sides. *WSB.*

As he peered at the inside of the hat, there was a strange fluttering sound above them, as though something was flying right over their heads. Sayyad and Cheikh looked up but saw nothing, and the sound faded. But Cheikh drew his head in and made a fearful grimace, as if a large hawk had flown overhead. Sayyad laughed and said, "What are you afraid of, Cheikh? There's nothing there, just the wind."

Sayyad returned his attention to the hat, turning it around and around in his fingers, and felt something hard and flat. He took out his penknife, carefully opened a seam in the hatband, and pulled out what had been sewn into it—a small key and a small piece of tightly folded paper. Gently he unfolded the paper; there was writing on it in tiny script, Nasrani letters which Sayyad could not read and numbers that made no sense. He slipped the key and the folded-up paper back into the hatband and put the hat on his head. It was a bit too large but he wanted to wear it anyway. He decided to go and find his friend Steetoo, who had taught himself to read and write and even knew some English from his experience with Nasrani tourists. Maybe Steetoo could tell him what the strange letters meant.

14

Of those who had been present in the cemetery, only Steetoo had seen Walter Harris's body materialize on the carpet before it and the carpet vanished. The body had looked completely restored, as though the earth had given it back. Harris merely seemed to be lying asleep on the carpet. Almost simultaneously, Harris's ghost, sitting on a nearby tombstone, had vanished.

Steetoo, being a curious boy, felt a sense of wonder rather than fear at what he had witnessed. Now I have a story that will impress even Kazim, he thought. Growing up in Tangier he had heard the street storytellers in the Kasbah mesmerize their audiences with tales of sorcery and magic. He had heard stories of talking fish, and of the souls of boys who inhabited snakes and scorpions. He had once dreamt of a cat who told him where a tourist had dropped his wallet. When he awoke he ran to the spot and there lay the wallet. Inside it where several hundred dollars in traveler's checks. He tried to cash them at a hotel but the clerk took them, called Steetoo a thief, and chased him away. He still had the wallet, along with a few other objects he had found in the street and hoped to sell at the flea market. But he had never heard a story involving a dead Nasrani flying away on a magic carpet. Alhamdulillah, he thought to himself as he looked down at the grave.

After the explosive flash of light, the donkey had started kicking its hind legs and braying, and Abdul untied it from the fallen vase. "Steetoo, let us leave this djinn-haunted place," he said, and led the donkey quickly out of the cemetery, with Steetoo following. As soon as Tweed recovered enough to realize he was alone, he ran to catch up with them.

"Abdul! What just happened? Where did the carpet go?"

"Perhaps to hell, I do not know. But that place is for the devil, and djinns, and Nasrani ghosts."

"Will you be at home tomorrow?" Tweed asked. "I need to talk to you."

"Oh yes, Señor Tweed. You owe me some money," said Abdul, "Well, come by, and, inshallah, maybe I am there."

Tweed felt a sharp pain in his chest and stopped. He was still shaking and he saw it had grown dark. He watched as Abdul, Steetoo, and the donkey turned into one of the medina streets and were gone. Once he had caught his breath he made his way home. The medina was alive with people shopping for food and preparing their evening meal. Several of his neighbors were outside, talking around their charcoal braziers. The savory aromas of fresh baked bread and grilled meat filled the air. The clouds had passed and the first stars were appearing above the rooftops.

Inside his house at last, Tweed staggered into the kitchen and collapsed in his one wooden chair. He felt the junk sickness returning, so he made some tea and put a drop of the djinn oil in it. Soon he felt better. Not quite as high as he had been at Abdul's, but a lot calmer than he had felt in a while. His stomach growled, and he decided that after a good wash he would go to a restaurant.

The cave-like Al Andalus near the Calle de los Arcos was one of his favorites. It only had four tiny tables, each covered with a plastic red and white checkered tablecloth. Jamal, the owner and cook, greeted him and Tweed ordered lamb brochettes, carrot salad, a small loaf of bread, fries, and a Fanta. Since Al Andalus served no alcohol, Tweed poured some Fanta into a glass and, after a quick glance around the restaurant, pulled a battered silver flask from his inside jacket pocket and poured a generous shot of vodka into the glass, quickly replacing the flask in his jacket. He took a drink and sighed with pleasure. The food tasted good and he felt his strength returning. A sense of peace gradually descended over him. He no longer felt some urgent duty nagging at his consciousness. In fact, the memory of everything that had occurred in the cemetery was vanishing like Abdul's carpet. By the time he finished his meal he had totally forgotten about Walter Harris.

Higher up in the medina, Abdul, Steetoo, and the donkey had reached the opening in the Kasbah wall that overlooked the strait. Steetoo felt the wind blowing across his face as he looked down at the lights of the fishing boats below. When they arrived at Abdul's house, Abdul asked Steetoo to return the donkey he had borrowed and thanked him.

"Steetoo, come back tomorrow and I will give you something. Now I must go in and lie down. Be careful when a Nasrani asks for your help. They are all friends of the devil."

"Ouakha," said Steetoo, taking the rope. After returning the donkey to the old bearded man who owned him, he ran toward the Zoco Chico. He was excited to have a new story to tell. And tomorrow Abdul would give him some money. As he neared Dar Baroud he heard someone yelling his name and looked up. It was Sayyad.

The sound of the shot and breaking glass interrupted Zodelia's reverie as she knelt in front of the tombstone on the garage floor, her fingers tracing the strange inscription. She quickly went into the storeroom and got a basket of potatoes, then back up the stairs into the kitchen, after locking the door to the garage behind her. She deposited the basket next to the sink and stood still and listened for a few moments. Hearing nothing more unusual, she climbed the stairs to the second floor and knocked tentatively on the door of Aicha's bedroom. Aicha asked who it was, then told Zodelia to enter.

Aicha was kneeling on the floor with a hand broom and dustpan, sweeping up the remnants of a broken glass. "Here, this is your job," she said, getting to her feet and handing broom and dustpan to Zodelia.

Zodelia immediately noticed the cut on Aicha's forehead and the trickle of blood. Glancing over at the table she saw the derringer and the box of bullets. "What happened?" she asked.

"Just a small accident," Aicha said.

Zodelia realized no more information would be forthcoming, so she merely swept up the shards of glass. As she crossed the room to empty the dustpan into the wastebasket, she glanced out of the open window into the garden, which was barely visible in the encroaching dusk. She stopped and looked again. Had she seen three figures there, strange Nasranis? Or were her eyes playing tricks on her? She turned toward Aicha, who was putting away the derringer and the bullets. She looked down into the garden again but now she saw nothing out of the ordinary. Zodelia dumped the glass in the wastebasket and put away the broom and dustpan. Aicha dismissed her wordlessly.

Downstairs in the kitchen, Zodelia looked out into the darkening garden again, but there was no one there. She tried to remember exactly what she thought she'd seen from upstairs. The image of three Nasranis, a woman and two men, the one older man sitting in the iron garden chair by the fishpond, passed briefly through her mind, then vanished abruptly. She shook her head and tipped the basket of potatoes into the sink to wash and peel them for dinner. From the bottom of the basket tumbled a slithering knot of huge black centipedes, spilling out of the sink and dropping to the floor with a rubbery sound. Zodelia jumped back and let out a scream that would have been heard all the way up the road in Tony Mahoney's studio, had not another Led Zeppelin sample been booming out of the monitor speakers at that very moment.

Next door, Just-Call-Me-Ishmael came out of his villa, locked up, and reset the alarm system. He walked across the expansive front yard to the watchman's cottage at the front gate and exchanged a few pleasantries with him while waiting for the taxi he had called. Tucked under his arm was a flat wooden case in which he had packed a rare pastel by Claude Monet, one of the series of views of Waterloo Bridge the artist had completed during his London sojourn in 1901. Just-Call-Me-Ishmael planned to catch the early ferry to Algeciras in the morning, and then the train to Zurich to arrange the sale of the Monet. The taxi arrived and he said goodbye to the watchman, saying only that he'd be away for a few days, and asked the driver to take him back into town.

In the Hotel Lutetia in the Avenue Prince Moulay Abdellah, Evangeline Marylebone sat on the edge of her bed, smoking a cigarette and drinking from a bottle of Flag beer. She was dressed, as was her habit, in black cargo shorts, a thin black muslin tank top, and black Doc Martens. Tribal tattoos in vivid designs snaked down her arms, and her ears as well as her nose and lips were pierced with silver rings and studs. Her hair was cut short and dyed black with a shank of green hanging down over her forehead; her natural blonde hair showed through at the roots.

The hotel was another faded relic of Tangier's colonial past, in this case the infamous "International Zone" years—it had hardly undergone any changes since it was built in 1933. Before Paul Bowles settled permanently in Tangier, he had lived for a while in the Hotel Lutetia. That was one of the reasons Evangeline had chosen it.

The French doors to the balcony were wide open and a cool breeze blew in off of the Bay of Tangier. The clouds reflected a last trace of pinkish-orange glow as the sun went down, and the lights of the harbor were beginning to twinkle and reflect in the waters of the bay below. Leaning against one of the French doors, also smoking and drinking a beer, was Piet, a young man from Amsterdam who Evangeline had befriended on the train from London to Tangier via France and Spain.

"What's so important about that old hat?" Piet said. "You act like it's some priceless heirloom."

"That's exactly what it is."

"Well, we'll keep looking for it, but if we don't find it, maybe you should go to the police."

"I'd rather not."

"Why not?"

Evangeline sighed and took a drag from her cigarette, followed by a gulp of beer. She got up and walked past Piet onto the balcony and looked out across the harbor. "It's a long story," she said.

Piet came out onto the balcony and leaned on the balustrade next to her. "I've got plenty of time," he said.

"You know who William Burroughs was, right?"

"Sure. I've read some of his books—*Junky*, *Naked Lunch*, *Nova Express*—and that biography, *Literary Outlaw*. And he's mentioned in books about Tangier, of course."

"Then you probably know who Ian Sommerville was?"

"Yeah, the English math wizard who collaborated with Burroughs and Brion Gysin when they were living in the Beat Hotel in Paris, working on the Dreamachine and the cut-up projects. Wasn't he Burroughs's lover at one point?"

"Right. Well, Ian was my uncle, and when he was killed in that car accident in 1976, his possessions were divided up among members of our family. My mother got a cardboard box full of stuff, mostly old tape reels and some journals and letters, plus a lot of mostly useless junk, but there was also an old fedora that had belonged to Burroughs. It had his monogram on the inside of the hatband. And that hat got handed down to me."

"And that's the hat you lost at the Café Hafa?"

"Yes, but there's more to the story. In one of his journals, my uncle mentions a thick manuscript that Burroughs locked away in a safe deposit box here at some point and never got back. You've read the biography, so you know Burroughs wrote like crazy during his years in Tangier. We know about the thousand or so pages that he referred to as the 'Word Hoard,' from which he took the material for *Naked Lunch* as well as much of *The Soft Machine* and parts of other books. One big chunk of the Word Hoard was the manuscript he called 'Interzone,' which Ginsberg and Kerouac helped him organize and type up in Tangier in 1957—what was eventually published as *Naked Lunch*. But according to Ian, Burroughs told him he'd written a mass of other material in his first years in Tangier, too, which he'd locked away before Kerouac and the others arrived. Something he called 'Ultrazone'— even weirder stuff that he just didn't want to have around him but couldn't bring himself to destroy. When Burroughs left Tangier in 1958, the Word Hoard went with him, but Ultrazone remained here. He told Ian he'd paid the safe deposit fee for fifty years in advance, so he could come back and get it some day."

"Wow," said Piet. "That's quite a story in itself. So this Ultrazone manuscript has just been sitting in a safe deposit box here all these years, unseen by anyone?"

"So it would seem. Then at some point Burroughs lost track of the key. He tried to retrieve the manuscript on a subsequent trip to Tangier, but the paperwork he'd originally signed had been lost, and the bank officials refused to give him access to the box without the key. He apparently had conflicted feelings about the contents of Ultrazone anyway and eventually gave up the idea of ever seeing it again."

"Did your uncle give any indication of what was in the manuscript?"

"According to Ian, Burroughs was trying to come to terms with the shooting of his wife, Joan, in Mexico in 1951—you know, in that drunken game of 'William Tell.' He was trying, through writing, to exorcise what he called the 'Ugly Spirit,' the demon he believed had caused him to kill Joan."

"But where does the hat come in?"

"When I first tried it on, I felt something sewn into the hatband. It turned out to be a small key and a folded-up piece of paper with a number written on it and the name and address of a bank in Tangier. Once I'd made the connection with what Ian had written in his journal, I sewed the key and the slip of paper back into the hatband and set out for Tangier, hoping to rescue Ultrazone from obscurity."

"Incredible. But maybe you should have kept the key in a safer place."

"Easy to say now. But if they hadn't been sewn into the hat, the key and the paper would have been completely lost long ago. I figured if that was good enough for Burroughs, it was good enough for me."

"We'll start looking again first thing in the morning. It's funny, but that guy we saw with your hat did sort of look like Burroughs."

"I thought that too! So he should be easy to find again."

"But they didn't call Burroughs *El Hombre Invisible* for nothing."

15

"Where'd you get the Nasrani hat?" Steetoo asked.

Sayyad explained how Cheikh had stolen the hat and the bottle of white powder from the Nasrani's apartment and showed him the key and the slip of paper with the strange writing. Steetoo glanced around and told Sayyad to put them back in the hat, suggesting they go to their hideout before taking a closer look. The streets of the medina, full of eyes and ears, were no place to discuss secrets.

They walked down through the winding streets to the harbor, then along the Avenue Mohammed VI, turning after a while into a narrow passageway between small shops and an old warehouse that had been boarded up for years. At the back of the warehouse, which was entirely obscured by high brick walls, Steetoo and Sayyad removed a couple of boards from a small window and climbed inside, replacing the boards behind them.

They went through the warehouse space into a small windowless room they had fitted out with two old chairs and a rudimentary table made of wooden packing crates. They called it their *oculto chabola*, their secret hideaway. In the corner was a mattress on which Steetoo sometimes slept. On the wall hung a calendar and a tattered poster of curvy Pamela Anderson in her red *Baywatch* swimsuit. Sayyad took out the key and the slip of paper from the hatband and passed them to Steetoo. In the flickering light of the candle he'd lit, Steetoo carefully studied what was written on the paper, looked closely at the key, then back at the paper.

"What does it say?" Sayyad asked.

"It's the key to a safe deposit box, with the number of the box and the address of the bank."

"What should we do with it?"

"We need to find out what's in that box."

"What if it's a lot of money, or gold, or jewels?"

"Then we'll be rich, and you can buy Cheikh a diamond-studded collar."

After leaving the rectory office, Moustapha walked slowly past the rows of wooden pews towards the church door. He passed two prominent plaques on the south wall, the first of which proclaimed, "Knowledge belongs to God — He who has the power and the glory." Its companion repeated five times the phrase, "Praise be to God for the grace of Islam." He paused at the plaque commemorating church founder Sir Hay John Drummond Hay and rubbed it with his fingers, as if to gain some power or good fortune. Hay had been British Minister to Tangier in the second half of the nineteenth century, a diplomat with immense influence in Tangier and throughout the kingdom, as well as a consummate sportsman with a passion for horse racing and hunting. Under his energetic example, pig-sticking in the Diplomatic Forest southwest of the city—on horseback, using native spears—became de rigueur for Tangier's adventurous upper-class British residents.

Moustapha sat down in one of the pews and recalled the time when the old wooden church organ had been dismantled. The wood had begun to suffer as a result of constant variations in temperature and humidity, as well as infestations of wood-boring insects that had a particular taste for the valves. Once capable of producing warm, mellifluous tones, the organ had become impossible to repair and was perpetually out of tune. It wheezed like a tuberculosis sufferer trying to catch his breath.

Moustapha had asked the Rector at the time, Arthur Evans, if he might keep as a souvenir one of the smaller organ flutes that were destined for the charcoal market. The one he picked out was about twelve inches long, with a sound hole and opening where the forced air from the organ bellows blew through it. With quiet determination Moustapha learned to play several clear notes on it by strategically placing two fingers over the valve. Though he had a reed flute that had belonged to his uncle—a Sufi who played with a group of Jilala musicians—he favored the wooden organ pipe and would often sit in his shack and play Berber song patterns during the afternoon siesta. He had even carved a crude hamsa design on each of the four sides. The hamsa, also called the hand of Fatimah, was supposed to offer protection to the owner.

Moustapha's eyes were moist as he got up and walked through the doorway. He paused again to look up at the square Moorish tower, then wandered listlessly to his shack. He touched each of his tools— a saw, a hoe, a shovel, and a pickax—then carried the shovel and a broom over to Joseph Dean's grave, where the two parts of the papier-mâché tombstone had disintegrated into lumps of soggy newsprint. Moustapha stuck the shovel blade under the wet paper and heaved it on top of a pile of cuttings and other refuse. In doing so he uncovered a cluster of black centipedes who had arranged themselves in the form of the letter "D." As soon as they were exposed, they scurried off in different directions. "May Allah protect me," said Moustapha. He swept the grave clean and placed cedar branches where Dean's tombstone had lain.

Returning to the shack he picked up his worn blanket, an old shopping basket, the organ pipe, and a heart-shaped stone the young daughter of a parishioner had once given him. As he left the cemetery by the main gate he glanced back and saw Zora sitting on the wicker stool outside his shack, staring at him with her intense green eyes.

Moustapha shrugged his shoulders. "Don't worry, Zora. I will get to the bottom of this chicanery and get Dean's tombstone back where it belongs. Yousef will feed you while I'm gone. Be careful, this is a place full of evil."

Zora regarded him with an impenetrable feline gaze. Moustapha turned and went through the gate, shutting but not locking it, since he no longer had the key. He scanned the cemetery and church grounds in the diminishing light of evening, then walked away down the street.

For months he had been wearing an old pair of leather sandals that were dirty and falling apart, so he stopped by the shoe stalls across the street from the church and bought a pair of bright yellow babouches. The new shoes lifted his spirits a little and he walked on to the Grand Socco mosque in time for Maghrib, the evening prayer. Outside the mosque he washed his feet carefully and threw the old sandals away. After prayers he put on his new shoes and decided to walk up to the Rue Amérique du Sud on his way to the Rue de la Liberté.

The ghosts of Burroughs and Dean arrived in the cemetery just after Moustapha had left. Like super-sensitive seismographs, they immediately felt the strange vibrations from Walter Harris's grave. They circled Harris's tombstone and Burroughs pointed out a rectangular area that sparkled as if it had been sprinkled with glitter. "Apparently something went down here."

"Or something went up," Dean suggested. "I don't sense the presence of Walter Harris at all, Bill. I wonder what else might have been going on. We should inspect my grave as well."

They drifted over to the low wall and steps leading to the lower cemetery, the least well-tended in the churchyard. The base of the high wall was overgrown with vines and the flat areas displayed patches of bare clay that glistened like bald men's heads. Burroughs and Dean moved slowly, peering at the broken remains of old tombs. Now the rain had ended, a half-dozen feral cats were lounging on moss-covered slabs of marble.

"This is definitely my grave," said Dean, pointing down at the covering of cedar branches. "But where's the fake tombstone?"

"There's your memorial," said Burroughs, nodding toward a lumpy pile of newspapers near the wall.

They floated over to what was left of the papier-mâché tombstone. The pages had come unglued and separated in places. "Jesus, what a mess," said Dean.

"Wait, this is interesting," said Burroughs. "A whole new spin on Gysin's cut-up technique. These disintegrating *Journal de Tanger* pages have melted and merged with a section of *Le Matin*. These could be the first tombstone cut-ups."

"Never mind the artsy-fartsy literary crap. I'm trying to get my damned tombstone back," said Dean.

Burroughs was still lost in his reverie. "Not *The Ticket that Exploded*, but *The Tombstone that Melted*. Who knows, maybe there's another book in all this."

At that moment the two ghosts tuned their psychic monitoring to Moustapha's movements nearby. Passing through the cemetery wall, they spotted Moustapha approaching Dean's Bar in the Rue Amérique du Sud. He paused, as if deciding whether to go inside.

"I don't think booze is what Moustapha needs right now," said Dean.

Dean quickly exercised the power of suggestion to make Moustapha feel nauseous from the smell of alcohol, tobacco smoke, and grilled sardines that wafted from the doorway.

"He seems lost," said Burroughs. "Like he doesn't know where to go next. Reminds me of me when I was alive and haunted these streets . . . Look, he's got his shack blanket and that shabby old basket."

"Maybe he's been fired from his job for all the craziness that's been going on at St. Andrew's. Let's follow him and see where he ends up," said Dean.

"Yeah. As the Mage of Tangier put it, *Let it come down!*"

Moustapha's thoughts were as tangled as a pile of wool before being carded. He had been tricked and vexed by Aicha and her dubious witchcraft, betrayed by the rain that had exposed the fake tombstone, and fired from his job as caretaker and watchman. The cemetery was still haunted, and he still owed Tarik at the bakkal five hundred dirhams. How could he explain to his sister what had happened? Her husband, obstinate tyrant that he was, would now likely forbid Moustapha from visiting their home. It seemed to him that his one chance to save himself was to steal back Dean's tombstone and restore it to its proper place before Rector McLean's deadline. But doing so would require battling Aicha, and he knew he wasn't strong enough to defeat her on his own. What he needed now was the help of a holy man or a sorcerer. From out of nowhere the wise and benevolent face of Kazim appeared in his mind's eye.

16

Everly Tweed stepped out of Al Andalus into the street and stood for a while trying to dislodge a stubborn piece of gristle stuck between his upper rear molars with a toothpick. It was dark, the streetlights were lit, and the people still going to and fro in the narrow streets of the medina were now just anonymous figures in hooded haiks, djellabas, and burnooses. Tweed spat out the dislodged gristle, tossed the toothpick into the gutter, and rubbed his hands together. What to do with the newly begun evening? He would have liked to go home and snort another line of Blue Messiah heroin, but that damned monkey had made off with it, as well as the hat. The monkey must belong to that neighbor kid with the flute, so maybe he could track him down and recover the heroin. The hat was obviously trouble. Might as well have a curse on it. Strictly hands-off. But maybe the kid would accept the hat in exchange for returning the glass vial. The Moroccans loved to barter. Tweed still had a bit of Abdul's djinn oil left, but he wasn't in the mood for that kind of a high, and it was too soon after last night's spectacle to return to the Café Triangle.

Coming down the street Tweed saw the crazy old Spanish man in a ratty wool poncho and battered black matador's hat, the one who always walked around Tangier calling "Paloma? Paloma?" Tweed had long wondered who or what Paloma was. An estranged girlfriend or wife? A cat or dog? A canary flown from its cage? The ghost of some long-lost loved one? It was a mystery and would likely remain so. Maybe the guy was just a complete loony. There were plenty of those in Tangier. Tweed watched him go down the street, glancing left and right, calling "Paloma? Paloma?" into the darkness.

Out of curiosity, Tweed decided to follow him. Maybe the mystery would be explained. Tweed took great pride in knowing the medina as well as he did, so he was surprised to see the Spanish guy turn into a narrow side street that was totally unfamiliar to him. The man was still ahead of Tweed but barely visible, the street was so poorly lit. Tweed heard his "Paloma? Paloma?" as he followed him around a corner into another street, then another, this one really just a passageway, and saw him stop outside what seemed to be a small café. The Paloma-seeker hovered at the window for a few moments peering through the glass, then moved on.

Tweed looked around the tiny intersection, then at the façade of the café, but recognized nothing. He wasn't even sure he was still in the medina. He walked up and looked through the window. The interior was decorated in the style of a nineteenth-century Parisian café, with marble-topped tables and simple wooden chairs, much brass and glass, and a zinc-topped bar running along one wall, everything bathed in a warm, muted light. It looked extremely cozy. There was no TV up in the corner as in every other café in Tangier, on which dumbstruck patrons silently watched the ubiquitous fútbol game or some ridiculous dubbed Spanish soap opera or game show. In fact, everyone inside seemed to be deeply absorbed in some action off to one side which Tweed could not see from where he stood.

He looked up at the sign above the door. CAFÉ DE NUIT it read, in gold Art Nouveau lettering on a red background. A chalkboard hung in another window. Tweed read, in English: LIVE TONIGHT – POETS AND STORYTELLERS. With no further hesitation, he stepped inside and found a table at the back of the room. Glancing around, he recognized Dr. Microbio in a dinner jacket and a bow tie, a pile of books and a notebook on the table in front of him.

On a low stage in the corner sat a young Moroccan reciting a poem. Tweed's Arabic was relatively good, but not so good that he could understand all the subtleties and nuances of Moroccan poetry. Judging by the rapt faces of the audience, the poet was pretty good. All Tweed could understand was something about a river in the woods, some birds having a conversation, and something about a graveyard and a tombstone. He sat up straight when he heard those last words. He wanted to think of it as a strange coincidence, but he knew all too well that there were rarely any coincidences in Tangier. How did that Arabic proverb go? "On the palm of fate we walk and do not know what is written." Or just *Mektoub*, as Moroccans were prone to say.

A beautiful dark-haired waitress with large brown eyes appeared at Tweed's table. She was so beautiful that it took Tweed a few moments to get his bearings after the initial eye contact. Taking a wild chance, he asked if they had any absinthe. If not in the Café de Nuit, then where else?

"Of course," she said in a deep, silky voice. "We have a Duval from Brussels, a Berger from Argentina, or a Pernod Fils from Tarragona."

Tweed's eyes widened. "A Pernod Fils 68 per cent?"

"Yes, it's one of the last bottles, from 1965."

Tweed rubbed his hands together in keen anticipation. "A Pernod Fils then, please."

"Very well," said the waitress and turned and headed for the bar.

The Moroccan poet had finished and stepped down from the stage to a loud round of applause. A tall, slim man with sharply chiseled features, dressed in a dark suit with a very narrow tie, his black hair pomaded and combed straight back, with a thin elegantly waxed moustache—he reminded Tweed of a young Salvador Dalí—got up onstage and introduced the next performer, first in accent-free Arabic, then in accent-free English. "And now, ladies and gentlemen, our special guest for the night, all the way from Hamburg, Germany, Mark Terrill." The applause was not as enthusiastic as it had been for the Moroccan poet, but the Tangerinos were notoriously nationalistic in all matters of pride, cultural or otherwise.

The waitress returned with a silver tray and placed a glass of absinthe, a small pitcher of water, a dish of sugar cubes, and a silver absinthe spoon on the table. Tweed set the absinthe spoon on top of the glass and placed a sugar cube in it, then slowly let a trickle of water run over the sugar cube and through the slotted silver spoon until the sugar had dissolved and the absinthe turned a milky white. He smiled and took a small sip. Wonderful, he thought. Just like the good old days.

Terrill stepped onstage and took a seat at the small table lit by a candle stuck into an old straw-wrapped Chianti bottle. He took a sip from a glass of red wine and leaned back in the chair, scanned the audience, and after a brief silence in which he seemed to be gathering his thoughts, he began to recite a story. Its title, he announced, was "The Travelers."

Having made one of their rare collective decisions, the travelers halted for a brief respite at a rest stop along the autobahn. They parked between two large trucks, adjacent to a weathered cement picnic table. From the back of their Volvo station wagon, Francine produced a wicker basket and placed it squarely in the middle of the cement table, on which could be seen stains and residues from previous roadside picnics. From the basket she took out a block of Dutch cheese, a half loaf of dark German bread, and a dusty, cobwebbed, vintage bottle of Coca Cola. The others looked on in various states of road-weary ambiguity and ambivalence.

From the autobahn came the sudden sound of screeching rubber, metal impacting against metal, and breaking glass. In the spirit of the prevailing ambiguity and ambivalence, Ralf stood up and half-heartedly began to slice the cheese. In the grass nearby lay the usual empty beer cans, crumpled cigarette packs, and used condoms, all waiting for someone to include them in some redundantly mundane and boring poem.

Cornelius lit a Cuban cigar and stared off into the stand of fir trees that defined the perimeter of the rest stop. He was overcome by an urgent desire to discuss the things he no longer cared about, which seemed to be increasing exponentially from day to day, perhaps even minute by minute, but decided against it. Instead, he dipped into an ongoing reverie in which a recent trip to the island of Crete was replicated in all its detail. There was the room in the hotel above the harbor with its polished stone floor on which the rainwater that had blown in under the door to the balcony had collected in a shimmering puddle; there was the squeaking bed with its ornate iron bedstead, the bedside table with its kitschy neo-Art Nouveau lamp, the hulking wooden armoire with its creaking doors, and the all-pervading fallow atmosphere of a mostly deserted holiday resort in Greece in the middle of winter.

Again the sound of screeching rubber, metal against metal, and shattering glass could be heard from the direction of the autobahn, bursting the bubble of Cornelius's detailed and comprehensive recollection.

Bread and cheese were passed around, and vintage Coke was poured into the white plastic cups that Francine had so thoughtfully included, where it foamed and effervesced with cheery familiarity, despite its advanced age. "Cheers," Francine said, raising her plastic cup. It was the first word spoken since their arrival, and although no one could possibly foresee it, it was to be the last during their brief interlude alongside the noisy autobahn.

The others raised their cups in silence, wordlessly acknowledging Francine's well-meant toast.

Brigitte returned from the toilet and fell upon the bread and cheese like a person starved. Ralf glanced down at an empty potato chip bag lying in the grass nearby and was immediately aware of the lines of a poem beginning to form in his head. It was a terrible habit. He quickly looked away and forced his mind to think of something else, but being the visual sort of person he was, he had no other choice than to think about what he saw, which happened to be one of the truck drivers climbing up into the cab of his truck. He was dressed in jeans and cowboy boots, a red and black checkered shirt, a black leather vest, and a black cowboy hat. Had they been in America, this would not have seemed the least bit remarkable to Ralf, but since they were in Germany, it struck Ralf as being most odd and incongruous.

The truck driver had left the door of the cab open while he got settled in his seat, and suddenly Ralf heard the familiar strains of Hank Williams's "Your Cheatin' Heart." He was immediately reminded of one of his first girlfriends, who had a BMW 2002 with an eight-track tape player and a meager collection of cartridges including a Hank Williams greatest hits collection, which, during the course of their relationship, they had certainly heard at least one million times, until one night the tape finally broke and became an impossible tangle of shimmering black tagliatelle.

There was another accident on the autobahn, this time apparently involving several vehicles in a series of thundering chain-reaction collisions. Sirens could be heard in the distance.

Having devoured the last of the bread and cheese, Brigitte leaned back and lit a cigarette, pondering the scene she had just experienced in the women's toilets. There had been a large, noisy group of gypsy women and their children, washing themselves and their clothes, while a portable gas samovar steamed on the floor in the corner. For the most part, the gypsies had ignored Brigitte and gone about their business, and Brigitte had followed suit, although one older woman seemed unable to take her eyes off of Brigitte.

After Brigitte had washed her hands and was combing her hair in the steamed-over mirror, she suddenly became aware of the older woman standing next to her, gesturing with the open palm of her hand. Brigitte started to open her purse to get out her wallet, but the woman shook her head and pointed at Brigitte's hand. Then Brigitte understood. She held her hand out, palm up, towards the woman, who took it in her own and began to study it with an expression of utmost earnestness. Without looking up, the woman began to speak, but it was a language that Brigitte couldn't even recognize, much less understand. She tried to discern from the tone of the woman's voice if what she was saying was positive or negative in nature, but the woman spoke in an even monotone that betrayed no emotion whatsoever, although it was obvious from her demeanor that what she was saying was of great import. Brigitte watched the woman's lips move as they contoured to the language she was speaking and noticed a small growth just below her left nostril, out of which grew three shiny black hairs.

There was a long, suspended screech of rubber, almost in slow motion, followed by the violent crumpling of sheet metal and the spraying of safety glass and suddenly Brigitte was aware of herself watching Francine packing the remnants of their meager roadside repast into the wicker picnic basket.

Cornelius and Ralf had gotten to their feet and were silently involved in a series of stretching exercises prior to getting back in the car and continuing their journey.

When the last of the plastic cups and the dusty bottle of Coke were packed away in the basket, Francine found herself absentmindedly staring down at the worn surface of the cement table, with its slight green shimmer of moss, and was immediately reminded of a recent walk she'd taken in Paris through Père Lachaise cemetery, ostensibly to see the graves of Colette, Edith Piaf, Sarah Bernhardt, Oscar Wilde, Apollinaire, and the meister of remembrance of himself, Marcel Proust, when actually she had been most interested in seeing the grave of Jim Morrison, the infamous Lizard King, although she'd been too embarrassed to mention this to her friends.

She'd had no idea where to look for Jim Morrison's grave, and couldn't bring herself to ask someone, but after a while she noticed little arrows scratched roughly into the sides and backs of certain tombstones and monuments, sometimes accompanied by the word JIM, and as she began to follow these crude signs they increased in frequency and complexity, sometimes including lyrics or quotes or poems. At one point she thought she heard music of some kind, and as she came around the corner of a large obelisk, she saw a group of people loosely gathered around a small plot, some standing, some sitting, one guy strumming on an acoustic guitar in an inept attempt at "Light My Fire," sung with a thick French accent.

Francine approached the grave, and saw the small bust of Jim Morrison's head, draped with beads and flowers and a pair of someone's sunglasses, a crudely rolled joint pressed between the stone lips. The people gathered there were all quite young, dressed in vintage hippie garb, in colored scarves and snakeskin boots and black velvet jackets and fringed leather vests and a lot of other things Francine hadn't seen since high school. They were passing around a joint, as well as a bottle of wine, talking in hushed tones, or just staring listlessly at the grave itself. The reverential atmosphere of the scene was impressive, but there was also something quite ludicrous about the entire scenario.

Francine thought about the rumor that Jim Morrison hadn't actually died, that he wasn't buried in Père Lachaise, that he was alive and well and writing poetry somewhere in North Africa. It was with no small effort that she suppressed the urge to laugh out loud, although the last laugh certainly would have belonged to the Lizard King.

Then she was suddenly swept up in a powerful reminiscence of another visit to another grave in another part of the world. It had been mid-winter and she was visiting friends in Boston. She wanted to drive up to Lowell to see Jack Kerouac's grave, but couldn't interest anyone in accompanying her, and ended up going alone. Somewhere on the turnpike there had been a sign for Walden Pond; a big, blue, state highway sign like all the others along the turnpike. She hadn't realized she would be passing so close to the idyllic setting of Thoreau's masterpiece and wondered what he would think of seeing his humble abode listed as just another exit along the turnpike.

Having never been to Lowell, Francine had no idea where to look for traces of Jack Kerouac, and since she was expected back in Boston for dinner that evening, and somewhat pressed for time, she finally asked someone on the street, who directed her to a downtown office of the state park system, where a woman in a ranger's uniform gave her a handful of leaflets and maps and described the route out to Edson Cemetery, where Kerouac was buried.

Francine wandered around town for a while, trying to soak up the atmosphere and get a feeling for the place. There was Lowell High School, and there was the Paradise Diner, the supposed inspiration for the last name of Sal Paradise. It was bright and sunny, but there was a driving icy wind that seemed to cut through everything, including her clothes. Despite the abundance of sun and light, Francine had no problem seeing Lowell as the dreary, red-brick mill town so often described by Kerouac. She went into the Boott Cotton Mills Museum, where one of Kerouac's rucksacks was on display in a glass case, complete with its well-worn contents. She looked closely at the small gas cooker, the battered aluminum mess kit, the plastic water bottle, the sewing kit, and a dog-eared little notebook with the pages full of penciled notes. In the same glass case was an old portable typewriter, worn and battered from years of constant use.

Afterwards Francine walked down the hill to the plaza where the Jack Kerouac Commemorative sculpture was located

and read all the inscriptions on the massive stone mono-
liths, but the wind was just too cold for her to linger, so
she got back in the car and headed out to Edson Cemetery.
The map she'd received was accurate and easy to read, and
she parked outside, walked in through the wide iron gate,
and continued to follow the directions on the map. It was a
large cemetery, the graves organized in neat rows, divided
by streets into a symmetrical grid of blocks, much like a
regular city neighborhood. The leafless trees formed stark,
jagged silhouettes against the bright blue winter sky, while
the leaves themselves swirled and skittered among the gravestones. Apparently she was the only person there.

Suddenly Francine found herself standing directly over
the grave of Jack Kerouac, a small rectangular slab of stone
set into the grass, with the words TI JEAN inscribed across
the top. Against her will, and in absolute contradiction
with her personal nature, she was overcome by a feeling of
immense sorrow and loss. She could feel tears forming in her
eyes, in which the bright winter sun was now refracting,
temporarily blinding her.

A long howl of abrading rubber was followed by a deafening
grinding and smashing of metal and glass as a large truck
jackknifed into the cars already stationary on the autobahn
after the previous accident. There was a muffled explosion
as a car's ruptured gas tank burst into flames. Francine
closed the wicker basket and started towards their car. The
others followed, and without exchanging a single word, took
up their places in the green station wagon. Ralf started the
engine, searched futilely for a tape with some country music
but gave up, put the car in gear, eased out the clutch, and
started towards the autobahn, where thick black smoke could
be seen coiling up into the sky.

Francine sorted through the cassettes as well, looking
for something by the Doors, and finding nothing, decided on
a tape of traditional Gypsy violin music, which immediately
launched Brigitte into another reverie, while Cornelius
chewed on the cold stub of his cigar, trying to decide just
what it was he really cared about least of all. From somewhere in the distance came the sound of police and ambulance
sirens, but they soon merged and mingled indistinguishably
with the sound of the violin music, which Francine had decided to hear a little louder. It went without saying that
the travelers were glad to be back on the road again.

After a somewhat hesitant silence, there was thunderous applause. Terrill stood up and took a bow. The MC came up on stage and shook his hand. Tweed didn't know what to think. Looking down at the table, he saw that he had drunk three absinthes. There was no way he would be able to pay for it all. Nonetheless he signaled to the waitress that he wanted to pay his bill.

What a strange story that had been. And what was with all these cemeteries and tombstones, Tweed wondered as he waited for the waitress to bring the bill. A definite surfeit of necropolitan imagery. The synchronicity was piling up far too high. It was getting to be much more than just uncanny. When the waitress brought the check, Tweed explained that he'd miscalculated the cost of the absinthe; he didn't have enough cash on hand and had left his wallet with his credit cards at home. She was friendly enough to believe the lie and accepted Tweed's offer to leave his gold pocket watch as a deposit until he could come back and settle the bill. He gave her the last of his cash as a token of his good will, designating half of it as a tip.

Tweed put on his cape and beret and left the café. The absinthe had definitely gone to his head, and as he tried to find his way home, he realized he was lost. It was the first time he'd been lost in Tangier in probably ten years. He wandered along various streets looking for some familiar landmark or vista, but for the most part it was too dark to see anything. Eventually he came to a wider thoroughfare with streetlights, and he followed that until gradually things started to look more familiar. He was somewhere behind the medina, skirting the edge of the Marshan, heading toward the Boulevard Pasteur.

Suddenly he heard the sound of screeching rubber, followed by the sound of metal crashing against metal, and the shattering of glass. As he came around the next corner, Tweed saw that two taxis had collided in the intersection. One had been flipped onto its left side so the driver's head in the broken window was only inches from the pavement. The driver of the other taxi had gotten out and was cursing the trapped driver while holding a bloody handkerchief to his own forehead. A crowd of men rushed to the overturned taxi and began rocking it back and forth until it landed upright. A few of them then picked up stones and smashed the back window in to help a passenger in the back seat. Others pried open the driver's door, dragged the stunned taxi driver out, and laid him on the sidewalk. It took a couple of men to pull the passenger out through the back window. Other than having a torn jacket and glass fragments in his hair he seemed unhurt, but either he'd been knocked unconscious or had fainted, so they laid him on the sidewalk near the dazed driver.

A few minutes later a Sûreté Nationale car arrived on the scene. The officer on the passenger side rolled down his window and shouted at the crowd to push the wrecked cars out of the intersection, which by this time was a log jam of cars, donkey carts, taxis, and a tour bus full of Spanish tourists. It seemed like everyone was leaning on their horn and adding to the commotion. Without investigating the accident or offering any assistance, the police drove off toward Avenue d'Espagne, leaving the crowd to sort things out.

Everly Tweed stood at some distance from the crowd, watching through his absinthe haze, then suddenly recognized the girl in black with the piercings and tattoos and her friend who had chased him earlier in the day. They were totally absorbed in the scene with the two crumpled taxis and the yelling drivers and did not notice him. Nevertheless, he pulled up the collar of his cape, pulled his beret down lower, and continued down the street toward the Boulevard Pasteur.

Witnessing the young Moroccan men yelling and jumping into action to assist the victims had caused Evangeline's cheeks to flush, and she felt her nipples harden against her tight muslin top. Piet noticed this and felt his sex beginning to stir. Unconsciously he reached out and clasped her left hand, but his touch was both unexpected and unwelcome and Evangeline, who was more excited than frightened by the spectacle, quickly withdrew her hand without even acknowledging Piet's gesture. Piet's erection at the sight of Evangeline's stiff nipples was a surprise to him as a gay man. Or was he responding to the same display of raw youthful masculinity that had excited her? He decided to leave the question for later, but it was definitely something he wanted to ponder in calmer surroundings.

17

Sickened by the smells emanating from Dean's Bar, Moustapha walked on to the corner of the Rue de la Liberté and down to the Grand Socco. The ghosts of Burroughs and Dean followed close behind as he made his way through the throngs of people. By now the Socco was filled with families heading to and from the big market and the shops that lined the Rue Siaghine and all the intertwined side streets. Vendors had spread out piles of sweaters, underwear, socks, and trousers on the sidewalk. Kids were hawking cigarettes, three for a dirham. Sellers of roasted peanuts, pistachios, and little candies were doing a brisk business. A few old women sat cross-legged behind baskets of Kleenex packets for sale. Some Berber women were selling bundles of sage and mint. The tiny open-air restaurants near the main medina gate were all busy, and the savory smells of grilled chicken and fish kebabs, french fries, and harira, the hearty lentil soup, filled the evening air. Old men in fine white hooded djellabas and white babouches passed by on their way back from evening prayers. Moustapha recalled his own experience as a child selling Gauloises cigarettes, two for ten francs. Just entering the communal gathering of the Grand Socco always lifted Moustapha's spirits, and his sadness at leaving St. Andrew's, perhaps for the last time, began to lessen.

When Moustapha reached the Zoco Chico, Burroughs and Dean dropped back and watched as he walked past the cafés and turned into Tarik's bakkal.

"Dean, I'd like to sit here in the Café Tingis," said Burroughs. "For old times' sake. From here I have a good view of the Café Central where Kiki and I used to sit drinking mint tea and smoking kif. Some of the most pleasant moments I had in Tangier were spent there. And we can still keep an eye on Herr Watchman."

"All right," said Dean. "There's always something to entertain one in the Zoco Chico."

During his walk from St. Andrew's, Moustapha had decided he should offer Tarik something in partial payment of the money he owed him. In this way he might restore the flow of baraka that had become thwarted by the tombstone fiasco. Tarik had a small shop where he sold candy, cigarettes, lighters, incense, various toiletries, ballpoint pens, pencils, tape, envelopes and stamps, cheap souvenirs, and postcards. He also ran an illegal currency exchange and made small deals in black-market goods.

When Moustapha arrived at Tarik's bakkal, an elderly American couple was looking at postcards and a small display of Moroccan Berber women dolls and toy camels made of leather. The woman looked to be in her late sixties, sturdy and ramrod straight. The man was perhaps a decade older. He wore khaki cargo pants, sandals over black socks and a Greek fisherman's cap that had never seen a fish or a fisherman. Tarik looked surprised to see Moustapha and they greeted each other without shaking hands. Tarik was originally from Bangalore, and had a long, pinched nose, large, expressive eyes, and a small mouth with yellow buck teeth.

"Are you here to beg, borrow, or steal?" asked Tarik. "You know your credit is no good with me. Not until I have the five hundred dirhams you owe." Tarik spoke in Moroccan Darija, and the Americans understood nothing of what was being said.

"I am here to offer you something toward payment of my debt," said Moustapha. "I have lost my job at St. Andrew's and so must barter and sell what I can until I find another job."

"What do you have to offer me? That old blanket? It's not worth the glue on a postage stamp. And I would have to charge you rent for all the fleas."

"I have something else," said Moustapha, reaching into his basket. "This wooden flute came from the St. Andrew's Church organ. It makes a sweet sound and since it is so old maybe you could sell it in your shop as an antique." Moustapha blew on the wooden pipe and by moving his fingers over the sound hole, played a string of simple notes. The American couple turned to listen, and the man said in broken French, "What a lovely sound. Is that a native flute?"

Moustapha blew a few more notes on it and wiped his mouth with his sleeve.

"Oui, monsieur. From the mountain villages. It is very old."

Tarik stood transfixed as the American asked if he might hold the flute and examine it.

"I've never seen anything quite like it. It isn't made like the others we've seen. Is it for sale?"

"Monsieur, this is the only flute like this in Tangier. You would have to travel far up into the Rif to find another one, inshallah," Moustapha said assuredly.

Tarik nodded his head in agreement with Moustapha and played along. "Monsieur, what he says is true. It is a great find. The wood is from a sacred tree which only grows near Ketama. It is called 'The Tree That Sings.'"

"How much would you want for it?" asked the man. He looked at his wife, who seemed more interested in the handful of postcards she had been looking at. She shrugged and said, "You wanted a souvenir and we're leaving early tomorrow morning, so you'd better make up your mind. But you'll have to bargain, you know."

"Combien? How much?" asked the man.

Moustapha rubbed the flute on his blanket to make it shine a little. "One thousand dirhams. It is a good price for such a treasure."

"A thousand dirhams?" repeated the man. "That's almost a hundred dollars! That's way too much. Anyway, I don't have that many dirhams on me. What about five hundred?"

Tarik blurted out, "Five hundred dirhams, monsieur? That is an insult. The flute is worth at least two, maybe three sheep."

"I'm sorry, I'm all out of sheep," said the American, hoping to leaven the situation with a bit of humor.

Moustapha blew a few more notes, wiped the mouthpiece and handed the flute to the American. "Here, I show you how to play. Just put your finger on the hole and blow through this end."

The man took the flute and held it to his lips. After he had awkwardly blown a few shrill notes, he noticed several Moroccans had gathered to watch.

"Well, it does have a nice sound. I can offer you six hundred for it."

"No, no, no. This flute is too precious. Nine hundred dirhams. And look, others are also interested to buy."

The man's wife had put the postcards back on the pile and was urging her husband to leave, as the growing crowd was making her nervous. But he was fully engaged in the transaction. "Eight hundred and no more. My wife and I are late for dinner, and we must be going."

Moustapha held up the flute and shook his head. "This flute is in my family for many years. I cannot sell for less than eight hundred fifty dirhams, Allah be praised."

The man turned to his wife, who was already digging in her purse. He took the money from her, then turned and counted out eight hundred fifty dirhams, which he placed in Moustapha's outstretched hand.

"Alhamdulillah!" said Moustapha and glanced at Tarik, whose face bore a flabbergasted expression. "Tarik, wrap the flute in that blue paper with the pink flowers on it."

Tarik reached for a roll of the gift wrap and deftly made a tight package of the old organ pipe and handed it to the American.

"Merci," said the man's wife and the crowd parted as they stepped out into the street.

"Shukran bezzaf!" said Moustapha. Then he turned to Tarik with the look of a National Lottery winner on his face. "Now I can pay what I owe. But first I want you to write a receipt for the amount and sign it."

"Moustapha, you have owed me this money for over a year. I think you should pay an extra hundred for my trouble and patience."

"You never said anything about that! Five hundred dirhams is what I owe you and that is what I will give you."

Tarik was about to curse but held his tongue. "Then pay me five dirhams for the wrapping paper. You know, you could not have tricked those Americans without my help. And it was in my shop."

Moustapha ignored his comments and carefully laid five one-hundred-dirham bills on the counter and then with a dramatic gesture placed a ten-dirham bill on top. "Safi," he said, then picked up his basket and left the bakkal.

Just-Call-Me-Ishmael woke with a jolt amid a cacophony of car horns. He was lying on his back on the sidewalk looking up into a circle of faces that looked back down at him with expressions of concern and curiosity. He tried to get up but an older man kneeling next to him placed a large, strong hand on his chest, indicating he should stay put.

"What happened?" asked Just-Call-Me-Ishmael.

"An accident," the man said. He had a neatly trimmed beard streaked with gray and wore a black wool burnoose. "Two taxis trying to be in the same place at the same time. It never works, but they never learn. How do you feel? Is there anything broken?"

Just-Call-Me-Ishmael flexed his arms and legs then shook his head. "I don't think so. Just a little shaken up." He glanced around for the wooden crate with the Monet pastel but didn't see it. "My package! It must still be in the taxi!" He tried to get up again, but was held down by two strong hands.

Underneath the battered but now upright taxi a large puddle of gasoline had formed. One of the headlights had also been knocked out of its mounting and now dangled from two wires, which were occasionally producing flickers of sparks. Then there was a flash, followed by a jarring explosion. The crowd emitted a collective cry of astonishment and quickly moved back as one, and Just-Call-Me-Ishmael felt himself lifted and carried along with it. "My package! I have to have my package!" he yelled at the top of his lungs, but in the panic and confusion no one paid any attention to his frantic entreaties.

The taxi was engulfed in flames, and the wooden crate and the Monet pastel were soon reduced to a pile of ashes on the charred back seat.

Mr. Garland stood on the balcony of his villa in the darkness, enjoying a last snifter of Fundador before retiring for the evening. He was worried that his big cats were not getting enough to eat because of the scarcity of inexpensive livestock. Chickens were cheap but the cats were not fond of feathers, and it took many chickens to make a meal. After all the animals had been fed, they settled in for the night and all was tranquil for a while. But then the macaques became unusually restless, scrambling frantically up and down the wire-mesh walls of their large enclosure, jumping in and out of the old oak tree that grew up through the roof of the enclosure, chattering and screaming and generally making a horrible racket.

Mr. Garland was also concerned about his neighbors, who were making increasingly frequent complaints about the noise and smell from his menagerie. Right now, though, he was even more concerned about just what the problem was with the macaques. They had gone through a phase of extreme agitation once before, and he thought he had solved the problem in a most clever fashion. For years he had given each of the macaques a daily ration of seven argan nuts in addition to their usual meal of fruit and vegetables—three nuts in the morning and four in the evening. Eventually the macaques let it be known that they were not happy with this arrangement, and he switched to four nuts in the morning and three in the evening. The macaques had been satisfied with what they apparently interpreted as an improvement, but perhaps by now they had seen through the subterfuge. Or their restlessness had another cause altogether.

While he pondered the situation, Mr. Garland gazed out over the roofs of the houses below him on the Old Mountain. As he took in the view of the town and the harbor beyond, a bright orange fireball suddenly leaped into the sky. A column of flames followed, generating a cloud of thick black smoke eerily lit from the flames below. What on earth was that, he wondered. A terrorist attack in some café? A bottled gas explosion from a cooking stove in some courtyard? He watched the flames and smoke coiling up into the night sky, and after what seemed like a very long time, he finally heard the sound of fire engines.

Burroughs and Dean watched from the Café Tingis as Moustapha walked out of Tarik's and turned into the Calle de los Arcos.

"I'm having trouble believing what just happened," said Burroughs. "Old Moustapha played those tourists like the marks they are."

"Should we see where he's going?" asked Dean.

"Naw," said Burroughs. "Let's stay put. We can catch up with him later. He may figure out a way to get your tombstone back with the money he conned. Right now he's probably headed for a restaurant on the Avenue d'Espagne for a nice dinner."

The sound of a muffled explosion from somewhere outside the medina caused everyone in the Zoco Chico to pause and look up.

"That can't be good, whatever it was," said Dean.

"No, not good. No bueno," said Burroughs, his voice breaking. Dean looked over and saw that tears were streaming down his face.

"Are you okay, Bill? Why are you crying?"

"That noise, it reminded me of the gunshot that killed Joan in Mexico City, and then that pitiful scene today at Aicha's. It's as though I never learned a thing, I'm doomed to repeat my mistakes over and over. And then I sensed the presence of *El Espíritu Feo*—the Ugly Spirit, as Brion called it. I feel the same heavy cloud of hopelessness hanging over me now that I felt just before I killed her. It's like some malevolent force has its scaly hands around my throat. As if I'm about to do something terrible and have no power to prevent it."

Dean felt a sense of dread beginning to press down on him. "I think I feel this Ugly Spirit too."

"What's worse is that there are times when I'm not sure I actually shot Joan. The Ugly Spirit continues to torture me with that gnawing uncertainty. But even if I didn't pull the trigger, I let it happen and I will always blame myself."

"You mean someone else might have shot her?" said Dean.

"I keep recalling there was someone or some thing standing just behind and to one side of me when the shot was fired. You know, there were several pistols in the apartment and several other people besides Joan and me in that room. My boyfriend, Lewis Marker; another friend, Eddie Woods; and Betty Jones. Maybe others as well. Everyone was drunk or on drugs. I had that Star .380 automatic with me because I was planning to sell it. Then after the shooting someone called my lawyer, Bernabé Jurado, but before he could get to me I had told the police I was drunk and had accidentally shot her. Then Jurado gets all the witnesses to say I or someone dropped the pistol and it just went off. I've told the story in so many ways to so many people over the years that I'm not sure myself exactly what happened."

"So it is possible you didn't shoot her, then. Maybe someone else fired the shot that killed her, and then left. But the Ugly Spirit wants you to believe you did."

"None of it ever made sense, Dean. It was just absolute insanity. Even now, sitting here again in the city I escaped to after her death, nothing is any clearer. But the Ugly Spirit continues to lurk, and I still have that sense of oppressive guilt. Funny, that lawyer ended up shooting his own wife and then killing himself. It's a continuum of evil that knows no end."

"Bill, we should try to find a shaman to contact the Ugly Spirit. Then you might learn the truth, and perhaps even destroy that devil, so you could begin to find peace."

"Years later in Lawrence, I did hire a Navajo shaman to exorcise the Ugly Spirit."

"What happened?"

"He said he got it out of me, but that it was still hanging around."

"That's not very conclusive, is it?"

"Not really. But I remember when I was coughing up the hairball that became *Naked Lunch,* I also produced hundreds of pages of automatic writing that later disappeared. They were meditations, if you will. Collectively I called them 'Ultrazone.' I would get high on majoun and type and type until I literally fell out of my chair. It was an attempt to drill into what was left of my soul to find the truth. I was wrestling for my life with the Ugly Spirit. I could sense Joan speaking to me, or rather through me, in those pages. I believed then it was her way of reaching out to help me heal. Joan and I used to play a telepathic game. We would each take a sheet of paper and draw a box with nine equal squares. We'd sit across the room from one another and draw an image in each square. When we compared them, the images were almost always identical. One night when I was living at the Muniria I had a vivid, almost super-real dream that Joan had come to Tangier to visit me and to tell me, not directly but telepathically, that it was time for her to leave the realm she was inhabiting. I asked her to forgive me, but without saying goodbye she was gone. I don't know what realm she inhabits now. I continued to dream of her even after I left Tangier, but she never spoke to me again. No communication at all. She must have said all she needed to say. But now that I am back in Tangier maybe it's time to try and locate that manuscript."

"You have no idea where these writings are?"

"I can't remember what happened to them. They might even still be here in Tangier somewhere, in a trunk or suitcase in the basement of a hotel. I had a safe deposit box in a bank here, but I lost the key and the number years ago. Can't even recall which bank. Thinking about those writings now, I believe Ultrazone was actually a record of the therapy Joan was offering me subconsciously. Whereas *Naked Lunch* was mostly drug-induced stream-of-consciousness scraps, gathered up by my friends then edited together and published by Maurice Girodias. It was really about being tormented by guilt and addiction. Of course, in life I thought drugs would bring me peace. An addict's delusion. As you know, Dean, drugs are not much use to the dead. I find it amusing that drugs were actually placed in my coffin. Here, look what they sent me off with."

From various pockets in his vest and jacket Burroughs produced three tightly rolled joints, a small packet of heroin, an Indian-head five-dollar gold piece, a pair of reading glasses, a ballpoint pen, and a Smith & Wesson snub-nosed .38 revolver, all of which he placed on the café table in front of them.

"No doubt they meant well," Burroughs continued. "It was certainly a nice gesture, but I never did believe in that Egyptian mummy afterlife shit. The fact is, if I had indeed made the big transcendence and managed to get all the kinks out of my karma, then the place I would be now would be somewhere far beyond the Western Lands, a place where drugs and guns and money and even the written word would be of no use whatsoever. Game over. End of the Word Virus. The ultimate liberation."

"And the Ugly Spirit? Was it when you were looking for yagé in South America that you first become possessed?"

"No, the Ugly Spirit took hold of me in Mexico before I ever took yagé. What a mind sucker. Like when a parasitic insect lays an egg in another insect. The larva infiltrates the insect's nervous system, takes control, and can then force the host insect to do something totally against its will and its own survival instinct. The parasite drives the host, let's say a land cricket, to abandon the safety of dry land and leap into the nearest body of water. As the host drowns, an adult parasite emerges ready to find and infect another host."

"Bill, you must find the right person to rid you of its curse. Perhaps your old friend Kazim can help, if he's still around. Otherwise you will continue to suffer in purgatory just as you did in your lifetime."

"I wonder sometimes if the Ugly Spirit didn't in fact dictate some of Ultrazone," said Burroughs, returning the items to his pockets. "The answer might lie in those pages. And you know, Dean, I do believe in exorcism. Exorcism of the text, you might say, like editing, crossing out passages, rubbing out the words, erasing the tapes. Ian Sommerville once showed me how to completely erase a reel of tape just by passing a heavy magnet over it. Maybe exorcising the Ultrazone manuscript would be the way to rid myself of the Ugly Spirit. But needless to say, the thought of unearthing Ultrazone, considering all it might entail, is a frightening one. Even to a ghost."

They sat there for a while in silence, contemplating the implications of what they'd been saying while watching the evening crowds drift by in the Zoco Chico. In the background could be heard the sound of fire engines.

"What the hell?" Burroughs suddenly exclaimed, sitting upright.

"What is it?"

"You see those two kids over there with the monkey on the leash?"

"Yes."

"The hat that one kid is wearing looks exactly like an old fedora of mine. Right down to the stains on the hatband."

"Isn't it the same one we saw that man wearing earlier today, the one who we thought was your dead ringer?"

"You know, Dean, for me Tangier was always a place where anything could happen, an open-air laboratory. Where reality was constantly being subjected to the cut-up technique, before Brion even introduced me to it. And that's exactly the feeling I'm having now, that the linear narrative of reality is being torn apart by something much stronger than the psychic cement that normally holds everything together. It's like what Don Juan was getting at with his ideas of the *tonal* and the *nagual*, the tonal being the sum of an individual's perceptions and knowledge, everything he can talk about and explain, including his own physical being, and the nagual being everything beyond the tonal: the inexplicable, the unpredictable, the unknown exogenous force. The nagual is everything that cannot be talked about or explained, only witnessed. And that, in turn, is very close to Kazim's personal philosophy about 'this world,' 'that world,' and the 'other world,' all existing simultaneously. Which may be a bit confusing to some people, because it sounds like three different worlds, but it's really a neither–nor kind of thing; the one world with its binary complements of rational and irrational, good and bad, right and wrong, and all those various man-made dualities, and then the other world, which both includes and precludes the world of duality, where all is one and one is all. Like what the Buddhists say, 'Not one; not other.'"

"So where does that put us, Bill, as a couple of old ghosts? Which realm are we in?"

"I'm not so sure myself, Dean. Wherever it is that we are, you've been here a lot longer than me. I'm still learning how to navigate this afterlife business. But I don't see why we have to just sit back and witness something that doesn't make sense. I suggest we discreetly follow those two kids and see what else we can learn."

18

Steetoo, Sayyad, and Cheikh were cutting through the Zoco Chico on their way to the apartment in the Rue Mohamed Bergach, where Sayyad lived with his older sister and their mother.

"Maybe you shouldn't be wearing that hat," Steetoo said. "What if someone recognizes it?"

"It belonged to the stupid Nasrani who lives next door. I'd see him before he ever sees me."

The ghosts of Burroughs and Dean were drifting along about ten yards behind the trio.

"Dean," Burroughs said, "How do we know if we're actually invisible? I mean, what if one of those kids turns around and can see us?"

"All I can suggest, Bill, is to try and bundle your psychic energies in such a way as to remain totally invisible. The will power of the dead is a potent force."

"When I used to walk through the streets of Tangier all those years ago, no one paid a lick of attention to me, which is how I got that moniker, *El Hombre Invisible*. Now here I am, dead as a doornail, ghosting through the Zoco Chico, worried about possibly being seen. The ironies never end."

Steetoo, Sayyad, and Cheikh turned into a side street that was lit only by a weak glow from occasional low-wattage streetlights. There was hardly any foot traffic now and Burroughs and Dean dropped a little further behind, just in case.

Cheikh, who had been prancing happily along at the end of his leash next to the two boys as they walked along, suddenly stopped and turned. Seeing the ghosts of Burroughs and Dean, he let out a vitriolic hiss.

"Shit," Burroughs exclaimed, "So much for remaining invisible. That damned monkey made us. Duck into this doorway!"

Cheikh was jumping up and down, emitting a frightful volley of screeches and hisses.

Steetoo and Sayyad turned to look behind them but saw nothing.

"What's the matter, Cheikh?" asked Sayyad.

"What's his problem?" asked Steetoo.

"I don't know. He did the same thing this afternoon when we were up on the roof, like he was seeing or hearing things."

"Maybe he's seen a ghost!"

"Ha!"

Steetoo and Sayyad turned and continued up the street, while Cheikh screeched and hissed and hopped up and down at the end of the now-taut leash as they walked along.

Burroughs and Dean dropped even further back, turning a corner just in time to see Steetoo, Sayyad, and Cheikh enter a large, non-descript apartment building in the Rue Mohamed Bergach.

"Shit," Burroughs said. "If we follow them inside the building, that monkey will make a ruckus and totally blow our cover."

"Are you sure it's your hat the kid is wearing?"

"Looks just like the one I bought on my first trip to London, when I took my first apomorphine cure with Dr. Dent."

"So what do we do now?"

"I'm not sure, Dean. The script is written in invisible ink."

As Burroughs and Dean pondered their next move, a dark figure emerged from the shadows, made its way unsteadily up the street, and stopped in front of a small narrow building next to the one the boys and the monkey had gone into. It was a man in a black beret and a long black cape, now somewhat clumsily searching his pockets.

"I wonder who that guy is," Burroughs said. "Looks sort of like Doctor Sax."

The ghosts drifted in a little closer for a better look.

"Bill, isn't that your dead ringer again?"

"Could be. Let's tag along and see what he's up to. Smells like he's been hitting the absinthe."

Everly Tweed finally found his key, unlocked the front door, and plodded up the stairs to his apartment. He was confronted again with the chaos the monkey had caused earlier in the day, his books and clothes strewn across the floor of the small apartment. He was much too zonked out to do anything about it now; he threw down his beret and cape among the jumble and flopped onto the banquette. Within a few minutes he was fast asleep, snoring loudly.

Burroughs and Dean floated up the stairs and passed through the locked door of Tweed's apartment as if it were a thin veil of smoke.

"Well, well," Burroughs said as they surveyed the ransacked apartment. "What a mess. Looks like he was burgled while he was out."

"I wonder how they broke in," Dean said, looking at the single window that faced the street below and the locked door, both of which were unscathed.

Burroughs glanced around as well, then looked up at the colored skylight and scratched his bony chin. Then he looked at the front door again. "Look at that worthless antique lock. You could pick it with a wet dishrag."

"I wonder what they were looking for. Doesn't look like there's anything much of value here."

"Except for some of these old books, which were apparently of no interest to the thieves. I must say, this guy is no slouch, intellectually—assuming he's read them all. A lot of these I had in my own library. Just this selection on the history of hypnosis is most impressive. Here's a copy of James Braid's *Neurypnology* from 1843, and Clark Leonard Hull's *Hypnosis and Suggestibility*, *Hypnosis in Criminal Investigation* by Harry Arons, and Ormond McGill's *Encyclopedia of Genuine Stage Hypnotism*. Amazing."

Burroughs then noticed some framed certificates and diplomas hanging on the wall above a small, cluttered desk in the corner. "Everly Tweed. That name ring any bells?"

"Can't say that it does. Look at this, though, apparently he's no stranger to the world of opiates as well," Dean said, pointing to the blue foil wrapper and the mirror on the table.

Burroughs came over for a closer look. "Well I'll be damned. I'd recognize those blue foil wrappers anywhere. That's from the Blue Messiah. I used to score heroin from him way back when. He also had some other poison from a village near Toubkal that was mighty potent. Made from mushroom-eating-donkey shit. I used to say one hit of that in the morning made a man feel as creepy as a hundred centipedes under a rotten log. The Blue Messiah must be getting on in years, if it's still him dealing that stuff."

"Maybe it's become a franchise, or his heirs took over the business," Dean said, picking up the blue foil wrapper and noticing the strange insignia stamped on the inside. The figure of a grinning creature seemed to be half-man, half-goat—and it had a major hard-on.

"Strange," Dean muttered, passing the foil to Burroughs. "I've seen this insignia somewhere else before."

"Any idea where?"

"In St Andrew's, I think, on a tombstone. Yes, I'm pretty sure that's where I've seen it."

"We could float on over to St. Andrew's and have a look," Burroughs suggested.

"Right now, in the middle of the night?"

"What are you afraid of? Ghosts?" Burroughs cackled dryly.

In the apartment building next door, on the other side of the wall from Tweed's apartment, Steetoo and Sayyad were sitting around a glass-topped coffee table in the main room with Sayyad's older sister, Mina, and their mother, Fatoma. Mina, whose taste was decisively European, had decorated the apartment. In the corner a television showed a Spanish soap opera with the sound turned off. On the walls hung cheap framed reproductions of Picasso, Matisse, and Miró paintings.

Sayyad had made up a story about buying the old Nasrani hat in the flea market, then finding the key and the paper sewn into the hatband. Mina worked as a secretary for a shipping company, and her English was quite good. After looking at the slip of paper, she agreed to go to the bank the next day with the safe deposit box key and see if she could claim the contents.

As Burroughs and Dean glided out of Tweed's window and set their course for the cemetery at St. Andrew's, Cheikh, who had been sitting on the windowsill of Sayyad's apartment looking down into the street, began to hiss and jump up and down again.

"What's the matter with Cheikh?" asked Fatoma.

"I think he's going crazy."

"Give him a banana. Maybe that will quiet him down."

As Burroughs and Dean made their way up the Rue Siaghine, the cafés in the Zoco Chico were filling up with members of the nouveau expat community. Most were middle-aged or elderly, European or American men dressed in the continental style: sport coat, shirt and tie, or sweater vest. One portly gentleman had wound a white opera scarf around his neck.

"Seeing that gaggle of graying wannabes just reminds me that all my old friends from the Interzone days are dead," said Burroughs wistfully. "These old birds look like roosting buzzards."

"I know what you mean," said Dean. "They bring back memories of the days when mine was one of the world's great bars, with a clientele to match."

"Surely you mean one of the great dives and notorious hangouts for smugglers, fugitives from justice, and out-and-out losers."

"Let's not forget, Bill, I had a steady stream of some of the most famous drinkers who ever staggered off into the Tangier night; Samuel Beckett, Jane Bowles, Errol Flynn, Ava Gardner, Ian Fleming, Barbara Hutton, Jean Genet, and—speaking of fugitives from justice—even a certain *hombre invisible*, who, as I recall, skipped out a few times without paying."

"Dean, I may have been a pervert and an addict, but I was never a deadbeat, especially when it came to buying drinks. I respect the profession of the saloon keeper too much. It's possible, though, that I was so high on occasion I forgot to pay. But let's not forget, some of your favorite *Naked Lunch* routines were probably fueled by your choice selection of whiskies. And didn't you used to add a pinch or two of cocaine to my gin and tonics?"

"A few times, when you brought along one of your sleazy scores. You looked like the glass-half-full-of-poison type, and I was hoping it might finish the job."

"Dean, old pal, I was doing a fine job trying to shuffle off this mortal coil myself, without any help from you."

"Well, I may have been dead longer than you have, but we're equals now," Dean laughed. "And all will be forgiven if you can help me get my tombstone back."

As the two neared the Rif Cinema they recognized the older American couple from Tarik's bakkal. There seemed to be some commotion and a small crowd had gathered. The man was cursing and shouting while his wife tried to pull him away. A street urchin had tried to snatch the brightly wrapped package out of the man's hand, but only succeeded in causing the man to drop it to the pavement, where it got kicked around in the foot traffic until a passing donkey trampled it with a loud crack. All that was left of the magic flute were shattered fragments. Some of the crowd were laughing and saying that the broken flute was a cheap fake. "Is not Moroccan," jibed a toothless old man in a skullcap and a frayed plaid overcoat. "Is cheap wooden toy." The crowd erupted in laughter. Exasperated by the commotion and the loss of his prize souvenir, the man picked up what was left of the wrapping paper and tore it into smaller pieces, then stomped on the wooden fragments that remained. Finally his wife dragged him away, and the onlookers quickly dispersed.

"I'd say it's a good thing Moustapha isn't anywhere around," said Burroughs. "That guy's wife looks like she'd like to cut off somebody's balls."

"It'll probably be her husband's," said Dean.

As Burroughs and Dean neared St. Andrew's they sensed the presence of a distinctive otherworldly energy behind the cemetery walls. It seemed familiar, but it was certainly one they hadn't been in contact with for quite some time. The smell of kif smoke cut through the cloying perfume of the datura blossoms, and there in the darkness, sitting on the tomb of Sir Reginald Lister, was another ghost, languorously puffing on a cigarette holder from which protruded a Benson & Hedges cigarette whose tobacco had been replaced by high-grade kif. The ghost wore a corduroy jacket over a white turtleneck sweater, and neatly pressed khaki slacks and brown suede shoes. Burroughs and Dean glided toward him through the tombstones.

"Paul Bowles? Can it be you?" Burroughs asked somewhat incredulously.

"Well, it depends just what you mean by 'Paul Bowles,'" the figure responded dryly. "If you mean Paul Bowles, the author of *The Sheltering Sky* and the composer of *The Wind Remains*, etc., etc., then no. That Paul Bowles never existed. As I said many times when I was alive, there was no such entity called Paul Bowles. But if you mean the ghost of the egoless figure that once walked the earth known as Paul

Bowles, then that would be him—or me, if there ever was a 'me.' To be honest, I'm still trying to come to terms with this very different variety of non-being."

"Same old slippery Paul," said Burroughs through a smile. "I was just talking to Dean about that. This afterworld business is certainly a whole new ball of wax. Good to see you again."

"I must say Bill, you seem to have enhanced your status as *El Hombre Invisible*. More like *El Hombre Transparente*, shall we say? It's good to see you, too."

"Imagine finding you here. I thought you were peacefully interred back in the States. Last time we met was back in '94, I reckon. You're looking well yourself, considering the circumstances; rather detachedly debonair, as always. So what brings you back to your favorite den of iniquity?"

Bowles took a drag of kif and slowly exhaled. "I have mostly been at peace since my passing. Not like during my last years in Tangier, when my flat was constantly overrun by nitwits of every stripe who had decided I was their guru and clung to my withering remains like insatiable leeches. Thank Allah for Abdelouahaid Boulaich, my driver and assistant. He did his best to filter the endless stream of drop-ins. He also kept an eye on the thieves trying to make off with valuable first editions from my library.

"Anyway, I heard from Jane that there was some trouble at the St. Andrew's Cemetery. Since I was originally planning to be buried here, I thought it might be a propitious opportunity for a visit. I like to watch and observe, as an 'invisible spectator,' to borrow the title of that sham of a biography of me. Also, I quite miss Tangier. Jane sends her regards, by the way."

"Why *aren't* you buried here?" asked Dean.

"Good question. It seems the church fathers decided my grave would attract too many unwanted visitors, à la Jim Morrison. They didn't want my final resting place to become a shrine for any Paul Bowles death-cult groupies. It was certainly the strangest rejection letter I ever received. So, as a joke, I began telling everyone who asked that I wanted to be buried in the Tangier pet cemetery. While I enjoy the peaceful view of Seneca Lake from the apple orchard where my ashes are buried in upstate New York, I'm far from happy there. Here I used to enjoy the sounds of drumming in the night, the calls to prayer, the occasional wedding procession passing by in the streets, whereas now the only sound is the intermittent thud of a falling apple in the grass. The only excitement at Seneca Lake is the annual National Lake Trout Derby." Bowles flicked the ash from his cigarette holder and smiled, his blue eyes sparkling in a shaft of moonlight shining down through the trees.

"Janey was buried in San Miguel Cemetery, just across the straits in Málaga, correct?" asked Burroughs.

"Well, one is *told* that her remains are there, but who knows exactly where? Anyway, as I once remarked, Jane isn't *there*. She moves about quite freely, as she did in life. She's given up the booze, though she does partake in the occasional snort of vermouth. She flits from party to party on Long Island, then checks out the lesbian bars from Cairo to Paris, constantly moving between the here-and-now and the hereafter. In fact she has stopped by Dean's quite a few times to make sure the stray cats are being well fed. That's when she heard about the necropolitan antics at St. Andrew's."

"The cats are well attended to, as always," said Dean.

"That certainly sounds like Janey," said Burroughs. "Always ready to have fun. You can't keep a good girl down."

"May I ask what all the commotion is about?" asked Bowles.

"It's a long story," said Dean. "Moustapha, the watchman who used to work here, got tricked by a conniving old witch named Aicha into letting her remove my tombstone for use in her diabolical magic."

"If you can call that two-bit gimcrackery of hers magic," Burroughs interjected.

"Moustapha was being harassed by some ghosts and asked for her help in ridding the cemetery of them, offering the use of a hat which allegedly belonged to Bill, but most likely belonged to Paul Lund," Dean continued.

"As remuneration he offered her datura plants and pieces of old tombstones—necessary ingredients, as you know, for her necromantic activities. She evidently employed the services of an imposter to portray Bill's ghost, which she hoped Moustapha would believe she had conjured by way of the hat, but the hat went up in flames, the ghost blew his cover, and the plan went askew. Nevertheless, Aicha took my tombstone, but by doing so released a centipede curse I had placed on it. Bill attempted to frighten her into giving up the tombstone by shooting a glass off her head but that didn't work. Moustapha tried to cover up the theft with a phony papier-mâché tombstone, but it melted in the rain and Moustapha got fired. Quite a mess, really. I just want my tombstone back where it belongs, and I'm sure Moustapha would like to have his job back."

"A little superstition can go a long way when it's misused," said Bowles. "In this case it seems to have backfired on everybody. Of course you know who Aicha's sister was—Cherifa, whose magic caused Jane's stroke and ultimate death. So in fact you're dealing with some very serious power-sisters here."

"Cherifa!" exclaimed Dean. "That name is still spoken with a sense of fear in Tangier."

"And rightly so," said Bowles. "I suggest you look up Kazim, that wise old Moroccan shaman. As far as I know he's still around. His insights into Moroccan black magic and superstition never failed to amaze me. If I had been in Tangier when Jane became ill, instead of on a boat returning from Ceylon, I would have gone to Kazim immediately to get the effects of the magic reversed. By the time I got back it was too late."

"Seems like we need Kazim's help to solve more than one problem," said Burroughs. "After we cure Dean's tombstone blues, I have to find my lost Ultrazone manuscript. The more I think about it, the more certain I am it's somewhere in Tangier. I suspect the Ugly Spirit has occupied its pages in order to manifest its malevolent agenda. The Ugly Spirit takes every opportunity to torment me still, but finding the manuscript might at last enable me to kill a rat with an Uzi, if you get my drift."

"Not sure I do," Dean replied.

"I'm not saying any more than that. You never know who might be listening," said Burroughs. "Even the dead spy on one another."

All the cemetery cats except Zora were by now blissfully asleep atop their favorite tombs. Unseen by the three ghosts, the mysterious turtle that always seemed to appear out of thin air winked at Zora as it moved slowly along the path behind Walter Harris's former resting place.

Dean led the way to where his tombstone had been and pointed out the dismal remains of the papier-mâché fake that Moustapha had left against a nearby wall. Bowles smiled and shook his head, always keen to relish a bit of schadenfreude.

Burroughs produced the blue foil wrapper from his jacket pocket and handed it to Bowles. "That weird insignia mean anything to you?"

"Of course," Bowles said. "The Blue Messiah. He was known mostly as a dealer, but he was, or is, also the head of some obscure primitive cult."

"I was just telling Bill I know I've seen that insignia somewhere among the tombstones, but I can't remember where," Dean said.

"Ah, yes," Bowles said. "When I was doing the research for my book *Points in Time*, I tried to find out more about the Blue Messiah and his cult. I came up against a wall of silence, but I did find the mausoleum in St. Andrew's with that insignia carved on the door. It's over here somewhere."

The three ghosts glided toward the back of the cemetery and stopped before a squat marble mausoleum surrounded by a rusty wrought-iron fence. On the door of the mausoleum, in weathered bas-relief and partly hidden under a thin growth of moss, was the half-man, half-goat insignia.

"Very strange," said Burroughs. "I mean, if it's a primitive Moroccan cult, what's this doing here in the Anglican Cemetery of the Church of St. Andrew?"

"Good question, Bill," said Bowles. "And one I've never been able to answer."

"Shall we have a look inside?" Burroughs suggested.

The three of them passed effortlessly through the iron gate and the thick marble door of the mausoleum into its dark, musty interior. Ghosts have their own light source, gathered from the earth's molten magnetic core, and by this residual light they could make out the tiered shelves on two opposite walls where several dusty cobwebbed coffins and urns rested in various states of decay and disintegration.

"Rather sinister," said Dean, looking around with an expression of mild disgust.

"But what's this?" Burroughs said, drifting toward the rear of the mausoleum. Embedded into the stone floor was a large trap door with an iron ring as a handle.

"We'd better investigate," Bowles said.

The threesome glided down through the floor and discovered a cavernous crypt-like room furnished with a large stone altar. There were several niches along its walls, as well as a red stone door. On the other side of it they found themselves in a natural grotto with walls of black stone that glistened with moisture. At the far end of the grotto, a flight of hand-carved stairs seemed to descend into eternity itself.

Wafting up from the darkness below was the tangy smell of the sea, along with the distant sound of the surf.

"How very interesting," Bowles said. "I'd always heard rumors about a system of catacombs and tunnels beneath Tangier that were used by smugglers during the International Zone days, and earlier by religious cults who practiced forbidden rites, even sacrifices there."

"Where do you think this comes out?" Burroughs asked.

"Somewhere along the coast west of the port, I would guess, perhaps by the Tombeaux Phéniciens. Mrabet used to fish from the rocks there and he told me he thought some of the caves were haunted by strange spirits."

"Well, I'll be damned," Burroughs said as he peered down into the bottomless darkness. "First the afterworld and now the netherworld. What's next, I wonder?"

"How about my tombstone?" Dean said.

"Of course, I forgot for a moment," Burroughs said. "We can continue our spelunking later."

Burroughs, Dean, and Bowles drifted back to the surface and through the iron gates of the cemetery, then down the Avenue d'Angleterre toward the medina. As they glided along Bowles commented on various landmarks as he recalled the earlier International Zone days. Trees had once filled the Grand Socco, he said, where now a large marble fountain stood. Following an episode involving a panicked donkey that trampled several people, causing serious injuries, the locals came to believe evil spirits that dwelt in the trees were responsible. They petitioned the authorities, and all of the trees were cut down. Several new restaurants now lined the Socco, while some of the old cafés above the vegetable market were gone. It was all a bit disorienting.

"I imagine I can still find Kazim's house," said Bowles. "Jane and I used to have a small place near his. We can see if a light's still on and, if so, perhaps pay him a visit."

The trio continued on as the lights began to go out in the small shops and the night grew darker and quieter. When they reached the patio of the Hotel Continental they sat down to admire the view of the port in the moonlight and the tiny flickering lights of the boats as they made their way out of the harbor toward the fishing grounds. In a few hours, dawn would break, and the boats would return filled with the night's catch. The only sounds to be heard now were muted conversations from the clustered houses and the sea breezes which blew through the medina alleys. One could imagine one was hearing the old city whispering its secrets to the sky.

19

Brunhilde Reinhart's ghost was still drifting around the garden of Aicha's villa on the Old Mountain, hovering in place from time to time to peer into one of the many windows. Zodelia had locked herself in the bedroom of the caretaker's cottage and refused to come out to prepare dinner. Mohammed pleaded with her to come to her senses, but she adamantly refused to come out until the last of the black centipedes had been removed from the premises. She told her husband through the locked door that he must call the exterminator first thing in the morning. Mohammed laughed silently to himself on the other side of the door. The exterminator. Right. Of course. Preferably one who knew how to get rid of curses.

Aicha was still troubled by the appearance of the trio of ghosts, as well as the giant black centipedes, and shaken by the apparent attempt on her life, but now she was most of all annoyed with her incompetent servants—and *very* hungry. There was no way she was going to bed without dinner, and if her servants weren't able to provide it, she would have to take care of it herself.

Black magic, extortion, sorcery, blackmail, trickery, seducing rich men and women in order to obtain money or favors—these were all areas in which Aicha displayed innate ability. But cooking and the preparation of food had remained a lifelong mystery. In the refrigerator she found eggs and some leftover eggplant and zucchini. Figuring she could manage to make some kind of omelette, she poured olive oil into a pan on the stove and lit the burner. As she cut up the vegetables, she had the feeling someone was watching her. She glanced up at the kitchen window and saw nothing, but the feeling of being watched did not go away and further agitated her already frayed nerves.

Aicha put down the knife and stepped outside onto the small landing at the top of the stairs that led down to the garden. She could see relatively well in the bright moonlight, but there was no one there, just a breeze coming off the strait and rustling the leaves in the bamboo grove. Still, she felt the presence of some spirit lurking nearby. From further up on the Old Mountain came the sound of screeching animals—Mr. Garland's macaques were creating even more uproar than usual. Aicha wondered if Mr. Garland had known what he was getting into when he acquired the macaques from a breeder on a farm in the countryside between Tangier and Asilah. The Barbary macaques, as they were properly known, were all descended from a single family that had been bred specifically to replenish the dwindling numbers of so-called "rock apes" who had lived on the Rock of Gibraltar since being brought over by the Moors, well before 1492. By the time the English captured Gibraltar in 1704, the rock apes were firmly established, and during World War I the British armed forces had taken charge of them, ensuring they were properly fed and cared for. They were even given names, often after some governor, brigadier, or high-ranking officer. And when the population of rock apes got dangerously low in the early 1940s, additional Barbary macaques were brought over from Tangier.

In the loud screeching that Aicha now heard, she thought she recognized something both mournful and baleful, laced with a tone of longing—something like the Portuguese notion of *saudade*—as though the macaques were yearning to be reunited with their brethren in Gibraltar. She wished the macaques would break free and somehow make their way across the strait. Besides the legend that as long as Barbary macaques remained on the Rock of Gibraltar the territory would remain under British rule, there was an even older legend that the macaques had originally arrived in Gibraltar by way of a subterranean tunnel that ran under the strait, beginning somewhere along the northern coast of Morocco and ending in Lower St. Michael's Cave in Gibraltar.

Aicha's reverie was interrupted by the smell of smoke. She turned and saw that the frying pan had overheated and the oil had caught fire. She ran back inside, grabbed an unwashed pot from the sink, filled it with water, and threw it on the flames. There was a loud crackling explosion and burning oil splashed across the wall behind the stove and up to the ceiling.

Aicha ran over to the caretaker's cottage near the front gate and banged on the door shouting "Fire! Fire!" until Mohammed answered. The two of them ran toward the kitchen, where flames were already visible in the window and the open doorway. Mohammed grabbed a garden hose and turned on the water, but the pressure was so low that the stream of water didn't even reach the top of the stairs. He threw down the hose and ran back to the caretaker's cottage to call the fire department.

By the time the first fire truck arrived, the flames were leaping out the kitchen window and doorway and had spread to the wooden roof. As it careened into the driveway, the driver miscalculated the turn and tore off one wing of the large iron gate with the truck's bumper. Several firemen jumped down and began to roll out hoses, making the connection to the fire hydrant in the street. The water pressure was low there, too, but with the help of the fire truck pump there was enough pressure to bring the flames under control after a brief but intense battle.

The firemen packed up their equipment and headed back down the hill. Aicha had complained about the broken gate and been told to take it up with the fire chief the next day. The kitchen was ruined and unusable, and while the rest of the house had survived intact, it was full of smoke and soot. She couldn't spend the night in the house until it had been aired and cleaned, and the kitchen would need substantial repairs. Mohammed suggested Aicha stay with them in the caretaker's cottage in the interim, but she wouldn't hear of it. She had already decided to take a hotel room in town until the house was habitable again. She went back inside to pack a small bag and call a taxi. As she swung open the bathroom cabinet door to get her toothbrush and toothpaste, a clump of shiny black centipedes fell with a thud into the sink, where they writhed and squirmed and began to reproduce until they were flopping out onto the marble floor.

It was nearing dawn when Moustapha finally returned to his sister Laila's house. He had spent several hours aimlessly wandering around the streets of Tangier, wondering what he was going to do about the missing tombstone and how he would explain to his sister and her husband about getting fired from his job at the cemetery. The lights were out, and he let himself in the house as quietly as possible. He went into the kitchen and was reaching for the jar of majoun when he heard the front door open. Moments later Ahmed was standing in the kitchen doorway, looking at Moustapha with an irritated expression. He was dressed in his blue fire department uniform, his face and hands smudged with soot and dirt, his hair plastered against his head from wearing his helmet.

"What are you doing up at this time of night?" Ahmed asked.

"I was going to ask the same of you." Moustapha replied.

"A busy night," Ahmed said, opening the refrigerator door. "A burning taxi in the Marshan, then a kitchen fire in a villa up on the Old Mountain. I'm tired, but I'm also hungry."

Moustapha watched as Ahmed rummaged in the refrigerator and finally took out the dish containing the leftover chicken tagine. He stood at the kitchen counter and gnawed on a chicken leg while looking absently yet disparagingly at Moustapha.

"Which villa on the Old Mountain?" asked Moustapha, out of curiosity but also to thaw the icy atmosphere with a bit of small talk.

"The one that old witch Aicha inherited—the sister of that other witch, Cherifa, who used to work in the grain market and put a spell on that crazy Nasrani woman."

Moustapha raised his eyebrows in surprise. "Was it a big fire? Was there much damage?"

"The kitchen mostly, the rest of the house we were able to save. But no one can live there until that mess is cleared up."

"So she's not there now?"

"No, she said she was going to take a room in a hotel. Why, what's it to you?"

"Just curious," Moustapha said, looking down at the floor.

After Ahmed had gone to bed, Moustapha sat at the kitchen table and dipped a spoon into the jar of majoun, which he washed down with a cup of strong black tea. Before he even felt the first effects of the majoun, he had a clear vision of what he had to do next. From the trunk in the spare room where he often slept, he took out a flashlight and a pair of gloves, which he placed in his shoulder bag. He quietly turned off the lights and left the house.

Moustapha walked through the quiet, dark streets and into the medina. Arriving at the Café Triangle, still open at that late hour, he went straight through to the back room, where Ravi Khan and Tony Mahoney and the Gnawa musicians were whipping up wild versions of Captain Beefheart songs to an enthralled audience.

Looking around the room as his eyes adjusted to the dim lighting, Moustapha saw Kazim at the bar at the back of the room, seated next to the two Mugwumps. He made his way through the crowd to the bar and approached Kazim.

"Peace be upon you," said Kazim.

"And you also," Moustapha replied.

Moustapha sat on a stool next to Kazim and explained what had transpired during the last twenty-four hours. He then told Kazim what he had in mind. Kazim listened intently, one eye on the musicians on stage, the other roving the audience in the smoke-filled room. Then he turned toward the two Mugwumps and spoke briefly with them, his words inaudible to Moustapha because of the music.

Kazim turned back toward Moustapha. "My friends are willing to help you—they owe me a favor, and a favor for you is a favor for me. They have a car parked down the street. They'll be ready to go as soon as they've finished their drinks and this song is over, which is the last of this evening's performance. I wish you luck, my friend."

"Thank you. I'm sure I'll need it."

"What will you have to drink?" Kazim asked.

"Just a tea, thank you."

When his tea arrived Moustapha sipped at it gingerly while he looked around the room. He didn't see Everly Tweed, or anyone else he knew, other than the musicians. In fact, he wondered just who all these people were and where they came from—he didn't recognize any faces from the streets or markets of Tangier. Meanwhile the majoun was taking effect and Moustapha's perception was beginning to warp accordingly. Despite his less-than-thorough understanding of the English language, he found himself listening intently to the strange lyrics of the song being played . . . *Who's afraid of the fallin' ditch . . . Fallin' ditch ain't gonna get my bones . . . Ain't my fault the thing's gone wrong . . .* and was surprised at how appropriate they seemed to his present situation.

When the song was over there was an uproarious round of applause and Ravi Khan, Tony Mahoney, and the entire Gnawa ensemble stood up and took several bows. Then the house lights came on and the crowd began to disperse, while the musicians packed up their gear.

The combination of the strong black tea, the majoun, and the bizarre lyrics had given Moustapha a sudden sense of empowerment. The two Mugwumps got to their feet and motioned to Moustapha that they were ready to leave. He was surprised to see just how tall they were, well over two meters. With their reptilian heads and tails, human bodies, and translucent skin they were formidable creatures indeed. Surely his mission could not fail in the presence of such beings. They introduced themselves as Marvin and Lee, although Moustapha had trouble telling them apart.

"Our car's just around the corner here," said one.

"It's a super-bad ride. You'll dig it." said the other.

Moustapha had wondered what language the Mugwumps might speak, but he hadn't been expecting it to be hipster English.

When they came around the corner he immediately recognized the metallic-bronze '66 Ford Mustang parked at the curb. It had belonged to Paul Bowles and been bequeathed to his driver, Abdelouahaid Boulaich, who had eventually sold it. Marvin unlocked the driver's door and sat behind the wheel. Lee opened the passenger door and Moustapha climbed into the back seat.

Moustapha marveled at the throaty roar of the V-8 engine as with a screech of burning rubber they started down the street. They made their way through the narrow streets until they turned onto the Boulevard Pasteur and headed toward the Old Mountain. The Mustang's interior was upholstered in fake white leather and, despite being only a two-door coupe, was large and roomy. With obvious relish, Marvin shifted through the gears with the four-on-the-floor transmission. As they roared by the Place du Koweit, Moustapha was humming along with the lyrics that were going through his head, *'n when I get lonesome the wind begin t' moan, Fallin' ditch ain't gonna get my bones.*

As they neared Aicha's villa, Moustapha told Marvin to slow down and drive past. Moustapha saw the gate was broken and wide open, and there were no lights in either the main house or the caretaker's cottage. He told Marvin to park in a dark side street around the corner, and from there they walked back to the gate and slipped inside. They went around to the back of the house and quietly up the stairs and into the smoky kitchen. Moustapha didn't know where the tombstone might be, but considering its weight and bulk, he decided to look first in the garage downstairs.

"Wow!" said Marvin as they entered the garage and saw the vintage pistachio-green Mercedes 290 SL. "Check this fucker out!"

"Super-bad!" exclaimed Lee.

While Marvin and Lee were admiring the old Mercedes, Moustapha searched the garage and found the two pieces of Joseph Dean's tombstone lying on the floor in the back. "Over here!" he whispered.

Moustapha was pulling on gloves as Marvin and Lee approached.

"What's with the gloves?" Lee asked.

"Just a safety precaution. Sometimes people have strange curses on their tombstones so they don't get stolen."

"Fuck that mumbo-jumbo-juju-voodoo shit," Lee said, bending over and picking up one half of the tombstone as though it was made of Styrofoam. "The curse has not yet been conjured that can fuck with the likes of us."

Marvin picked up the other half of the tombstone and the three of them climbed the stairs, Moustapha leading the way with the flashlight.

"We gotta see how we can get our hands on that 290 SL, man," Marvin said. "Make that Aicha bitch some kind of offer she can't refuse."

They retraced their steps to the back door and down into the garden. Moustapha switched off the flashlight and they made their way toward the front gate through the patches of moonlight shining down through the tall eucalyptus trees.

Zodelia was still too nervous and agitated to sleep. She was alone in their bedroom while Mohammed slept on the banquette in the living room. Thinking she heard footsteps in the driveway, she went to the window and pushed aside the curtain. Her jaw dropped in sheer disbelief at what she saw in the bright light of the full moon. Walking toward the front gate were two extremely tall figures who looked like a cross between a man and a lizard, with a fan-like crest of cartilage running down their spines and stopping just short of their long tails; each carried a piece of the tombstone she'd seen in the garage. Leading the way was a shorter man in a light-colored djellaba and a straw hat. Zodelia fainted and fell back onto the bed.

Marvin and Lee loaded the two halves of the tombstone into the trunk of the Mustang, then the three of them got in and Marvin started the engine. Moustapha loved that sound. Lee took out an old-fashioned 8-track tape cartridge from the glove compartment and slipped it into the vintage player mounted under the dashboard. As they headed back down the Old Mountain toward St. Andrew's, the Mustang was filled with the sound of Steppenwolf's "Born to be Wild," the three of them enthusiastically nodding their heads in time with the music and the two Mugwumps singing along, *Get your motor runnin', head out on the highway, lookin' for adventure, and whatever comes our way . . .*

20

Burroughs, Dean, and Bowles were still lost in their reveries on the terrace of the Hotel Continental. The call to Fajr, the early morning prayer, would soon echo through the Medina. In the east, the first few blushes of salmon-pink were already glowing along the horizon. Suddenly the silence was broken by squealing tires, the roar of a powerful engine, and the thumping bass notes of a car stereo.

"What in the world is that *awful* racket?" Bowles asked.

The noise grew louder. They looked down and saw a metallic-bronze '66 Ford Mustang flash by on the boulevard below and screech around the corner into the Rue du Portugal.

"Say, Paul," Burroughs said, "Didn't you used to have a car like that?"

"That *is* my car—or rather, it *was*."

"Did you see who was in the front seat?" Dean asked. "Looked like a couple of Mugwumps."

"So that's where my Mustang ended up," said Bowles. "Abdelouahaid must have sold it. But to those creatures?"

"Mugwumps?" Burroughs repeated, somewhat puzzled.

"If you gentlemen will excuse me, I think I'll have a closer look."

While Burroughs and Dean remained on the terrace, entranced by the moonlit bay and the pre-dawn calm, Bowles rose up and followed the Mustang as it zoomed up the hill toward St. Andrew's.

As their car approached the church, Marvin switched off both headlights and engine and they coasted silently down the street to park alongside the wall of the cemetery. Moustapha waited for Marvin and Lee to lift the two tombstone slabs out of the trunk, then pointed along the wall. "Venir por aquí," he said. "I no longer have a key to the locked gate but I know a way to get inside without being seen."

Marvin and Lee followed him until they reached a thick growth of cane. The Mugwumps' translucent skin glittered green and magenta in the moonlight and seemed to glow from within. Moustapha pushed the cane aside to reveal an opening in the wall that had been filled in with stones, broken pottery, and sticks. He cleared the rubble out of the way and Marvin and Lee made their way inside.

"So where do we drop this load, man?" asked Lee.

Moustapha raised his index finger to his lips and silently motioned toward Dean's grave site. Bowles, hovering nearby behind a weathered obelisk, watched as the two Mugwumps lowered the tombstone halves carefully into place, exactly where they had lain since 1963.

Marvin looked at Lee and said, "This is like a reburial, so before we leave we ought to say a few words for old Dean, don't you think?"

"Absolutamente," said Lee. "And there's a song by Blind Lemon Jefferson that might be perfect for the occasion. I'll just change the lyrics a little, if you'll allow me."

"Be my ghost, er, guest," said Marvin.

"Let me get my gear."

Lee went back through the wall to the Mustang and returned with a guitar case and a small battery-operated Pignose amplifier, which he set on the ground next to Dean's grave. He produced a 1960 Supro Val Trol guitar, plugged it into the amp and checked the tuning.

Bowles floated a little closer. Being a great fan of the blues and, like his wife Jane, a love interest of the late great torch singer Libby Holman, he didn't want to miss this. Moustapha, excited by the return of Dean's tombstone, climbed atop the tomb of Major Harry Twentyman and looked on wide-eyed as Lee began to sing softly.

Well, there's one kind of favor I'll ask of you
Well, there's one kind of favor I'll ask of you
There's just one kind of favor I'll ask of you
You can see that my grave is kept clean

And there's two green Mugwumps following me
And there's two green Mugwumps following me
I got two green Mugwumps following me
Waiting on my burying ground

Did you ever hear that coffin' sound
Have you ever heard that coffin' sound
Did you ever hear that coffin' sound
Means poor old Dean is underground

Did you ever hear them church bells tone
Have you ever hear'd them church bells tone
Did you ever hear them church bells tone
Means poor old Dean is dead and gone

Well, my heart stopped beating and my hands turned cold
And, my heart stopped beating and my hands turned cold
Well, my heart stopped beating and my hands turned cold
Now I believe what the bible told

There's just one last favor I'll ask of you
And there's one last favor I'll ask of you
There's just one last favor I'll ask of you
See that my grave is kept clean

As soon as Lee had finished, Marvin said, "Right on, Daddy. Let's blow this creamery." The two Mugwumps simultaneously said "Pasta Lumbago" to Moustapha, grabbed the guitar and amplifier, flicked their tails, and hopped back through the opening in the wall. A deep throaty roar came from the Mustang's four-barreled, 302 cubic-inch V-8 engine, followed by the screech of spinning tires as Marvin gave the gas pedal the heavy-metal treatment. Moustapha ran to the opening, pushed aside the cane, and saw a ghostly cloud of white smoke in the street that smelled of burning rubber. The car's taillights glowed red like the eyes of a devil as they disappeared into the distance.

"Allah protect me," said Moustapha. He climbed out through the hole in the wall, filled it up behind him, and walked swiftly toward the Rue de Hollande.

Bowles hovered in the darkness for a few moments, bemused by what he had witnessed. Then he produced his cigarette holder out of thin air and took a few puffs of a firmly packed kif cigarette. There was a faint fluttering sound in the air and almost instantaneously he was back at the Hotel Continental seated next to Dean and Burroughs.

Burroughs turned towards Bowles and said, "What's with the rather self-satisfied look? And what did you find out? What kind of otherworldly mischief are those Mugwumps up to now?"

Bowles took another long drag, exhaled slowly and said, "I've got some news to die again for, Dean. It seems your tombstone has been recovered and replaced, though for how long is anyone's guess."

Dean rose from his chair and hovered about three feet above his two compadres. "I'll be damned! Not literally of course, but I won't believe it, even from a ghost, until my spirit actually feels those cold broken slabs of granite."

"Well," said Bowles, "Follow me."

A shower of sparks flashed on the terrace and the three of them were back in St. Andrew's churchyard hovering over the grave. Dean looked dumbstruck as he stared down at the stones:

DEAN
MISSED BY ALL
AND SUNDRY

DIED
FEBRUARY 1963

"It's really back! And not in three or four pieces but the same two halves in which it was originally laid back in 1963. I remember it being transported here in a harness of woven hemp slung between two donkeys. Somehow the donkeys got spooked, and the harness broke just inside the gate. The tombstone fell and split almost dead center. I suspected at the time that some of the more privileged persons interred here weren't too thrilled to have me join them and were making a clumsy attempt to keep me out. The dead can be so snobbish."

It occurred to Burroughs that this was an entirely different explanation for the two-piece tombstone than the one Dean had given him before. He was about to call him on it but decided not to. Much of Joseph Dean's past was veiled in mystery; there always seemed to be multiple versions of the stories he told.

"But now it's back and I feel like celebrating," Dean continued. "Hey Bill, any chance we can score some special 'spirits' for the occasion?"

"If you mean coke, you're crazy," said Burroughs. "That's what put you here in the first place. Remember, I was resting comfortably with my cats and the rest of the Burroughs clan in St. Louis until I got word of some stupid shenanigans involving a bogus fedora, a witch, and your desaparecido tombstone. And the plot just keeps getting thicker. I used to say, If cats don't need no junk, Bill don't need no junk. But as the popular adage goes, 'Never say never again.'" Burroughs's tone became increasingly vehement as he continued his rant.

"As pleased as I am for you, Dean, I still have to corner that goddamn Ugly Spirit and go all 'Wild Boys' on his or her ass. And to do that I need to locate my lost manuscript. What's more, if I ever see another alleged 'Burroughs fedora' I'll be tempted to persuade Aicha

149

to take a shit in it. If I could get my ghostly hands on a good old Colt Peacemaker I'd settle a lot of scores in the nagual realm. As I've said before, nonviolence is not exactly my program."

"Why don't we all just calm down," said Bowles soothingly. "Who knows, one success may lead to another and yet another, then we can all celebrate. I might even be able to find some satisfying 'spirits' for us to partake of. Meanwhile, as long as we're here, I'd like to delve some more into those subterranean realms we discovered earlier. I haven't been able to stop thinking about that."

"OK, Mage, lead on," said Burroughs.

Bowles looked around for the mausoleum, but it wasn't where they remembered it being. They drifted up and down between the rows of tombs until they reached the back of the cemetery, where they spotted a strange-looking turtle. As soon as they made eye contact, the turtle was transformed into the very mausoleum they had entered before.

"Speaking of the nagual, I haven't seen a shape-shifter like that since I was in Guatemala many years ago," Bowles said.

Again they passed through the thick door of the mausoleum and the stone floor like flour falling through a sieve, and continued down into the grotto from where stairs descended into the void. They followed the narrow twisting stairs at a steep angle and found themselves in a large echoing chamber with a high curved ceiling made of brick, perhaps of Roman or Phoenician construction. Five hall-like passageways led out of the chamber. Bowles suggested they take the center one. The passage continued for some distance, taking several turns, slanting lower then climbing abruptly upward until it stopped at a high stone wall. Bowles reckoned they were somewhere beneath the medina, perhaps near the ruins of one of the fortifications left after the British had bombarded the city in 1684 under Samuel Pepys.

The wall was massive, but the three of them passed through it like fog through a boxwood hedge, Bowles commenting that its various layers of stone, brick, and mortar suggested an ancient edifice that had undergone various phases of reconstruction. They found themselves in a small room in the back of an apparently abandoned building, which contained an old mattress, a couple of backless wooden chairs, and a crude wooden table made of packing crates, as well as several empty Coca Cola bottles and a small aluminum pot for making tea. On the wall hung a tattered poster of Pamela Anderson.

"A hideout for contrabandistas?" Bowles suggested.

"A veritable thieves' den," said Burroughs.

After floating around to examine the space more carefully, they made their way back to the main chamber.

"That was a bit of a disappointment," Bowles said. "Perhaps the other passages lead to more rewarding destinations. At least it confirms my belief that there are tunnels beneath the city. Perhaps there's a whole network of passages along which magic spells travel back and forth from sender to victim."

"Or an underground railroad to the Western Lands," mused Burroughs.

Dean took the opportunity to retell a story about the time workmen doing plumbing repairs in the dining salon of his bar accidentally broke through the floor and discovered a sealed-up room, perhaps part of a Roman house, which held the skeleton of a camel. Dean said the workmen were so terrified they immediately closed up the hole and left without even collecting the money they were owed. He had to hire Spanish plumbers from Algeciras who completed the job without further problems, but tales of a haunted ancient brothel or torture-chamber beneath Dean's Bar began to circulate in Tangier. For months the overly cautious would only walk past it after crossing to the other side of the street. Perhaps, he thought, one of these tunnels might lead to that mysterious room.

"So which passage shall we try now?" Bowles said.

"How about the one on the far right," said Burroughs. "There's an ominous odor of decay coming from its entrance that I find appealing."

With Bowles leading the way, the three ghosts glided down the dark tunnel. They had gone quite a distance in a more or less straight line when the tunnel curved sharply to the right and ascended abruptly. They felt and heard percussion instruments being played in an oddly syncopated, almost haphazard rhythm.

The tunnel ended at what seemed to be a large door in the ceiling. Moving carefully through it, the three ghosts found themselves in a cavernous, elaborately decorated theatre. The high domed ceiling was decorated with faded and peeling images of painted angels and swirling clouds. On both sides were balconies with ornately carved railings. Below were rows of seats, separated by a wide aisle that presumably led back towards the entrance. Private boxes sat below the balconies. The place was in a dilapidated state, everything covered in a thick layer of dust, with a few old light fixtures protruding from the walls. Dean looked up and saw they were behind the proscenium arch at the back of the stage, on which was piled the detritus of old stage sets and broken seats.

"Es increíble!" said Dean. "I know this place; it's the Gran Teatro Cervantes! When it was built in 1913 it was the greatest theatre in all of North Africa. Operas, plays, dancers, Andalusian orchestras, Flamenco—you name it, it all happened here. But it's been closed for decades now."

"Caruso sang here," Bowles added. "And Shakespeare's *Othello* was performed in Arabic."

The fumbling rhythmic sounds they had heard earlier began again. "Wait," said Bowles, squinting and cocking his head slightly. "I recognize that beat. It's either Gnawa or a poor attempt at a Jilala rhythm." Bowles moved forward until he was downstage, close enough to peer over the edge. On the dusty floor, strewn with trash and fragments of plaster, sat the ghosts of Brian Jones and Brion Gysin, struggling to play a native djembe drum and a pair of krakebs, the large metal castanets that are essential to Gnawa music. They were not having much success handling the instruments, and Bowles could sense their frustration.

"Playing a musical instrument when you're dead isn't easy," said Jones, as he continued his ghostly rapping on the djembe.

"Unless you're the Grateful Dead of course," quipped Gysin. "'Exterminate all rational thought' was a concept best applied to music," he continued. "But it only works if you can manipulate the fucking instruments. Give me a minute to see if I can get a better hold on these krakebs and then let's start again."

"I wish I still had my Vox Teardrop Mark III," Jones said. "That guitar wrote most of the greatest Stones songs. Maybe I'd do better with that."

Burroughs and Dean glided to the edge of the stage so they were just behind Bowles, looking down over his shoulders. "Well I'll kiss a mandrill's ass," whispered Burroughs. "Never expected to see Brion again, especially not in Tangier. And with the original Stone-Meister himself. This is a helluva reunion."

For the next few minutes the three remained silent and listened. Gysin and Jones were so intent on getting a decent percussive groove going that they were totally unaware they had an audience.

"Look, Brion," said Jones. "The reason I asked you to join me in this session was because I finally heard another group with enough

soulful power to make me want to try a comeback—in my case, a res-
urrection—and you were the one who originally introduced me to the
thousand-year-old rock n' roll music of Joujouka. When I felt the vibes
from Ravi Khan and Tony Mahoney's jams with the Gnawa orchestra,
I had the same feeling as when I first heard Elmore James. They just
need a little more of that old mystical Gnawa juice, you know, trance
music that connects with the spirit world. Tomorrow night is the big
rave before they go on tour, so we don't have much time."

"I understand, Brian. I'll keep working at it until we're good enough
to slip in and join Khan and Mahoney. Fuck, they won't even know
we're in the group. We'll be the invisible back-up band. But what a
fantastic place to have a concert!"

They finally got together a few grooves that hinted at the magically
hypnotic qualities Brian Jones had been talking about, with a nod to
"Sympathy for the Devil." When they stopped, they were surprised by
the sound of applause from above. Looking up, they saw the ghosts of
Burroughs, Dean, and Bowles, clapping and smiling.

"Bill! Paul! Dean!" Gysin exclaimed. "What a wonderful surprise!
What on earth, or off of it, are you doing here?"

"Well, Brion," Burroughs drawled emphatically, glancing at Dean
and Bowles with a knowing look. "That's getting to be a long story."

"We have nothing but time, Bill," Brion answered. "All the time in
eternity."

Through the boarded-up windows of the Gran Teatro Cervantes
came the wavering pre-recorded call of the muezzin to Fajr, echoing
through the medina from speakers mounted on the many minarets of
the city. The Port of Saints now glowed golden violet in the first light
of the day, and in the palm trees the starlings had begun their insistent
nervous rustling.

21

Mr. Garland was an early riser, up at dawn to oversee the feeding of his
menagerie, who were already clamoring for their first meal of the day.
But as he was getting dressed in his bedroom, he was aware something
was missing from the typical early-morning acoustic background—
the sound of the macaques. He stepped onto the balcony and looked

toward their large enclosure—it was empty.

He went downstairs and found Ali, the watchman and grounds-keeper, who had no explanation for the missing macaques. He too had heard them in the night and thought they sounded particularly restless. He started to offer possible explanations, putting the blame first on the full moon, then on evil spirits, but Mr. Garland was not in the mood for any Moroccan superstition codswallop and quickly cut him off. He told Ali to check with the neighbors to see if anyone had heard or seen anything. Of all the animals in Mr. Garland's possession, the macaques were dearest to him. He had given them all names, and each of them had its own individual personality.

A closer look at the macaques' enclosure established that the macaques had apparently broken out on their own, without any human assistance from outside. Not without a certain reluctance, Mr. Garland called the police. He hated dealing with the authorities, but in this case he had no choice—he absolutely had to get his macaques back, and any kind of help would be welcome. It wasn't the material worth of the animals that mattered most, it was his close emotional bond with them, in particular with Bruno, the large shaggy male and self-appointed leader of the group.

After explaining to the police what had happened, Mr. Garland tried to calm himself by putting a favorite LP, *The Late Great Townes Van Zandt,* on his vintage Technics turntable. He cued up the song "Pancho and Lefty," turned the volume way up, and went back out on the balcony with his morning cup of tea while he waited for the police to arrive. The detective he'd talked to on the phone said they wanted to inspect what he called "the scene of the crime," although as far as Mr. Garland could tell no crime had been committed—the macaques had simply broken out of their enclosure and escaped. He couldn't understand why, as he did his best to look after them and treated them well. But if the Moroccan police preferred to see it as a criminal act, maybe that would provide them with the necessary motivation to find them.

Mina was a little nervous when she arrived at her job in the office of Maghreb Marine in the Avenue Mohammed V. In her purse was the key her brother Sayyad had given her, along with the folded paper on which was written the bank's name and the safe deposit box number. Anticipation of what might be waiting in the box had cost her some sleep, and kept her from concentrating on her work now. In her mind's eye she saw it filled with gold, jewels, and other riches, then she visualized herself on a shopping spree in Paris, then sunning herself on the deck of her yacht in Monaco, prior to an evening of cruising the casinos . . .

Mina's responsibilities included a trip to the post office and the bank every morning to pick up and deliver registered mail and deposit checks. She planned on using that opportunity to find the bank where the safe deposit box was located and see if she could gain access to it. According to the slip of paper, it was called Interbank, located at the Place Brahim Roudani. There was no listing for Interbank in the phone book but she had noticed there was a branch of the Bank of Gibraltar at that address.

Promptly at ten, Mina gathered the outgoing mail and checks to be deposited at her company's bank, slipped them into the brown leather attaché case she always took with her, and walked up the Boulevard Pasteur and the Avenue Belgique to the Banque Populaire du Maroc. She was on friendly terms with the teller, an older lady named Fatima, and asked if she knew anything about Interbank. Fatima told her that it was originally the Bank of Gibraltar but had been renamed Interbank during the International Zone era. Then, when Tangier rejoined the rest of Morocco after the restoration of full sovereignty in 1956, bringing an end to the International Zone, it had reverted to its old name.

Mina walked back through the Place de France, passing the Café de Paris, crowded with the morning contingent of locals, tourists, and faux bohemians, plus the usual attendant shoeshine boys, beggars, and hustlers. She headed back down Avenue Mohammed V toward the Place Brahim Roudani, her thoughts firmly on the safe deposit box. Whatever was in it had been languishing there since at least 1956, and given the amount of smuggling and other illicit business that had gone on during the International Zone years, there was a good chance the contents would prove to be valuable.

When she reached the Bank of Gibraltar, Mina stood outside on the sidewalk for a moment to compose herself. Her manner should in no way raise any suspicions. She tried to assume a confident air and walked into the vestibule. Quickly she scanned the counter and approached a woman teller who had a somewhat sympathetic appearance. She explained the purpose of her visit, having decided in advance not to offer any explanation for wanting access to a safe deposit box that had in all likelihood not been opened in almost fifty years. She was relying on the code of discretion that prevailed among banks, trusting they would respect her privacy.

The teller looked at the safe deposit box key and excused herself, saying she would be right back. Mina watched her walk toward the rear of the bank, where several employees were seated at large desks, and speak with an older man with a balding head and a thick black moustache. The man looked over at Mina and down at the key, then replied to the teller. He stood up and walked further into the interior of the bank, taking the key with him, and spoke with a corpulent man with white hair who sat at an even larger desk. Mina felt her nervousness increasing but tried to control it.

After conferring for what seemed to Mina an eternity, the man with the moustache went into an office at the very back, disappearing from view. Mina looked down at her fingernails, then at the grain of the marble of the countertop, then at the pen in its holder on the end of a small metal chain. She had reached the point where she was considering leaving and abandoning the entire venture when the man with the moustache came out of the office and approached the counter, gesturing for Mina to step around it and follow him.

"This way, please, Madame."

Mina hesitated for a moment but decided to go with him. They walked to the rear of the bank and down a spiral staircase into the basement. The man opened the huge steel door of the vault and invited her to step inside. He handed the key to her and from his vest pocket produced a similar key, which he slipped into one of the two locks of safe deposit box number 251914. Mina noticed it was one of the medium-sized boxes, not the smallest, which raised her hopes further. He gestured for her to slip her key into the other lock, they each turned their key, and he pulled out the box.

"Follow me, please," he said, and they walked out of the vault and into a small room with a desk and two chairs. "I'll wait outside until you are finished." He set the box on the desk and left the room, shutting the door behind him.

Mina sat down and looked at the box. She closed her eyes and slowly lifted the lid. Then she opened her eyes again. After a moment of pure bewilderment, she felt her heart sink. The images of prosperity she'd been entertaining all morning long fell with a silent crash to the floor, splintered like the shards of a broken mirror.

Inside the box were a pistol, a box of bullets, a large folding knife, several glass syringes with needles, a kif pipe, a mildewed leather pouch of kif that had dried to dust, and several glass ampoules labeled Eukodol. Underneath them was a huge stack of paper as thick as several phone books. She cautiously lifted out some of the sheets with the tips of her fingers. They were typewritten pages, dog-eared and dirty, some with ugly stains and even small, charred holes in them, as if they had been lying around exposed to all sorts of abuse before being gathered up and placed in the box. The first page bore the word ULTRAZONE, typed in capital letters in red ink and underlined. Below that, typed in black ink, was a name, William S. Burroughs. The name meant nothing to her, or . . . maybe she had heard it somewhere, but she didn't know where. She dropped the pages back onto the pile, sat back in the chair and sighed deeply. So much for shopping in Paris and lying on the deck of her yacht in Monaco.

"Merde!" she said out loud.

"Madame?" said the man through the door. "Is everything alright?"

"Yes of course, I'll be through in just a moment."

Mina transferred the contents into her attaché case and closed the lid of the safe deposit box. After they had returned the box to its place and locked it, she thanked the man with the moustache and wished him a good day. When she stepped outside into the warm Tangier morning, it seemed even warmer after the cool interior of the bank.

So deep was her disappointment and so engrossed was Mina in her thoughts that she failed to see an old blind beggar in a black burnoose shuffling along the sidewalk towards her and ran right into him. He staggered, the burnoose that had covered his head flipped back, and Mina saw his brown leathery skin, the white stubble of a beard, and closely shorn white hair. The beggar's eyes were two colorless orbs rotating in the sockets of his skull.

She dropped the attaché case, which landed on the ground with a thump and burst open, spilling its contents onto the sidewalk. As she quickly kneeled to gather them up, a sudden gust of wind picked up several sheets of paper, sweeping them further down the street. A gaggle of young street urchins who had been standing in a nearby doorway came running out and chased after the windblown pages as they went wheeling down the Avenue Mohammed V like a flock of crazed white gulls.

22

Everly Tweed was unable to sleep. He couldn't even lie still anymore. The junk sickness, brought back to life once he'd tasted the Blue Messiah's product, was now a writhing, clawing *thing* trying to take over his consciousness from deep within. He sat up to wipe the cold sweat off his brow and retched. He needed another fix, and not just a few drops of djinn oil. That was kid's stuff, and it was time for the real thing. But where could he score? And with what? He'd spent his last dirhams on absinthe in the Café de Nuit. He focused on piecing together the blurry incidents of the recent past. That vial of heroin the monkey had snatched up along with the fedora. Where was it now?

Tweed glanced up at the multi-colored skylight and the wheels of his junk-sick mind began to turn like a children's wind-up toy. He cleared the books and clothes from the floor directly under the skylight, then slid the table so it was positioned under the skylight and placed a chair on top of the table. Carefully he climbed onto the table, then stood on the chair so he could ease open the skylight. Poking his head out, he looked around the rooftop. There was no one to be seen, so he lifted himself up through the skylight and stood on the roof, blinking in the bright Tangier sun. Its glare, reflected off the bay and the walls of the whitewashed buildings all around him, was overwhelming. He felt weak and dizzy and stumbled backward, almost falling into the open skylight.

After a few minutes the wave of nausea had passed, and his eyes had adjusted to the harsh light. The walls of the buildings on either side were windowless and some stories higher than his own building. So where had the kid and his monkey come from? He walked to the rear of the roof and looked down into a narrow courtyard hung with freshly washed laundry. To the right, at the back of the building next door, he could look down onto the rear balcony of the apartment directly next to his own. It held a table and chairs along with propane gas bottles, a few potted plants and herbs, two parakeets in cages suspended from a makeshift trellis. Several wooden crates were stacked against the wall. The door from the balcony into the apartment was open, but Tweed heard no sounds from within, only the usual chatter of voices and TV echoing up from the courtyard.

That must be where the kid and the monkey live! By climbing onto the crates, they would have been able to get to the roof where he now stood. So it was theoretically possible for him to climb down to the balcony the same way and search the apartment for that precious little vial. Turmoil raged within him, a battle between the urgent demands of his junk sickness and what one might call common sense.

Tweed trembled as he tried to figure out the easiest way to get down there. Looking around him, he saw in one corner a rickety-looking wooden ladder that painters must have left behind. It looked to be just about long enough to reach down to the balcony. He needed all his strength to lift the ladder into position and slide it down the side of the wall to the floor of the balcony below. Then he slowly made his way down, until he felt tiles under his feet. He was breathing hard and sweating from the junk sickness as well as his fear of being caught in the act. A throbbing pain ran from his left shoulder down his arm, as if it were being squeezed by a large and powerful hand. Sooner or later he would have to see a doctor about that.

Tweed stepped around the wooden boxes, almost tripping over a laundry basket. He looked under the table, behind the gas bottles, and in the wooden crates, but found nothing but useless clutter and a bag of seed for the parakeets. But something glinted among the potted plants on the other side of the table near the door that led into the apartment. Getting down on his hands and knees, he crawled over to the plants and saw a small bottle was wedged between the stems of one of the plants. Excitedly he removed the rubber stopper and saw it still contained the precious white powder. Wiping his brow with his sleeve, he began to rejoice. I just have to get back up the ladder and I'll have the fix I need, he thought.

As he turned to crawl back to the ladder, he glanced into the open doorway and saw the old fedora lying on the kitchen table next to a loaf of bread. On impulse he jumped up and grabbed it, then started climbing the ladder. With the last of his strength he pulled it up after him and put it back where he'd found it.

Getting down through the skylight was a precarious enterprise but Tweed managed to grasp the rim of the skylight and slowly lower himself until he felt the chair under his feet. Then he stepped down onto the table and steadied himself before jumping to the floor. He fell backwards against the wall, the vial and the fedora clutched tightly to his chest.

Tweed went into his kitchen and dug through the wooden box where he kept his tableware, picking out a large silver soup spoon. Behind a burlap curtain under the counter he located his last set of works. The inside of the syringe was coated with a green film, and the needle tip held a white crystal residue. He removed the needle, wiped the crystals off it, and poured some water into a cup, then filled and emptied the syringe several times to make sure the plunger worked. After reattaching the needle, he checked to see it was clear.

His junk need was about to overwhelm him, so he didn't want to boil the works. But a thought flashed into his squirming brain: I'll mix the djinn oil with the Blue Messiah's junk. It'll be the perfect drug cocktail to blow away all the weird shit I've been through in the last couple of days. Tweed poured the rest of the djinn oil Abdul had given him into the spoon, added the Blue Messiah's heroin, stirred them together with a small knife and heated the mixture over a burner on his stove until it dissolved into a milky liquid. Carefully filling the syringe, he walked into his bedroom and sat on the bed.

Tweed rolled up his sleeve and made a fist with his left hand. His shoulder still ached but the veins in the crook of his arm stood up nicely. With a satisfied grin he stuck the needle into the fattest vein he could see and slowly pushed the plunger in, then pulled it back just enough to see a red cloud swirling inside the syringe. That's the golden ticket! he said to himself, and rammed the plunger home.

With the first rush Tweed felt like he had made a bungee jump from the earth to the moon. His toes dipped into the cold, powdery lunar soil before he was whipped back across space and plunged into the deepest part of the deepest ocean on Earth. He kept going down, deeper and deeper, being tossed and rag-dolled into the submarine-crushing depths of an unimaginable void. His eyelids were being ripped off and his pupils expanding in a vain search for the tiniest speck of light. Finally, as though a curtain had been abruptly lifted, there came multicolored explosions that turned into psychedelic visions of glowing larvae and maggots crawling upward through his intestines and his throat. His mouth opened wide, and he vomited a stream of putrefaction into a coffin of alabaster. Looking up he saw a pulsating cloud etched with furls and ridges like a human brain. A bolt of lightning pierced the cloud, which began to rain drops of blood that covered him, soaking through his clothes to his sweaty skin.

The djinn oil had lit the fuse of the Blue Messiah's junk and it was

Lift Off, All Systems Go. Tweed found himself astride a mile-long thousand-wheeled locomotive that streaked across the desert like a rocket sled. It headed straight for a mountain of black granite which had only a tiny tunnel opening. Just before the locomotive reached the tunnel it was transformed into a gold-flecked blue serpent which slipped effortlessly into the opening and plunged into the darkness of a huge bottomless cavern. Tweed wrapped his arms around the serpent's neck as it formed a circle, with the serpent's mouth grasping its own tail. He was riding the ouroboros. The pain in his left arm intensified as he gripped the serpent tighter and tighter. The ouroboros began to spin like a roulette wheel; Tweed lost his grip and was flung into the abyss. As he fell, one image appeared out of the darkness: *Sadak in Search of the Waters of Oblivion*, an early nineteenth-century painting by John Martin, which Tweed had seen once in James Ridley's book, *Tales of the Genii*. The image disappeared as he continued to drift downward, and gradually he felt a state of almost perfect bliss envelop his being.

Then everything stopped. In a state of near paralysis, Tweed found himself looking into the yellow eye of a turtle. The eye blinked once and the turtle disappeared. Tweed slowly turned his head and saw he was lying on his back on a smooth, flat surface. He looked down and realized to his astonishment that he had come to rest on Walter Harris's tomb in St. Andrew's Cemetery. Even more astonishingly, a group of tourists stood over him, commenting on the tomb and the Moroccan zellige tiles that covered it. The tourists seemed completely unaware that Tweed was lying there. "What are you staring at?" he said out loud. No response. "Well, won't someone please help me up?" The crowd ignored him and moved down the path to the next row of tombs. "Fuck the lot of you then," Tweed shouted. I must still be high from that fucking atom bomb I cooked up, he thought. But even if I'd had an overdose, I wouldn't drag myself back here, of all places.

In fact, he didn't feel high at all. He didn't feel junk sick, either. He didn't feel anything except a strange weightlessness. I've heard of *The Incredible Lightness of Being*, he said to himself, but this is beyond lightness. This is like nothingness; as if I'm on the verge of disappearing in some magic act. He stood up just as a man and woman were walking toward him. Before he could excuse himself or move out of the way, the couple passed right through him as if he weren't there. The realization that something had changed significantly began to overtake him. He stood motionless as the clucking gaggle of tourists made its way along the cemetery wall and out through the gate to their waiting bus.

Tweed didn't know how long he had been under the influence of his drug cocktail, but the shadows cast by the tombstones indicated it was mid-morning. He was gazing around the now vacant cemetery, trying to figure out what had happened, when he heard voices. At the back of the cemetery three figures stepped into view as if they had materialized out of thin air. Paul Bowles, Joseph Dean, and William Burroughs.

While schmoozing with Gysin and Brian Jones in the Teatro Cervantes, Burroughs had felt the presence of the Ugly Spirit somewhere nearby, and his GPS (Ghostly Positioning Sensor) alarm was activated. He felt the Ugly Spirit's vibrations were coming from somewhere in the Avenue Mohammed V, and the word ULTRAZONE flashed before him in a blaze of neon red, then faded to a fuzzy afterimage. Burroughs told Dean and Bowles he needed to find out what was going on, and the three ghosts quickly made their way through the tunnel and up to the mausoleum entrance in St. Andrew's.

Dean was the first to spot Tweed and said, "Well, what do we have here, Bill? It appears that your double has decided to join the party." Before Tweed could say anything, Dean greeted him with "Welcome to Zero Zero Land."

Tweed was certain he was still high, or he was dreaming. He reminded himself that the best thing to do when a dream becomes more real than "reality" is to just go along with it—like being hypnotized. When I wake up or come down, I probably won't remember any of this, he thought. Without replying to Dean or acknowledging the others, Tweed slowly turned and walked down the path toward the gate. I'll just walk back home and when I wake up I'll be where I was when I got high, he told himself. It's always worked before.

As he passed through the cemetery gate Tweed felt a powerful wave roll over him. Everything seemed more sharply in focus. The light was brighter. The street sounds were clearer and the smells more intense. As he walked along he realized he could hear the thoughts of the people passing by. Still, no one seemed to notice his presence. The walk back to the Rue Mohamed Bergach seemed to take only seconds rather than minutes, and he found himself back in his flat, standing in the kitchen. There on the counter were the two vials and the empty spoon. Aha! I was right, he thought. I was dreaming while I was still high and now I'm awake and starting to come down. He turned and headed to his bedroom. When he reached the doorway he looked down at the bed and saw a figure lying there, eyes and mouth wide open, a syringe dangling from its arm. For a moment he failed to recognize the body as his own.

Evangeline and Piet were sitting at a table outside the Café de Paris, having a breakfast of croissants and café au lait after what had turned into a long night. After witnessing the accident with the two taxis, one of which had then burst into flames, they had wandered down the hill in the direction of the harbor and into a dark, hole-in-the-wall bar called Lord Nelson's Pub. It was just the sort of dreary yet slightly menacing dive, full of unsavory characters, that appealed to both of them. They found an empty table in the corner and ordered a couple of beers. The interior decoration had originally intended to replicate an English pub, but all such references had gradually disappeared under a patina of dust and age, not to mention a hodgepodge of generic maritime knickknacks. It seemed to be a typical harbor bar, full of dock workers in blue overalls, seamen, and fishermen; there were no other tourists to be seen. The floor was littered with crumpled tissue-like napkins, chicken bones, olive pits, and peanut shells from the tapas that were served with each order of drinks. Kif smoke hung in the air. The television suspended from the ceiling in one corner was turned on, but the sound was off, and out of a dusty ghetto-blaster behind the bar came the sounds of Egyptian pop music. Evangeline and Piet felt right at home.

Several beers later, the place had become even more crowded, and they were joined at their table by two middle-aged men with long hair and beards. Soon the four of them were engaged in a lively drunken conversation. The two men, a Chilean named Arturo and a Mexican named Ulises, were both poets, they said. They had been part of a group known as the Visceral Realists, who were active in Mexico City in the mid-seventies. They'd spent a lot of time and energy back then trying to track down an obscure poetess in northern Mexico whom they considered the "mother" of Visceral Realism, dating back to the movement's conception in the 1920s. Cesárea Tinajero was her name. In the twenty-some years since their thwarted quest for the poetic grail, Arturo and Ulises had been knocking around North America,

Europe, the Middle East, and Africa, living a hand-to-mouth existence. They'd been stranded in Tangier for months, trying to scrape together enough money to get back to Spain. To the young Europeans they seemed like true vagabonds, infused with a powerful poetic integrity and radiating authenticity. Evangeline later told Piet that the two men seemed like modern-day versions of Arthur Rimbaud and Paul Verlaine, or Jack Kerouac and Neal Cassady.

When Lord Nelson's Pub closed in the early morning hours, the four of them walked down to the beach, where they sat on the sand in the silvery moonlight and smoked a few rounds of the men's very strong hashish. Piet bought a chunk of it from them, to replenish his own stash but also to help out the down-at-heel poets. They talked and laughed and traded more stories until the first blush of pink began to glow in the east and the call to morning prayer rasped out of the loudspeakers. Then they said farewell and parted ways, Evangeline and Piet walking back to the Hotel Lutetia while Arturo and Ulises headed toward the harbor and the abandoned café where they were camping out.

At the Café de Paris, Evangeline was poring over a map of the city as Piet read in his tattered copy of John Hopkins's *Tangier Diaries*, ignoring the endless pleas of the shoeshine boys while laughing to himself at Hopkins's description of sitting outside that very café and speculating that Tangier must be the only city in the world where there were more shoeshine boys than there were shoes.

Out of the corner of his eye Piet was distracted by sudden movement. He glanced up to see some kids running down the Boulevard Pasteur chasing sheets of paper being blown along by a strong breeze. They were a bunch of grubby street boys, dodging cars and taxis, weaving between the pedestrians on the sidewalk and the trees planted along the curb, laughing and leaping in the air. One by one they managed to grab all the sheets except one that had been swept upward beyond their reach. Piet watched as the piece of paper finally fluttered down and landed in the branches of one of the trees lining the sidewalk in front of him. One of the kids came running and tried to climb up into the tree, but the branches were out of his reach and the bark too smooth for him to get a foothold. He looked up at the piece of paper with a bemused and frustrated expression.

Piet pulled one of the metal chairs over to the tree and stood on it. He could just reach high enough to pluck the piece of paper from the branches and climbed back down to hand it over to the boy. It was a yellowed and stained sheet of letter-size paper, covered on both sides with typewritten text. Piet wondered why the kids were so excited about gathering up all the pages. Most likely it was just a frivolous game to pass the time that otherwise went by slowly and uneventfully for Tangier street urchins.

Piet handed the piece of paper to the kid and watched him run off triumphantly to join his friends.

"What was all that about?" Evangeline asked.

"Just kids having fun with some trash blowing down the street."

She glanced briefly in the direction in which the boys had disappeared and began folding up her map.

"Let's go back to the Café Hafa," she said. "Maybe if we describe the guy who made off with my hat someone could tell us who he is or where we might find him."

"Good idea."

Under the cover of night, Bruno and his fellow macaques had made their way through the gardens and winding streets of the Old Mountain down to Merkala Beach. From there they worked their way between the rocks along the coast in the direction of the harbor. Before it was light they had disappeared into a narrow cleft in the rocks at the base of the cliffs and entered the subterranean network of tunnels known only to smugglers, lost souls, ghosts, Blue Messiah cultists, and a few fishermen.

23

Just-Call-Me-Ishmael was still unsteady on his feet after the accident, and a couple of concerned citizens took him in their car to the hospital, where he was admitted for observation. After X-rays and a thorough check-up, he was released the next morning. Other than a few aches and pains and a nagging headache, he felt okay, and decided to walk back to his apartment, figuring the fresh morning air would do him some good. He took a shower and changed his clothes, took several aspirin, and then called a taxi to take him up to his villa on the Old Mountain again. The Monet pastel was a total loss, and he needed another work of art to take to Zurich. He had a few Gauguin pastels he figured he could bear to part with, from Gauguin's early Impressionist phase before he left for the South Seas. Or maybe he should take a collage by Kurt Schwitters. But time was running short for him to get to the travel agency and make his ferry and train reservations.

To save time, he went downstairs to wait for the taxi. While he was standing in the doorway of his building, a bent-over old man came shuffling along the sidewalk and seeing Just-Call-Me-Ishmael, approached him with an upturned empty hand, the universal sign of the beggar. Looking closer at the man's face, Just-Call-Me-Ishmael saw that the entire right side had been eaten away by some kind of cancer. What looked like the man's cheekbone was partially exposed, and tiny white maggots wriggled in the festering wound.

He looked away in disgust, but the man stayed put, the palm of his hand resolutely protruding into Just-Call-Me-Ishmael's peripheral vision. He dug into his pocket, scooped out all the coins he had and dropped them into the empty palm, which quickly receded from view. The man mumbled something and shuffled off just as the taxi pulled up to the curb.

Just-Call-Me-Ishmael gave the driver the address of the villa and told him to hurry. They went zooming up the street and were making good time until they became trapped in a traffic jam. He leaned forward to squint out of the front window of the cab and saw that there had been a bad accident. A taxi had run into a donkey that was pulling an old wooden cart filled with tires. The donkey's body was sprawled across the street, its belly split open by the impact, guts slithering onto the pavement like a ripped-open sack of eels. Blood streamed across the street and into the gutter. As always, a crowd had gathered, and as always, there was much cursing and yelling, hysterical accusations flying back and forth, and no sign of the police. Just-Call-Me-Ishmael told the driver to turn around but behind them was a gridlocked mass of cars, trucks, and taxis, all of them honking loudly.

After the initial jolt of seeing his own lifeless body, the truth began to wash over Everly Tweed in waves. Evidently he'd been having either an out-of-body-experience or a near-death-experience. I must have skipped a dimension or two on those last kicks, he thought. Hah, there I am, he mused, looking down at his body sprawled on the unmade bed, *like a patient etherized upon a table.* Old Tom Eliot sure nailed that one.

Tweed moved from the bedroom to the salon and glanced up through the window facing the street to the hard blue of the Tangier sky. It was a Bowlesian sky, cold and indifferent, a blue emptiness with a blazing white orb of sun burning a hole in it, offering no shelter whatsoever as Tweed puzzled over the transformation he had apparently undergone. He went back to inspect his body more closely. In an out-of-body experience the body is in a state of limbo, between the worlds of the living and the dead. Tweed was well read in such matters, having spent years studying the literature of trance, illusion, hallucination, and medically induced coma. As for near-death-experiences, he had read many stories of people who had "come back" from death's door or the final threshold of the unknown. Most described their experiences as euphoric and above all peaceful. They had experienced no fear or anxiety. But those people hadn't actually died. Tweed was feeling anything but euphoric, faced with the grim realization that there was no way back.

As he examined his body he noticed purple blotches on his arms and his face. Lividity appears after the heart has stopped pumping blood, when blood begins to pool near the skin surface, one of the first signs of death. "Well I'll be damned," said Tweed out loud, then thought better of the expression. If I am indeed dead, I don't want to have to watch my body rot in this dingy apartment. He checked to see his apartment door was unlocked, as well as the front door at the bottom of the stairs, then made his way to Kazim's house.

Kazim was one of his few friends in the world and certainly the wisest person he knew. Tweed figured that if he could get Kazim to be the one who discovered his dead body, then the matter of its disposal would be attended to swiftly and discreetly. After slipping vaporously through the two heavy wooden doors of Kazim's house, Tweed's ghost found him reclining in a bamboo and leather papasan chair fast asleep. Lying there he resembled a large pear lodged in a catcher's mitt. On the small table next to him was a plate of cookies and a half-finished glass of mint tea. David Bowie's "Golden Years" was playing softly in the background. Tweed listened as Bowie sang, *Don't let me hear you say life's taking you nowhere . . .* and smiled wryly at the irony. He began to project a potent post-hypnotic suggestion into Kazim's mind, so that when he woke he would feel an urgent need to go to Tweed's flat and check on him. Kazim took a couple of deep breaths, sighed, and began to stir. Unsure if his ghost might be visible to his friend, Tweed ducked behind one of the archways leading to the interior garden.

Kazim's eyes shot open. He was instantly wide awake and felt his heart beating rapidly. He called for his housekeeper, Habiba, and asked her to bring him his dark brown djellaba, telling her he had to visit someone. Kazim often left the house abruptly and nothing in his manner seemed unusual. Habiba opened the large main door for him and handed him his cane. It was past noon and the sunlight cast stark shadows at odd angles along the twisting medina alleyways. The effect reminded Kazim of the Expressionist film sets in *The Cabinet of Doctor Caligari*. When he had first heard the film mentioned many years before, he had heard the title as *The Cabinet of Doctor Calamari* and had imagined a man with tentacles instead of arms and legs.

When Kazim arrived at Tweed's building he rang the buzzer, but there was no answer. As he wondered what to do next, he noticed the door was open. He went up to Tweed's flat and knocked loudly three times with the heavy brass knocker. Hearing nothing from the other side of the door, he tried the latch and found it was open as well. Meanwhile Tweed's ghost hovered on the roof and peered down through a pane of clear glass in the multi-colored skylight. Kazim stepped inside and his nostrils were filled with a sweetly putrid odor. As if led by an unseen hand, he made his way to the salon, turned and then stopped at the entrance to the bedroom. There lay Tweed's body, the eyes wide open but glazed over like those of a dead fish.

Kazim steadied himself with his cane and stepped back. Tweed's body had turned a purplish gray, and there was a distinct smell of death in the room. Kazim was surprised but not shocked. Drug overdoses had become fairly common among the aging expatriate community in recent years. "I am sorry, Mr. Tweed. May Allah grant you mercy," he said half out loud. He sat down at the table in the salon and calmly reflected on the situation. Soon a plan began to take shape in his mind.

First he would look for any cash or valuables that might be in the apartment. Anything Tweed had left behind would enable Kazim to make the necessary final arrangements. He went from room to room and with Tweed's invisible guidance discovered a well-hidden stash of English pound notes in an old biscuit tin. He also found Tweed's passport on a bookshelf with some old electric bills, a resident visa, and a few faded Tangier photo postcards that had never been mailed. He knew where to find the spare apartment keys and dropped them into the hood of his djellaba.

Kazim returned to Tweed's body and, using a towel, carefully removed the works from Tweed's arm. He gathered all the drug paraphernalia in the bathroom and kitchen and wrapped everything in the towel, then placed the bundle in Tweed's canvas shoulder bag. He needed to remove any evidence of drug use from the house, so the authorities would not have to get involved.

He lifted a worn Moroccan carpet from the salon floor and draped it over Tweed, then picked up the canvas shoulder bag and left, setting the apartment door latch to lock from the inside. On the roof Tweed's ghost hovered motionlessly at the edge of the skylight and watched over his body as if he were attending a wake.

Back at his house, Kazim called Habiba into his meditation room. He showed her the canvas bag and said it must be disposed of immediately, as it contained highly potent magical materials capable of causing great evil. He asked Habiba to take the bag to the cliffs high up in the medina and drop it into a cistern which opened into the sea, so that the poisons would be swept away with the tides and out to sea. After handing her the bag and some money, he warned Habiba not to look inside it, as doing so might bring harm to her. Habiba nodded, put on her haik and veil, and left.

Kazim's next step would be to contact Dr. Microbio. For an agreed sum, he was sure the good doctor would be willing to prepare a death certificate and have signed copies delivered to the Moroccan authorities. Tweed had told Kazim long ago that he had no living relatives, so there was no one to inform, and the disposal of his remaining possessions would likely be left to his neighbors. Kazim had to work fast, though. Moroccan burials traditionally take place within twenty-four hours of death or before sunset. Though autopsies were rarely performed on Moroccans in Tangier, the death of a foreign national was a different matter. But once Dr. Microbio had specified a natural cause of death, no autopsy would be required.

Kazim picked up his cane and Tweed's money and headed for the doctor's office in the Rue de la Liberté.

Mina watched the street urchins chase the sheets of paper that had escaped from the briefcase when it burst open and been blown all the way down to where the Avenue Mohammed V became the Boulevard Pasteur. Then she kneeled and quickly gathered up the rest of the stack of paper and the other contents of the briefcase. The old blind beggar was still standing nearby, apparently somewhat stunned by the impact of their collision, but no one else had seen the pistol, the knife, the syringes, and the other paraphernalia that had also fallen out of the briefcase. When everything was back inside, she clicked the briefcase shut and got to her feet, just as the street urchins approached from down the avenue, waving the papers in the air.

"Did you get them all?" she asked.

"Yes," they said in unison, although one of the kids had in fact seen several pages go fluttering past the parapets of the mirador next to the Café de Paris and out over the rooftops of the medina.

One of the kids, who was bigger, older, and dirtier than the rest, collected the sheets from the other kids and approached Mina. "Even one that was stuck in a tree in front of the Café de Paris. A Nasrani helped me get it out of the tree. So what are these papers worth to you?"

Mina wasn't sure if they were worth anything at all, but she wanted to have them back.

"What are they worth to *you*?" she countered.

"A thousand dirhams!"

Mina laughed and started to walk away from him.

"Five hundred!" the kid yelled after her.

Mina stopped and turned around. "I'll give you each fifty dirhams."

"Give us each a hundred and you can have them back."

"Seventy-five dirhams. No more."

The boy looked down at the dirty yellow pages with the strange words typed on them, then at his companions. One of them nodded, and the older boy held out the pieces of paper toward Mina with his left hand while extending the upturned palm of his right hand. The exchange took place, and the kids ran off laughing down the street. Mina kneeled again to open her briefcase and put the other pages inside. As she was doing so a shadow passed over her. She looked up and saw the old blind beggar. "Are you aware of what you have in your possession?" he said in a low, raspy voice.

Mina looked at him in a state of perplexity. Was he blind or not? His eyes seemed to be nothing more than two boiled quail eggs, rolling around uselessly in their sockets.

"I may not be able to see what you can see," he went on, "But you can't see what I see. That's the difference between us. I see a force of unimaginable darkness, one that has lain dormant for many years and just now been brought back to life. This force can only bring evil to its owner, for soon it possesses whoever has taken custody of it. Do you understand?"

"What are you talking about?"

Before the beggar could continue, another violent gust of wind swept down the avenue, threatening to blow the loose pages down the street again. Mina quickly stuffed them into the briefcase and snapped it shut. She got to her feet, took one last critical look at the blind man, and started off down the Avenue Mohammed V. She'd been away from the office for too long already, and she still had to go to the post office.

24

Kazim arrived at Dr. Microbio's office to find a crowd of Moroccans standing and sitting in the tiny waiting room and the hallway outside. He went to the head of the line, where the assistant, Abdallah, recognized him and ushered him into the doctor's private salon. Within minutes Dr. Microbio arrived, wearing a bloody surgeon's smock. Beads of sweat stood out on his forehead, and his hair was damp and matted.

"Kazim! Salaam alaikum. What a pleasant surprise. Please excuse the chaos. I had to leave suddenly to euthanize a poor donkey which had been horribly injured by an automobile. Now there is a mob of patients waiting to see me. Some days are worse than others. What can I do for you?"

Kazim told him about finding Everly Tweed's body, the drugs, and the need for his help and absolute discretion in facilitating the burial.

"Is the body still in the apartment?"

"Yes," answered Kazim. "I covered it with a carpet."

"The warm weather means that decomposition will be rapid, so it's good that you covered the body. And the carpet could be useful in transporting it here. I have a cold room in the back and can have some blocks of ice delivered. That should keep the body sufficiently cool for a day or two."

"Fine," said Kazim. "I am hoping a burial can take place by tomorrow at the latest. I will arrange to have the body brought here. You know Moustapha, the St. Andrew's cemetery watchman?"

"Of course. He's been working there for years."

"I'll need his cooperation to obtain a coffin and ensure that Tweed's body is buried with minimal fuss. But I will need a signed death certificate from you to keep the authorities from getting involved, especially the police."

"Um, yes, that can be done. But there is a risk for me, you understand. He is not Moroccan."

"I understand, doctor. But we are old friends, and I think we can agree on a price. I assume payment in English pounds is acceptable?"

"Absolutely," said Dr. Microbio. "I will prepare the paperwork while you have the body brought here. What do you prefer that I list as a cause of death?"

"A heart attack," said Kazim.

"Perfect. Myocardial infarction it will be."

The two men came to terms and shook hands, then Dr. Microbio showed Kazim out through a door that opened into a narrow alley behind the building. "This is where you should have the body brought. Ring the buzzer here and my assistant will open the door. If the body is rolled up in the carpet, then no one should take any notice."

On his way back to Tweed's apartment, Kazim spotted Moustapha walking briskly up the street toward St. Andrew's.

"Moustapha!" he called out.

Moustapha turned and waited for him to catch up.

"Salaam alaikum, Kazim."

"Salaam, Moustapha."

There was a small café nearby and Kazim motioned for them to step inside, where he ordered two glasses of mint tea. "I assume you and Marvin and Lee were successful in your mission?" Kazim asked.

"Yes, the tombstone is back where it should be and I'm on my way to St. Andrew's now to show Rector McLean and then hopefully get my job back."

"Well, the rector is obliged to be a man of his word, so there shouldn't be any problem. And I have a proposition for you that may give you more bargaining power in your negotiations with Rector McLean."

Kazim told Moustapha of Everly Tweed's sudden death and the need for an expedient burial. Moustapha was jolted for a moment to hear of the death of his recent tormenter, while also feeling it was somehow fated that a man who had played at being a ghost to deceive him should now in fact be dead. He recovered himself to assure Kazim that arranging the sale of a plot would certainly please the rector. The financial health of the church had suffered considerably with the decline of the British and expatriate population. The meager offerings collected each Sunday were only a scant addition to the dwindling funds of the Tangier Diocese. Some speculated that it was because of the accusations and rumors that at least one church member had engaged in immoral activities, which had brought St. Andrew's unwanted scrutiny by the Tangier authorities. Times were changing. It was possible that the church might even have to close. In any case, Moustapha knew how much the few remaining plots were selling for and told Kazim there was a nice spot in the very back of the cemetery near a cane brake which barely concealed a compost heap.

Kazim cautioned Moustapha to be careful when speaking to the rector about the deceased. "If the rector asks, say the family wants the affair to be very private. Tell him that payment for the plot will be in cash and that you will arrange for the internment."

"Ouakha, Sidi Kazim," said Moustapha.

"Once you have confirmed the price, send a messenger to my house and I will get you the money."

"Alhamdulillah," said Moustapha enthusiastically, and the two shook hands and parted.

While Moustapha hurried to St. Andrew's, Kazim made his way through the streets of the medina to Lord Nelson's Pub, down near the port. There were always men hanging around the bar eager to earn a few dirhams, no questions asked. Many were addicts of one drug or another, including alcohol, and willing to do just about anything. A heavy haze of kif smoke hung like a blue cloud inside the bar, even at this early hour. Kazim knew the café owner and asked him to pick out two men who would be no trouble and who could keep their mouths shut. The owner looked around at the rogue's gallery of faces in the bar and the corners of his mouth drooped in dissatisfaction.

"Not such a good selection today. Maybe those two over in the corner playing cards," the owner said somewhat unenthusiastically. "I don't know them well. They're from the Rif and have only been in town for a while and are looking for work. Any work."

Kazim went over and introduced himself to the two men and sat down at their table. Hassan and Mansour, both in their mid-thirties, were broke and hungry and ready to take on any task. Kazim explained the situation and what he needed them to do, and they quickly agreed on a price.

Hassan and Mansour followed Kazim to Tweed's apartment. When Kazim lifted the carpet and the two men saw Tweed's body sprawled on the bed amid the detritus of scattered books and clothes, they glanced at each other, then lifted the body and began rolling it up in the carpet. Kazim saw an old fedora lying on the bed and briefly considered tossing it in with Tweed's body as it disappeared into the folds of the carpet. But wherever it was that Tweed was headed now, the hat would probably do him little good.

Kazim gave Hassan and Mansour two hundred dirhams each and told them to rent a handcart and deliver the body to the rear entrance of Dr. Microbio's office in the Rue de la Liberté, promising them each another two hundred dirhams when they had completed the job. One was to wait with the body in the flat while the other went to find a cart. When they left the flat they were to lock the door behind them. Kazim wished the two men luck and left to alert the doctor to the body's imminent arrival.

Aicha had taken a taxi into town after the fire in her villa and checked into the Hotel Dar Sultan. She was extremely tired but also angry and agitated and had hardly slept. In the morning she showered and dressed and called down for breakfast. Although she'd had no dinner the night before, she was not the least bit hungry, but she hoped the sight and smell of breakfast would restore her appetite. While she was waiting, she opened the door to the small balcony and looked out over the roofs of the medina and the Bay of Tangier, sparkling brightly in the sun. As she reviewed everything that had happened recently, the telephone by the side of the bed rang. It was Mohammed, calling from the villa to tell her what Zodelia said she had seen during the night: the man accompanied by the two strange creatures leaving the villa in the middle of night carrying the two halves of the tombstone.

Aicha was furious. "What do I pay you for? Are you a watchman or are you a lazy useless dirty dog lying around waiting for someone to throw you another scrap of meat?"

Without giving Mohammed a chance to explain or defend himself, she slammed down the phone and went back out onto the balcony. The anger had taken possession of her entire being like some powerful spell. Whoever was responsible for stealing the tombstone from her villa was in for some serious trouble. It had to have been Moustapha, he must have recruited those two Mugwumps who hung around the Café Triangle. The sort of revenge that was called for would be the most cruel and all-consuming that she could possibly conjure up.

As Aicha began to formulate her plan, she felt a sharp pain in her lower abdomen. She'd been half-aware of the pain the entire night but had blamed it on missing dinner and the stress associated with the fire and having to sleep in a strange bed. But now the pain was something she could no longer ignore.

By the time Kazim arrived at Dr. Microbio's office, the ice had been delivered to the cold room and arranged in a coffin-shaped rectangle on the tiled floor.

Dr. Microbio showed Kazim the signed and completed death certificate.

"I believe this will be satisfactory," he said. "I left the name blank."

"That's probably best. I've already disposed of the passport and any other identification. Under name just put Unknown European."

"Certainly, as in John Doe," said Dr. Microbio.

"If Moustapha is able to arrange the purchase of the plot in St. Andrew's then the burial could even take place today," said Kazim.

"I certainly hope so. I don't want the corpse to get any riper than it already is. I'll have the body doused with lye powder as soon as it arrives. That should help mask any odors of decay and will speed decomposition. By the time it is buried there should be no way of identifying the body, if there were to be an investigation. After it leaves here my assistant will scrub the room with carbolic acid. All very tidy, don't you agree?"

"As always, Dr. Microbio, you ply your trade with a deft hand," said Kazim.

"Compliment graciously accepted, thank you."

Kazim was exhausted by the time he reached the Grand Socco

and stopped to have a quick meal of chicken kebabs, salad, fries, and a Coke. He finished eating with a hearty belch and resumed his walk home. Along the way something on the sidewalk caught his attention. He glanced down and saw it was a tarot card. He bent to look closer; it was Le Pendu, the Hanged Man. Kazim reached down to pick up the card but thought better of it and continued up the street, pondering its significance. He would have to look it up in his library when he got home.

A young Moroccan boy was sitting on his front step when he arrived. At the sight of Kazim, the boy jumped up, bowed, and handed him a folded slip of paper. On it were Moustapha's scrawled figures for the cost of the plot, the coffin, the digging of the grave and burial. The total came to four thousand dirhams, or nearly three hundred pounds. Kazim told the boy to wait and went inside. Habiba had not returned from disposing of Tweed's bag, and this worried Kazim a little. But whatever happens, it is Allah's will, he thought to himself.

He had put most of Tweed's money in a safe place in the salon, carrying the rest with him in the hood of his djellaba. When he put all the bills together and counted them, he had a little over one thousand pounds—more than enough to pay Dr. Microbio, Hassan and Mansour, and the expenses of Tweed's burial, with something left over for his trouble. He wrote *Agreed. Meet at the Café Triangle after Asr* on the slip of paper and told the boy to return it to Moustapha. He handed the boy five dirhams as a tip, but the boy remained standing there until Kazim added another five dirhams.

After all the exertions of the day, Kazim needed to rest and so he plopped himself down in his papasan chair. He was soon dozing and began to dream that he was on a long trip south into the desert, where there were beautiful oases with lush gardens, citrus orchards, date groves, fragrant flowers, and many songbirds. Just as the dream was starting to take an unexpectedly sensuous turn, he looked up at the crest of a giant sand dune which appeared over the top of the palm trees and saw wooden gallows, with the silhouette of a man dangling upside down at the end of a rope. There came the sound of splashing water and Kazim was awakened by the sound of Habiba at work in the kitchen. He got up and went to find out if she had done what he asked. She stood at the sink vigorously scrubbing a bunch of turnips.

"Habiba, did the canvas bag find its way to the sea?"

Habiba jumped and dropped the turnips in the sink. She turned to Kazim with a troubled look. "Before I even reached the cistern two boys jumped out of a doorway in the medina and grabbed the bag from under my arm. They disappeared before I could even call for help."

"Would you recognize them if you saw them again?"

"One wore a djellaba with the hood up and the other had pulled the hood of his sweatshirt over his head, and they were both wearing sunglasses, so I couldn't see their faces."

Kazim shook his head. "This city is going to the dogs."

<h1 style="text-align:center">25</h1>

After Kazim left Tweed's flat, Hassan and Mansour unrolled Tweed's body from the carpet. Hassan pried open the corpse's mouth to reveal several gold-filled teeth and inlays. They tried to pull the chunky gold signet ring from Tweed's finger, but it wouldn't budge. The two men searched the apartment and in a plastic bucket under the kitchen sink they found a rudimentary assortment of rusty old tools, including a hammer, a couple of screwdrivers, and a crescent wrench. On the kitchen counter was a bread knife, long but not particularly sharp.

Tweed's ghost, still perched on the roof and peering through the skylight at the activity below, watched in horror as Hassan used the hammer and screwdriver to chisel out the gold fillings and inlays, while Mansour hacked away at the ring finger with the bread knife until the large signet ring, dripping with blood, dropped into his hand.

Hassan left the apartment and walked around until he saw an old man sitting on an empty two-wheeled handcart. He asked if he could rent it for an hour or so, gave the old man the two hundred dirhams as a deposit, and wheeled it back to Tweed's apartment, where the two of them rolled the body up in the carpet again, lugged the unwieldy burden down the stairs, and placed it in the cart. Making sure the doors were locked behind them, the two of them started pushing the handcart through the medina toward the Rue de la Liberté.

As they passed a small bar-café, Mansour signaled to Hassan to stop.

"I need a drink," Mansour said. "To calm my nerves."

"You always need a drink, even when your nerves are calm. But you can't get a drink in the medina, and anyway we can't just leave this cart here in the street."

"This is a special place. We can park the cart over there in the shade and keep an eye on it from that table just inside the door."

Hassan reluctantly agreed and they went inside and sat down. An elderly waiter appeared at their table. Mansour ordered two mint teas; one "green" and one "red." The waiter flashed an almost imperceptible smile and went over to the kitchen area. Into one empty tea glass he placed a handful of fresh mint leaves and filled the glass with piping hot green tea. From somewhere out of sight he produced a bottle of Johnnie Walker Red and poured a generous amount into another, empty tea glass. He dropped a sprig of fresh mint into it, placed both glasses on a brass tray, and brought them over to Hassan and Mansour.

The waiter left and Hassan pulled out his pipe and his leather bag of kif, but there were only a few crumbs of kif in it, not even enough for one puff. "Mansour, loan me some money so I can buy some more kif."

"You just got two hundred dirhams."

"I gave it to the old man as a deposit on the handcart. When I get the change I'll pay you back."

"That's what you always say, then I never see my money again."

Hassan laughed and held out his hand to show Mansour the bloody gold fillings and inlays, a grim reminder of their suddenly increased fortune. Mansour grudgingly handed Hassan a hundred-dirham note.

Hassan went over to the bar and talked with the young qahouaji who was washing glasses. The qahouaji pointed to two young men in the corner playing dominoes and smoking kif. Hassan soon rejoined Mansour at the table by the door and began filling his pipe with the newly bought kif.

"This smells beautiful," Hassan said. "Like the fragrant cedar forests on the mountains above Chefchaouen."

He lit the pipe and filled his lungs until they almost burst, then gradually let out a huge blue cloud of smoke that almost filled the tiny café. "Ah, this is very good, very strong. You should try some, Mansour."

"You know I'm a drinker not a smoker."

"You're missing out on something truly special."

Hassan reloaded the pipe and passed it to Mansour, who filled his lungs with the strong, savory smoke. He held the smoke in as long as he could and then exhaled, smiling knowingly at Hassan.

"Hassan, I am kiffed," said Mansour. "I think I am becoming a chameleon and soon no one will be able to see me."

"You know the proverb: 'A chameleon can only change its color, but never its skin.'"

They laughed and continued to smoke and drink, joking and telling stories, oblivious to the passing of time. When the kif was gone and the money was running low, Hassan rubbed his face and turned to look out the door. He sat upright as though he'd received an electric shock.

"What is it?" asked Mansour.

Hassan jumped to his feet and ran outside, Mansour directly behind him. They stood in the street, somewhat blinded by the bright sun after the dark café and disoriented from the kif and the whiskey. But one thing was very clear to them: the handcart with the body wrapped up in the carpet was nowhere in sight.

When they reached the Café Hafa, Evangeline and Piet went into the terraced garden. The view across the deep blue waters of the strait was breathtaking, with the little whitewashed port of Tarifa plainly visible on the Spanish coast. They looked around and found a waiter they had seen there the previous evening, told him about the incident with the hat, and gave him a description of the man who had helped recover the hat from the tree and then disappeared. The waiter had witnessed the incident and told them the man they were looking for was Moustapha, the caretaker at the cemetery at the Church of St. Andrew.

Evangeline and Piet gave the waiter a healthy tip and thanked him. When they arrived at St. Andrew's cemetery, there was no one in the watchman's shack inside the gate. Nor was anyone to be seen in the cemetery, except for a number of cats and a lone turtle basking in the sun.

"You hear that sound?" Piet asked.

"What sound?" Evangeline answered.

"Sounds like someone digging, back there somewhere," Piet gestured toward the rear of the cemetery.

The two of them walked toward the source of the sound and saw a man standing chest-deep in a freshly dug grave. He was sweating profusely as he continued to dig with steady, determined strokes, as if it were something he'd been doing his whole life. From where they were standing, they couldn't be sure if it was the man from the Café Hafa.

"Excuse me, do you speak English?" Evangeline asked.

When he turned around they saw his eyes widen with surprise and recognition.

"Ah," Moustapha said, "Yes, a little."

"We wanted to know if you have the hat I lost at the Café Hafa."

"Ah yes, the hat," said Moustapha.

"Yes, I'd like to have it back."

Moustapha set the shovel down and climbed out of the grave, mopping his brow with a handkerchief and then wiping his hands. "Madame, please, I did not steal your hat. I wanted to give it back but then I fell all the way down the hillside to the beach. I had to hurry for an important appointment and when I finally got back to the Café Hafa it was closed."

"That's okay," Piet said. "No one is saying you stole it, we just want to get it back. It's a family heirloom that used to belong to an important American writer. Where is it now?"

Moustapha looked somewhat puzzled. "Which American writer?"

"William S. Burroughs."

Moustapha briefly lost his footing in the loose dirt and almost stumbled backwards into the open grave.

"Where is the hat now?" Evangeline repeated.

"I don't know."

"What do you mean, you don't know?" she asked, somewhat irritated.

"It was stolen from me, here in the cemetery, last night."

"And who stole it?"

Moustapha hesitated, wondering if he should tell them Tweed's name, or if that would just make everything more complicated, not to mention angering Kazim. But he had no desire to be involved in any further lies. Things were difficult enough. Glancing over the woman's tattooed shoulder he saw Zora crouching by a tombstone, seemingly nodding her head in a gesture of encouragement.

"An Irishman named Everly Tweed," Moustapha said.

"Do you know where he lives?"

"No. But that doesn't matter because he no longer lives there."

Piet's patience with the old Moroccan was rapidly dwindling. "So where does he live now? Do you know the address?"

Moustapha turned toward the half-excavated grave and pointed down into its cool, moist shadows. "There, that's his new address."

Evangeline and Piet looked at one another in consternation. Neither was sure if they could believe the old gravedigger. All Evangeline could think to ask was, "So when will the funeral be?"

"Later today, inshallah," said Moustapha.

The ghosts of Burroughs, Dean, and Bowles were lingering behind some gravestones just within earshot as Evangeline and Piet interrogated Moustapha.

"Old Tweed seems to be quite a multi-faceted character," Burroughs said.

"You mean *was*," corrected Dean.

"Either way, I'm sure we haven't seen the last of him, in one form or another. But what does that couple want with my old hat? Are they talking about the same hat we saw one of those two kids with the monkey wearing last night? And how did those kids get the hat from Tweed if he stole it from Moustapha? This is getting *very* confusing. I sense the Ugly Spirit at work here."

The three ghosts suddenly felt the presence of a fourth and turned to see Brunhilde Reinhart approaching from the front gate.

"Well, Dean, I see your tombstone is back where it belongs," Brunhilde said.

"Yes, I'm most pleased about that. But Aicha must be steaming mad."

"Absolutely," Brunhilde said. "She set the kitchen on fire while trying to cook herself dinner last night and now she's staying in the Hotel Dar Sultan."

"Jane stayed there for a while, many years ago," Bowles recalled in a wistful tone.

"Well, that's all fine and dandy but I need to get my manuscript back. And I want to get to the bottom of this hat thing," said Burroughs gruffly. "I'm going back to that apartment where we saw the kids with the monkey and my hat. Since Tweed was their neighbor, there has to be some connection. Anyone care to join me for a little detective work?"

The four of them lifted off toward the medina.

Aicha could no longer stand the pain in her lower abdomen, which had been increasing steadily all morning. Now it felt like there was a fire burning deep inside her. She raised herself from her prone position on the bed to glance at the untouched breakfast tray and grimaced. She tried to get up, but the pain was too intense, almost blinding her, so she called the hotel desk and said she needed a doctor right away. The clerk offered to call an ambulance, but Aicha said it wasn't an emergency; she just wanted to see a doctor, preferably in the privacy of her own room.

A few minutes later the desk clerk called back and said that no doctors were available for house calls, but there was a doctor's office just down the street, where they could see her right away. Aicha forced herself to get up, threw some items in her handbag, and slowly descended the stairs, wincing with each step.

She left the hotel and turned in the direction of the Rue de la Liberté. The pain came in waves, and she hoped she could make it to the doctor's before it got any worse. She turned around 180 degrees and continued walking backward. A minute later she swiveled around again without breaking step and continued down the sidewalk.

Several patients were sitting in the waiting room but Aicha, now white in the face and on the verge of fainting, was quickly shown into the doctor's office by one of his assistants. Dr. Microbio took one look at Aicha and said to Abdallah, "Appendicitis. We have no time to lose."

Aicha was laid out on a gurney and wheeled into an inner salon that served as the operating room, where she was anesthetized by Abdallah. From a stand in the corner a large gray parrot watched the proceedings with keen interest. As soon as Aicha had slipped into a deep sleep and been prepared for surgery, Dr. Microbio began to operate. The sweat was beading on his brow already, and his breathing was somewhat laborious, interspersed with occasional grunts. The tip of his tongue appeared between his pursed lips from time to time like a tiny naked mole rat peering out of its hole.

Abdallah was worrying that he had misjudged the amount of anesthetic he had administered to Aicha when the lights in the operating room flickered and then went out. It was dark as night in the windowless room. For several weeks now the water pressure had been wavering, and during the last few days the power had unexpectedly failed on several occasions. The government was installing a new transformer just outside of town and apparently the job was not going smoothly.

Abdallah was still unfamiliar with the operation of Dr. Microbio's brand-new continuous-flow anesthetic machine, and totally overwhelmed by the challenge of trying to switch to manual control by the unsteady light of a candle. Aicha's breathing stopped, her heartbeat began to falter, and she started to turn blue. Dr. Microbio dropped the scalpel in a steel tray with a resounding clank and ran around to where Abdallah was fumbling with the machine. In the ensuing struggle between man and machine there were only losers. Dr. Microbio tried CPR and got out the portable defibrillator, only to find that the batteries were completely dead. And so was Aicha.

When Moustapha arrived at the Café Triangle shortly after the afternoon prayer, Kazim was already seated in his usual place sipping a glass of mint tea, his pipe and kif bag lying on the table in front of him.

"Sidi Kazim!" Moustapha exclaimed and kissed Kazim's hand. "Señor McLean has given me my job back. And it was partly because of you."

"Allah provides everything, Moustapha. What is the status of the grave?"

"Everything is ready, just as you wished. Where is the body?"

"At Dr. Microbio's office in the Rue de la Liberté. You know it?"

"Certainly."

"Go and buy a cheap coffin and take it to the back entrance of Dr. Microbio's office. Ring the buzzer on the alley door. The doctor's assistant will be expecting you. He will help you place the body in the coffin and carry it out to the cart. Take it to the cemetery and bury it immediately. No ceremony, no rituals, just the burial. And do not ask any questions when you pick up the body. Do you understand?"

"As Allah is my witness, Sidi Kazim. My mouth will be filled with stones."

Moustapha returned to St. Andrew's to fetch his handcart, then made his way through the medina to the woodworkers' quarter, where he bought the cheapest coffin he could find. He was glad to have his job back and to be working again and whistled an old Om Kalthoum song as he wheeled the handcart with the coffin through the crowded streets to Dr. Microbio's office. That Dean's tombstone was back where it belonged and Tweed would no longer be around to practice his devilish trickery both seemed good omens. There would probably be more trouble with Aicha, but Moustapha was now feeling confident enough to deal even with that.

He rang the buzzer at the rear entrance to the doctor's office, and after a couple of minutes, Abdallah appeared, looking somewhat befuddled. He helped Moustapha carry the wooden coffin inside and into the cold room, where Moustapha saw a corpse wrapped in a white sheet laid out on several blocks of ice. Wordlessly, the two men placed the corpse into the coffin and Moustapha closed the lid. They then carried the coffin back outside and placed it on the handcart, and Moustapha set off toward the cemetery.

Kazim finished his last glass of tea, said his farewells, and left the Café Triangle. On the way home he had the feeling he was being followed. Thoughts of Everly Tweed crossed his mind and he wondered if Moustapha would manage to take care of everything according to his instructions. On numerous doorsteps along his route, he saw cats curled up asleep. They reminded him of how much he wanted to lie down and rest. The skies to the east toward Gibraltar were growing darker and women could be seen on the rooftops taking down their laundry. Aromatic smoke from charcoal burners wafted through the streets.

When Kazim got home he went to the salon to recover his strength while he waited for Habiba to tell him when dinner was ready. The business of Tweed's death and the hasty burial arrangements he had needed to make with Dr. Microbio and Moustapha had left him exhausted, but he also felt a pervasive underlying unease. He sat back and reflected on all that had happened recently. There is death, praise Allah, which every creature that breathes must face. But there are also those spirits which become trapped in one of death's many dimensions. They linger, trying to solve problems that they could not solve in life, or to exact revenge, or counteract some curse placed on them or their family in life. I feel a struggle is about to take place in Tangier between some of these spirits.

Kazim went to his bookcase and looked at several leather-bound volumes before pulling out his copy of Ibn Khaldun's *The Muqaddimah*. Sitting down in his papasan chair, he searched for a particular passage and started reading: *Real dream vision is an awareness on the part of the rational soul in its spiritual essence of glimpses of the forms of events. While the soul is spiritual, the forms of events have actual existence in it, as is the case with all spiritual essences. The soul becomes spiritual through freeing itself from bodily matters and corporeal perceptions. This happens to the soul in the form of glimpses through the agency of sleep, whereby it gains the knowledge of future events that it desires and regains the perceptions that belong to it.*

Kazim read the passage twice then closed the book and set it on the table beside him. Those are the words of a saint, he thought. Perhaps if I sleep I will learn about those uneasy spirits, how events may unfold, and whether Tweed has found peace. Kazim closed his eyes and was soon snoring as the westerly rays of the setting sun streamed through the colored glass in a large window at the rear of the inner courtyard, covering his body in geometric patterns of green, red, yellow, and blue.

26

When Aicha died in Dr. Microbio's operating salon, her ghost left her body like the smoke from an Ashura festival bonfire. Aicha understood very quickly she was now free of a vessel that had become feeble, wrinkled, and worn out. As a moth emerges from the confines of its chrysalis, so Aicha began to flex her wings as a surge of energy electrified her spirit. She first rose high above Tangier, so she could see the entire city shining brightly. The view from Cape Spartel to Cape Malabata was stunning: to the northeast she could clearly see the Rock of Gibraltar, and to the east Jebel Musa, the "Mountain of Moses." Then she descended to hover just above a huge swimming pool on one of the grand estates on the Old Mountain. Gazing into the mirror-smooth water Aicha beheld her reflection. She was young and beautiful again! She wore a bejeweled qaftan of red silk and necklaces strung with amber, silver coins, and precious stones. The largest ornament was a gold filigreed hand of Fatima studded with tiny pearls. On her feet were slippers of red velvet embroidered with gold thread. Heavy silver and gold bracelets adorned each wrist. Her fingers sparkled with gold rings set with sapphires, opals, emeralds, diamonds, and rubies. As a final touch she wore a veil of sheer black silk set with tiny diamonds that resembled stars in a night sky.

Aicha's ghost was a magnificent vision of power and was almost flawless—except that in the middle of her forehead was a crimson scar in the shape of a serpent. It was her birthmark, one she shared with her sister Cherifa and which she had always hidden from public view beneath a layer of makeup. In this other world it would forever be revealed, as the mark of a sorceress. It would be her ghost's beauty mark, like the famous mole above Marilyn Monroe's lip.

Aicha flew back to her villa, where she saw that the fire damage was not as bad as it had first seemed. Workmen had begun the repairs. Despite their incompetence on this occasion and others in the past, Aicha was glad she had bequeathed the property to Zodelia and Mohammed in her will, in exchange for their promise to continue to serve her faithfully for as long as she was alive. Her will also contained instructions for her burial at a spot in her garden overlooking the strait, and she knew she could trust the pair to carry them out. So exalted was her ghost with its escape from her decrepit body that the vengeful thoughts she had harbored towards Moustapha over the matter of Dean's tombstone were dispersing like a puff of kif smoke in a stiff breeze.

She was curious to see what had become of her earthly body. Her ghostly powers were still new to her, although not entirely strange— she had after all been a witch who often slipped between the two worlds. In a way the spirit world was her natural abode. She knew she now had far greater powers—transmigration, teleportation, and telekinesis, as well as the potential to appear to those who possessed psychic or clairvoyant capabilities. What's more, as a former witch she knew her powers were far superior to those of William Burroughs, Joseph Dean, Brunhilde Reinhart, and all such wannabe ghosts. She could conceivably teleport inert matter, even human beings, through time and space, whereas Burroughs and Dean would probably have difficulty teleporting a sack of couscous from one side of the Fez Market to the other. Such was the destiny of inveterate junkies and alcoholics who had long since sold their souls and psychic potency to the devil in return for kicks.

Aicha's curiosity sent her soaring back up into the sky and in an instant she found herself in the cold room of Dr. Microbio's office, where Abdallah and Moustapha had lifted her corpse and were placing it in a plain, unfinished coffin made of old shipping crates. One side of the coffin still bore a packing label for canned cat food. Not exactly the kind of end I was expecting, she thought, but still, I'm glad to see that body go.

Aicha hovered in a dark corner as the two men placed the coffin on a handcart. She thought Moustapha might be able to see her ghost and did not want to disrupt their work. The fact that it was

Moustapha who was removing her body from Dr. Microbio's, and on a rickety handcart, seemed odd to her, so she decided to follow him. She had assumed that her body would be transported by van to her villa for burial in accordance with Islamic law, as she had specified in her will for the eventuality that she did not die at home. But where were the van and driver? She supposed she could teleport her body back to the villa herself, but perhaps that task was better left to the proper authorities.

Moustapha turned the cart around and proceeded downhill toward the Avenue d'Angleterre. As it bounced along the street, hitting loose stones and potholes, the cart shook and the coffin shifted from side to side, at one point almost sliding off the cart. "I'm sorry, Señor Tweed," Moustapha murmured under his breath. "We're almost there."

In a matter of minutes he had reached the side gate of St. Andrew's and maneuvered his cargo into the cemetery. Aghast, Aicha moved closer, but remained out of sight behind the tombstones and shrubbery, muttering foul oaths. For a moment Moustapha thought he heard a woman's voice, but after glancing around and seeing no one he continued on to the grave he had dug earlier and parked the cart. He considered trying to lower the coffin into the grave by himself, but he did not want to risk a mishap that would anger Rector McLean.

In life Aicha's beliefs were a peculiar synthesis of native rituals, folkloric superstition, and the practice of magic by casting spells and conjuring djinns and demons, combined with aspects of the Islamic faith and seasoned with occasional charlatanry. Nevertheless, her adherence to the Koran and its laws was unwavering, and she was horrified at the scenario that seemed to be unfolding. An Islamic funeral must follow certain practices, which include the ritual washing of the body, wrapping it in a white shroud, and positioning the grave so that the head of the deceased is facing Mecca (this grave had been dug on a north-south axis, she calculated). And of all the conceivable abominations in Aicha's culture, burying a Moslem in a Nasrani cemetery was perhaps the worst. It was said by some that the body of a Muslim would reject the very earth it was laid in if it were buried in the vicinity of infidels. Her anger was increasing by the moment as Moustapha rubbed his stubbly chin and tried to figure out who might help him lower the coffin into the grave. The fact that she had been in this same cemetery so recently trying to trick Moustapha only added to the absurdity of the situation. Then she recalled the matter of the tombstones from Dean's grave that had been stolen from her, and her rage grew greater still. But what could she do?

Finally Moustapha decided he would get Nazeer, a part-time cemetery gardener, to help him. Nazeer was a notorious gossip, but for a few dirhams he was usually willing to help as long as the job was not too demanding. He could often be found napping at a nearby café at this time of day.

Some fifteen minutes passed before Moustapha returned with a yawning Nazeer and showed him the coffin on the cart and the freshly dug grave.

"I thought you had lost your job," said Nazeer.

"It was just a misunderstanding. Everything is good now."

"Another Nasrani to plant, eh?" said Nazeer. "Pretty soon there won't be any more of them left. Who is this poor devil? Someone I knew?"

Remembering what Kazim had said about keeping quiet, Moustapha simply pointed to one end of the coffin and Nazeer moved into place. He felt a sudden chill as he realized he had already violated Kazim's instructions by telling the young Nasrani couple the name of the person being buried. His confusion about what he was supposed to say and not say was making his head spin. "No, you don't know him, and neither do I," he said.

"This is as light as goose down!" exclaimed Nazeer as he began to lift his end of the coffin. "Are you sure you aren't burying a mouse?"

Moustapha lifted his end and sure enough the coffin seemed almost weightless. He looked at Nazeer with a puzzled expression and with the blade of the shovel he pried open the lid slightly to peer inside. What he saw made him cry out.

Nazeer could see the panic in Moustapha's eyes. Together they removed the lid and looked inside the coffin. It was as empty as the freshly dug grave.

"Well, Moustapha," said Nazeer, a sardonic grin revealing his crooked teeth. "So this is what you woke me from my siesta for? It looks like your dead Nasrani has gone for a walk."

Trying to mask his astonishment and growing fear, Moustapha exclaimed, "This is some stupid mistake! They must have loaded the wrong coffin on the cart. Now I will have to go back for the body. This has made me very angry. And I will make them pay for my trouble."

"*Your* trouble?" said Nazeer. "You drag me over here to this infernal cemetery to help you bury what? A Nasrani zombie? I want my money now—twice over, in case a curse has been placed on me that I will have to have removed!"

Moustapha had agreed to pay Nazeer fifty dirhams and did not want to argue since he might cause trouble. He was already imagining him telling the qahouaji at the café about the empty coffin. If word got back to Rector McLean, he would lose his job for good.

"Ouakha. Here is the fifty I promised plus fifty more."

"I hope you find your zombie," Nazeer said with a smirk. As he left he tripped over a small tombstone and almost fell.

After leaving the Church of St. Andrew, Evangeline and Piet walked to the main post office in the Avenue Mohammed V. They looked up Everly Tweed in the Tangier telephone directory and Evangeline jotted down his address. As they neared the medina on their way to the Rue Mohamed Bergach, they came upon a crowd gathered around a man and a woman involved in a loud argument. The man kept raising his hand as though he was going to hit the woman and she kept ducking out of the way while continuing her tirade of insults and curses. Finally the man struck her. There was a murmur among the crowd, but no one intervened. The man raised his hand again and Evangeline stepped forward. Piet put a restraining hand on her shoulder and said, "I wouldn't, if I were you. This isn't London, you know, and people here have a different concept of domestic strife. Let them settle it their way and let us worry about finding your hat."

Evangeline considered what Piet had said and was about to turn and continue up the street when the man struck the woman again, so that she screamed. Evangeline brushed Piet's hand away and forced her way through the crowd. She went directly up to the man and gave him a hard shove backwards with both hands. He was so surprised that he stumbled on the curb and fell backwards into the street. Another murmur rippled through the crowd, this time much louder.

The man lay there and stared up at Evangeline with a look of disbelief and smoldering rage, his eyes like glowing coals.

"*Never* hit a woman," Evangeline said calmly and resolutely, wagging a raised finger at him. She turned on her heel and rejoined Piet, and the two of them continued up the street, the crowd looking after them in collective astonishment. Piet felt his member stiffen as he walked beside her. Evangeline's courage and aggressiveness had both startled and aroused him, while at the same time making him feel weak and subservient. For a moment he pictured her dressed head-to-toe in black skintight leather, circling him with a riding crop while he sat naked, tied to a chair in some dungeon-like room. He imagined her saying the same words to him, "Never hit a woman," as he cowered before her.

Abruptly Evangeline stopped and turned to Piet, her eyes flashing in anger. "Don't you have any balls? Don't you know how to act like a man?" Piet stood weak-kneed as his cock throbbed and the first pulses of an orgasm shook his loins. When the moment had passed, he answered, "Uh, that's a question I'm still trying to figure out." Evangeline didn't seem to notice his crisis and continued walking, while Piet lagged a few paces behind her, sperm dripping down his leg.

Sayyad had just showered and went into the kitchen to make himself a tuna sandwich with the bread he'd bought that morning. He noticed immediately that the fedora was not on the table where he'd left it when he returned from the market. He looked around the kitchen and on the balcony, but it was nowhere to be seen. He found Cheikh in the living room and asked him if he knew where the hat was, but the macaque just shrugged his shoulders.

Sayyad went back onto the balcony and looked in the stems of the plant where he had hidden the bottle with the strange powder. It was gone, too. He gazed around the balcony and then up at the roof, studying it closely while different scenarios ran through his head. He whistled once and Cheikh came out onto the balcony. Sayyad fixed the long leash to his collar and arranged the wooden packing crates so that the two of them could climb onto the roof.

Meanwhile the four ghosts had arrived in Tweed's cluttered flat and hovered over the disarray of books and clothes and personal belongings on the floor.

"Hmm," said Bowles. "I never would have thought the smell of death could be offensive to a ghost, but that's exactly the effect it's having on me."

"Definitely smells like someone checked out here," said Burroughs.

"And what might this be?" Dean queried, looking at the floor next to the bed. The others floated over and looked over Dean's shoulder at the hacked-off finger lying in a pool of blood.

"Ach, Gott," Brunhilde said, turning away in disgust.

Then they saw the bloody kitchen knife and the hammer and screwdriver lying nearby.

"Well," said Bowles with a sigh. "As Shakespeare had Othello say, 'He that is robbed, not wanting what is stol'n, let him not know't, and he's not robbed at all.'"

"Exactement," said Dean.

"Hey, look at that," said Burroughs. "There's my old fedora lying on the bed."

He picked it up and gazed at it with an absent-minded expression as he ran his hands over the crown and around the brim, triggering a chain of long-lost memories. "Something is coming back to me . . ."

The other three looked expectantly at him as he turned the hat over and looked more closely at the sweat-stained band inside, probing it with his fingers. "Now I recall I sewed a key and a folded piece of paper into the hatband, sometime before I left Tangier and went to live in the Beat Hotel. Look, here's a slit in the hatband, but there's nothing in it."

"What sort of key? And what was on the paper?" asked Dean.

Burroughs fingered the hole in the hatband as though he might coax the answer out of it. "It must have been the key to the safe deposit box where I stashed the Ultrazone manuscript, along with a few odds and ends, a junkie's survival kit of sorts. So the paper would have the name of the bank and the box number."

Just then a shadow passed over the skylight, followed by a scraping sound, as though someone was trying to pry it open.

"Everybody into the kitchen," Burroughs said, tossing the hat on the table as he passed by.

The four ghosts whooshed into the kitchen and took up positions where they could just see around the doorway into the other rooms. They'd come to understand that even as ghosts there was always the danger they might be seen.

The skylight opened a little and a monkey's head appeared. The animal climbed inside and was lowered down on his leash by an unseen hand up on the roof. He scampered over to the table and snatched up the fedora, then glanced around the room. Slowly his gaze came to a halt as he peered into the kitchen. He let out a scream that sent a chill even down the spines of the ghosts, then quickly shimmied up the leash and out of the open skylight. The skylight slammed shut and they heard footsteps crossing the roof and fading away.

After a long wordless interval the ghosts came back into the salon and looked up at the skylight, now casting its colored light throughout the room, where the smell of death still lingered like some unseen presence and a sense of mystery yawned like the veritable abyss.

Zodelia looked into the garden from an upstairs window in Aicha's villa, where she was cleaning all the surfaces to remove the pervasive smell of smoke, and saw a long white package lying on the tiled walkway beside the fountain. She ran downstairs and out the back door to see what it was and met Mohammed coming from the caretaker's house with an earnest look on his face.

"Mohammed, there is a large package lying by the fountain." she shouted.

"Zodelia, I was just coming to tell you. Someone called a few minutes ago. They said Aicha had died while undergoing an operation in town. They said her body would be delivered here at the house for burial. But if that's Aicha's body, apparently the van that brought it has already come and gone. I didn't see or hear anything."

"Who was it that called?" asked Zodelia, shaking as the news began to sink in. A thousand thoughts raced through her mind.

"A woman, but she didn't say who she was and I didn't recognize her voice. She just said the body would be here soon, and then the phone went dead."

Together they walked over to the fountain. As they approached the object, which was wrapped in a white sheet, they each felt a tingling at the nape of the neck.

"You look, Mohammed. I am afraid."

Mohammed knelt slowly beside the body and carefully pulled back the sheet. It was Aicha. Her eyes were wide open and her jaw was clenched shut as if in anger. Mohammed noticed that her usual heavy makeup was smeared and had flaked off in places. Then he saw the serpent scar on her forehead.

"Allahu Akbar! It is Aicha."

"Alhamdulillah!" said Zodelia. "I know where to find her will."

When Zodelia had returned with the will and told him exactly where Aicha wanted to be buried, beside a strawberry tree with a view of the strait, Mohammed dug a grave with determined haste. Her

body slipped easily into the loamy garden soil, and when he had filled
and tamped down the grave site, Zodelia planted a bougainvillea in
the freshly turned soil. The two of them recited the Salat-al-Janazah,
the funeral prayer in which pardon is sought for the deceased and for
all believers who have died before them, and washed their hands in
the fountain. A sudden breeze blew through the leaves of the eucalyptus and pine trees and the branches swayed to and fro.

27

The runaway macaques were hiding out in the subterranean tunnel
system until it grew dark. Then they planned to head down to the
harbor to find a truck they could stow away in, a truck that was taking the ferry to Algeciras. From there they would make their way
to the Rock of Gibraltar. The long-anticipated reunion of the clan
was inevitable. But it was a long wait, and the macaques were very
hungry, having missed their usual breakfast at Mr. Garland's. Bruno
designated two large strong males, Pancho and Lefty, to go and find
food for the group.

Pancho and Lefty had gone some way into the network of tunnels
with no sign of an outlet to the city above, until they came to a stone
alcove with a wooden trap door. When they pried it open and peered
inside, there was a smell of sewage, a faint trickling sound, and a shaft
of light just ahead of them. They dropped onto a narrow pathway that
ran alongside the sewer bed and saw daylight streaming through an
iron grating. Looking through it, they realized they were at sidewalk
level, and across the street was a row of market stalls.

They pushed up the grating and climbed out, set it back in
place, and scurried under a beat-up Renault delivery truck that was
parked by the curb. It was siesta time, so there were relatively few
people in the street. Some of the vendors had draped cloths over
their stands while they napped in the shade or drank tea in a nearby
café. All seemed quiet, so Pancho and Lefty darted out from under
the truck, grabbed four big rattan baskets from a stand selling all
kinds of wickerwork, and stuffed them with melons, oranges, bananas, kumquats, grapes, and apples from one of the stalls. Then
they dashed back across the street, only to see two men unloading

a large wooden crate from the back of the Renault van and setting it down directly on top of the iron grating, blocking their escape route.

The macaques looked at each other in desperation. Meanwhile one of the market stall vendors had seen the theft and sounded the alarm. Pancho and Lefty fled down the nearest dark alley, lugging the four baskets of fruit with them.

The four ghosts still hovered in Tweed's foul-smelling flat, trying to piece together the puzzle.

"Let's recap and see if we can figure this out," said Burroughs, placing a bony finger on his bony chin. "Somehow Moustapha gets ahold of the fedora at the Café Hafa—my old fedora, which had somehow come into the possession of the young European couple. He then has some kind of clandestine rendezvous in St. Andrew's cemetery, apparently with this Tweed character and Aicha. Tweed winds up with the hat, and Aicha makes off with Dean's tombstone. At some point the kid with the monkey from next door steals the hat, and then later Tweed somehow gets it back. Then Tweed dies, or is killed, or OD's, or whatever, and the kid with the monkey steals the hat back again."

"That's a well-traveled hat," Bowles said with a grin.

"But who's responsible for the grisly amputation?" asked Dean.

"Who knows," Burroughs replied.

"And where is the key and the paper with the bank information?" asked Brunhilde.

"Another good question."

The door buzzer sounded. They looked at each other, then floated to the front window and looked down into the street, where they saw the young couple they'd seen talking to Moustapha in the cemetery.

"Most likely that's the question that's on *their* minds as well," said Bowles.

As was her habit, Mina left the office of Maghreb Marine and walked home for lunch. She had transferred the contents of the safe deposit box to a shopping basket of woven straw and covered them with a sweater. As she turned into the Rue Mohamed Bergach she saw a young couple, evidently European tourists, waiting at the front door of the apartment building next to hers. The woman was dressed in a black shirt and shorts and had many tattoos and piercings. They were ringing a buzzer, but no one seemed to be answering.

Mina ignored them and went inside. Her mother and Sayyad were waiting for her expectantly as she came into the living room and set the basket down on the coffee table next to a pile of magazines.

"So what was in the box?" Fatoma asked, her kohl-lined eyes wide with anticipation.

Mina took out the pistol, the box of bullets, the folding knife, the syringes and needles, the kif pipe, the mildewed leather pouch, the glass ampoules, and the huge stack of paper.

"That's all there is?" asked Sayyad in disbelief.

Their mother sighed and slumped back on the couch.

Sayyad picked up the somewhat rusty automatic pistol and aimed down the barrel at an invisible enemy. "Pow, pow!"

"Put that down!" Mina said gruffly.

Sayyad reluctantly set down the pistol and picked up the knife, unfolding the blade so that it clicked into place.

"Can I keep the knife?" he asked.

"No! I'm keeping all this together until we find out who it belongs to and what it's worth."

"It's just a bunch of evil rubbish," said Fatoma. "Anyone can see that."

"If someone went to the trouble to put it in a safe deposit box all those years ago, then it must be worth something," Mina said.

"Bah! Maybe you could get a few dirhams at the flea market and at least we could use the papers to line the bird cages," said Fatoma.

"Aw, let me have the knife," pleaded Sayyad.

"No!" Mina said.

Sayyad folded the knife and put it back on the table next to the other items. "What about the key and the piece of paper that were in the hat? Can I have those back?" Sayyad asked.

"Let him have them," Fatoma said. "They're of no importance anymore."

Mina slid the key and the paper across the table and Sayyad slipped them into his shirt pocket.

"I'm going out to find Steetoo," said Sayyad as he got up from the couch and turned toward the kitchen. "I'll be back for dinner."

In the kitchen Sayyad took a small sewing kit from a drawer and sewed the key and the piece of paper back into the slit in the hatband of the old fedora. He then put on the hat and whistled for Cheikh, who came bounding into the kitchen from the balcony. Sayyad clipped the leash to Cheikh's collar and said, "Come on, we're going out."

Evangeline and Piet had rung the buzzer of Everly Tweed's flat three times but there was no response. They looked up at the windows but saw only the North African sky reflected in the glass.

"What do we do now?" Piet asked.

As Evangeline was considering their next move, the door of the adjacent apartment building opened and a boy with a macaque on a leash stepped into the street. She and Piet both did a double take when they saw the kid was wearing the Burroughs fedora.

"Hey," Piet said. "Look at that . . ."

Evangeline put her finger to her lips. She stepped toward the kid and said, "Wow, what a fantastic animal! What's his name?"

Sayyad's English was not very good, but he understood what the Nasrani woman with the tattoos and silver piercings was asking. "Cheikh," he answered.

"Can I pet him? Will he bite?"

"No bite."

Evangeline patted Cheikh on his head and scratched behind his ears. "What kind of monkey is he?"

Sayyad had to think for a minute. "A Barbary macaque. Same as ones on Rock of Gibraltar."

"Aha, a macaque with a pedigree. He's *very* beautiful."

Sayyad smiled with pride, and Cheikh was clearly enjoying the attention.

"That's a cool hat you have, by the way. Would you like to sell it? I could really use a hat like that. The sun is so intense here in Morocco."

Sayyad took off the hat and looked at critically. "This hat very important to me. It was given me by my father before he went to Algeciras to work in shipyards. I can't sell it."

"I'll give you twenty dirhams for it," Evangeline said.

Sayyad pursed his lips and shook his head, then put the hat back on, making clear that it was going to stay there.

"Fifty?"

Sayyad continued shaking his head, but a sly smile began to form on his pursed lips.

"Seventy-five?"

Sayyad stopped shaking his head, slowly removed the hat, and began to study it closely again.

Piet took out his wallet, slipped out a brown hundred-dirham note, and began rubbing it between his fingers.

Without saying anything, Sayyad handed the hat to Evangeline and took the hundred-dirham note from Piet.

"Oh, thank you so much," Evangeline said, slipping the hat on her head as though for the very first time. "And look, it fits perfectly."

Sayyad looked down at the face of King Hassan II on the hundred-dirham note, then turned it over and looked at the picture of the crowd of men and the giant bird on the reverse, then carefully folded it and slipped it into his pocket.

While Sayyad was preoccupied, Evangeline took off the hat again and furtively slid a finger around the inside hatband. The metal key was still there. She smiled to herself and put the hat back on.

"What's your name?" Evangeline asked.

"Sayyad."

"Well, Sayyad, I'll always think of you and Cheikh whenever I wear this hat. And your father as well, of course. Thank you so much."

"You're welcome. You need guide for medina? Want to see Kasbah? Want to buy some kif?"

"No, thank you. We have everything we need."

Evangeline petted Cheikh one last time, and she and Piet turned and headed down the Rue Mohamed Bergach in the direction of the Hotel Lutetia.

Sayyad watched the two Nasranis walking away and smiled, patting the folded hundred-dirham note in his pocket. He and Cheikh went back inside to stash the money in his room before going to look for Steetoo.

28

The four ghosts had observed the proceedings from Tweed's window.

"That was a slick piece of work, you've got to give them that," Burroughs said. "Now they've got the hat back, although without the key for the safe deposit box. That must be in the apartment next door. But as long as that damned monkey is around we can't take a look without him blowing our cover."

"Meanwhile the unsavory aromas here are really getting to me," said Bowles.

"And the smell of death will certainly attract the Ugly Spirit," said Burroughs. "No defense except to get out of here pronto and consider our next move. As Brion always understood, the Ugly Spirit is an evil possessing force. It can easily be transmitted from one person to another, just like herpes or Ebola."

"Ghosts can be possessed by other spirits, too," added Dean.

"Yes," said Burroughs. "It's a sad fact that you can never trust another ghost, especially one who likes to linger around corpses or around addicts looking for a fix. It's just the way things are. Always watch your back."

That was enough for Bowles. "I had my fill of possession with Cherifa and Jane! Why don't we head out to the Caves of Hercules, to where we scattered Brion's ashes back then? That should be a place of refuge from the Ugly Spirit for a while. And the view is magnificent, of course. We can search for the key later on."

"Then let's go," said Dean, echoed by Brunhilde, whose ghostly antennae were picking up on the presence of some encroaching evil as they hovered in Tweed's apartment, though none of them could know that on the other side of the wall the Ugly Spirit was even now shaking off almost fifty years of hibernation in the dusty mildewed pages lying on the coffee table.

"Let's stop by the Teatro Cervantes and pick up Brion and Brian," Burroughs suggested.

"Excellent idea. This way," said Bowles, and the ghostly quartet moved swiftly through the window and out across the rooftops of the medina, dodging the spiky minarets and dipping down just long enough to gather Brion Gysin and Brian Jones into their entourage. They soared up into the brilliant sky again and headed west, curving around Cap Spartel, where the Atlantic meets the Mediterranean, then south to the cliffs overlooking the caves.

As they neared the grotto, Bowles said, "Should any of you sense a heavy presence of anxious spirits, it will be because we are very close to where an airliner crashed in 1965. Some fifty passengers perished in these waters. Many of the bodies were picked up by fishing boats, others washed up on the beach. Imagine how the local folk must have felt. The passengers were mostly Swedes and Germans so it must have seemed like an invasion of dead Teutons. I was told by a Moroccan who lived nearby that it was quite a horror show."

"Wouldn't be the first time a lot of blondes lost their scalps in Morocco," drawled Burroughs. "Both the upper *and* lower ones."

"Probably won't be the last, either," said Dean. "I remember there was an Austrian banker who came through Tangier back in the sixties. He hired a car and told the driver to take him into the Rif so he could find a farm boy to fuck. As they rode along he would spot a man in a field and say to the driver, 'Stop and ask how much.' After a few futile attempts during which the driver would converse with the farmhand in Darija, they finally stopped near a group of men standing by a small cedar grove. After a brief exchange between the driver and the men, the Austrian was led from the car and down a hill out of sight from the mountain road. The men gagged him, tied him to a tree, and raped him repeatedly over the next eight hours. Many male members of the local tribe returned several times to obtain pleasure from the Austrian's now limp body. By morning he was dead, probably from a heart attack. His body was dragged behind a pickup to a ravine, where it was unceremoniously dumped for the jackals to feast on."

"'A Distant Episode' revisited," said Bowles with a smile.

There were a few restaurants and fishermen's cafés on the cliffs above the cave opening, which offered a spectacular view out over the Atlantic. Legend says the ancient Phoenicians carved the opening through the cliff wall. From inside the cave the opening looks like a strangely deformed head. From the outside it resembles a map of Africa. Some believe the cave is bottomless and connects to a subterranean tunnel that passes beneath Tangier and under the Strait of Gibraltar—the tunnel through which the Barbary macaques are said to have reached the Rock of Gibraltar. Another legend says that Hercules stayed in the cave before he performed his eleventh labor, collecting the golden apples from the Garden of the Hesperides. To get there, Hercules had to smash through the great Atlas Mountain which connected Europe with North Africa. In splitting the mountain in two he created the Pillars of Hercules and the Strait of Jebel Tarik, now known as the Strait of Gibraltar.

"I believe the presence of Hercules can still be felt here," said Bowles. "Together with the ghosts of the air crash, who are most likely still stumbling around on the beach and hills looking for their lost luggage, that should keep the Ugly Spirit at a safe distance."

"I'm glad you suggested we get out of Tangier, Paul," said Burroughs. "The feeling that I was being hunted down by the Ugly Spirit, combined with the noxious atmosphere, were almost enough to bring back my old junk sickness."

Dean, Brunhilde, Brion, and Brian had already found a peaceful spot to recline in the scruffy grass on the cliffs and were contemplating the waves, the seabirds, and the fishermen along the shoreline, while Brion and Brian supplied light musical accompaniment on castanets and an old three-stringed gimbri Brian had found in the Gran Teatro Cervantes. Every so often Dean would look over at Brunhilde and try to look into her ghostly eyes, which had the gaze of infinity. He wasn't looking for love—love was an ephemeral, biochemical emotion that died with the body. What he was trying to do was read her thoughts and fathom her ghostly essence, a desire based on a much more eternal impulse than mere love. Brunhilde was at this moment lost in another dimension, however, and barely noticed Dean.

Taking everything in with the eyes of a painter, Brunhilde was admiring the colors of the sky, water, and rocks. She could see it as a colorful large-scale canvas painted in dynamic Expressionist strokes, like a Max Beckmann landscape. And when she looked around at the others, it occurred to her that this gathering of ghosts lounging around in the grass looked very much like a weird afterworld take on Manet's *Le déjeuner sur l'herbe*, a thought which pleased her greatly.

After Nazeer had left the cemetery, Moustapha sat down on a small stone bench near the open grave and tried to think what to do next. For Nazeer's sake he had pretended there had been a mix-up at Dr. Microbio's, but he knew it wasn't so—he himself had helped place the body in its shroud into the coffin. Now he was left with an empty grave, an empty casket, and no body. Looking around the cemetery would be fruitless—that was the last place anyone would try to hide a body. But why would anyone want to steal the body of a dead Irishman? If he even *was* Irish. The Nasranis all looked alike anyway. Anglaish, Amereekans, Français, all alike. He covered the open grave with some branches from the compost heap and an old tarp, on top of which he shoveled a thin layer of dirt to conceal the opening. Then he pushed the cart with the empty coffin back up the hill to Dr. Microbio's. He rang the buzzer at the back door several times, but no one came.

After Aicha died on the operating table, Dr. Microbio had closed his office and sent his staff home, then retired to his apartment upstairs. He had planned on closing early today in any case, since he had been invited by the owners of a new bookstore on the Boulevard Pasteur to attend the first in a series of "literary soirees," which would feature readings by local and international writers, accompanied by live music, hors d'oeuvres, and an open bar. He slipped out of his bloody smock and took a shower, then put on his dinner jacket and bow tie.

Moustapha rang again. The office must be closed, Moustapha thought. By the Saints of Joujouka, this is making me crazy. Is it possible that someone removed Tweed's body from the coffin? But when, and where, and how, and above all why? Could those Nasrani ghosts be playing games with the dead?

He considered going to Kazim's house and telling him what had happened but feared his anger. Anyway it was getting late. The longer he postponed the burial the greater the chance the coffin would be discovered to be empty. Moustapha decided to wheel the cart and coffin back to the cemetery, where he removed the tarp and branches and carefully slid the empty coffin into the open hole. Then he gathered some rocks, pieces of broken tile and pottery shards, and wood scraps and tossed them into the open coffin. After replacing the lid he set to work filling the grave.

What do I know about these things? he thought as he shoveled. I am a Muslim and these Nasrani are like djinns. Always playing tricks and making trouble. They can go to hell. And with that he spat into the grave. But after this final curse he felt a cold shiver run up his spine that frightened him and he hurriedly finished the job. He tamped down the earth as flat as he could make it, put the handcart and shovel away, and took one last look around the cemetery before closing and locking the gate for the day. He went to the nearest hammam, bathed himself with olive oil soap and buckets of steaming hot water, put on a clean djellaba, and went to the mosque.

From the rooftop of his flat, Tweed's ghost had watched Hassan and Mansour load the rolled-up carpet containing his body onto the handcart. As they started off down the street, Hassan pushing from behind and Mansour steering at the front, Tweed swooped down and

followed them. The two men seemed too low down on the evolutionary ladder to be capable of any kind of clairvoyance or psychic vision,
so he did not fear being seen by them.

When Hassan and Mansour parked the handcart in the shade
across the street from a small café and bar and went inside, Tweed
hovered nearby, keeping an eye on both the handcart and the door
of the café. Several people walked by in the narrow street, but no
one seemed to pay any attention to the handcart with the rolled-up
carpet. But then a man in a tattered, dirty djellaba, the hood pulled
up over his head so that his face was almost invisible, passed by the
handcart and stopped. He came back and stood looking down at the
rolled-up carpet on the handcart, then glanced around the street.
Tweed suddenly recognized him. It was Abdeslam, a taxidermist and
purveyor of magical supplies for witches and sorcerers, a regular figure in the medina. Tweed didn't know him personally, but Abdeslam
had a reputation in certain circles. Should you need a snakeskin or a
scorpion's stinger or some newt's eyes or eagle feathers or tiger claws
you went to see Abdeslam. If he didn't have what you were looking
for, he knew where to get it. Tweed watched as Abdeslam bent over
and peered into the rolled-up carpet. When he stood up again, Tweed
could just make out a slight smile on his unshaven face. Abdeslam
looked around once more, then started pushing the handcart down
the street, further into the depths of the medina.

29

Tweed followed the man as he wheeled the handcart with his corpse
through the narrow twisting streets until he stopped in front of a
massive wooden door. Abdeslam unlocked it with a large key and
pushed the cart inside. After a quick look up and down the street,
he shut and locked the door behind him. Tweed passed through the
door and found himself in a narrow courtyard, at the other end of
which was another large wooden door. Abdeslam unlocked the second door, pushed the cart through, and locked that door behind him
as well. Tweed followed and was then in an even smaller courtyard
shaded by the leaves of an ancient fig tree in its center. Off to one side
was an outbuilding that Abdeslam had converted into his workshop

and store, where his wares were on display. Stuffed jackals, lizards, and turtles were mounted on wooden stands, and the heads of antelopes and other exotic animals hung from the walls, which were also festooned with garlands of feathers, skins, and dried herbs. Stacked on the ground were wooden buckets and straw baskets full of other, unrecognizable items, many of which seemed to be of an animal nature. Even to a ghost, the smell was almost overwhelming.

At the rear was a sort of altar built into a niche in the wall. It consisted of a slab of marble on which lay a human skull, flanked on one side by an hourglass and on the other by a single red and white tulip in a small glass vase. Tweed wondered if it was an intentional homage to the painting by Philippe de Champaigne or just a weird coincidence, a Moroccan take on the *vanitas* tradition.

Abdeslam wheeled the cart to the back of the workshop and unrolled the carpet. Grabbing a rope from a block and tackle mounted on an iron beam in the ceiling, he tied it around the ankles of Tweed's corpse, which by now smelled quite ripe, and hoisted the body so it was suspended head down. He then placed a plastic ten-liter bucket directly underneath it. Tweed didn't even see where it came from but suddenly a knife flashed in Abdeslam's hand, making two deep lateral incisions either side of the neck, severing both jugular veins. It was sickening to watch, but Tweed couldn't tear his eyes away from the grisly spectacle as the blood drained out of his body into the yellow plastic bucket.

Abdeslam took a green pack of Marquise cigarettes out of his djellaba and lit one while he watched the bucket filling. If he was lucky, and if the body hadn't been dead for too long, he might get a half a bucketful. Mr. Harper, the strange Englishman who lived in a villa in the Marshan, was one of his regular customers. He was interested in one item and one item only: human blood. Abdeslam could usually find enough live donors to supply Mr. Harper, but their number had begun to dwindle lately, and Abdeslam had been hard-pressed to keep his client satisfied. Once this blood had been transferred into glass vials and properly refrigerated, as Mr. Harper insisted, no one would know the blood was from a corpse and not a living donor.

As Abdeslam had hoped, the yield was around five liters. That would keep Mr. Harper happy for quite a while, especially if it was doled out to him in small, precious-seeming portions, each with a label denoting an individual "donor." Abdeslam put the bucket in an beat-up stainless-steel refrigerator in the back corner and lowered the body onto the handcart. He rolled it up in the carpet again, then wheeled the cart back through the two wooden doors and out into the street, locking each door behind him.

Hassan and Mansour stood in the street debating what they should do now that the handcart with the body was gone.

"We can just forget about it and be happy we made an easy two hundred dirhams," Mansour suggested. "After all, we have the gold fillings and the ring as well."

Hassan rubbed his kif-red eyes and looked up and down the street. "I want the rest of the money we are owed. And I want to find the thief who stole the cart and the body."

"Alright, you know best," Mansour said with obvious resignation. "Where shall we look first? The lost and found?"

Hassan looked at Mansour with narrowed eyes, suppressing the laugh he felt welling up inside him. "Very funny," he said. "You go that way, I'll go this way, and we'll meet back here in half an hour."

"Ouakha. Half an hour."

They looked up and down every street and alley, even the narrowest passageways, but the handcart was nowhere to be seen. Hassan considered asking some of the shop owners in the area if they had seen the cart going by, but decided against it. If the body had been discovered in the meantime it would just mean trouble for them.

After a half an hour futilely searching the streets of the medina, Hassan and Mansour met back at the café where their problems had begun.

"It's gone, we'll never see it again," Mansour said.

"Don't be such a pessimist. It's gone, but who's to say we'll never see it again?"

"So what do we do now?"

"I need more kif," Hassan said, turning toward the door of the café.

"And I could use another whiskey."

Half an hour later, the kif and the whiskey had lessened their anxiety somewhat, but they were all out of kif and almost out of money.

"Now what?" inquired Mansour.

Hassan disliked the way Mansour was always asking him questions, as though he had all the answers. He looked down at the empty glasses, the full ashtray, and the empty kif bag and felt a yawning emptiness inside himself as well. Suddenly he had the odd sensation that someone was looking at him. He glanced around the café, but no one was paying any attention to them. The kif must be playing games with his mind. He turned and looked out the door and a spasm convulsed his body. The handcart with the rolled-up carpet was right there where they had parked it over two hours ago.

Hassan jumped up and ran outside, with Mansour at his heels. He slipped his hand inside the rolled-up carpet and felt the cold clammy flesh of the corpse inside. He looked at Mansour and smiled. "You see? What did I tell you?"

Mansour stood there with his mouth slightly ajar. "I should not have smoked all that kif," he said, looking down at the handcart with its grisly cargo. "Now the whole world is backwards and upside down."

"That's not the world, that's you," Hassan said. "Come, we have to hurry."

They wheeled the handcart as fast as they could through the medina, barely avoiding accidents with other carts, pedestrians, and donkeys. Coming around a sharp curve the bundle slipped off the handcart and fell to the pavement with a dull thud. Luckily the carpet remained rolled around the body and they could load it back onto the handcart without its contents being revealed. They came rattling around the corner of the alley behind Dr. Microbio's office and Hassan rang the buzzer. No one answered, so he rang and rang again.

"The doctor must be gone already," said Hassan, glancing around the alley.

"What do we do now?" Mansour asked sheepishly.

"We either leave the whole package here and take the handcart back, or we leave the body here wrapped in a sheet and sell the carpet later at the Casa Barata market. Once it's been washed it should bring another two hundred dirhams."

"I don't like your plan," said Mansour. "But let's do this quickly. I am afraid we will get caught with the body."

Hassan hurried around the corner to the Rue de la Liberté and bought a sheet from a street vendor. When he got back, Mansour was pacing back and forth in the alley.

"Mansour, I have a sheet, so help me unroll the body and wrap it up. Then we leave."

They lifted the rolled carpet off the cart and onto the sheet. The corpse seemed lighter to them now, and its skin had shriveled somewhat. Once the body was tightly wrapped in the white sheet it resembled an oversized joint lying there in the alley. Hassan and Mansour rolled up the carpet, placed it on the cart and headed down the hill.

"I know a place below the Kasbah ramparts where the women still wash clothes in a stream that flows into the sea," said Hassan. "They pound them against the flat rocks, then lay them out in the sun to dry. We can pay one of them to wash the carpet. Then we will sell it, inshallah."

They dropped off the carpet with the laundry women and went to return the cart. After some haggling, Hassan agreed to pay the cart owner fifty dirhams and recovered the rest of his deposit. Then they headed for the newer part of town outside the medina. First they stopped at the Ranch Bar and had a couple of Casablanca beers each and several tapas: saffron rice with chunks of grilled swordfish, marinated carrot salad, grilled sardines, bread and olives.

"You know, Mansour," Hassan said, licking his fingers and wiping them on the little triangular bar tissues. "I think we should just take the carpet and leave Tangier. Sooner or later someone will link us to the body or the carpet and we will have nothing but trouble."

"I'm ready to leave this moment," said Mansour.

"But we must be careful, and consider the best way to take. We should stay away from the neighborhood of Dar Baroud and definitely not go back to Lord Nelson's Pub. I know a safer way to get to the washing place and get the carpet. We can go down to the port, then along the outside of the old Portuguese walls. Where the wall ends is close to where the women wash the clothes. Once we get our carpet, we roll it up tight and get a big taxi to take us back to Chefchaouen."

"And say good-bye and good riddance to Tangier, where a man survives by separating dead Nasranis from their fingers."

"Yes, it would be much less messy to separate them from their dinero," said Hassan.

The two of them stepped out into the late afternoon. Already the dark blue sky was turning faintly golden toward the west. Hassan led Mansour down one of the steepest streets in Tangier. Sections of sidewalk were missing, as if large pieces had been completely and randomly removed. The street grew narrower until it was bordered on both sides by the back walls of abandoned warehouses. The sun was effectively hidden, and the street was already dark and gloomy.

"You sure this is the right way?" asked Mansour.

"Of course, just follow me."

The two miscreants continued cautiously down toward the port. A strange silence descended, punctuated intermittently by a peculiar rustling sound. They stopped to listen for footsteps but there was no one else about. Further up the hill they could hear a man's voice calling "Paloma? Paloma?" Hassan looked down and saw two sheets of paper in the middle of the street. They seemed to give off a phosphorescent glow. Thinking they might be of value, Hassan bent to pick one up, but when he touched it an electric arc shot up from it and burned his fingers. He jumped back with a yelp, and the sheets of paper rose up and flew towards Hassan and Mansour, wrapping themselves around their faces, covering their noses and mouths. They tried to rip the paper away, but its grip was too strong, and they would have suffocated if the papers had not suddenly fallen away and floated upward, away over the roofs of the buildings.

"That was the Nasrani's spirit, I am sure of it," said Mansour. "Forget the carpet, Hassan, before more evil djinns find us."

Hassan was holding his injured hand. In a small, child-like voice he whimpered, "By the Seven Saints of Marrakech, we are cursed."

30

When it became clear that the gridlock resulting from the accident with the taxi and the donkey would last some time, Just-Call-Me-Ishmael paid off the taxi driver and started walking. He turned his head away as he passed the scene of the accident, not wanting to be confronted with the gory spectacle of the donkey's guts spilled across the street. As he did so, he glimpsed Dr. Microbio stepping out of the crowd in his white smock, carrying a leather valise. When he reached the Avenue Belgique he hailed another taxi and gave the driver the address of his villa on the Old Mountain.

The watchman was surprised to see him back so soon. Just-Call-Me-Ishmael said only that he'd forgotten something. He'd given much thought to which work of art he could now part with, after the tragic loss of the Monet drawing in the burning taxi the night before. From a large metal storage cabinet he selected a small unframed work by Kurt Schwitters, one of his typical Merz collages from the early 1920s, employing various found objects and text fragments, including wire, wallpaper, bus tickets, and newspaper texts. It would bring a tidy sum in Zurich.

Just-Call-Me-Ishmael had carefully packed the drawing in a small, flat wooden crate and was preparing to leave when the lights flickered and dimmed, signaling the onset of yet another power outage.

"Shit!" he hissed loudly.

His hope of catching the afternoon ferry to Algeciras was fading as fast as the lights in the shuttered house. Without electricity the security system was totally disabled, and he would be locked in until the power returned, a prisoner in his own villa.

Once he had safely hidden the hundred-dirham note in his room, Sayyad whistled for Cheikh and left the apartment again to find Steetoo and tell him about the disappointing contents of the safe deposit box. As they were cutting through a back street in the medina on their way down to the harbor, Cheikh suddenly began chattering and screeching.

"What is it now, Cheikh?" Sayyad asked, somewhat annoyed.

Cheikh pranced up and down and strained at the leash.

Then Sayyad saw what Cheikh had seen, two macaques further down the street, each lugging two large rattan baskets. Cheikh broke Sayyad's grip on the leash and went scampering down the street to join them.

Although Pancho and Lefty had never met Cheikh, there was a strong sense of mutual recognition between the three of them, which they verified with some serious scent-sniffing. They were, after all, from the same bloodline, dating back many generations. Cheikh asked Pancho and Lefty what they were doing and where they were going. They explained about breaking out of Mr. Garland's menagerie, the other macaques waiting in the tunnel system, and their plan to smuggle themselves onto the ferry and join the rest of their family who had been resettled in Gibraltar many years ago.

"You should come with us," Pancho said to Cheikh. "It will be a giant reunion."

"Hmm, I don't know," Cheikh said, considering Pancho's proposition. "Sayyad and his family are good to me. I have everything I need."

"Do you have your freedom?" asked Lefty, motioning at Cheikh's sturdy leather collar and long leash.

It was a rhetorical question, and Cheikh's silence was the answer.

Pancho shrugged. "You know best," he said.

"But maybe I can help you," Cheikh said. He told Pancho and Lefty about the boys' secret hideout by the harbor. From there it would be easy to locate a truck that would be taking the ferry to Spain. Cheikh took one of the baskets of fruit and the three of them set off down the hill, Sayyad trailing in puzzlement behind them.

A fair-sized crowd had gathered in the brand-new Lumières de la Ville bookstore by the time Dr. Microbio arrived. There were a number of young Moroccans, but it was mostly Europeans, both tourists and long-standing members of the Tangier expatriate community. He got himself a glass of red wine from the bar and helped himself to the tapas. Across the room he recognized Madame Delacroix, a French writer of postmodern pulp-noir fiction who had lived in Tangier for decades, and went over to say hello. Soon they were engrossed in an intense discussion of the fiction of Sartre and Camus, weighing the pros and cons of *The Stranger* and *Nausea* and debating the relevance of French Existentialism at the turn of the millennium. Dr. Microbio was so enthralled by the debate that he was unaware of the splash of red wine that appeared on his white shirt and the glistening saffron-yellow globs of paella on his dinner jacket.

Their lively conversation was interrupted by an announcement from the owner of the bookshop, a balding, gray-bearded expat American named Horace Pixley, himself an accomplished poet, welcoming the guests to the first of his literary soirées. After a short speech outlining the intention of the soirées and plans for other events at the bookstore, he introduced the evening's first guest, the American poet Francis Poole, a former Tangier resident and teacher of English at the American School, friend of Paul Bowles, and editor of *BLADES*.

Poole took the stage and told the audience he was always glad to be back in Tangier. He said he would read poems from his forthcoming collection, *Snakeskin Raincoat*, took a sip of wine, and without any further ado, began reading:

WEST OF CEUTA
Algeciras-Tangier

From my deck chair
on the Ibn Batouta
the water spreads west
like a blue tablecloth.
To starboard
four mounds of spice
pour into the sea.
The hills of Tarifa.

The Berbers standing at my feet
unwrap their parcels,
legs spread as if to steady
the roll of the ship.
Orange peels fall to the deck.
Loaves of flat white bread
sliced open
to hold the soft goat cheese.

To port, the towering forehead
of Jebel Moussa, Mountain of Moses,
sheltering the tiny fishing boats
bobbing in its shadow.

Topside at the rail
a Spanish girl's red dress
catches on a nail of breeze
revealing the smooth brown pillars
of her thighs.

Nearby an old Moroccan
wearing a white djellaba
removes his slippers and
kneels on the deck to pray.

West of Ceuta
a giant's craggy jawbone juts out
from the cliffs
with scattered houses erupting crazily
like errant teeth.

In our wake, dolphins
diving over and under each other.
Is that a mermaid or a merman
porpoising with them?
I glance up and behold
the diamond glint of a jet
scratching the hard blue sky.
This is all quite a show.
Something to put down
on a postcard once we arrive.

Lens cap off
I try to focus on the clean incision
made by the bow
as we cut a wide arc
toward the African coast.

Just as I snapped the picture
there was a flash of silver scales
across the water
and an odor of damp hair
on the wind.

HIS OWN TWO FEET
Tangier

At dusk the streets are nearly empty.
The walls of the buildings glow flamingo.
A young boy walks up the hill pushing
a wheelbarrow filled with the hooves of cattle.
The smell is rich.
He smiles at the tourists who are
sickened at the sight of his burden.
They are headed down to the market place
to buy shiny leather jackets, belts and slippers.
As they pass
the boy's own two feet
become hooves, flint-hard and deadly.
He hears them click against the rough stones
of the street, growing sharper
as he pushes on.

THE BIG FEAST
Tangier

At dawn on the morning
of the Aid el-Kebir
I awoke and through
our bedroom window
saw a fish on the sidewalk
gleaming like a fragment of
some dissolving dream.

From our terrace, smoky light
and the smell of burning hair.
A group of boys were squatting
around a fire pit
dug at one corner
of the soccer field
roasting sheep heads on
sharpened sticks.

Below in the courtyard
buckets of blood
a black ram's skin
splayed out on the tiles
and Mina, the young concierge,
barefoot and erect,
holding a huge sheep liver
in her left hand
knife in her right
looking up at the sky
and yelling for
water.

The applause that followed was enthusiastic and unanimous. Dr. Microbio looked around with a feeling of deep satisfaction. He was in his element, surrounded by books and book lovers, poets and writers, and all things literary; away from clamoring patients, sickness and disease; away from blood and the boring treadmill of the operating table. Someday he would write his own *Lord of the Flies,* or *The Stranger,* or a collection of pioneering avant-garde poems, and become a literary celebrity, attending book launches and readings throughout the world, his books glowingly reviewed in the most esteemed periodicals and displayed in the window of the Librairie des Colonnes.

His expanding illusions of grandeur were suddenly deflated by the sound of severe coughing just to his right. He turned and saw Madame Delacroix with her hand to her mouth, her eyes bulging and her face a waxy gray. Just as she slumped and began to fall, Dr. Microbio slipped an arm around her waist and guided her into an overstuffed chair next to a table piled with books.

Horace Pixley came rushing over and asked what was wrong.

"I don't know yet," said Dr. Microbio. "But there's no time to lose. Call a taxi and I'll take her to my office. It will be quicker by far than one of those slow-motion Tangier ambulances."

31

After Dr. Microbio summoned him to assist in an emergency, Abdallah reluctantly turned off the TV and headed to the office in the Rue de la Liberté. When he turned into the alley, he immediately saw the body wrapped in the white sheet lying by the back door. He was tempted to unwrap the sheet to see who it was, but the sickly-sweet smell of decay discouraged him. He rang the buzzer and the doctor's most trusted assistant, an older, turban-wearing Egyptian named Khufu, opened the door. He greeted Abdallah then looked down at the body. The two men placed it on a wooden litter and moved it inside, setting it down in the cold room on what remained of the blocks of ice. Khufu went to get Dr. Microbio, since it was highly irregular to have bodies dropped off with no name or identifying paperwork.

Dr. Microbio had been attending to Madame Delacroix, who, fortunately, had only been struck with an attack of what she called "nerves," apparently as a psychosomatic response to some of the unusual imagery she had been exposed to at the literary soiree. Madame Delacroix was a tough writer but a sensitive soul. Dr. Microbio gave her a sedative and sent her home in a taxi, saying he would send her his bill later. He was now sitting in his office contemplating all that had happened that day, still wearing his old white double-breasted dinner jacket and his now red- and yellow-spotted dress shirt. He had a stethoscope around his neck and on his head he wore an antique round physician's head mirror, more for effect than for any practical purpose. The parrot in the corner was mumbling semi-unintelligible phrases and epithets in Arabic, French, Spanish, and English.

Khufu stuck his head in the open door and asked what they should do with the newly arrived body.

"Body?" asked Dr. Microbio, looking up from his desk. "What body?"

A lit cigarette clenched between his teeth, the doctor followed Khufu to the back room.

"What *is* this? Some kind of cadaver bazaar?" asked Dr. Microbio. "Wasn't the body that was here a few hours ago picked up by what's-his-name, the cemetery worker?"

"Yes, it was taken by Moustapha to be buried in St. Andrew's," said Khufu.

The doctor pulled back the sheet covering the face. "For Christ's sake. This is the body he was to take to St. Andrew's. What happened to Aicha's body, Abdallah?"

Abdallah stood downcast, shaking his head.

"Pardon me, sir," said Khufu. "But the other body was wrapped in a sheet just like this one. They looked the same. And Moustapha said nothing when he took it."

"You two stay right here. Don't answer the door or let anyone in. I will take care of this," said Dr. Microbio.

"It shall be done," said Khufu with a slight bow. He picked up some sticks of sandalwood incense and lit them.

Dr. Microbio walked rapidly to his office, called Mr. Garland, and told him about the unidentified body. "I've looked at it, and it has been drained of blood. No doubt the work of someone we are both familiar with, unfortunately. He must have wanted to get rid of the corpse and so had it brought here. I'm reminded that there are still those around here who like an occasional chilled glass of blood."

"Yes," Mr. Garland said. "Sounds like a typical Abdeslam job. So what is the good doctor suggesting?"

"Mr. Garland, you can have this body, no questions asked. I assume your menagerie of meat-eaters might appreciate it, even though it is somewhat depleted. I have it on ice to keep it as fresh as possible. If you send a couple of your men here right away, I will turn it over to them and forget any of this ever happened."

"In other words: no deposit, no return," said Garland with a chuckle. "Though there will be, um, deposits in the end. I greatly appreciate your offer and I'll have the body picked up toute suite. The price of meat has gone up dramatically in the main market and buying a large sheep or goat is even costlier. And now there's a shortage due to the Aid el-Kebir feast. My poor beasts have lost weight in the past month—that's one reason they're constantly roaring and bringing the wrath of my neighbors down on my head."

"Very well, Mr. Garland. We will be doing each other a favor. I know nothing and your lions and tigers will say nothing. One might describe it as a sort of Tangier sky burial."

"Or we might say this will be just another Nazarene thrown to the lions. Gladiator, my dearest male and king of the pride, will be especially grateful."

An old Citroën van pulled up behind Dr. Microbio's office a short while later, and two of Mr. Garland's workmen, aided by Khufu and Abdallah, loaded Tweed's body in the back. Tweed, who had been hovering nearby the entire time, decided that things had definitely gone too far. The desecration of his corpse by Hassan and Mansour, and then Abdeslam's bloodletting, were disturbing enough. But he absolutely could not contemplate Mr. Garland's big cats ripping his flesh to shreds and devouring it. That was not his idea of resting in peace.

Tweed's ghost slipped back into his body, wrapped in its white sheet and now lying on the floor of the van. Mr. Garland's men slammed the back doors shut, and the van sped off toward the Old Mountain.

The two lost manuscript pages that had almost smothered Hassan and Mansour had by now joined up with other errant pages scattered throughout the medina and arranged themselves in a pile behind a potted cactus plant next to the wall of the old Spanish Post Office in the Zoco Chico. These pages contained some of the most malignant passages dictated to Burroughs by the Ugly Spirit—crucial parts of its viral matrix, in fact. They began to shuffle and resequence themselves, forming entirely new texts—the word virus was expanding and mutating. It was the Ugly Spirit's evolutionary mandate to reproduce the new texts by making its own clones of Ultrazone. Once these pages had accumulated enough power, they would be able to take control of the rest of the manuscript, resulting in a new incarnation of the Ugly Spirit that would make *Naked Lunch* seem like a Girl Scout handbook. From there Ultrazone would continue to procreate and take over other texts. Then the next phase could begin—to assume complete control of the souls of Burroughs, Paul Bowles, and Brion Gysin. Once those three longstanding targets had been subdued, their psychic powers could be used by the Ugly Spirit to extend its control to other victims. The Word and all possible permutations thereof would eventually become the property of the Ugly Spirit.

Burroughs's determination to confront and defeat the Ugly Spirit was shared by Bowles and Gysin, both having had ill-fated encounters with the Ugly Spirit in the past. Bowles had come to reconsider his initial explanation of Jane Bowles's stroke. He had long believed the stroke and Jane's subsequent decline and death were the result of a magic plant used as a control agent by her lover, Cherifa. The roots of the plant Cherifa gave Jane had been tangled around a tiny packet of *tseuheur*, a black magic potion that contained pubic hair, nail clippings, dried blood, and lizard's feet. But after learning more from Burroughs about the Ultrazone manuscript, Bowles had begun to suspect the Ugly Spirit was to blame. For his part, Brion Gysin felt his whole life had been a series of losing battles with the Ugly Spirit, from his inexplicable exclusion from the Surrealist movement by André Breton to the overnight loss of his legendary restaurant, the motorcycle accident outside Tangier in which he lost part of his foot, and his grim, grueling death from colon cancer in Paris. He had many reasons to want to destroy the systems of control exercised by the Ugly Spirit. But it was a tall order the ghosts faced. Somehow they would have to locate and completely destroy every page of the manuscript.

When Sayyad and Cheikh had left and Mina had gone back to work, their mother made a cup of tea and sat on the couch absentmindedly watching a Spanish game show on TV. After a while she turned the TV off and looked at the items lying on the coffee table. The pistol and the syringe gave Fatoma a bad feeling. The mere sight of them sent a shiver up her spine. And the stack of yellowed and stained typewritten pages lying beside the magazines seemed to radiate their own kind of evil. She set down her tea and took a handful of pages from the top of the pile. Setting them aside, she placed the rest of the stack in the bottom of the straw basket along with the other items, so she wouldn't have to look at them anymore, then put the basket behind the couch out of sight.

Fatoma next took the remaining handful of pages onto the balcony, removed the soiled newspapers from the cages of the parakeets and the big parrot, and replaced them with some of the yellowed sheets of paper. As she was removing the old newspaper from the last of the cages, a sudden breeze caught a few sheets still lying on the table and blew them across the balcony rail and out over the adjacent rooftops. She watched them swirl in the early evening sky until they dropped out of view behind a building in the next street.

Back in the living room, Fatoma picked up a copy of *Paris Match* and began leafing through it, more out of boredom than from any real interest in its contents. But something was wrong. Instead of the usual gossip columns adorned with colorful pictures of celebrities and garish advertisements, there was just text, page after page of it, apparently in English, not French. Fatoma had learned some English while Mina was studying it, so she started reading. But these were hardly normal sentences, nor could she discern any real sense in them. What she did understand was so disgusting, so obscene and blasphemous that it made her eyes hurt. It was obviously the work of a depraved mind, and maybe not even a human mind, but rather a Nasrani devil.

Fatoma let the magazine drop to the table and raised her hands in a protective gesture against horror and evil, while reciting appropriate lines from the Koran. Then she pulled the basket out from behind the couch, dug out the rest of the yellowed sheets of paper and began reading the uppermost page. It was more wild rantings in a voice that seemed utterly evil, and a host of bizarre characters with otherworldly names doing vile and unspeakable things to one another. Fatoma slumped down on the couch, overcome with a sense of total bewilderment. Her hands were trembling. She glanced at the words on the typewritten page and then at the words in *Paris Match*, which now seemed to be part of the same text. But how could that possibly be?

32

Aicha was pleased that Mohammed and Zodelia had carried out her burial precisely as she had instructed. Despite various minor transgressions over the years, they deserved to inherit her property. Mohammed knew how to deal with workmen and would make sure the repairs were made to the villa. He was also a good Muslim and only smoked kif in the evenings after the day's work was done. They were simple country folk and had been faithful servants. Allah provides, thought Aicha. Alhamdulillah.

Now that the corporeal part of her journey into the afterlife had been satisfactorily taken care of, she felt an extra sense of liberation. She had no attachment to her villa, although it still resonated as "home" to her, a familiar place she could visit whenever she liked to see what was going on, and the garden with its view of the strait was a wonderful place to meditate. Aicha no longer held any enmity toward Moustapha, either. He was among the living and had his own problems. And although the negligence of Dr. Microbio and his assistant was partly responsible for her death, she did not blame them—it was basically an accident, the will of Allah. As for the episode with Burroughs's hat and the attempt to drive out the Nasrani ghosts from St. Andrew's cemetery in exchange for various *materia magica*—they seemed like nothing more than curious memories from her past life. Dean's tombstone was now just a piece of material detritus for which she no longer had any need.

After visiting her villa Aicha looked around for other things to see and do. There were seemingly no limits to her ability to move about. She circled above Tangier several times, visiting her old hangout, Le New York Bar, and floating down the Boulevard Pasteur past the Café de Paris at the Place de France. She didn't go to St. Andrew's cemetery, not because it was a Nasrani cemetery but because it lacked any meaning for her. The medicinal plants and herbs and other graveyard objects useful in casting spells and working magic were irrelevant to her in her new state. Her old needs had evaporated like a mist. She had a feeling of almost perfect freedom—but not quite.

Aicha now inhabited a different plane, one which had its own reality. She could sense the presence of other spirits, especially those in need or in some sort of crisis, and this more keenly than most new ghosts. After all, she had been a sorceress in life and still had memories of that calling. She already knew that the ghosts of Burroughs, Dean, and Brunhilde, now joined by Paul Bowles, Brion Gysin and Brian Jones, had been moving about Tangier searching for something. It wasn't only the problem of Dean's missing tombstone they had been trying to solve. Other sinister forces were at work, she sensed. She had long heard rumors of a Burroughs manuscript that had been lost in Tangier, one that had supposedly involved a fateful collaboration with *El Espíritu Malo*. The evil spirit contained in those pages was evidently gaining strength and posed a threat to both the living and the spirit inhabitants of Tangier, and she realized her powers might be needed to deal with the threat.

Failing to locate Burroughs and his ghost cohort in Tangier, Aicha followed her GPS out to the Caves of Hercules where they were still sprawled on the cliffs enjoying the ocean view. Bowles was the first to sense her approach, but in his typical watch-and-wait-and-see-what-happens manner, said nothing to Burroughs and the others. Burroughs was still preoccupied with the Ugly Spirit and how best to search for the Ultrazone manuscript. His determination to ultimately defeat the Ugly Spirit was becoming more insistent, now bordering on the obsessive.

Dean was relaxing after the stresses and successes of the past two days. From time to time he glanced over at Brunhilde, admiring the fine lines of her face. He was still wondering if something like sexual attraction was even possible between the dead. What purpose could it serve when the dead were unable to procreate? Or was sexual attraction just a symptom of something greater, something that transcended life and death? Although the idea of something like eternal love seemed more like a topic for bad poetry or a kitschy love song.

Brion Gysin's ghost was alert on multiple levels as usual, and he was the first to see Aicha, resplendent in her finery, as she settled on one of the cliffs above the caves. But though he saw her clearly, he failed to recognize her in her new incarnation.

"Hey Bill, we have company. And I'm not sure if it's for good or ill," said Gysin.

"At this point I'm not so sure there's a difference," said Burroughs. "Who and where?"

"Look above and behind you on that rock," said Brion.

Burroughs turned and squinted. After a few moments a wry smile formed on his thin ghostly lips. Burroughs recognized a fellow spirit, but not yet as Aicha, now looking decades younger.

"I guess we're attracting dead drag queens now," he drawled. "Don't go making any friendly gestures to the thing. Maybe it will fade away. Though I have no problem with drag queens—never did—as long as they keep their distance. Actually dressed in drag myself a few times with Allen and Jack. There are lots of drag queens at the

Djemaa el Fna in Marrakech. It's Moroccan street theatre, to entertain the country folk and titillate tourists. When I visited Marrakech with Paul once, I had four of them following me around, hiking their skirts and exposing their codpieces. Despite their makeup, you could see they needed a shave. Finally I had to ask Paul to deal with them, which he did, though he appeared a little disappointed not to see one of them fuck me in the ass. My asshole was whispering 'Let 'em!,' but Paul wouldn't cough up the dirhams it would have cost to turn the trick. I figured he should have been willing to pay, since, as you know, Paul likes to watch."

Bowles said nothing but smiled almost imperceptibly and took a long drag from his cigarette holder, while keeping a wary eye on Aicha perched on her rock above them.

"Speaking of whispering assholes, no worries about that 'talking asshole' now," said Gysin. "After all, the dead don't have assholes. Don't need them either."

"Right. And I don't miss mine one bit," said Burroughs. "As my uncle Ivy Lee once said, 'Dead assholes don't talk.'"

"I sure missed mine when it was surgically removed in a Paris hospital, but that's all history now," Gysin said.

"Yeah, good riddance to bad assholes," Burroughs said. Even Gysin had to laugh.

Aicha had initially felt insulted at being called a drag queen, but the feeling passed quickly. Listening to the ghosts talking, she was struck again by the uncanny resemblance between Burroughs and Everly Tweed and wondered what had happened to Tweed since their last meeting in the cemetery. This group seems to be hiding out from something, she thought. Perhaps from *El Espíritu Malo*? I need to know more about this evil djinn before I get involved. My powers are new to me and there is still much to learn.

By now the sun was sliding down to the horizon and evening was fast approaching. The clouds in the western sky turned bright orange, then red, then purple.

"Definitely what one would call a mandrill-ass sky," muttered Burroughs.

Dean glanced over at Brunhilde, but she seemed totally absorbed in Brian Jones, who was reminiscing quietly with Paul Bowles about the Master Musicians of Joujouka and Jones's classic recording of their music, *The Pipes of Pan*. Jones listened as Bowles recounted his own trips into the Rif to record indigenous tribal music, much of which had all but disappeared as a result of government "modernization" programs.

Brion Gysin looked back at where Aicha had stood and saw only a large, mottled-white seagull, standing on one leg and facing the sunset, its head tucked low.

"Hey, Bill, the drag queen has apparently taken a powder," Gysin said.

"Or morphed into a seagull."

"That's entirely possible," said Bowles, slowly getting to his feet.

"What do you mean?" asked Gysin.

"That drag queen was Aicha. I'm surprised no one else recognized her, despite her changed appearance. I felt it as soon as she arrived, the presence of another ghost."

"Aicha? A ghost?" Burroughs repeated, obviously puzzled.

Gysin gathered up some nearby stones and started throwing them at the seagull. Burroughs soon joined in.

"Fuck off, you old witch! You good-for-nothing useless whore!" Burroughs yelled.

"Go back to hell or wherever it is you came from!" shouted Gysin.

Unscathed and only slightly perturbed, the seagull flapped its wings and lifted off into the evening sky, soaring gracefully out across the waves of the Atlantic as they reflected the last golden rays of the setting sun.

Dean, Brunhilde, and Brian Jones were on their feet again as well. "What the hell," said Dean. "Aicha a ghost now? I wonder how that happened?"

"Maybe it's time to head back to Tangier and see what's going on," said Gysin.

"It might be safer if we all stay together," said Burroughs. "As I said before, even ghosts can have their mojo depleted by evil entities, and I don't want to end up a piece of limp ectoplasm." Burroughs pulled the snub-nosed .38 revolver out of his jacket pocket and gave the cylinder an impressive spin. "At first I thought it was ridiculous that they buried me with this thing, but there's nothing like the feeling of a nice warm piece in your hands, you know."

"Just like John Lennon said," Brian Jones added.

"And look what happened to him," Brunhilde said ominously.

"Bullets wouldn't be much use against the Ugly Spirit, of course," Burroughs sighed.

The six ghosts moved as one into the dank depths of the grotto.

"Follow me," said Bowles. "My assistant Abdelouahaid once showed me where the opening is that allegedly leads to the network of tunnels beneath Tangier. I now believe we can follow it to that underground chamber beneath St. Andrew's cemetery."

"I don't ever want to be caught dead again in that cemetery," said Brunhilde. "Enough is enough, if you know what I mean. I'm over my murder but some of those highfalutin British fancy-pants ghosts are just *insufferable*. That Katherine Doolittle, and Claire de Menasce and her husband, Commander Howell—the epitome of stuck-up snobs!"

"Just stick with us stuck-up ghosts, Brunhilde," said Burroughs with a smile. "Strength in numbers has worked for me before. Anyway, there's no need for us to hang around St. Andrew's—my Ultrazone manuscript is no doubt somewhere outside the old boneyard. Paul, you lead."

With that they disappeared into the tunnel.

The van made its way up the Old Mountain road, Tweed's body rolling across the floor in back each time it went around a curve. Tweed reanimated his corpse's vocal cords and began emitting a low groan at every curve, each one louder than the one before.

"Do you hear that?" asked the workman in the passenger seat. "What's that noise?"

"What noise?" asked the driver.

They listened for a moment but heard nothing other than the noise of the engine.

Then they went around another sharp curve and Tweed let out an even louder groan.

"*That* noise!"

The driver shrugged and made a dismissive gesture. "Probably just a wheel bearing. They're always going out on these old Citroëns."

The electricity had returned on the Old Mountain, so Just-Call-Me-Ishmael locked up his villa and set the alarm, then made the rounds of the property with the watchman, making sure all the motion-activated lights were functioning. The watchman told him about the fire next door the previous night. Just-Call-Me-Ishmael asked if anyone had been hurt; the watchman said no. Afterwards the two men waited in the pool of bright electric light just inside the front gate until

Just-Call-Me-Ishmael's taxi arrived. The flat wooden crate tucked under his arm held the Schwitters collage. He'd missed the six p.m. ferry to Algeciras, and although he still had time to catch the midnight ferry, he decided to postpone his crossing until tomorrow.

When the taxi arrived, Just-Call-Me-Ishmael recognized Farid at the wheel and wished him good evening as he climbed in the back seat.

"Good evening, Monsieur Just-Call-Me-Ishmael. Where to?"

"Drop me in the Grand Socco, please, as usual."

With a squeal of spinning tires they started down the Old Mountain road, much too fast for Just-Call-Me-Ishmael's taste.

"How have you been, Farid?"

"Not well. I just got out of the hospital."

"Hopefully nothing serious."

"Just some evil djinns. But you should be careful, monsieur. Those evil djinns and your neighbor Aicha seem to be working together."

"Yes, I heard there'd been some strange goings-on there recently. Farid, must you drive so fast? I'm not in a hurry."

"As you wish, monsieur."

Just-Call-Me-Ishmael was unable to detect any reduction in the speed of the taxi.

"Farid, do you know the story of the tortoise and the hare? It's an old fable by Aesop, but there must be some Moroccan equivalent."

"I know nothing of any tortoise or hare. How does the story go?"

Just-Call-Me-Ishmael told Farid the story, without any further commentary, in the hope that the moral of the story would be self-evident to Farid.

They screeched around two more corners while Farid was clearly considering the implications of the story.

"So, the stupid lazy hare lost the race. Just shows you how important it is to keep moving and stay ahead. If a tortoise passes you, you know you're moving too slow. I think that's obvious enough without having to write a story about it. We have much better stories here in Morocco. Is this Aesop a famous writer?"

Approaching them in the opposite direction was the Citroën, with Tweed's body still rolling to and fro in the back of it. As it rounded another curve and the cadaver smashed against the wall of the van, Tweed this time let out a noise that was something between an agonized groan and a scream of anger. The two men in front both turned around and saw Tweed's body sitting upright. The soiled sheet in which it was wrapped was now unraveling to reveal its pale face and bloody toothless mouth, eyes wide open and looking from side to side, as Tweed willed it to stare at both of them as menacingly as he could. The passenger let out a scream of horror and reached impulsively for the door handle, while the driver turned around to steer the van, only to be completely blinded by the lights of an oncoming vehicle, hurtling directly toward them.

33

The stray pages from Ultrazone that had gathered themselves behind a cactus by the wall of the old Spanish Post Office in the Zoco Chico were rustling and buzzing with the nervous industriousness of a beehive. Words were swallowing other words, digesting them, shitting them out as new words. Other words were enveloping still other words in balls of sticky ectoplasm which then split and divided into more globs containing yet more new words, like cells dividing under a microscope. The new words formed into new sentences, new paragraphs, new texts, new chapters, until there was no more room for them in the yellowed typewritten pages. So the words began to look for a new home, a new context they could colonize, from where they could spread the Ugly Spirit's insidious directives.

The old Spanish Post Office was closed, and the last postal worker had gone home. On the other side of the wall, inside the post office, were the rows of metal boxes from which patrons collected their mail, each with its number and a tiny glass window in its door. In the silent darkness of the shuttered building, the letters, postcards, bills, periodicals, and advertising flyers waiting in those post office boxes were undergoing a strange metamorphosis. One by one, word by word, sheet by sheet, every single printed surface began to resemble the yellowed typewritten pages of the Ultrazone manuscript. The letter that had previously stated *Dear Sirs, Thank you for your letter of 23.11.2000 inquiring as to the delivery of 35 cases of our El Quazzania brand olive oil. We can offer you the following prices* . . . now began *Lee on all fours on the floor of a Marrakech hotel room getting sucked off by the Talking Asshole* . . . *Lupita adjusting the dial of the radio to broken neon*

*arabesques . . . a rotting corpse floating in the oily waters of the harbor . . .
old newspapers blowing down an empty Kansas City alley . . . A postcard
bearing the words Dear Marcel, Thank you for the check and the fine pres-
ents from Paris. Here the weather has been very hot and dry. Last weekend
we drove out to Sidi Kacem and then to Volubilis for a picnic . . . had been
transformed into The Frisco Kid shouts 'No Good. No bueno!' . . . a smell
of abyss and nothingness . . . 'Annie Laurie' was a code tune just enemy
intercepted . . . a distant hand lifted . . .* And so on, throughout each and
every post office box, all waiting to be opened the following morning.

By the time Evangeline and Piet recovered the Burroughs fedora from
the kid in the Rue Mohamed Bergach, the banks had closed. They
would have to wait until the next day to find the Interbank and try to
get into the safe deposit box. As they entered the lobby of the Hotel
Lutetia on their way to their rooms, they heard a short "Pssst!" from
the direction of the reception desk to the left of the door. They looked
over and saw Ali, the desk clerk, beaming at them. "Hello, my friends,
how are you?" Ali was maybe in his mid-twenties, with a permanent
three-day beard and a halo of curly black hair surrounding his smiling
face. He always seemed to wear a short-sleeved Hawaiian shirt and
faded blue jeans.

It occurred to Evangeline and Piet that Ali was always smiling. He
was also the only one they ever saw at the reception desk, whether
it was day or night, weekday or weekend. Other than the silent and
somnolent maids they passed in the hallways or on the stairs, Ali appeared to be the only person who worked there. He was always there,
smiling, friendly, and helpful. He had changed money for Evangeline
and Piet at far better rates than they would have received at any bank.
He had offered them excellent kif and hashish at bargain prices, occasionally even a free joint.

One afternoon when Piet was passing through the lobby alone, Ali
had invited him to a corner of the otherwise deserted dining room,
where a beautiful young woman was sitting, drinking a glass of cognac
and smoking a joint. The panoramic windows behind her offered
a stunning view of the harbor below. The three of them shared the
joint, and in the course of the conversation it became apparent to Piet
that the woman was a prostitute and Ali was subtly offering her services to Piet. Beautiful and attractive as the woman was, and enticing
as Ali's veiled proposition seemed, Piet would have been too stoned

to go through with it, even if he had been completely certain about the direction of his sexual desires. When he looked more closely at the woman's face, trying to imagine the two of them on intimate terms, Piet noticed some pockmarks and a small scar on her chin that seemed to denote some underlying wickedness that sent a shiver up his spine. He extracted himself from the situation as diplomatically as he could and went to his room, where he fell into a troubled sleep, haunted by a nightmare in which Ali and the prostitute were up on the roof, looking down through a hole in the ceiling, speaking to one another in Arabic while Ali probed down into his room with something resembling an extra-large coat hanger, like something out of a painting by Salvador Dalí.

Evangeline and Piet stopped at the bottom of the stairs and Ali came over. "You're well? You have everything you need?"

"We're fine, Ali. Thanks. Look," Evangeline said, taking off the fedora, "I even got my hat back."

"Excellent," Ali said. "You can wear it to the party tonight."

"What party?" asked Piet.

Ali glanced around conspiratorially before continuing. "That's what I wanted to tell you about. It's really more like an illegal rave, in the old Gran Teatro Cervantes in the Rue Anoual. There's a great local band called the Apostles of Pandemonium, and they're leaving tomorrow to tour Europe. Entertainment of the highest quality, I can guarantee you that."

"What time will it start?" asked Evangeline.

"Probably not before midnight, like most raves."

"Will you be there?" asked Piet.

Ali shrugged. "I don't know if I can get away. But you two should definitely go."

"Okay, Ali. Thanks for the tip," Evangeline said. "Maybe we'll see you there."

"If you need any extra 'party favors' before going to the party, just stop by the desk and let me know."

All Farid could see were two blazing headlights as his taxi came around the curve. Whoever it was, they were on the wrong side of the road and coming right at them. Just before the taxi and the van collided, Farid cranked the steering wheel hard to the right. His taxi shot off the road and through a narrow space between a tree and the high stone wall of a villa, then plowed into a long hedge which brought it to a shuddering stop.

The van swerved in the other direction and went careening off the other side of the road, bursting through the wall of a decrepit abandoned villa and spinning a full 360 degrees with such force that the back doors flew open and Tweed's corpse went hurtling out as if fired from a cannon. The body rolled down the hillside and finally came to a stop on a cracked stone patio beside an empty swimming pool, the bottom of which was layered with soggy eucalyptus leaves, pine needles, and a few dead rats.

Tweed's ghost rose up out of his body again and hovered overhead, assessing the situation. He could hear voices up on the road, but no one seemed to be moving in the wreckage of the van, which had come to rest against the sturdy trunk of a large oak tree further up the hillside, steam billowing from its smashed radiator. Clouds of dust swirled in the slanting rays of light from its one intact headlight.

Wow! Tweed thought. I haven't had that much fun since I hypnotized the Queen's corgis on that BBC special about hypnotism back in the seventies! But now what?

Having saved his body from being thrown to the lions, Tweed still faced the problem of getting it back to St. Andrew's, where it belonged. As an oxygen-breathing, blood-pumping human being Tweed had been an accomplished hypnotist, but he had never really mastered the art of telekinesis. Sure, he could send a fountain pen rolling across a table or give a pair of reading glasses a nudge across a desk, maybe even dislodge a ring of keys from a hook on the wall, the usual little tricks—but moving large inert objects from one place to another had never been his forte. Maybe now, in this other realm, things might be different. He certainly hoped so.

Tweed looked down at his body lying on the patio and began to concentrate on an image of the body making its way back to St. Andrew's and into its grave. He tried several times, but the body didn't even so much as quiver. Frustrated and disappointed, Tweed glanced around and his eyes came to rest on the dead rats in the empty swimming pool. As an experiment, he started to imagine one of them rising up out of the pool. He focused all of his psychic energy and made such a concerted effort that he felt cold drops of ghost-sweat forming on his brow. Gradually, the dead rat began to move, almost imperceptibly at first, but then, shakily but steadily, it rose into the air. Tweed felt empowered and attempted to channel this new energy into his efforts, but the rat abruptly stopped in mid-air, began to tremble, then dropped like a stone into the muck of rotting leaves in the bottom of the pool with a resounding *splat*.

It was useless—this was a material problem and it required a material solution. Tweed needed some physical assistance from a living person. But who could he ask? Various scenarios flickered through Tweed's troubled ghost-mind. Should he try to contact Kazim again and somehow get him involved? Or maybe Abdul and his magic carpet?

Moustapha was walking up the Boulevard Pasteur toward his sister's house, where he hoped dinner would be waiting for him. After his visits to the baths and the mosque, he felt clean and revitalized, physically and spiritually. He might even have been able to enjoy these sensations if not for the matter of Tweed's missing body and the empty coffin buried in St. Andrew's. If that were somehow to be revealed, Moustapha would certainly lose his job again, this time for good.

As dusk turned to evening, the lights in the streets and in the shop windows and cafés came on and the streets slowly filled with the usual evening crowds, tourists and locals stepping out for dinner, to do some shopping, or simply to promenade along the boulevard, to see and be seen. As Moustapha passed his regular café he saw there was an empty table outside amid all the occupied ones and decided to sit for a while. The waiter greeted him, briskly wiping the table and rearranging the chairs with a professional flourish. "Good evening, my friend," said the waiter. "What became of your precious hat, the one that belonged to the famous writer?"

Moustapha shook his head and made a dismissive gesture with his hand. "Never mind that cursed Nasrani hat. Nothing but trouble."

"What did you expect?" replied the waiter with a knowing air.

Moustapha shrugged and ordered a mint tea. When the waiter left, Moustapha pondered his reply. Yes, what did he expect? It seemed like one of those unanswerable questions that was an answer in itself. Moustapha suddenly recalled some fragments of what Kazim had said to him in the Café Triangle the other night about the "other world."

Moustapha's metaphysical reverie was interrupted by the sound of familiar English voices nearby. He glanced around and saw Ravi Khan and Tony Mahoney engaged in conversation with two other

Nasranis at a table a little further down the sidewalk. He knew who Ravi and Tony were, but they didn't know him, and he felt free to eavesdrop. They were discussing some kind of party they were preparing for that evening, obviously something more than another performance in the back room of the Café Triangle. They used many technical terms relating to sound and logistics that Moustapha didn't understand, but he clearly heard them mention the Grand Teatro Cervantes. This surprised him, since the theater had been closed for years, and was supposedly little more than a crumbling ruin, hardly suitable for a public event. What kind of party could they be planning?

Moustapha hoped to learn more but Ravi and Tony and the other two Nasranis abruptly got to their feet and shook hands, saying they would see one another later at the "big bash." Moustapha watched them walk down the boulevard until they disappeared in the crowd, then finished his tea and walked on to his sister's house, still wondering about what he'd overheard.

34

Pancho and Lefty followed Cheikh to the deserted warehouse by the harbor, with Sayyad in tow. Steetoo was in the secret hideout, about to eat a meager meal of leftovers he'd gathered in the streets of Tangier—the remains of an Eric's hamburger, a half-eaten tuna fish and french fry sandwich, and an inch of warm Pepsi in a plastic bottle were laid out on the packing crate. A sputtering candle provided the only illumination. "Who's that?" Steetoo asked, getting to his feet when he saw the two other macaques with their baskets of fruit.

"I don't know," Sayyad said, "We saw them in the medina and they started following us. I think they've been talking with Cheikh."

"Talking? Are you m'hashish again?"

"I don't mean talking like you and I talk, but like animals talk."

"So what were they saying?"

"How would I know? Look, they're doing it now."

Cheikh and Pancho and Lefty were chattering back and forth, discussing how to bring the rest of the macaques to the warehouse, which was indeed the perfect location from which to look for a truck that would be taking the ferry to Spain. Lefty scanned the room, then went over to the back wall and touched it with his paw. With his eyes closed, he began lightly tapping the wall in various places. "Do you know what's behind this wall, Cheikh?"

"No, why?"

"It's hollow. It could be a tunnel," Lefty said thoughtfully, still tapping. "Maybe it's part of the same tunnel system we used before and will lead us back to the others. They must be very hungry by now." He went out into the warehouse and returned with some rusty iron reinforcement bars. He handed one to Pancho, and the two of them started picking away at the wall, quickly breaking through the thin layer of whitewashed plaster and digging into the brick underneath, which soon began to crumble under the force of their repeated blows. Their shadows cast by the single candle loomed large on the wall behind them as they worked.

"What do you think they're doing?" asked Steetoo.

Sayyad shrugged. "Cheikh, what's going on?"

Cheikh looked back at Sayyad, who saw something in Cheikh's eyes he'd never seen before—a look of sheer feral determination that caused him to take a step backward. Cheikh picked up another of the iron bars and joined Pancho and Lefty, who were quickly carving out a large hole in the brick wall.

Sayyad set down one of the big baskets of fruit next to Steetoo. "Here, help yourself. This will taste better than that garbage you're eating."

The two of them sat peeling and eating oranges and bananas, watching curiously as the hole in the wall grew larger.

Tweed's ghost still hovered at the edge of the empty swimming pool. He was staring into its dark depths, pondering his next move, as though perhaps the answer to his problem lay hidden down there in the murk, when he heard a deep growl behind him. A massive and muscular black dog with a studded leather collar stood just a few meters away. All his life, Tweed had been afraid of dogs. He had been bitten and attacked more than once as a child—and again as an adult by stray dogs in the streets of Tangier. He felt that fear coursing through his being again now and was about to flee in an instinctual effort at self-preservation, but then he relaxed and laughed. The guard dog stopped growling, cocked his head, and looked at Tweed with a puzzled expression.

"What's the matter, doggie, never seen a ghost before?"

The dog's ears flattened, and he lowered his head a bit.

"Don't worry. As much as I'd like to get even with you and your kind, you don't have to be afraid of me. In fact, you might even be able to help me."

Tweed shut his eyes and began to envision a scenario, which he then projected into the dog's mind. Fuck that telekinesis shit, Tweed thought. Bring on the trusty old hypnotism.

The dog now perked up his ears, raised his head, and looked directly at Tweed. Then he turned and trotted over to Tweed's corpse. Gripping the collar of Tweed's jacket, the dog started dragging the body across the patio towards a two-meter-high boxwood hedge that formed a labyrinth. It pulled Tweed's corpse through the entrance of the labyrinth and disappeared. Several minutes later it reappeared without the body and looked expectantly at Tweed's ghost.

"Thanks, sport. I owe you one."

The dog wagged its tail and went trotting off into the darkness.

Tweed glanced up toward the road to see the driver stagger from the smashed cab of his van, his flashlight now stabbing the darkness. Tweed silently lifted off into the night sky and headed toward town and Kazim's house.

In the beam of his flashlight the driver saw that the back doors of the van were wide open and the body was no longer inside. Cursing under his breath, he wrenched open the passenger-side door. The other workman, dazed and shaken but with only a small cut on his forehead, stumbled out of the wreck. "That's what happens when you drive too fast," he said, rubbing his head.

"Never mind. We have to find the body; it flew out the back as we went through the wall. It must have rolled down the hill there," the driver said, pointing the beam of light toward the swimming pool below.

The two of them made their way down the hillside, the driver sweeping back and forth with the flashlight, but no body was to be seen. They stepped onto the patio and peered down into the empty swimming pool. "It can't have just disappeared. It must be here somewhere," the driver said.

"Maybe he wasn't really dead. That would explain his sitting up and screaming."

"Don't be foolish. That was some kind of djinn, or a Nasrani ghost. If you're not afraid, it won't hurt you. Are you afraid?"

The workman felt the growing lump on his forehead and peered into the darkness around them. "Yes, I am."

"Pull yourself together and follow me."

They made their way around the pool, looking into the shrubbery and even up into the trees, passing by the labyrinth and stopping beside a fenced-in tennis court, completely overgrown with weeds.

"Now what?" asked the workman.

"What do I know? The body is gone, that's all I can say. We'll have to come back when it's light and look again."

"If he's not already on his way back to Tangier."

"Don't be ridiculous," the driver admonished impatiently.

"Mr. Garland will be very angry with us."

"That goes without saying."

The two men had just started up the hill toward the road when the huge guard dog burst out of the shadows behind them, barking ferociously. They fended it off by throwing rocks until they made it up to the road and through the broken wall, where they saw Farid and Just-Call-Me-Ishmael standing by the taxi, whose front end was buried in a hedge. Farid immediately launched the usual curses and accusations at Garland's workmen, which returned with a volley of their own, while the dog kept up his furious barking from behind the broken wall.

When their loud and angry exchange had reached a stalemate, Farid asked the two men to help him get his vehicle out of the hedge. Just-Call-Me-Ishmael, the crate with the Schwitters collage tucked safely under his arm, stood and watched as the three of them struggled with the taxi. Once it was back on the road Farid got in and turned the key, but the engine would not start. He got out and opened the hood. With the help of the van driver and his flashlight, he tried to figure out what the problem was.

Just-Call-Me-Ishmael could see that the situation was hopeless and their efforts would be in vain, but their stubborn personalities would not allow them to admit defeat. They would probably stand there looking at the engine and making useless suggestions for some time to come. He told them he would continue on foot. Maybe a car would pass by and give him a lift. The three men were so absorbed in a disputative conversation about fuel pumps and carburetors they barely noticed his departure.

Burroughs, Bowles, and the other ghosts were making their way through the long tunnel from the Caves of Hercules back to Tangier, moving slowly and carefully as they approached each turn. They all felt a real sense of danger—underground tunnels sometimes followed parallel energy lines that ran through the earth's crust, crisscrossing and connecting with sites of great power, energy chakras such as Stonehenge, the Mayan pyramids, and the Great Pyramids of Giza. Even ghosts had to be careful not to disturb any lines of terrestrial electromagnetic energy. It would be like touching the third rail.

After passing what felt to him like the halfway point between the caves and Tangier, Bowles said, "I'm sure this will bring us to the subterranean hub beneath St. Andrew's, from where we can enter the crypt beneath the mausoleum."

"The last time we looked for that mausoleum it wasn't there. Then it reappeared out of thin air. How do you explain that?" asked Burroughs.

"I assume it's some sort of self-defense system the Blue Messiah came up with, so that the entrance to the tunnel system is not accessible to every mere mortal who happens by."

"Like the conning tower of a ghostly submarine. Only visible when there is a need to surface," said Gysin.

Eventually they reached the cavern-like room where the five tunnels converged and followed the passageway and stairs that led to the crypt beneath the mausoleum. As they neared the top of the stairs they saw that the red stone door to the crypt was slightly ajar, and a weak light shone from within.

"Wait a minute," Burroughs said. "Wasn't that door shut the last time we went through it?"

"I believe it was," said Bowles.

"I *know* it was," Gysin added.

"What's that weird noise?" asked Brunhilde.

From the crypt came an almost imperceptible rustling and murmuring. The ghosts peered around the red stone door into the crypt and saw the room was full of macaques, some lying around, others huddled together sleeping, still others intently picking fleas from their neighbors' fur. A few oil lamps normally used for various rituals had been lit—by Werner, a macaque with exceedingly advanced technical abilities—and cast a warm, wavering glow through the room. Abruptly they all stopped what they were doing and turned toward the doorway. One particularly large and stately looking macaque stepped forward and addressed the ghosts in his simian language, which the ghosts were able to understand perfectly.

"Who are you and what do you want here?"

"We were about to ask you the same thing," said Burroughs, looking into the curious eyes of the crowd of macaques.

35

Tweed's ghost slipped through the locked front doors of Kazim's house like a Mikado stick passing through whipped cream. He found Kazim asleep in his papasan chair, where he'd nodded out earlier. From the kitchen came the sounds of someone preparing dinner. The smell of frying onions and garlic and cumin and ginger titillated Tweed's nostrils but he felt neither hunger nor the desire to eat. Tweed focused his psychic energies to peer into Kazim's mind and see what, if anything, was going on in there. At first he could make out only random blurred images, flickering like a badly tuned TV set, but then a regular narrative of events seemed to be unfolding. Kazim was dreaming, his eyeballs nervously twitching beneath his eyelids, and Tweed shut his own eyes in order to witness that dream.

Kazim's dream narrative came into focus and Tweed could see the two men from the crashed Citroën van making their way down the hillside toward the swimming pool, their flashlight's beam sweeping back and forth in the darkness. They walked round its perimeter, shining the flashlight off to the side as well as down into the bottom of the empty pool. The large black dog with the studded collar appeared at the edge of the patio and started barking, running back and forth from the patio to the entrance of the boxwood-hedge labyrinth until the men followed the dog into the labyrinth, where they discovered Tweed's body, still partly wrapped in the torn and bloody sheet. They carried it back out to the patio and the driver told his companion to wait by the body while he went to find a way to contact Mr. Garland.

Next door was another villa with a small gatehouse where its care-taker lived. An old Moroccan man opened the door when the driver knocked and asked if there was a phone he could use, explaining there had been an accident. When Mr. Garland answered the phone and heard what had happened, he was furious, but told the driver to wait at the old villa until another truck came to pick up the body.

When a small pickup rattled down the darkened road about fifteen minutes later, he flashed his light and the truck pulled over. The two men made their way down to the patio, and together with the other workman carried Tweed's body up the hillside and deposited it in the back of the pickup, covering it with an old tarpaulin.

The scene now shifted to Mr. Garland's estate. The truck pulled around to the back of the main house, where the animals were kept. Mr. Garland stood there with a gas lantern, which hissed brightly in the darkness. He told the men to take the body to the cats' cage, open the hatch in the roof and slide the body down the chute into the enclosure.

When Tweed's body landed face down on the floor of their cage, the two Bengal tigers jumped back, snarling ferociously. The large male lion, Gladiator, merely bared his fangs and let out a low growl to signify his dominance. He approached the cadaver and pushed at it with a huge forepaw, rolling it over in the dust. Then, in one fluid motion, Gladiator clamped his jaws on Tweed's neck, lifted the entire body and shook it violently. The two tigers reacted swiftly, each lung-ing for one of Tweed's legs, which they pulled apart like a wishbone until the bones snapped. Each tiger then dragged a leg to a different corner of the cage and began to devour it, while Gladiator ripped open Tweed's chest and tore out the heart as deftly as any butcher.

Kazim shifted uneasily in his chair, as though he might awaken at any moment. Tweed opened his eyes again and quickly moved behind one of the arches that opened onto the interior garden. The dream narrative had broken off, replaced by isolated images flickering past, including a glimpse of a passage from a book Kazim had been read-ing: *The soul becomes spiritual through freeing itself from bodily matters and corporeal perceptions. This happens to the soul in the form of glimpses through the agency of sleep.*

Like flashcards from another world there followed a rapid-fire series of disconnected images—an old hat bursting into flames, a glass perched on the head of an older woman shattered by a gunshot, a thick manuscript being lifted out of a bank deposit box, pages of it being blown around the city, other pages being read by a different woman in her living room, the typewritten words changing, morphing, continuously altering their meaning until she dropped the pages in fear and disgust. The figure of a beautiful young woman dressed in Moroccan garments of the finest materials and adorned with precious jewels, a serpent-like mark on her forehead, then a lone seagull with a piece of paper in its beak, swooping down as it approached the city of Tangier. Then the flow of images abruptly ceased, as if the power had suddenly gone out in a movie theater.

Tweed was determined that this dream narrative should never become reality. His corpse had been abused enough as it was; there was no way it would become the daily special at Mr. Garland's. He rubbed his hands together in anticipation of the task ahead and went to work, envisioning a concise but detailed scenario in which his corpse would be retrieved from the boxwood labyrinth at the deserted villa and transported to St. Andrew's, then projecting that scenario deep into Kazim's mind.

Kazim awoke with a start and sat upright as if he'd been prodded with a red-hot poker. Without a moment's hesitation he went to the far corner of his interior garden and yanked the gray canvas tarp off a vintage three-wheeled motorcycle. The Harley Davidson, powered by a 45-cubic-inch flathead engine and with a utility box mounted on the back, was a memento from Kazim's smuggling days. He'd received it as payment in lieu of cash from some Americans back in the heyday of the International Zone.

Although seldom used, the Harley was in immaculate condition and Kazim kept it well maintained, the fuel and oil regularly topped off and the battery fully charged. He straddled the trike and kicked the starter, and the engine roared to life. Habiba came running out of the kitchen and yelled at him, "What are you doing? What will the neighbors say?"

"Fuck the neighbors. Open the front doors. I have some urgent business to attend to."

"What about dinner?"

"Keep it warm. I won't be long."

While Habiba opened the front doors, Kazim pulled out a WWI leather aviator's helmet, goggles, and a matching pair of gauntlets from the utility box. Whipping off his turban, he donned helmet, goggles, and gloves, revved the engine, and flashing Habiba a mischievous smile, roared around the perimeter of the garden, through the archway, across the front room and out the open front doors into the night, the folds of his djellaba flapping behind him.

As Kazim turned into the Avenue Belgique, he recognized Moustapha plodding along the sidewalk on the other side of the street. He pulled up to the curb and whistled, then waited for Moustapha to cross.

"Get on board, my friend," Kazim said, motioning behind him. "We have work to do."

"Work? Now? What kind of work?" Moustapha asked incredulously.

"A dream told me where to find Tweed's body. Let's go."

Moustapha stood immobile in a cloud of bewilderment.

"Come on," Kazim prompted impatiently. "We don't have a moment to spare."

Moustapha climbed on, Kazim revved the engine, and they went thundering off in the direction of the medina. Moustapha was impressed at Kazim's ability to maneuver the Harley through its narrow streets and alleyways, which in places were only a few inches wider than the rear wheel span of the trike. As they approached the Kasbah, they turned into a street that overlooked the strait, bordered by a low wall on one side and a row of narrow houses on the other. The lights of Spain twinkled in the distance. Kazim cut the engine and dismounted. "Wait here," he said, pushing up his goggles and removing his gloves. "We need one important thing before we continue."

Kazim crossed the street and rapped on a large wooden door covered with metal studs, using its brass doorknocker in the shape of a hand. After a pause, he heard the key turn in the lock and the door creaked open to reveal Abdul peering from the dim interior.

"Salaam alaikum, Abdul."

"Salaam as salaam, Kazim. What brings you here at this hour?"

"I need to borrow your tapis magique. Has it returned from Malta?"

Abdul furrowed his brow and looked over Kazim's shoulder at the Harley trike and Moustapha. "Yes, it's here. A faithful magic carpet always returns to its owner, like a homing pigeon. For what do you need it?"

"Our mutual friend, Everly Tweed, has met with an untimely end. I need to transport his body to St. Andrew's so it can be properly buried."

"I always thought of St. Andrew's as a place of peace and quiet, but these days there seems to be much action there."

"There are many strange goings on in Tangier right now. As though some kind of evil spirit has descended upon the city."

"Or perhaps awakened from a long slumber."

"Who knows?" Kazim said, shrugging his shoulders. "The carpet?"

Abdul disappeared inside, returning shortly with the carpet over his shoulder.

Kazim took the carpet and Abdul handed him a red velvet bag with green drawstrings. "You will need this too, the talisman and the spells. Are you sure you can manage it?"

Kazim looked at Abdul as though he had asked a very stupid question.

"It is a very fickle carpet," Abdul said. "Like a crazy cat or a woman. I wish you luck."

"Thank you, Abdul. Consider this a favor which I will repay generously on another occasion."

They said farewell and Kazim and Moustapha folded the carpet and stuffed it into the utility box on the back of the trike. Then with a loud roar they went jouncing down the potholed street towards the Old Mountain.

Kazim and Moustapha immediately saw the jagged hole where the van had crashed through the wall. The scene was deserted; Kazim maneuvered the trike through the hole and turned off the engine and lights. Steam was still wafting from the smashed hood of the Citroën van, and the engine was still ticking. Down the hillside a dog barked repeatedly. Kazim produced a flashlight and took out the carpet, which he placed over Moustapha's shoulders, then the two of them made their way down the hill to the empty swimming pool and into the labyrinth. Tweed's body lay at the center, still partially wrapped in the bloody, dirty sheet, and emitting a foul odor. Moustapha thought he might throw up but managed to stifle the urge.

The two men carried the body back out to the patio and laid it on the rolled-out carpet. Kazim took out the talisman and the papers with the various spells and, with the help of the flashlight, tried to make sense of what was written there. He started reading aloud in a language Moustapha had never heard before, until the carpet began to glow with a flickering blue light. Moustapha took a few steps back. The carpet began to quiver, barely noticeably at first, but slowly it rose into the air, still quivering, as though straining under its macabre load. Kazim leafed through the papers and began reading from a different page. The carpet moved a little to the left, then to the right, just above the edge of the pool, as though it was having trouble deciding in which direction it should go. Kazim shuffled through the papers again, impatient now, apparently not finding what he was looking for. The carpet shook and tipped to one side, and Tweed's body slid off it and fell into the vegetal morass below.

In the crypt beneath the mausoleum, Burroughs was endeavoring to give Bruno a coherent account of the events of the last two days, without getting too entangled in the increasingly complicated web of detail. Above all, he wanted to explain the backstory of his old manuscript and to stress the dangers it posed as host to the Ugly Spirit.

"So I'm on a mission, my friend," he concluded. "Together with my spectral comrades, I must find and destroy every page of that manuscript."

Bruno scratched his head and nodded, although Burroughs couldn't tell if everything he'd said had really sunk in. After all, he'd never talked to a macaque before, and was uncertain what the limitations of understanding actually were between man and monkey. He thought of something Wittgenstein had said: "If a lion could talk, we could not understand him." Was the bridge of genetic similarity sufficient for the transfer of meaning back and forth between the human world and the ape world? And, just as importantly, between the material world and the spirit world?

Bruno then explained to Burroughs and the other ghosts their plan to rejoin their relatives on the Rock of Gibraltar, the first step of which was to cross the strait by stowing away on the ferry to Algeciras.

"What about the tunnel from Tangier to Gibraltar?" Bowles asked. "Or is that just another myth?"

"It's no myth," Bruno answered. "But it's full of water now and completely impassable. That's why we need to get on the ferry."

"That shouldn't be too difficult," said Gysin. "There are always fruit and produce trucks heading over to Spain."

"Do you have everything you need for now? What about food and water?" Burroughs asked.

"We sent out a couple of scouts a while back, but they haven't returned yet."

"Well," Burroughs said, "we wish you the best of luck. Tangier seems to be changing, and not for the better. You may as well get out while the getting is good."

"Our thoughts exactly," said Bruno.

"Okay, team," Burroughs said to the other ghosts. "We've got work to do. Let's surface and see what's happening in the Port of Saints."

Bruno and the other macaques watched in fascination as the ghosts floated effortlessly up through the stone trap door and disappeared from view.

The ghosts then drifted out of the moss-covered mausoleum and through the tombstones and obelisks, gathering again just inside the front gate. "Let's spread out, do some reconnaissance, and meet back here in an hour or so," Burroughs said to the others. "Then we can—"

Burroughs was interrupted by the loud roar of the Harley's flathead engine as Kazim and Moustapha pulled up. The ghosts slipped back into the shadows, out of the glow of the single street lamp at the gate.

Moustapha jumped down and unlocked the cemetery gate, and the ghosts watched as Kazim and Moustapha detached a lengthy bundle they had tied to the top of the utility box. As they passed by with their load on their way into the cemetery, the ghosts could see that both of them were covered in black slime. They could also see that what they were lugging was Everly Tweed's body, his bashed and bloody face poking out from one end of a rolled-up carpet.

Staying just out of sight, the ghosts followed Kazim and Moustapha and watched as they set their burden down next to a freshly covered grave at the rear of the cemetery. Moustapha fetched two shovels and a gas lantern, and they began to excavate the grave. Eventually the ghosts heard the sound of the shovels hitting the wood of a coffin. Moustapha pried open the lid, removed the debris he'd filled it with earlier and together with Kazim unrolled Tweed's body from the carpet, then eased it down into the coffin and closed the lid.

The ghosts suddenly felt the presence of another spirit form and turned to see the ghost of Everly Tweed approaching in the darkness.

"Just in time for your own funeral," Burroughs said quietly.

Tweed glanced at Burroughs, then at the other ghosts. "What is this?" Tweed asked. "Some kind of Tangier alumni afterlife convention?"

"Something like that," Burroughs answered. "From the Interzone to the Afterzone by way of the Ultrazone."

"What?" Tweed looked perplexed.

"Never mind," said Burroughs. "Right now a period of solemn silence is in order, don't you think?"

The ghosts turned their attention back to Moustapha and Kazim, now shoveling dirt back into the grave on top of Tweed's coffin. At one point Moustapha stopped digging and from under his burnoose produced the paper packet containing the ashes of the first fedora. He contemplated its contents for a moment, then tossed it into the grave, where it was soon covered with dirt. When they had tamped down the earth and leaned their shovels against a tombstone, they sat down on the marble slab of an adjacent tomb to catch their breath. Kazim produced his sebsi and bag of kif.

Moustapha eyed him with a reproachful expression. "You think this is the right time to smoke?" he asked.

"Couldn't be better," Kazim replied confidently, touching the flame of his brass lighter to the plug of kif and inhaling deeply. Still wearing his leather aviator's helmet, with the goggles pushed up onto his forehead, he looked particularly bold, the lines of his face exaggerated by the sharp light of the gas lantern on the ground next to the rolled-up carpet.

Moustapha watched Kazim exhale a large cloud of blue smoke, which slowly rose out of the light of the lantern and disappeared into the darkness.

"May Everly Tweed's spirit rise into heaven as easily as that cloud of kif smoke," Kazim said in a pious tone. He then refilled the pipe and passed it to Moustapha, who now saw Kazim's gesture in a different light. Moustapha lit the pipe, inhaled deeply, and exhaled a blue cloud of his own, which slowly drifted up toward the stars, as the two men gazed in respectful silence.

After a while, Moustapha broke the stillness. "Tonight at a café I overheard Ravi Khan and Tony Mahoney talking about a party they were planning for later tonight in the Grand Teatro Cervantes. Do you know anything about that, Kazim? The Grand Teatro Cervantes has been closed for years, after all, so what kind of party can it be?"

"It's a 'rave' of sorts," Kazim replied. "It's also a final dress rehearsal for the Apostles of Pandemonium, the band that they've assembled with the Gnawa musicians. A spontaneous illegal party to celebrate the start of their European tour. It should be great fun. You should come along."

"I don't know . . ." Moustapha said thoughtfully, looking at the moths circling the glass shield of the lantern. They were trying desperately to get through to the bright hissing flame, in which they would disappear with a sizzle and a puff of acrid smoke if they ever reached it. For some reason he felt like one of those moths.

"Everything is as it should be now, here in the cemetery," Kazim said. "A little celebration is certainly in order."

"Hmm, maybe," Moustapha said, staring into the bright white flame of the lantern.

Burroughs gave a signal to the other ghosts and they retreated to the cemetery entrance, where they gathered in the shadows just outside the pool of light cast by the single street lamp.

"You know," Burroughs said to the others, "I might have actually preferred a quiet, straightforward interment like that, rather than the circus that surrounded my own in St. Louis. And *then* we all had to wait after Patti Smith got dropped off by taxi at the front gate and insisted on *walking* all the way to the grave. Jesus fucking Christ."

"Prima donnas always spoil the fun," Gysin said.

"So, Mr. Tweed," said Burroughs. "Would you care to give us *your* account of what's been going on. I'm sure you have a most interesting tale to tell."

Tweed began with the phone call he received from Aicha, followed by the meeting with her and Moustapha in the cemetery and his bungled attempt to impersonate Burroughs's ghost, then took them all the way through the story up to the events of an hour ago, when his body was retrieved by Kazim and Moustapha from the labyrinth at the deserted villa on the Old Mountain and returned to St. Andrew's, sparing him the inglorious destiny of ending up as big cat food.

"You've certainly been put through the wringer," Burroughs said.

"Incredible," Bowles said with a smile. "I couldn't have come up with a more macabre tale myself."

"My apologies for impersonating your ghost," said Tweed. "Most disrespectful, I must admit. But I needed the money and it seemed like a harmless ruse at the time."

"Don't worry about it," Burroughs said. "Desperate men make desperate moves. But all that doesn't change anything. We still have to find the Ultrazone manuscript and destroy it before it destroys us and everybody else."

"What is this manuscript?" asked Tweed.

Burroughs was getting tired of repeating the story, but it was only fair to inform Tweed, since he was involved in it and had ultimately lost his life as a result of all that had taken place since Moustapha first dug the old fedora out of his trunk, thereby setting the whole mechanism of chicanery in motion. He told the story once more, right up to their encounter with the Barbary macaques in the crypt below the mausoleum.

"So Aicha is dead?" asked Tweed. "I wonder what *her* ghost is up to?"

"Certainly nothing good," Burroughs replied.

There was a sudden fluttering above them, and a large mottled-white seagull swooped down out of the darkness and perched on one of the pillars supporting the iron gate of the cemetery. Clasped in its beak was a sheet of paper.

The ghosts all looked at the seagull, and the seagull looked back at the ghosts.

"That's a strange mark on its forehead," said Bowles.

"Looks like a serpent," said Gysin.

The seagull opened its beak and the piece of paper floated to the ground. As Burroughs moved forward to pick it up, the seagull flapped its wings and disappeared into the night.

Burroughs picked up the paper and studied it in the light of the street lamp.

"What is it, Bill?" Dean asked.

After a long pause, Burroughs looked up at the other ghosts with a blank expression. "It's a page from the Ultrazone manuscript."

"How the hell did—"

Before Gysin could finish his question he was interrupted by the sound of the muezzin's pre-recorded call to Isha, the evening prayer, *Allahu akbar, Allahu akbar . . . ,* issuing more or less simultaneously from the loudspeakers on the many minarets of the city and echoing across Tangier's rooftops as they slipped behind the veil of night.

36

The muezzin's last call to prayer echoed away into the night, replaced by the usual evening Tangier soundtrack—the honking of cars and taxis, the occasional barking dog, some wind-blown fragments of an Arabic pop song, a yowling catfight, and a ship's horn bellowing forlornly from the harbor below. The ghosts still hovered just inside the gate of St. Andrew's cemetery, gathered now around Burroughs and looking over his shoulder at the yellowed page of the Ultrazone manuscript he still held in his hand.

Again they heard the fluttering noise, and the seagull swooped down with several more pages in its beak, which it released directly above them before disappearing into the darkness. The ghosts snatched the pages out of the air as they drifted down and unanimously confirmed they seemed to be more of the manuscript.

"Where's all this coming from, I wonder?" asked Gysin.

"Yeah, and just who is that feathered courier?" added Burroughs.

"Perhaps it's Aicha," said Bowles.

"Why do you say that?" asked Dean.

"That mark on its forehead; it looks exactly like Aicha's birthmark, the one she always tried to conceal with make-up," Bowles replied.

"Well, wherever this page came from, there is obviously more," said Burroughs. "That seems to be what our avian messenger is trying to tell us."

Brunhilde started giggling loudly.

"What's so funny?" asked Burroughs.

"This is great stuff. You must have been out of your mind when you wrote it."

"I'm not so sure it even was *my* mind that came up with it all."

"What do we do now?" asked Dean.

"First let's gather up these pages and stash them somewhere before they fall into the wrong hands again. Then we should spread out across Tangier and try to tune into the location of the rest of the manuscript. It's obviously no longer in the safe deposit box, since it's accessible even to a seagull. Then meet back here in one hour."

While the ghosts scoured the city's streets and alleys in search of the manuscript pages, Tony Mahoney, Ravi Khan, and their associates were getting ready in the Gran Teatro Cervantes. The rows of seats had been unbolted and cleared away, along with the piles of accumulated trash and debris, so while the place still had a dilapidated appearance, there was now ample room for dancing. A portable generator had been set up in an adjacent vacant lot to power the sound system and lights, which were now being connected by countless lengths of cable. Several makeshift bars had been set up underneath the balconies and were now being stocked with crates of Stork and Flag beer, as well as a complete cocktail bar, and next to that was a long food bar which would be serving up tapas and snacks, as well as hashish cookies, majoun, and other psychedelic delicacies. The Gnawa musicians were backstage tuning their instruments and warming the skins of their drums over a small brazier, tapping and turning the drums repeatedly until the right tones began to sound. They worked without speaking but not without a smile now and then, the light from many candles glinting off the occasional gold tooth.

Brion Gysin was the first to locate some pages of the manuscript, lying in the gutter in the Rue Mohamed Bergach. Tweed had returned to his apartment and from the roof above had located the pages now lining the bird cages on the balcony of Sayyad's apartment. He sensed there were more pages within the apartment, but decided not to look further, for fear of being spotted by that damn monkey, having learned already from the others that the highly developed sensory perception of some animals allowed them to see ghosts or other spirit forms that humans generally could not. The parakeets were in alarm modus and Tweed hurriedly removed the pages, since it wouldn't be long until someone came out to see what all the commotion was about.

Burroughs found the nest of pages behind the potted cactus beside the old Spanish Post Office in the Zoco Chico. As he quickly gathered them up, he detected more malevolent energy nearby. He slipped through the wall into the post office and soon found the source. Through the glass windows of the post office boxes he could see that the Ugly Spirit had already cloned every bit of correspondence into more Ultrazone madness. He slipped back outside, and his attention was drawn involuntarily to the street signs on the corner of the building opposite where he was hovering in the shadows. He watched in fascination as the white letters on the enameled signs began to squirm about, gradually breaking apart into a sort of white snow which then reformed into entirely new words. Where it had previously indicated "Rue Khatimi" the sign now read "Rue Dr. Benway," and "Rue Almohades" had now become "Rue Frisco Kid". Burroughs realized now that they were dealing with an uncontrollable evil force of a higher order, and that he and his fellow ghosts were totally out of their league. It was time for Plan B.

Burroughs was waiting inside the cemetery gate as the other ghosts returned, some with several manuscript pages, others with just a page or two, while Dean arrived empty-handed. Burroughs collected the sheets of paper and looked them over. All together, they added up to less than forty pages.

"Well," said Burroughs, looking with a dour expression at the meager sheaf he now held in his hand. "This won't do at all, will it? No bueno." He turned toward Tweed. "Now that your hypnotic powers have been revitalized, do you think you could take on another mass hypnosis job?"

"Who do you have in mind?" asked Tweed.

"Those Barbary macaques in the crypt. If we show them these pages and get them on the scent, you could hypnotize them and they could move out under the cover of darkness and probably do a better job than us in retrieving the rest of the manuscript. Their agility and sheer numbers already give them a big advantage over us."

"I'd be happy to give it a try, although I can't guarantee anything. But I do have *some* experience putting animals into a trance—long ago when I had a summer engagement at the Grand Theatre in Blackpool. And I did once hypnotize the Queen's corgis on the BBC!"

"God save the queen, it's an Ugly Spirit regime," muttered Burroughs, looking despondently at the brittle yellowed sheets in his hand. In that same moment he noticed a subtle flickering across the uppermost page. Looking closer he saw that the letters were in motion, swarming about like trails of ants. Some of them worked their way to the edge of the page and then leaped onto Burroughs's hand. Others followed until there was a steady stream of letters moving up Burroughs's arm. "Goddam word virus!" he exclaimed, throwing down the pages. "It's coming after me!"

Pancho and Lefty had finally broken through the back wall of the warehouse and crawled into the opening. Pancho sniffed the dank air. "Yes, this must be one of the old tunnels. It should take us to Bruno and the others. Cheikh, hand us those baskets of fruit, if you will."

Cheikh passed the baskets through the hole in the wall and then stuck his head inside to speak with Pancho and Lefty. "Once you've all eaten, come back here with the rest of the clan and we can search for a suitable truck. By tomorrow evening at the latest you should be on the ferry to Algeciras."

"Thank you, Cheikh. You've been most kind," Pancho said.

"It's the least I can do."

"And do consider joining us," Lefty added.

"I'll think about it."

Pancho and Lefty disappeared into the darkness of the tunnel, lugging the baskets of fruit.

Steetoo picked up the candle and went over to look inside the hole. It smelled dank and mysterious. "Where do you think this goes?" asked Steetoo, peering into the darkness.

"No idea," Sayyad said, looking over his shoulder. "But I'd like to know how they knew it was there."

"I don't think Cheikh is going to tell us."

"No."

"Let's see where it goes."

"I'd rather not."

"Are you afraid?" Steetoo asked.

"I didn't say I was afraid, I just said I'd rather not. That's different. I just don't think it's a good idea."

A chilly, musty draft from the netherworld suddenly blew out the candle, plunging them into darkness.

"And we need a better light," Sayyad added.

"*Kharra!*" Steetoo cursed, as he groped his way across the room to the box of matches on the table. He relit the candle and jammed it into the top of an empty wine bottle. "What about the safe deposit box? Did you find out what was in it?"

Sayyad made a dismissive gesture with his hand. "Just worthless old junk; a rusty knife, an old revolver, a bunch of papers and some other stuff. Nothing of any real value."

"It must have been valuable to someone, or they wouldn't have gone to the trouble of locking it all away, right? What kind of papers?"

"Just a bunch of old yellowed typewritten pages, all in English."

"Hmm, I'd like to have a look. Where are they now?"

"At home. I'll bring you some tomorrow and you can see for yourself."

The lights and sound system were all now in position in the Gran Teatro Cervantes, and the Apostles of Pandemonium were setting up their gear for the sound check. Tony Mahoney plugged his 1958 Gibson Les Paul Sunburst into a stack of Marshall amplifiers and hit the first few chords of "Stairway to Hell," which resounded like thunder in the vast expanse of the theater, loosening a few clumps of plaster from the ceiling over the stage. Ravi looked over at Tony and they exchanged mischievous grins.

"Did you hear that?" Gysin asked, looking in the direction of the Gran Teatro Cervantes. "What the hell was *that*?"

"A Gibson Les Paul guitar," answered Brian Jones with a knowing smile. "I'd know that lovely sound anywhere."

"They must be warming up for the rave in the Gran Teatro Cervantes," Burroughs said, scratching his arm where the black letters were crawling about on his translucent ghost-flesh. "Let's see if we can orchestrate our telekinetic powers and flip that broken piece of tombstone over on top of the manuscript pages so they stay put," he said. "There's no way I'm touching them again. The Ugly Spirit is obviously determined to get me by any means possible. Everly, you've held on to one page for the monkeys, right?"

The ghosts gathered in a circle and shut their eyes, concentrating on the slab of marble lying at their feet. It began to tremble and slowly rose into the air, then unsteadily into position above the pages of the manuscript. It hovered there for a few moments, then dropped with its full weight on top of the pages, sending up a cloud of dust.

"Well done," Burroughs said. "Everly, let's descend into the crypt and see if we can enlist the services of those macaques. The rest of you should maybe head over to the Teatro and we'll meet up there. Hopefully we'll have good news for you all."

"Best of luck, Bill," said Gysin, lifting off with the others and disappearing into the velvety blackness of the night.

Burroughs and Tweed floated into the mausoleum and down through the stone trapdoor, like two toothpicks passing through a slab of Jell-O. The macaques were still milling about, restless with hunger and growing concerned about how long Pancho and Lefty had been gone. Bruno looked puzzled as the two ghosts appeared before him, glancing first at Burroughs, then at Tweed, then back at Burroughs.

"Don't worry, my friend, you're not seeing double. This is Everly Tweed; I told you about him earlier. He's going to help us locate the manuscript. We could use your help as well, if you're willing."

"How could we help?" Bruno asked.

"Well, the manuscript is apparently no longer in the safe deposit box where it had been all those years. It now seems to be scattered all over the city. We've tried to retrieve it but there aren't enough of us. I'm sure you and your comrades would have much better luck, if we show you a page of the manuscript and you are willing to let Everly hypnotize you for the task."

Bruno looked around at the other macaques, then back at Burroughs. "What's in it for us?"

"I suspect you could use our assistance in your efforts to get to Gibraltar."

Again Bruno looked at the others, and after a round of collective eye contact the majority of them nodded their heads in unison.

"Okay, we'll do what we can. But what do you mean, he would hypnotize us?"

"Everly will put you into a trance, which will focus your attention and increase your awareness. Once you have absorbed the image of the manuscript, we hope you will be primed, like super-simian blood-hounds, and able to locate every page wherever it is to be found. When you return with the manuscript and it's all accounted for, Everly will take you out of the trance. It's safe, it's painless, and hey—it's just a state of mind."

From his back pocket Tweed pulled out the folded page of the Ultrazone manuscript and with his other hand he reached into his front pocket for the miniature monkey skull on a leather cord, his trusted tool for optical fixation. But before he could even raise the it into the air in view of the macaques, Burroughs grabbed it and enclosed it in his fist.

"That little trinket may have served you well in the past," he said quietly, "but in the present circumstances it might be perceived as rather inappropriate. You catch my drift?"

Tweed's startled expression gave way to one of reluctant acquiescence.

"Here," Burroughs said, producing the Indian-head five-dollar gold piece from his vest pocket. "Try this instead."

Tweed held up the gold coin, which glinted warmly in the light of the oil lamps, and the macaques moved in closer. He handed the brittle yellow typewritten sheet to Bruno, who glanced at it quizzically and gave it a disdainful sniff before passing it around.

"Repeat after me," Tweed said. "Your power is high among us; your power is high among us . . ."

Moustapha got to his feet and collected the two shovels. From the edge of the grave he picked up the gas lantern, which now cast angular flickering shadows between the tombstones. "I have to lock up the cemetery and go to my sister's. I thank you for straightening out this impossible mess, Kazim. I will be forever in your debt. These dead Nasranis have been one big headache."

Kazim brushed the dirt from his djellaba. "Think nothing of it, Moustapha. How can we mortals live in peace when the dead are in turmoil?"

Moustapha jumped with a start as something went racing by in the darkness, but when he raised the lantern he saw nothing. Then he heard a rustling between the tombstones, and he and Kazim turned to see a large group of macaques scampering through the cemetery toward the front gate. Zora jumped on top of a crooked obelisk, her tail as wide and bristly as the trunk of a date palm.

"Where did they come from?" Moustapha asked astonished.

"Indeed," said Kazim. "And where are they going in such a hurry?"

37

The macaques had stood on each other's shoulders until Bruno, at the top of the pyramid, could push open the stone trap door. They all pulled themselves up into the mausoleum and wrenched open the door just wide enough for them to slip out into the cemetery. From there they fanned out into the city in all directions in search of the Ultrazone manuscript.

Bruno shot through the gate of St. Andrew's cemetery like a rocket sled on greased rails. He knew exactly where he was going, without actually knowing it. The mandate was implanted in the very fiber of his being. He went flying down the Rue d'Angleterre and across the busy Grand Socco so fast that many passersby thought it was a panicked dog dashing down the street. He was just a blur of brown fur. The few who did recognize him as a Barbary macaque didn't realize it until Bruno was already out of sight.

He raced under the big keyhole archway on the other side of the Grand Socco and down the narrow Rue Siaghine. Here it was much more crowded, and Bruno had to weave his way in and out of the evening crowds. Often he had to leap up over tables and chairs or display stands in front of cafés and shops as he made his way down the hill at breakneck speed. Crossing the bustling Zoco Chico he continued down the Rue de la Marine until it became the Rue Dar Baroud. He continued at full speed as the street curved to the left past the Terrasse Borj al-Hajoui and the Café Texas.

Now he cut left into the Rue Beni Arross, then right into the Rue Vicente, and came to a sudden stop at its intersection with the Rue Mohamed Bergach. Somewhere up the street to his left, that's where he would find the manuscript, he was sure. On the corner was the Hamburguesa, doing a brisk business at that late hour. Bruno hadn't eaten all day and the smell of the hamburgers made him feel faint with desire, even though he had never eaten meat in his life. He felt himself wavering, torn between locating the manuscript and trying to snatch some food from the plate of an unsuspecting customer. It would only take a moment; he'd be gone before anyone realized what had happened. The juices in his mouth began to flow and his nostrils grew wider and wider.

It had been a long, bloody day, a day of many defeats and few victories, and Dr. Microbio decided he needed something to unravel the knot of tension deep inside him. After changing into more leisurely attire and putting on his favorite tweed jacket, his trusty pen and notebook in the inside pocket in case he should be struck with a flash of literary brilliance, he said good-bye to Khufu and Abdallah, locked up his office, and left for a well-earned nightcap in the Café de Paris.

He was immersed in his thoughts as he walked up the Rue de la Liberté, staring down at the sidewalk. A brightly colored card by the curb, about to fall into the gutter, caught his attention. He recognized it was a tarot card and bent to pick it up. Before coming to Tangier, the doctor had tried his hand at fortune telling and tarot readings in Gibraltar, mostly for English and Spanish tourists. It had not been a success, but he remembered the meanings of most of the cards. There she is, he thought: Justice sitting on her throne, a double-edged sword in one hand and scales in the other. A reminder of cause and effect— sometimes a warning as well. He slipped the card in his jacket pocket and continued up the street.

The tables outside the Café de Paris were all occupied by locals and tourists, but Dr. Microbio found a free table just inside one of the open glass doors, near the main entrance. It was actually a good location, as he had a prime view of the street and the Place de France, without being directly exposed to the endless entreaties of beggars and hustlers. He ordered a mint tea and placed his Mont Blanc fountain pen and a newly purchased Moleskine notebook in front of him on the table. Remembering the tarot card, he placed it next to his notebook, where he could study it more closely and ponder the potential ramifications of such a find. He had just taken the first sip of his tea when he noticed a familiar figure working his way down along the tables outside, gradually approaching the entrance of the café. It was Just-Call-Me-Ishmael, looking for a familiar face so he could strike up a conversation and hopefully mooch some small change or a cigarette.

It occurred to Dr. Microbio for the first time that there was something inconsistent about Just-Call-Me-Ishmael's appearance; if he was really as down and out as he professed to be, shouldn't he look *more* shabby and threadbare? As it was, he appeared somewhat rumpled, with a trace of five-o'clock shadow, his hair a tousled mop, but he looked reasonably healthy and well fed, with nothing of the gauntness of a true pauper.

Looking through the doorway, Just-Call-Me-Ishmael recognized Dr. Microbio, waved, and approached with the unmistakable rolling gait of a former seaman.

"Good evening, Doctor."

"Good evening, Just-Call-Me-Ishmael."

"May I join you, or are you expecting someone?"

"A visit from the muse, perhaps, otherwise no one. Please, have a seat," Dr. Microbio said, motioning toward the empty chair.

"Maybe the muse is already here," Just-Call-Me-Ishmael said, pointing at the tarot card as he sat down.

"Oh, I found it on the sidewalk on my way here."

"Well, that's a bit of a coincidence. Look what I found in the street earlier this evening while making my rounds."

Just-Call-Me-Ishmael threw down another tarot card on the table, which landed right next to Justice. It was The Sun.

"Ah, yes," Dr. Microbio said, quoting from memory; "You have great resources at your disposal, but constrain yourself, since it's possible to have too much."

"Ha!" exclaimed Just-Call-Me-Ishmael loudly. "I don't even know where my next meal is coming from and you're talking about great resources. Your humor is commendable, to say the least."

"That's the given meaning of the card. I didn't make it up."

"So what does yours mean?"

"We are judged by the consequences of our actions. If you have caused pain to others, now is the time to make amends. And if you have been wronged, you may soon receive redress."

"Well, I would drink to that, except I'm totally without resources at the moment."

The two men exchanged knowing glances and Dr. Microbio motioned to a passing waiter and ordered two mint teas.

"I also found this," Just-Call-Me-Ishmael said, producing a folded page of yellowed paper from an inside pocket of his jacket. He spread it out on the table next to the two tarot cards.

"What is it?" the doctor asked curiously, peering down at the paper through his slightly smudged nickel-rimmed glasses. There were unappetizing stains on the paper and a charred hole near one corner.

"Damned if I know, but it's some of the craziest shit I have ever read."

Dr. Microbio picked it up gingerly with his fingertips and started reading. It was in English, but it hardly made any sense. It seemed to be someone's poor attempt at Surrealism. But there was no detectable narrative holding it all together; it was all just juxtaposition and collage, much of it downright disgusting and, as far as Dr. Microbio was concerned, of no literary value whatsoever.

"Someone's dilettantish attempt to make a second cup of tea from William Burroughs," he said dismissively, dropping the page and brushing his hands together with obvious disgust.

"What if it's the genuine thing?" countered Just-Call-Me-Ishmael.

"Preposterous!" Dr. Microbio exclaimed. "And how would you account for its provenance? It just fell out of the sky and landed in the street?"

At that moment there was a loud commotion on the sidewalk. Raised voices and yelling and a woman's shrill scream, followed by the sound of breaking glasses and cups as patrons jumped up from their chairs. A macaque jumped through the open doorway and landed on the table between Dr. Microbio and Just-Call-Me-Ishmael. The two men stared in stupefaction into its yellow eyes, and the animal stared back at them with a menacing expression, then grabbed the yellowed sheet of paper and leaped out the open glass door, upsetting the glasses on a table outside as it scampered away down the street.

The two men looked at each other wide-eyed.

"What the . . . ?" Dr. Microbio began, but he was unable to finish.

"Never mind," said Just-Call-Me-Ishmael confidently and patted his jacket pocket. "I've got another page right here."

Evangeline and Piet decided to go out for dinner, then maybe to a bar for a few drinks before heading over to the rave. As they were crossing the hotel lobby toward the front door, they heard a "Pssst!" from the direction of the reception desk. Ali had a mischievous smile on his face, which was not unusual, but there was something more pronounced about it this time. He motioned them over with a wave of his hand and the three of them stepped into the empty lounge with its panoramic view of the harbor below, a myriad of lights reflecting in the waters of the bay.

"You're going to the rave later?" Ali asked.

"Yes," Evangeline said. "After dinner. Will we see you there?"

"I hope so, but I can't be sure. Here, I have a little something for both of you."

Ali produced a small blue glassine packet from his shirt pocket and handed it to Evangeline. She felt something small and hard inside. "Should I open it?" she asked.

"Yes, by all means."

She carefully unwrapped the tiny package and saw two tiny blue pills inside. On the inside of the wrapper was a curious logo, a grinning half-man, half-goat creature with an erect cock.

"Ecstasy," Ali said, nodding approvingly. "Every raver's friend."

"Wow, great," said Piet. "What do we owe you?"

"Nothing, my friends, it is a free sample from a very good colleague. I am promoting his wares, which are the finest in Tangier. If you want more, just ask Ali."

"'Just ask Ali,'" Piet repeated with a chuckle. Evangeline pocketed the tiny package, and they thanked Ali profusely, saying they hoped to see him later that night. They stepped outside and started walking down the Avenue Prince Moulay Abdellah. They had no particular destination; the plan was to wander down toward the harbor until they found a restaurant that looked appealing and affordable.

It was a fine evening, and everyone seemed to be out for a stroll.

They turned left into the Rue Jabha al Watania, and then right into the Rue Anoual, passing the Gran Teatro Cervantes on their left.

"The place looks like a total ruin," Piet said, as from inside the building came the sounds of loud music with deep bass tones that vibrated the street below their feet. "Must be the sound check."

"Yeah. Supposedly only rats and stray cats have been living there for years. I doubt they'll find the Apostles of Pandemonium to their liking."

"So who owns it?" Piet asked.

"I read that Spain sold it back to Morocco and it's supposed to be totally renovated and reopened soon."

They continued down the Rue Anoual until they came to the Rue de la Plage, then turned right toward the harbor. On the opposite hillside loomed the old Jewish Cemetery. When they reached the Boulevard Mohamed VI they walked along the wide promenade across from the train station, stopping occasionally to read the menus posted outside the doorways of the many restaurants and cafés there. They decided on Restaurante El Pescador, where they found an empty table outside with a view of the harbor lights just beyond the train station. The patrons at the other tables were a mix of tourists and locals. Evangeline ordered a fish tagine and Piet ordered grilled squid, along with a bottle of Cap Blanc white wine. Neither the food nor the wine was anything spectacular, but they were reasonably cheap and satisfying.

"That Ali guy is quite a character," Piet said, stirring some sugar into his espresso.

"Yeah, but he seems to mean well. That's what counts."

"I don't think I'd trust him, though. He's a bit *too* accommodating, you know what I mean? 'Just ask Ali.' Makes me wonder what's his motive."

"Is that how you judge people, by what ulterior motives they might have?"

"Don't you?"

From further down the promenade came a man's voice calling "Paloma? Paloma?" and they turned to see a figure in a ratty wool poncho and a battered black matador's hat making his way along the promenade. Even after he had passed them by and disappeared in the direction of the port they could still hear him occasionally calling "Paloma? Paloma?" as he walked along.

Piet decided to change the subject. "So what's your plan tomorrow?"

Evangeline drained her espresso and sat up straight in the wooden chair. "I'll be at the front door of the bank in the Place Brahim Roudani when they open at nine."

"Even if the rave goes all night?"

"Yes."

"And if you find the Ultrazone manuscript in the safe deposit box?"

"I'll book a ticket on the ferry to Algeciras and a train ticket from there back to London as soon as possible, to get the manuscript back home safe and sound. That really is the only reason I came to Tangier. Once I've looked through it, I'll contact some editors and agents and see if there is anything that can be done with it."

"And if the manuscript is not in the safe deposit box?"

"I'll burn that bridge when I come to it."

Piet looked down at the dregs in his cup. He felt a strong attraction to Evangeline and didn't want to watch her get on the ferry and sail out of his life tomorrow. But what could he do to make her stay longer, long enough for him to sort out his inner conflict? Was that even something he was going to be able to resolve?

After leaving the restaurant they continued along the promenade in search of a bar or café where they could have a few drinks before it was time to head over to the rave. Most of the places they passed were too bright and garish and full of tourists. Lord Nelson's Pub had been a real bona fide dive and they both enjoyed a bit of local color, or even downright weirdness, but the places they were passing now all seemed enveloped in the same pathetic torpor and were anything but inviting. They seemed more like a sort of Club Med purgatory.

"Hey," Piet said. "How about that place?"

Evangeline looked up at the hand-lettered sign hanging above the doorway of a small bar-café wedged between two restaurants: THE GOLDEN SARDINE. She smiled. "Like the Bob Kaufman book. That's a good omen."

There were only two outside tables, both of which were occupied, but the evening had grown a little cool, so they stepped inside and took a table near the window with a view of the harbor. Strange psychedelic music filled the air and a series of peculiar primitive looking paintings hung on the walls. The clientele seemed mostly local, but more like hipster-student types than dockers and seamen. The bartender came over to their table.

"Do you have a bottle of Cap Blanc?" asked Piet. He wanted to sound like he knew what he was talking about, even though he had never heard of Cap Blanc prior to their meal at El Pescador.

"Sorry, no white wine," answered the bartender. "Only red, a Halana Merlot."

Piet glanced at Evangeline and she nodded. "I can still switch from white to red, as long as the night is still young."

The waiter left and Piet looked over at the vintage Wurlitzer jukebox in the corner of the room. "What the hell is this crazy music?" he said and walked over the jukebox.

"So what are we listening to?" Evangeline asked.

"'MK Ultra Boogie' by the Albert Hofmann Blues Band, apparently. Sounds like Michael Bloomfield on acid. The flip side is called 'A Bicycle Built for the Blues.'"

"Wasn't Albert Hofmann Bob Dylan's manager?"

"That was Albert Grossman. Albert Hofmann invented LSD."

Once the waiter had brought the bottle of wine and two glasses and returned to his post behind the bar, Evangeline took out the glassine package, carefully unfolded it, laying it out flat on the table between them. The tiny blue pills looked like two minuscule eggs in a little blue bird's nest.

Burroughs and Tweed floated out of the mausoleum and hovered in the dark of the cemetery. Burroughs involuntarily scratched at his arm, but the itching seemed to know no end. They heard Kazim's Harley Davidson fading away as he went roaring home for a late dinner, while from the watchman's shack near the front gate they heard Moustapha putting away the shovels and the lantern.

Tweed turned to Burroughs with a sly smile. "While we're waiting for those apes to return with the goods, how about we have a little fun with Moustapha?"

"What do you have in mind?" Burroughs whispered back.

"Wait here until I give you a sign."

Moustapha was just shutting and locking the door of the shack when he heard a voice behind him and jumped. His nerves were still jittery after all that had transpired in the last few days.

"Hey, Moustapha, how's tricks?"

He turned around and saw the ghost of Everly Tweed. Or was it?

"Tricks? What tricks? What do you want?" Moustapha asked, his voice trembling with uncertainty. "I've seen to it that you received a proper burial. We have no further business, surely? What more do you want from me?"

"Nothing, Moustapha. Just wanted to say thanks for taking care of my remains. I also wanted to let you know that Walter Harris will no longer be troubling you. He's on his way back to Malta, by way of a magic carpet."

"Magic carpet?" Moustapha repeated incredulously.

"Yes. And now I'd like you to meet someone."

Tweed snapped his fingers and out of the darkness appeared the ghost of William Burroughs, who took up his place next to Tweed. Moustapha felt the blood leaving his brain and heading for his feet. His hands began to tremble, and little points of light flashed at the periphery of his vision. He looked at Tweed, then at Burroughs, then back to Tweed. There was a sudden rushing and swirling, but everything remained inert. Then it was like someone sliced through his knees with a machete and he collapsed in a heap on the mosaic paving stones, the ring of keys falling from his open hand with a loud clank.

38

Breaking through the wall of the warehouse into the tunnel had been exhausting work, and Pancho and Lefty now struggled to make their way to the crypt where the others were waiting for them. They had only eaten a few apples and oranges in the course of the entire day and their energy level was severely diminished. In the darkness of the tunnel their eyes were failing them. They were going by feel, but even that was proving insufficient.

"You know where we're going?" asked Lefty, trailing behind Pancho as they dragged the heavy baskets of fruit along.

"I think so."

They had in fact taken a wrong turn and were in the tunnel that led to the backstage area of the Gran Teatro Cervantes. From directly above them came the sound of extremely loud music with pulsing tones that seemed to vibrate the walls of the tunnel. "What *is* that noise?" asked Lefty.

"I don't know, Lefty, but it ain't Townes Van Zandt."

"Wait a minute," he said, halting and tilting his head to listen more intently. "It's that crazy song we've been hearing the last few weeks from just down the road where that music producer lives."

"I think you're right," Pancho agreed, listening to the chord changes and hypnotic beat of "Stairway to Hell." "But where's it coming from?"

"We must be close, so let's follow the tunnel and see. We can leave the baskets here and then come back."

They soon reached the end of the tunnel where the trap door led up into the Gran Teatro Cervantes. The music was now much louder. They tried to push open the trap door, but it hadn't been opened in years, and by now they were too weak to do so.

"Well," said Pancho. "It's not where we want to go anyway. Let's get the baskets and retrace our path. We must have missed the turn that leads to the crypt."

"Okay, but let's take a quick break first. I need a banana or two to get my strength up again."

At the corner of the Rue Mohamed Bergach and the Rue Vicente Bruno was engaged in a vigorous battle between his animal instinct and the powerful hypnotic trance into which Tweed had placed him. He could almost taste the hamburgers which were practically within his reach, but at the same time he could see in his mind's eye the Ultrazone manuscript lying in the basket in Sayyad's living room, and the ferry heading to Algeciras, and, just across the bay, the Rock of Gibraltar jutting up from the blue waters of the Alboran Sea.

Drawing on an inner strength he was not even aware he possessed, Bruno turned away from the Hamburguesa and went bounding up the Rue Mohamed Bergach. He stopped in front of a nondescript building and looked up at the windows. He saw a light in one of the windows and a colorful glow pulsing on the ceiling of the room where he needed to go. On the left side of the building, where it butted up against the building next door, a drainpipe ran from the roof all the way down to the street. He shimmied up it until he was level with the window and by craning his neck with an arm grasping the windowsill for support, he was able to peer inside the room. Two women were sitting staring at a flickering object. On the floor nearby Bruno could see the rattan basket that he knew contained what he was looking for. What he could not see was the television screen, which was angled away from him. The two women were watching a popular French cooking show with Spanish subtitles. But there was something wrong with the TV, or with the transmission, because the Spanish subtitles kept breaking up and reforming into English words. Mina could read them, but they had nothing to do with cooking, they didn't even make sense—like, breakthroughs in gray rooms, the 23 Screwball Department, and other nonsense. She kept pressing different buttons on the remote control, but nothing seemed to solve the problem.

Bruno shimmied further up the drainpipe and onto the roof of the building next door. He ran across the roof, skirting the multi-colored skylight, then let himself down onto the balcony of the apartment where he knew the manuscript was. The door from the balcony into the kitchen was open. Two caged birds started chattering nervously, but Bruno told them he was there to remove an evil spirit from the house, and the chattering stopped as quickly as it had begun.

"We know about it," one of the parakeets said to Bruno. "Fatoma lined our cages with papers infused with some strange spirit. Then just a while ago the ghost of our Nasrani neighbor appeared and re-moved them again. Very strange. We tried to tell him there were more pages inside, but he didn't seem to understand. He was in a hurry and seemed very afraid."

"Afraid?" repeated Bruno, looking puzzled. "What does a ghost have to be afraid of?" He took a deep breath and ran into the kitchen, down the hall, and through the open living room door. The two wom-en screamed in perfect unison, the younger one dropping the remote control, the older one throwing up her hands in sheer terror. Bruno grabbed the rattan basket with the manuscript and dashed out of the room and onto the balcony before the women even had a chance to move. He shoved a couple of wooden crates into place and scrambled up onto the roof, and was soon racing back down the Rue Mohamed Bergach, the basket clutched tightly under one arm. He had already turned the corner and run a hundred meters down the Rue Vicente when he suddenly stopped, raced back to the Hamburguesa, grabbed an XL High Atlas triple cheeseburger out of the hands of a shocked patron sitting outside, and shot back along the Rue Vicente, wolfing it down as he raced toward St. Andrew's.

In the wavering light of the single candle in their hideout, Steetoo was telling Sayyad about the episode in the cemetery with Abdul, Everly Tweed, the magic carpet, and the ghost of Walter Harris. Steetoo was prone to exaggeration, so Sayyad wasn't sure he should believe the entire story. He had no problem with the concepts of ghosts and djinns, having seen several himself, but the part about the magic carpet seemed a bit far-fetched. Still, it was certainly a good story and Steetoo told it well. Sometimes that was the most important thing—not whether the story was true or not, but how it affected you. Sayyad remembered his grandfather recalling the days before there was a television in every café, when storytelling played a central role in people's lives—both as communication and as entertainment. In a way, storytelling allowed the illiterate to be literate. His grandfather had been a gifted and respected storyteller himself, apparently. Unfortunately those storytellers were now gone, and many of their stories with them, since it was an oral tradition. These days people were just sponges, sitting in front of their TV screens and soaking up whatever trash was projected their way. And no TV could ever take you where a magic carpet could take you.

Steetoo had finished his story and the candle was burning low. The two boys sat together in silence for a few moments, savoring the thought of the ghost of Walter Harris and his earthly remains on their way to Malta.

Sayyad was first to break the silence. "I have to go home now," he said. "Or my mother will start to worry. Tomorrow I'll bring you some pages of that stuff from the safe deposit box. Maybe you can figure out what it says. Maybe it's an even crazier story than the one you just told me, and we can sell it and get rich."

They bid each other good night, and after Sayyad and Cheikh had crawled out the window into the narrow alley behind the warehouse, Steetoo replaced the boards from within.

The ghosts of Burroughs and Tweed had retreated into the dark interior of the cemetery, but they could still see Moustapha, who was just now struggling to his feet. He looked all around and quickly gathered his keys and shoulder bag in his trembling hands, then went through the gate, locking it behind him and walking briskly away without looking back.

"I know that was a mean trick," Tweed said. "But I couldn't help myself."

"Totally harmless in comparison to what else has been going on."

"And it *was* Moustapha who started all this trouble."

"You're right about that," Burroughs said, scratching at his arm again. "Jesus, this damn word virus is worse than a junk itch."

Hearing a noise from the direction of the cemetery entrance, Burroughs and Tweed turned to see one of the macaques bounding over the gate with a handful of papers and heading toward the mausoleum. Soon more arrived, each of them carrying more pages.

"Looks like your powers are still with you, Everly. Well done. We never could have managed that by ourselves."

"I just hope I remember how to pull them out of the trance."

"Shall we go below and see what they've turned up? First we should collect the other pages from under that tombstone there. I think the two of us can manage it. But I'm not touching a single page again. No way."

"No problem, I'll take care of that. The Ugly Spirit and I have no issues."

"Not yet."

Tweed gathered up the handful of pages that had been under the tombstone, and he and Burroughs descended into the crypt. Using an old human tibia bone that was lying on the floor, Burroughs began poking through the growing pile of papers that the macaques had deposited on what had apparently been a sacrificial altar.

"Can't believe I wrote all this stuff," Burroughs said, shaking his head as he scanned various pages.

"But maybe you didn't," Tweed said.

"Ah, good point."

More macaques arrived by the minute, dropping down through the open trap door of the mausoleum, and the pile of manuscript pages on the altar continued to grow.

Then Bruno's head appeared in the open trap door, bearing a victorious smile as well as a smear of mustard from the triple cheeseburger he had devoured along the way.

"Look what I've got," he said, lowering the rattan basket into the waiting paws of a couple of the taller macaques.

"Oh God," Burroughs said, taking a few steps back. "I can feel the Ugly Spirit growing stronger now. And it doesn't feel good."

Tweed removed the thick bundle of pages from the basket and placed it with the other pages. When the last of the macaques had returned and all the pages were piled up on the altar, he then arranged them into a single stack. "Wow," he said, standing back to look at it. "That's thicker than the Central London phone book."

"Thicker than the London and Manhattan phone books put together," Burroughs said. "Jesus Christ, what was I thinking?"

"How do we know it's all here?"

"We don't," Burroughs said. "It's not as if I numbered the pages, after all. We'll just have to trust that the apes did a thorough job, thanks to your hypnotic spell. Of course, if there's even a single page still unaccounted for, it could conceivably start self-reproducing at any time."

"A sort of ticking Ugly Spirit time bomb."

"Exactly."

"So what now?" Tweed asked.

"While you pull our furry friends out of that trance, I'll look for a place to stash the manuscript until we come back from the rave. It should be safe here for the time being, under the eyes of our Barbary macaque security force. Tomorrow we'll figure out a way to destroy it. Burn it, drown it, drop it in an acid bath—I don't know what's best. Maybe the rave experience will suggest a solution."

Tweed placed the entire manuscript in the rattan basket, then pulled the Indian-head five-dollar gold piece out of his pocket and turned toward the macaques, who were all looking at him with expressions of tempered expectation.

"Repeat after me," Tweed said. "Your power is high among us; your power is high among us . . ."

Burroughs was meanwhile scouring the interior of the crypt. In a niche carved out of the stone wall at the rear sat a cobwebbed miniature sarcophagus, not much bigger than a microwave. He slowly tested the lid, which he was just able to lift. Lying inside were a few dry animal bones—maybe those of a dog or a cat—otherwise it was empty. There was just enough room to fit the basket with the manuscript inside.

When Tweed had all the macaques' attention focused on the gold coin he held between his fingers, he shouted "One, two, three, four, *five*! Back to reality—*look alive!*" He now clenched the coin tightly in his fist so that it disappeared from view. There was a collective sigh from the macaques, and a palpable release of tension. They looked at one another with slightly startled expressions, touching each other as though to check if it was indeed reality they found themselves in again.

"Well done, Everly. Now put that basket with the manuscript in here," Burroughs said, pointing at the open sarcophagus. Tweed did as he was told and replaced the stone lid.

"Bruno, where did you find that basket with the bulk of the manuscript?" Burroughs asked.

"In an apartment near the harbor."

"You know what street?"

"You said to collect manuscript pages, not street names."

"Yeah, okay. What about landmarks?"

"There was a hamburger place on the corner," Bruno said, his tongue flicking at the dab of mustard in the corner of his mouth.

"That sounds like my street," Tweed said.

"And next door to your place is where that kid with the monkey lives, right?"

"Right. With his sister and their mother. I see them in the street sometimes."

"So when the kid had my hat, he must have found the key in the hatband and somehow retrieved the manuscript from the safe deposit box. Then the hat was given back to the girl. I wonder if she knows about the key?"

"Maybe that's why she's here in Tangier," Tweed suggested.

Burroughs turned back to the macaques. "Bruno, you and your crew please keep an eye on that sarcophagus until we get back from the rave," he said, pointing. "No one is to open the lid or touch what's inside. In the morning we'll get you guys lined up with a truck to Spain. Tomorrow night you'll be eating bollos de hornazo and English marmalade with the Rock of Gibraltar firmly under your hairy asses." Burroughs and Tweed bid the macaques farewell and floated through the open trap door and out through the mausoleum like smoke going up a chimney.

After leaving Dr. Microbio at the Café de Paris, Just-Call-Me-Ishmael decided to return to his apartment for a while before heading over to the rave at the Gran Teatro Cervantes. He wasn't much of a party person, but the rave was an excellent opportunity to cultivate the public image of his fictional alter-ego. To be seen mooching drinks and cigarettes from the rave-goers would further cement his reputation as an impoverished mendicant in the Tangier collective consciousness. No one could imagine in their wildest dreams the wealth of Gauguins, Cézannes, Pissarros, Beckmanns, and Van Goghs slumbering in captivity in his villa on the Old Mountain.

As he walked along, he recalled the strange scene at the Café de Paris with Dr. Microbio. Where had that monkey come from? It almost seemed like he knew what he was looking for when he grabbed that yellowed manuscript page. But how could that be? And if he did know, why didn't he try to get the other page Just-Call-Me-Ishmael had in his pocket? He couldn't make sense of it all and pushed the scene out of his mind again.

When he reached his apartment in the winding Rue Bab Assa, he unlocked the multiple high security locks after glancing around to make sure he wasn't being observed, and let himself in, locking the door again behind him. It was a two-story apartment, with a kitchen, bathroom, and tiny living room on the ground floor, and two small bedrooms upstairs. He got a bottle of beer from the fridge and went up the steep narrow stairs to his bedroom. By the mirror on the dresser was the crated Schwitters collage. Taking the tarot card and the folded page of the manuscript out of his jacket pocket, he set them down on the dresser and hung his jacket on the back of a chair. He opened the single window and looked across the narrow street, where he had a view of a tiny bit of the harbor through a small gap between two buildings. He could see the bow of a ship and a crane swinging back and forth in the bright lights of the long mole. After all these years, the sight of ships and harbors still gave him a sort of romantic rush. And coupled with the knowledge that his upcoming trip by ferry and train would revitalize his bank account, he could look into the immediate future with confidence.

He sat on the edge of the bed and took a large gulp of his beer. Although the Schwitters collage was neatly packed up in its crate, ready for delivery to the Zurich auction house, Just-Call-Me-Ishmael decided he wanted one last look at it, his final chance to spend some time alone relishing its bizarre Merz imagery before he had to part with it for good.

He carefully removed the collage from its crate and propped it against the mirror, next to the tarot card and the manuscript page, then returned to the bed and leaned back with his feet up, sipping at his beer, fully absorbed in the collage, as someone else might watch their favorite TV program.

But something was amiss. Just-Call-Me-Ishmael rubbed his eyes and sat up to look closer at the collage. The text fragment from a German newspaper glued in the lower right corner seemed to be swimming in and out of focus as if it were alive. He scooted over to the side of the bed and, his feet on the floor, looked even closer at the collage. The words had stopped swarming about and were lined up in orderly sentences again. But they were no longer in German; they were in English now, in the typeface of an old typewriter—a typeface that was somehow familiar. He unfolded the manuscript page and looked at it. The typeface was identical. In fact, the writing in the newspaper fragment in the Schwitters collage was now just a continuation of the text on the manuscript page, more pseudo-Burroughs madness. What the fuck was going on?

39

It was close to midnight when Evangeline and Piet finally left the Golden Sardine. On their way to the Gran Teatro Cervantes they decided to make a loop through the medina by way of the stairs at the Bab Dar Dbagh gate. As they walked along the Rue des Postes in the direction of the Zoco Chico and passed the Rue Skiredj, Piet came to a halt and started laughing.

"What's so funny?" Evangeline asked, also aware of the subtly increasing psychic riptide occasioned by the Ecstasy pills they'd taken.

Still laughing, Piet pointed up at the corner of the building, where two blue and white enameled street signs were just visible in the low-wattage light of a street lamp. The sign that had earlier read "Rue des Postes" now indicated "Rue Talking Asshole," while "Rue Skiredj" had become "Rue Spare Ass Annie."

"Wow, that's pretty good stuff Ali gave us," said Piet, still grinning.

Evangeline stared at the signs. "I don't think that's the Ecstasy."

"What do you mean?"

"It's unlikely we'd both be having the same hallucination at the same time. I see 'Rue Talking Asshole' and 'Rue Spare Ass Annie'—is that what you see?"

Just hearing Evangeline say the names made Piet start laughing again. "Yeah, that's what I'm seeing, and that's what I'm hearing. Holy shit!"

"Someone must have changed the signs."

"Maybe the city did, to honor the late great William S. Burroughs."

"Here in the medina, where it's mostly Muslims? I doubt it."

"Maybe we should ask Ali," Piet said, unable to get the grin off his face.

They continued up the street at a leisurely pace, marveling at the variety of colors, sounds, and smells, all now much more intense than before. It was a roller-coaster ride of sensations: one minute they would be struck by the psychedelic designs on a wall of tiles, or the incredible color combinations of the facades of successive buildings they walked past, or a woman's intriguingly beautiful eyes peering out of an otherwise veiled face amid the crowds; then they would see a passer-by with a shriveled arm, or a club foot, or a hare lip, or whose face had been partly eaten away by some horrible skin disease. Multiple autonomous realities seemed to be operating simultaneously, each vying for the dominant role, each reality dependent on yet another in an endless continuum of revelation.

When they reached the Rue Siaghine they turned left toward the Zoco Chico. Piet looked up at the street sign: "Rue Izzy the Push." Under any other circumstances it might have mystified or even worried him, but right now it just seemed funny. Extremely funny. That there was no rational explanation for the changing street signs seemed totally irrelevant. As they neared the Zoco Chico they were set upon by a group of would-be "guides," mostly kids, all clamoring for their patronage. "You want see Kasbah?" "You want buy kif?" "You want cheap hotel?" "Where you go? That wrong way!" Evangeline shook her head and made a gesture with her hand as if brushing away a swarm of pesky mosquitoes. This just seemed to encourage them more. They fell in behind Evangeline and Piet and followed them as they walked along, their exhortations increasing in frequency until they merged into an indecipherable loop of noise that trailed behind them like an annoying sonic cloud.

When they reached the Gran Teatro Cervantes and went through the opening in the high wrought iron fence that surrounded the building, the kids dropped back. From within the Teatro came a steady, almost subsonic drone, underpinned by a strange cyclical rhythm.

Evangeline and Piet followed the other rave-goers around the corner of the building to a side door where people waited in line. They hadn't been told anything about tickets or invitations and, seeing the line of people, Piet became a little apprehensive about whether they would be admitted. He thought about asking someone else in line but decided against it, reluctant to appear not in-the-know. Evangeline didn't think about it; she just figured they'd get in.

As they neared the door they saw two burly Moroccan bouncer types flanking the entrance, dressed in shimmering metallic-blue satin djellabas and matching turbans, with jeweled scimitars tucked into their belts. They eyed the potential ravers with piercing expressions of unsettling neutrality that conveyed the sense of a human X-ray machine. Just as it was their turn, Evangeline recognized Ali's face inside the doorway. He stepped forward and said something to one of the bouncers, who signaled Evangeline and Piet to enter. A woman in a strange costume of studded black leather that revealed much white skin, and with a spiky platinum-blonde Mohawk streaked with iridescent blue and eyes encircled with raccoon-like black make-up, reached forward with a rubber stamp and firmly marked the inside of Evangeline and Piet's wrists.

"Welcome," said Ali with a toothy grin and a knowing look. "Great that you made it. Things are just getting under way."

Pancho and Lefty crawled up the last stone steps and into the crypt, collapsing at the feet of Bruno and a group of macaques in conversation. When the rattan baskets of fruit hit the ground, they flopped over and spilled their contents. Apples, oranges, pears, bananas, and melons went rolling across the floor of the crypt in a soft, thudding cascade, rapidly followed by the sounds of the macaques falling on the fruit and devouring it in a ravenous assault.

"What happened? Where have you been?" asked Bruno forcefully but with a note of almost fatherly concern.

"We got lost. Took the wrong tunnel," Lefty said, sitting up and reaching for a watermelon that had rolled to a stop against his leg.

Pancho explained about the truck parking over the grating and cutting off their return route, and how they had then wandered through the streets until they happened on Cheikh and Sayyad. How they were then led to a disused warehouse down by the harbor, where they discovered an arm of the tunnel system behind the back wall of the warehouse. Pancho also told them of Cheikh's offer to help them find a truck headed for Algeciras on the ferry.

Bruno in turn told Pancho and Lefty about their group being hypnotized by Tweed and ferreting out the scattered manuscript pages, which were now collected and stashed in the crypt, and of the ghosts' offer to help them find a truck going to Spain in return for having brought back the manuscript, which the ghosts planned to destroy.

Bruno was the oldest of the macaques—probably somewhere in his twenties, no one knew for sure. He was still physically fit and frisky, but was clearly moving towards the end of his life, and there was considerable speculation among the macaques as to who should succeed him as the group's leader, and when. There were two factions: one held that Bruno should remain their leader for as long as he lived, given his wealth of experience, and distrusted anyone who might question his authority; the other, the younger and more forward-looking faction, had concluded it was time for Bruno to step aside and let Pancho take over, given the latter's relative youth, his exemplary bravery, and his general disposition, which was that of a born leader.

Group decisions often ended in a standoff now, with the Bruno faction winning out by default. Since the macaques were twenty-three in number, any one of them could theoretically tip the vote the other way, but it hadn't happened yet. Pancho had enormous respect for Bruno, who had been their leader for as long as he could remember, and he did not relish the thought of challenging his authority. But he also saw that Bruno's decision-making ability sometimes seemed to be impaired. It was clear to Pancho and the youth faction that it would be best if Bruno stepped down—for the safety of the group, and also to spare Bruno any potential indignities that increasing age, even senility, might bring. But Pancho had so far been reluctant to initiate any action that could be interpreted as disrespectful to Bruno, or as a grab for power. Diplomacy underpinned by logical arguments would be essential.

"So what's the plan," Pancho asked as he got to his feet. He wanted to be on eye level with Bruno for any possible confrontation.

"We wait here until the ghosts return," Bruno said matter-of-factly, as though it was something hardly worth repeating.

Pancho waited a few moments before replying, hoping that other macaques might realize for themselves the inherent weakness in Bruno's plan. But the crypt was filled with the sounds of the other macaques consuming the bounty of fruit, and this seemed to be occupying their attention, although some had cocked an ear in the direction of Bruno and Pancho, curious to see how the discussion might develop.

"Would it not perhaps be better to move as a group through the tunnel to the warehouse, where we'd be closer to the harbor, and where Cheikh can better assist us?" Pancho suggested.

"The ghosts already said they would help us."

"The ghosts?" repeated Pancho questioningly. "The ghosts of some *old white men*? The same kind who robbed us of our freedom and kept us in captivity all these years? Surely we can't trust them more than a brother macaque?"

A barely audible murmur swept through the crowd of macaques. They stopped eating and looked up at Bruno and Pancho.

"We made an agreement," Bruno said. "It's a matter of honor for us to uphold our side of the agreement, which was that we would wait here and watch over the manuscript until the ghosts return."

With a loud cracking noise, Lefty broke open the watermelon on the stone floor and noisily bit into a chunk of the red juicy fruit, spitting out the seeds as he ate.

"Maybe we should vote on it," Pancho said, looking around at the others.

"If you feel it's necessary. I think you will find that the majority is with me," Bruno said confidently as he peeled a banana.

"Okay," Pancho said. "How many of you are for staying here in the crypt and waiting for the ghosts to return and help us?"

Eleven paws went up.

"And how many are for moving down the tunnel and regrouping in the warehouse, where our brother Cheikh has undertaken to help us?"

Another eleven paws were raised.

Only Lefty had not raised his paw either time, busy as he was gobbling watermelon. Everyone looked at him in anticipation as pink juice trickled down his hairy chin. He looked into their expectant faces with his yellow eyes and continued munching on a large mouthful of melon. He spat out a few more shiny black seeds, scratched himself nonchalantly under one arm, and then raised his left paw.

"So it's decided," Pancho said. "Once we've eaten we leave for the warehouse."

"We can't leave the manuscript unattended," Bruno objected. "I gave our word."

"We'll take it with us."

"But how will they find it?"

"They're ghosts. They'll find it."

The newly established dance floor of the Gran Teatro Cervantes was crowded with colorfully decked-out ravers from seemingly all walks of life—tourists as well as locals—all merged together in a sea of bodies bobbing to the music of the DJ, who had set up on the center balcony at the back of the huge room. Classic acid house tracks were being blasted through the theater by a wall of speakers and subwoofers on either side of the stage. Many were dancing the Melbourne shuffle, which had just recently made a comeback on international dance floors. Smoke from the kif, hash, and incense mingled with the clouds of white mist that the fog machines emitted periodically and was illuminated by colored spotlights and lasers sweeping back and forth across the room, punctuated by the flickering of a strobe light.

Multicolored fluorescent designs on the clothes worn by many of the ravers glowed brightly in the light of the banks of black lights. Some wore gloves with fingertip LED lights and formed sweeping gestures of light by waving their arms in time with the music. From the balconies more partygoers looked down at the dance floor, drinking from plastic glasses and passing around thumb-thick joints. Around the perimeter of the dance floor, just underneath the balconies, fire-eaters, snake charmers, magicians, and acrobats provided an ongoing show. A giant mirror ball suspended from the center of the ceiling slowly rotated, sending shafts of color jabbing through the fog and smoke, while tiny spots of light coursed around the entire room like a psychedelic carousel.

Evangeline and Piet made their way around the back of the crowd to one of the improvised bars and ordered glasses of wine. Although Ali had said things were just getting underway, it seemed to them as if they'd walked into something that had been going on forever. There was something primordial and communal about the scene that seemed to exist independently of time. It was the party that was always going on somewhere in the world. While they waited for their wine, Piet tapped Evangeline on the shoulder and pointed to a large banner hanging from the ceiling down to the floor. It was made of a shimmering blue material that wafted in the shifting air currents and at its center was a giant red sparkling logo—that grinning figure again, half-man and half-goat, legs spread to show his erect cock. Other such banners were suspended at intervals throughout the vast room.

The ghosts of Burroughs and Tweed slipped into the Teatro through an upper-story broken window like two pigeons returning to their roost. They were on the balcony at the back, just behind the DJ's podium. They drifted forward to the railing but stayed in the shadows, not wanting to risk being spotted by anyone who might possess the ability to see them. They looked down in awe at the scene below, the pulsing crowd, the hovering clouds of colored smoke and fog, a huge screen behind the stage onto which were projected colorful flashing computer-generated images and designs. The entire building vibrated to the rhythm of the acid house bass lines.

Burroughs yelled to Tweed, "23 skidoo, the joint is jumping!"

"Hey," Tweed said, looking over toward the podium. "Look who the DJ is."

Dressed in an iridescent blue djellaba with a pair of headphones clamped over his blue turban, rocking back and forth to the music, a broad smile across his ebony black face revealing pearly white teeth that clenched a smoldering joint, was the Blue Messiah himself, his left hand tweaking the knobs of a Roland TR-909 drum machine, his right hand massaging the keys of a TB-303 synthesizer.

40

As soon as Sayyad and Cheikh stepped into the apartment, Cheikh put his nose to the floor and began sniffing back and forth frantically.

"What is it, Cheikh?" Sayyad asked.

"Is that you?" he heard Mina asking from the living room.

"Yes, of course, who else?"

Mina seemed nervous as she came down the hall.

"What's wrong?" Sayyad asked, unsnapping Cheikh's leash and hanging it by the door.

"While Mama and I were sitting in the living room, a macaque burst into the room, grabbed the basket with the papers and ran out again!"

"Another macaque?"

"Much bigger than Cheikh. And it was like he knew exactly what he was looking for. He ran back out onto the balcony and disappeared over the rooftops. Mother almost had a heart attack!"

Sayyad and Cheikh went into the living room and looked at where the basket had been. Then Sayyad said some comforting words to his mother and went out onto the balcony. Cheikh was still sniffing everywhere, following the scent of the intruder.

Sayyad stood and listened to the sounds of the night, which at that moment consisted of the metallic banging of cargo hatches and the groaning of hydraulic cranes from the harbor below. And from somewhere not too far away came the pulsing beat of very loud music. He gazed up at the stars and speculated about the macaque stealing the basket with the papers. Was it maybe one of the two they'd met today? But they were not much bigger than Cheikh. Perhaps it was another member of their clan. But why steal the basket with the papers? What value could they hold for a macaque? His speculations were ruptured by Mina's voice from the kitchen.

"Are you hungry, Sayyad? There's kefta and salad and bread. We've already eaten."

He looked at the jagged skyline of the medina against the soft silky glow of the night sky and went back into the kitchen.

Just-Call-Me-Ishmael was overwhelmed by the generosity of the ravers who by now had filled the Gran Teatro Cervantes. As he made his way around the perimeter of the dance floor, stopping to linger at the various bars set up under the balconies, it seemed like anyone he asked for a drink or a cigarette was more than happy to fulfill his wish. Soon he was quite drunk. Not so drunk that he didn't occasionally think about the strange episode of the Schwitters collage in his room earlier, and the scene with Dr. Microbio and the macaque at the Café de Paris, but both those incidents now seemed part of another world, their significance slowly fading as the Ecstasy some cute raver girl had given him began to take effect, drawing him into an entirely other world.

The Blue Messiah was subtly shifting musical genres in preparation for the grand finale of the evening. He had worked his way through sets of acid house and drum 'n' bass and was now playing a set of dub techno before transitioning to acid trance—the perfect prelude for the live show that would follow. On the stage, roadies and technicians were uncovering instruments and amplifiers, adjusting microphones and lights in readiness for the appearance of the Apostles of Pandemonium.

Hidden in the wings behind musty curtains, the ghosts of Brian Jones and Brion Gysin watched with growing anticipation as the stage was prepared for the band. A roadie was removing electric guitars from a large flight case and standing them up in racks—beautiful Telecasters, Stratocasters, Gibson SGs, Les Pauls, and other vintage electric guitars of inestimable worth.

"Oh wow!" Jones gasped. "Look at that! A white Vox MK III teardrop just like I had!"

"Well," said Gysin. "Even ghost wishes can be granted. You've got your work cut out for you now. When the show gets going, you can plug into one of those spare amps and let it rip. They'll never know what hit 'em."

Steetoo woke up in the darkness with a start, certain there was someone else in the room. He groped for the matches and lit the candle, then looked around the room until his eyes met those of Pancho and Lefty. Then another macaque crawled through the hole in the wall, followed by another and another, until the little room was almost full.

"What do you want?" Steetoo asked, knowing he would receive no answer. Although they were half his size, he was vastly outnumbered and not entirely unafraid. The largest macaque, who also appeared to be the oldest, stepped forward as though he wanted to answer Steetoo's question. But no answer came forth, and the big macaque looked at the other macaques with a puzzled expression.

Pancho looked around the room, then went over and pointed at a wall calendar hanging by a single nail hammered into the cement wall. It was from the FRS ferry company. He jumped up on a wooden crate and with the calendar still on the wall, he flipped through the pages until he came to a large photograph of the Rock of Gibraltar, then pointed at the picture and looked at Steetoo.

"You want to go to Gibraltar?"

Pancho nodded, along with many other macaques.

"And how do you want to get there?"

Pancho flipped through the calendar again until he came to a photo of a large blue and white ferry, the *Morocco Star*, which plied the route between Tangier and Algeciras. He pointed at the ferry and looked at Steetoo again.

"Ah, you want to take the ferry to Algeciras. As paying passengers?"

Pancho shook his head and flipped through the pages once more until he came to a photo of a line of trucks waiting to board the ferry. He tapped on one of the trucks with a hairy finger.

"Okay, I get it. You want to stow away on a truck that is taking the ferry to Algeciras, and from there make your way to the Rock of Gibraltar. Right?"

The macaques grinned and jumped up and down, chattering and showing their large yellow teeth.

"Why didn't you just say so?" said Steetoo with a smile.

Steetoo looked at the battered old alarm clock on the makeshift table next to the candle. It was just after two a.m.—a good time for stealthy reconnaissance in the harbor.

Steetoo pointed at Pancho. "You come with me," he said. "The others will have more space if they wait out in the big hall, through here."

Steetoo opened the door of the little room and stepped into the main part of the warehouse, empty except for a few derelict trucks and some old washing machines and refrigerators stacked in a corner. From a street lamp outside, a thin shaft of light shone in through a dirty window high in the warehouse wall, but the warehouse was mostly dark. The macaques followed Steetoo, Bruno still clutching the basket with the manuscript under his arm.

The macaques made themselves as comfortable as they could in the gloom, while Steetoo and Pancho went back into the hideout. Steetoo removed the boards from the window and the two of them climbed out into the narrow alley. Once he had replaced the boards, they walked to the Boulevard Mohamed VI and turned left toward the harbor. Many large trucks were already parked there for the night, waiting to board ferries to Algeciras, Marseille, Barcelona, or Genoa in the morning. Street lights cast broad pools of orange-hued light throughout the harbor, but there were also large areas of shadow, and Steetoo and Pancho kept to these as much as possible while moving along the lines of parked trucks.

The harbor was almost deserted. One old cargo ship was being unloaded, and every now and then a large forklift zoomed past Steetoo and Pancho, who slipped into the shadows until it had gone by. In some of the trucks the drivers were sleeping or watching TV in the sleeping berths behind their seats. Steetoo made out muffled laughter, sirens, gunshots, and music from different TV shows as they scurried along. At one point Steetoo held up his hand and pointed at a truck with a large canvas-covered bed. He walked slowly along the side of the truck, stopping now and then to peer under the canvas to determine how full the truck bed was. Then he went around to the front of the truck and carefully climbed on the front bumper so he could look into the cab. In the street light's orange glow he scanned the documents he saw lying on the dashboard: clearance from customs and a ticket for the ferry to Genoa. Steetoo stepped down and they continued, repeating the process with other trucks until Steetoo found what he was looking for: a large red and yellow truck with a gray canvas-covered bed carrying cases of olive oil. The truck had cleared customs and was booked on the one p.m. ferry to Algeciras. He carefully undid some of the lashing and peeked under the tarp. If they moved some of the cases around, there would be room for all the macaques just behind the cab. Departure was less than twelve hours away.

Try as he might, Sayyad could not sleep. He lay there, with Cheikh curled up in his basket at the foot of the bed, and tossed and turned, thinking about the pile of pages that had been taken, about the other macaques, the key in the hatband of the fedora, Everly Tweed, the European couple, and how it all might fit together. But he could make no sense of it.

He got out of bed and dressed as quietly as possible. Cheikh was ready to go immediately, as though he had been waiting. They slipped into the hall and Sayyad attached the leash to Cheikh's collar. Silently he unlocked the door, eased it shut behind them, and locked it again.

The Rue Mohamed Bergach was deserted and silent at that late hour. They passed the Hamburguesa, now closed but still emitting greasy and savory aromas, and continued down the hill toward the harbor. As they neared the narrow alley off the Boulevard Mohamed VI where the deserted warehouse was located, Sayyad saw a familiar figure emerge from the shadows. It was Steetoo, accompanied by a macaque.

"Who's that with you?" Sayyad asked. Cheikh was jumping up and down.

"One of your furry friends. He came back through the tunnel, with about twenty of his clan. They want to stow away on a truck going to Algeciras."

"How do you know that?"

"I'm learning to speak macaque. You know I'm good with languages," Steetoo said with a smile. "But what are you doing here in the middle of the night? Won't your mother be angry if she finds out you're gone?"

"They're all asleep, they won't even know. But I couldn't sleep. That manuscript I was telling you about from the safe deposit box—it was stolen, right out of the living room before my sister and mother's eyes—by a macaque!"

They both looked at Pancho and Cheikh, who were quietly having their own conversation. Pancho was telling Cheikh how Tweed's ghost had hypnotized the others and how they had all gone off to find the manuscript and bring it all back to the crypt. It must have been Bruno who found the basket full of pages in Sayyad's apartment. Then the Burroughs ghost had stashed the manuscript in the crypt, and Bruno had agreed they would watch over it until the ghosts returned, in return for help in stowing away on the ferry. He went on to explain about the disagreement and the vote, and how they had all come down the tunnel to the warehouse, and now Steetoo had found a truck for them that was headed for Algeciras.

"Let's go inside and see if they brought the manuscript with them," said Sayyad. "I get the feeling it's something valuable."

"I told you that already," said Steetoo.

The four of them climbed in through the window and put the boards back in place. They found the macaques eating the last remnants of fruit they had brought with them, Bruno still protectively holding the rattan basket with the manuscript.

"That's it," Sayyad said, pointing at the basket. "But I don't like the idea of trying to take it from that big macaque."

"Me neither. But if they take it with them on the ferry, we'll never see it again."

"So what do we do?"

"I don't know. Let's go in the back room and think about it."

Steetoo and Sayyad returned to their hideout, while Cheikh stayed with the other macaques.

Pancho stepped up to Bruno: "We found a ferry that is leaving for Algeciras tomorrow at one p.m. I think we should go now and get settled in the truck while it's still dark. We have to rearrange the cargo so that we have enough room but can't be seen if anyone peeks inside." He looked down at the basket with the manuscript. "What are you going to do with that?"

"We take it with us. I said I would look after it and that's what I'm going to do," Bruno said adamantly.

"But we know it's contaminated with some kind of evil spirit! Why bring it to Gibraltar and risk infecting everything there? Just leave it here, in crazy fucked-up Tangier, the ghosts will find it and destroy it eventually. We don't need their help, we already have our ferry."

Bruno started to speak but Pancho cut him off. "And please don't give me that 'honor' crap again. There is no honor between Barbary macaques and old white men."

A murmur swept through the other macaques, all of whom had gathered around Bruno and Pancho with only two exceptions. Lefty was sitting on top of an old washing machine picking lice from the fur of Loretta, a particularly becoming member of the group he'd long been attracted to. With the prospect of freedom and a new life on the Rock of Gibraltar ahead of them, the thought of starting a family had entered Lefty's mind for the first time.

"Let's vote," Pancho said. Bruno shrugged his shoulders, then nodded halfheartedly.

Pancho turned to address the other macaques. "How many of you are for taking the manuscript with us and seeing it is returned to the ghosts?"

Eleven paws were raised, while Cheikh looked on.

"How many of you are for leaving the manuscript here and being rid of it and rid of the ghosts?"

Another eleven paws went up. Gradually, all the macaques turned to look at Lefty, who had not raised his paw, occupied as he was with picking fleas out of Loretta's fur. Lefty eventually looked up into the expectant faces of the other macaques and then lazily scratched his left armpit, then scratched the back of his head, and then slowly raised his left paw.

"Okay, settled. We leave the manuscript here. Let's move out. We have work to do and it will be getting light soon."

Pancho turned to Cheikh. "What about you? Are you coming with us? It's probably your only chance to experience freedom."

"Freedom?" Cheikh repeated in a pondering tone. "I understand what you're saying, but I see it differently. You will all be free now, it's true—free to fend for yourself, free to deal with camera-toting tourists who want to feed you junk food, free to be a living spectacle on a lonely lump of rock in the sea, free to be exposed to illness and disease by feral cats and dogs and harbor rats, free to be exposed to the elements and the vicissitudes of nature. As for me, my owners are good and mean well. I am loved, well fed, and well taken care of. I have no worries. I am spared the contingencies of fending for myself. I'm free to contemplate the meaning of existence and the nature of reality. I can lie back on the couch and question the very existence of God. Not even God can do that."

Pancho and the other macaques looked at Cheikh blankly. Pancho reached out his paw and bumped paws with Cheikh. "Peace be with you, brother," he said.

"With you as well," Cheikh replied. "I wish all of you the best of luck in your new life."

41

Laila and Ahmed had already eaten dinner and were in the living room watching television, while Moustapha ate dinner alone in the kitchen after arriving home late from the cemetery. Moustapha had never told his sister about losing his job—he knew that would make him the target of Ahmed's anger and discontent, even more than usual. Ahmed might have even used it as an excuse to kick him out of the house, something he'd threatened on several occasions in the past. But now that Moustapha had succeeded in retrieving Dean's tombstone and gotten his job back, there was no need to mention the entire incident.

Moustapha was feeling much better about his situation in general. Not only had he successfully retrieved and replaced Dean's tombstone in the cemetery, he had also paid off his debt to Tarik, and Ravi Khan would soon be leaving on tour with the Apostles of Pandemonium and therefore not be disturbing the peace and quiet of the cemetery. What's more, Walter Harris's shadow would no longer be falling in the wrong direction, day or night, his remains and ghost now having been resettled in distant Malta, if the ghost of Everly Tweed was to be believed. But could he trust what a ghost had told him about another ghost?

When Moustapha finished eating, he washed and dried his dishes and put them away. He found the jar of majoun at the back of the shelf and spooned out a generous mouthful, washing it down with a glass of tea. He looked up at the kitchen clock and saw it was close to midnight. When he had first heard about the rave at the Gran Teatro Cervantes, it piqued his curiosity slightly, but he had no intention of going. He didn't enjoy large crowds and loud music, but after his experience in the Café Triangle with the strange music that lulled him into a dizzying trance, he realized that events like that could also be a source of enjoyment. He hadn't been inside the Gran Teatro Cervantes in many years and he was intrigued to see what had been done to make a decrepit ruin of a building functional again, if only for a night. And when he thought of the challenges he'd faced recently and how they had all seemingly been resolved, he felt a surge of pride. Some kind of celebration was definitely in order. Moustapha stuck his head in the living room and told Laila and Ahmed he had forgotten something at work and was stepping out. He would see them in the morning.

When he arrived at the Gran Teatro and made his way to the side door, Moustapha saw there was a long line of people waiting to get in. Normally this would have deterred him, but the majoun had kicked in on the walk over from his sister's house and the loud music emanating from inside was already having a magnetic effect, making him even more eager to get inside and experience it firsthand. He kept looking over the shoulders of the people in line in front of him, watching the two big bouncers scanning the people in line. Some were being let in while others were turned away. Moustapha could not tell what criteria the bouncers employed; their decisions seemed totally arbitrary. Maybe it was just people's appearance, in which case Moustapha realized his straw hat and coarse brown burnoose would not improve his chances. Maybe he should have changed from his work clothes into something more appropriate, except that he had nothing appropriate.

As Moustapha neared the entrance and looked closer at the bouncers, he realized one of them was Bachir, the nephew of his brother-in-law. He wasn't sure if that was good or bad. But when Moustapha finally stepped forward to be approved or refused, Bachir looked at him with a derisive grin. "What do you want here? This is no place for country-bumpkin gravediggers."

Moustapha was at a loss for a suitably cutting retort, but the majoun spoke for him: "The gravedigger's respect for the dead knows no bounds. But a corpse can be buried deep, or it can be buried shallow. Respect for the gravedigger is like money in the bank."

Bachir looked at him with a puzzled frown. "Step aside and let the others pass," Bachir said impatiently, giving Moustapha a gentle nudge in the chest.

Moustapha watched from one side as the bouncers continued to sort through the long line of people. He considered going back home, but something about the music seemed to draw him in, pulling at him like an invisible undertow, seducing him like a strange sultry spirit. Then he saw the familiar figure of Kazim just inside the doorway, still wearing his leather flying helmet with the goggles pushed up onto his forehead, but now dressed in a stylish black djellaba with a fine gold pinstripe that seemed to Moustapha particularly chic.

He had not recompensed Kazim for his assistance, but when he thought about it again now, he wasn't sure he really owed him anything. Kazim hadn't actually done any magic or cast any spells, as Moustapha had been hoping, he had merely acted as a middleman in dealing with the Mugwumps and burying Tweed's body. Come to think of it, as long as he had known Kazim he had never seen him actually conduct any kind of sorcery, good or bad. And his attempt at commanding the magic carpet had been anything but convincing. All Kazim ever really did was talk—about crazy stuff like other worlds and other minds, interzones and ultrazones and other quasi-philosophical stuff that didn't make much sense to Moustapha. Perhaps Kazim was a charlatan, a stylish fake. Then again, perhaps philosophy *was* a kind of sorcery, a sorcery that takes place only in the mind?

Moustapha laughed and reminded himself to compliment his sister yet again on her excellent majoun. He waved and caught Kazim's attention, and Kazim gestured for him to step closer. Kazim whispered a few words into Bachir's ear, at which Bachir gave Moustapha a hyper-critical look but then waved him through the open door into the Gran Teatro. His eyes were as big as goose eggs as they scanned the colored clouds of smoke and fog lit by the sweeping lasers, the crowds of people dancing to the music booming from the huge wall of speakers and the huge blue banners suspended from the ceiling, undulating in the shifting air currents.

Brunhilde and Dean stuck to the shadows of the Gran Teatro at first, but as the evening wore on and they saw the hugely diverse and colorful crowd, it seemed highly unlikely to them that anyone would recognize them as ghosts, even if they could see them. Many people were dressed in recognizable costumes—Marie Antoinette, Karl Marx, Mae West, Albert Einstein, Fidel Castro. There was even an older-looking man with a snow-white pompadour and chrome-rimmed sunglasses and a flashy white body suit stretched over a bit of a beer belly who was doing a pretty good job of looking like an older Elvis.

"Maybe it *is* Elvis," Brunhilde said, after Dean had pointed him out.

"Yes," said Dean. "And maybe that's Janis Joplin, and over there Jimi Hendrix and Jim Morrison."

"We should tell Brian Jones, I'm sure he'd like to reconnect."

"I don't think we need to worry about being recognized ourselves. Shall we dance?"

"I'd love to, Dean."

They moved out into the surging crowd.

Meanwhile the Gnawa troupe had come onstage and begun to jam along with the Blue Messiah's acid trance music, its castanet players and drummers locking into the rhythm, while the gimbri players created a throbbing drone on the bass strings with their thumbs. The house lights were slowly dimmed and the huge video screen behind the stage now showed a video loop of a Dreamachine, its revolutions precisely synchronized with the beat of the music.

"Well, look at that," Burroughs said, pointing at the house-high image of the spinning Dreamachine. "Brion's invention has outlived him well."

"Haven't seen one of those in years," Tweed said. "This could become a veritable alpha-wave rave."

Tony Mahoney and Ravi Khan were now on stage as well, plugging in and checking their amps and effects. Gradually they too merged into the groove, joined by a drummer, bass player, and keyboardist. Soon the groove became totally infectious and overwhelming. Almost everyone was dancing or in some way physically reacting to the music. Moustapha stared up at the image of the revolving Dreamachine, letting his body be taken over by the powerful and hypnotic music, unable to resist. On either side of the stage were two large structures of scaffolding covered with papier-mâché so they looked like marble columns. On top of the columns were ornate iron cages in which Marvin and Lee, the two Mugwumps, were go-go dancing, their translucent reptilian skin glowing eerily in the flashing lasers and colored spotlights.

Paul Bowles was up on the balcony just behind the DJ's mixing desk, looking over the Blue Messiah's shoulder as he tweaked the knobs and deftly changed records on the turntables. A lit kif cigarette smoldered in the end of the holder clenched between Bowles's teeth as he tapped with the fingers of his right hand to the rhythm of the music on top of one of the aluminum flight cases.

Burroughs and Tweed had stepped out of the shadows and were at the edge of the balcony looking down at the spectacle, both of them rocking and swaying to the music, Burroughs now and again scratching at the pestering itch that was working its way up his arm. Down on the dance floor Brunhilde was spinning like a whirling dervish while Dean was trying to update his foxtrot and swing dance steps to something more contemporary. Brunhilde glanced up at Ravi onstage and was struck by the look of intense concentration on his face as he played. It was the part of the boyish enthusiasm that had always attracted her to him. She would have loved to go onstage and give him a kiss right then, but she knew it was neither possible nor necessary. He was doing what he liked doing best and he was doing it extremely well, tapped into the mystical source that enabled him to become one with the music. He didn't need help from her, not in this world nor in any other. He'd made it on his own terms, and she was infinitely proud of him. Still, a little kiss might have been nice . . .

Piet and Evangeline had worked their way through the crowd and were dancing just below the stage. Although the beats per minute remained constant, the groove seemed to get deeper and wider, becoming almost four-dimensional in its volume and power. Combined with the Ecstasy and kif and majoun and other mind-altering substances they had consumed, the music was creating vast arrays of hypnogogic images in the brains of almost everyone present, so that the gradually morphing sense of reality was becoming an all-embracing collective experience.

Piet glanced up at the stage to try and figure out how the musicians were creating such a powerful sound. What he saw confused him at first, but then a smile broke across his face. He tapped Evangeline on the shoulder and pointed toward the stage. Together they watched in awe as a pair of iron castanets and a white Vox MK III teardrop guitar, suspended in midair at the back of the stage, both appeared to be played by invisible hands.

"Just ask Ali!" yelled Piet to Evangeline as the band launched into the thundering intro of "Stairway to Hell" and it felt like the entire Gran Teatro Cervantes was about to lift off toward some distant unknown universe.

42

There was a pale orange smudge on the horizon in the otherwise pastel blue of the eastern sky as the weary ghosts lifted off from the Gran Teatro Cervantes and headed for St. Andrew's cemetery. It had been a long night, and even ghosts can only expend so much energy before they need to recharge their spectral metabolisms. It was time to collect the Ultrazone manuscript and consider its final destruction. And the macaques needed a lift to Gibraltar. After the night-long barrage of beats, bass, and acid trance, the scratchy pre-recorded call to morning prayer emanating from the minarets seemed to the ghosts like an ironic twist.

Brian Jones's ghost had decided to stay behind and join the Apostles of Pandemonium. In a way, it was the sort of super-group he'd always dreamed of. Now he could kick out the ghost jams in high style, without that egomaniac Jagger telling everyone what to do. The others drifted through the door of the mausoleum and descended into the crypt below to find it deserted. The oil lamps had burned out during the night, and it was cold and dark; in the air hung the stale odors of banana peels, date pits, melon rinds, orange peels, and macaque shit.

"What the hell?" Burroughs said to no one in particular as he peered into the gloom. "Where'd they all go?" He flew over to the sarcophagus in the wall niche. Except for the dry animal bones at the bottom, it was empty. "Damn!" he exclaimed.

"Maybe they got impatient and went on ahead to the harbor to find a truck," Dean said.

"The first ferry for Algeciras leaves at six a.m. That doesn't give us much time. How many trucks do you think are down there now at the harbor waiting to board the ferries? We're fucked. *Where is that damn manuscript?*"

"They must have taken it with them," Tweed said.

"Why? What good will it do them?"

"You told them to look after it," Brunhilde reminded him.

"Shit," Burroughs said, kicking at a human skull that was lying nearby and sending it skittering across the stone floor. "Let's go topside again. This place is giving me the creeps. It's like an orgone accumulator that only accumulates negative energy, a giant petri dish breeding spores for the Ugly Spirit."

They floated out into the cemetery, now suffused with the soft salmon-colored light of dawn, and gathered in a circle near Dean's broken tombstone, making themselves comfortable on the surrounding graves.

"Now what?" Tweed asked.

"If it was anything else, we could put our heads together, bundle up our ghost radar energies, and probably locate the manuscript. But as we know, the Ugly Spirit will do all it can to jam our radar. Animals seem to be impervious to that, but now we don't have any more animals at our disposal," Burroughs said.

"What about those cats over there?" Gysin suggested, pointing toward several nearby cemetery cats, including Zora, basking in the early morning sun. "They've got good noses. Couldn't they be hypnotized as well?"

In the time it took the other ghosts to turn their heads and look, the cats had all vanished into the most inaccessible recesses of the cemetery.

"Cats are too smart," Tweed said. "I've tried it before."

"It's more likely they'll hypnotize you," Paul Bowles added.

There was a fluttering noise above them and they looked up to see the now familiar seagull descending with something in its beak. As it swooped low over their heads it opened its beak and a piece of folded paper dropped to the ground at Burroughs's feet. "Brion, have a look and see what that is. I don't want to touch it."

Brion picked up the paper and unfolded it. "It's the schedule for the Tangier-Algeciras ferry."

"Great," Burroughs said. "What good is that going to do us?"

"Wait a minute. Someone's marked an X by the one p.m. ferry. Look here . . ." Brion held up the brochure.

"What does that mean?" Brunhilde asked.

"It means we're going to be on the one p.m. ferry to Algeciras," Burroughs said, as he looked up at the seagull flapping away into the distance.

Piet had promised Evangeline he would accompany her to the bank in the morning, but now he was regretting it. They had been dancing all night and he wanted nothing more than to fall into bed and sleep for the rest of the day. Whereas Evangeline wanted to eat breakfast and freshen up a bit before going to the bank. There wasn't time for a leisurely breakfast at the Café de Paris, so the meager hotel breakfast would have to do. She wanted to be at the bank promptly at nine when they opened the doors.

On their way back to the hotel, Piet saw more of the same madness they had noticed last night on the street signs: "Rue Agent K9," "Boulevard Mr. Bradly Mr. Martin," and so on, all the way back to the hotel. It didn't seem as funny now and was starting to demand a plausible explanation.

When they entered the hotel, Evangeline headed straight for the dining room, where they were just starting to serve breakfast. In the Lutetia that meant nothing more than a baguette, butter, and jam, perhaps a hard-boiled egg, and coffee with hot milk. Piet stood in the lobby, looking back and forth between the dining room on the left and the stairs on the right that led to his room. Then he saw Ali at the reception desk, who looked up and gave Piet a smile and a thumbs-up sign. He looked as if he'd just woken up from a refreshing sleep, although Piet had seen him dancing the whole night through. How did he do it? Piet wondered. Piet smiled and returned the thumbs-up gesture, then went into the dining room.

At one minute before nine, Evangeline and Piet were standing outside the bank, which no longer bore the name Interbank, as written on the scrap of paper, but was now the Bank of Gibraltar. From her map, Evangeline figured it must be the right one, given its location in the Place Brahim Roudani, even as on the street sign its name was reshuffled before her eyes into "Place Hauser and O'Brien." An elderly Moroccan man in a threadbare uniform unlocked the door from the inside and let them in. The air-conditioning chilled their skin, and there was a persistent musty smell. Of the three tellers at the counter, one reminded Evangeline of her father and another of an old boyfriend; the third was a somewhat more friendly-looking woman. Evangeline greeted the woman and produced the key. She had thought up a story to explain why she was here, wanting access to a safe deposit box that had presumably lain untouched since well before she was born, but decided that she would say nothing at first and see what happened.

After the teller had walked to the back of the bank and consulted at length with a male colleague, who in turn took the key to another man behind a large desk, where another long conversation ensued, the first man came forward and ushered her and Piet behind the counter and down a spiral staircase into the vault. Two minutes later she was sitting in a small room with the safe deposit box in front of her, Piet standing off to one side.

Evangeline held her breath and lifted the lid. She gasped loudly, and let it fall shut again, then buried her head in her hands. Piet stepped over, lifted the lid, and looked inside. It was empty, except for an old matchbook cover. Piet picked it up and read what was printed on it: *ACME EXTERMINATORS, Chicago, Ill.*

As they walked down the Avenue Mohammed V toward the Café de Paris, Piet could feel Evangeline's disappointment loom between them like a solid barrier. She walked along with her head down, completely lost in her thoughts. He wanted to say something consoling but couldn't think of anything that didn't sound trite, even if he meant it well.

Suddenly Evangeline stopped and looked up at Piet. "That boy with the monkey—he has something to do with this."

"How do you know?"

"I just know it. He had the hat with the key in it for some time, and who knows what happened during that time."

"But if he found the key and got the manuscript from the bank, why would he have sewn the key back into the hat?"

"I didn't say I knew everything—just that he has something to do with all this."

"That neighbor of his who died had the hat for a while, too."

"He's dead. He can't help us. But the kid can. Come on!" Evangeline said, turning around and starting in the opposite direction.

"Where are you going?"

"Are you coming with me or not?"

When they turned the corner by the Hamburguesa into the Rue Mohamed Bergach they saw the street was empty. They walked to the apartment building where they had first seen Sayyad and Cheikh and looked at the buzzers next to the door.

"Which will you ring if you don't know his last name? They're mostly in Arabic, anyway," Piet said.

Evangeline pressed each of the six buzzers several times.

They saw movement through the textured glass, and an old lady in a flowered qaftan opened the front door.

"Hello," Evangeline said. "Do you speak English?"

The woman made a gesture with her hand that might have meant "a little bit."

"The boy with the monkey—he lives in this building, yes?"

The lady nodded her head.

"Can you show me which one?" Evangeline asked, pointing at the buzzers.

The lady pointed at a buzzer with no name next to it, and Evangeline pressed it long and hard.

"Thank you very much," Evangeline said.

The woman smiled and stepped back into the hallway, shutting the door behind her. From somewhere in the building came the sound of flute music.

Evangeline pressed the buzzer again. The music stopped.

There was a noise from up above and they looked up. A window opened and Sayyad stuck his head out and looked down. "What do you want?" he asked.

"Hello Sayyad, remember us? How are you? How's Cheikh?"

"We're okay. What do you want?"

"We thought maybe you could help us."

"What kind of help?"

"We're looking for something. Maybe you'd like to be our guide? We'll pay you."

"I'll be right down."

Sayyad's head disappeared and the window slammed shut.

"Let me do the talking," Evangeline said to Piet as they waited.

The front door opened, and Sayyad stepped out into the street.

"Where's Cheikh?" asked Evangeline.

Sayyad leaned his head against his folded hands. "Sleeping on the couch."

On the walk over from the bank, Evangeline had already figured out the best approach. She said to Sayyad: "Those papers that were in the safe deposit box at the bank—they belong to me and I need to get them back."

Sayyad looked shocked and stepped back toward the doorway. "What papers? I don't have any papers!"

"Sayyad, I didn't say that you did. I'm not accusing you of anything. But I think you might know where they are, and that you could help us find them. We will make it worth your while."

"How much is my while worth?"

From her jeans pocket Evangeline produced a crisp two-hundred-dirham note. "I'll give you this now, and four more when I get the papers back."

Sayyad eyed the two-hundred-dirham note that Evangeline was holding up in front of his face. "A thousand dirhams all together?"

Evangeline nodded.

"Let me get Cheikh and I'll be right back down." Sayyad reached for the two-hundred-dirham note but Evangeline raised it out of his reach.

"That can wait until you come back."

43

Just-Call-Me-Ishmael had only slept a couple of hours but he forced himself to get up and get dressed. His hangover was severe, if not totally debilitating. Normally he would have shown it more attention and even respect, but he wanted to get booked on the lunchtime ferry to Algeciras and catch the next train to Madrid, where he would spend the night. He had a strong urge to visit the Museo del Prado and stand for a while in front of Hieronymus Bosch's *The Garden of Earthly Delights*, bathing in its ambiguous, surreal imagery. It always energized him in a way he couldn't explain. He also wanted to indulge in some decent tapas and wine in his favorite bodega. The second-rate equivalents served in Tangier had never been an adequate substitute. The following morning he would continue by train to Zurich and arrange the sale of the Schwitters. He hadn't looked at the collage since he'd packed it up in its crate again the previous night. Hopefully whatever had caused the strange textual disturbance was no longer an issue. The incident seemed so unreal this morning that it had merged into his memory of the general psychic disorder caused by the Ecstasy he'd taken and the majoun brownies he'd eaten, combined with the amount of alcohol he had consumed, to say nothing of the many joints he had shared during the course of the night.

Leaving the crated collage and his overnight bag in the apartment, he carefully locked the door behind him and walked toward his usual travel agency in the Boulevard Pasteur. It was a bright clear day with a slight breeze—a perfect Tangier day, but also a good day to travel. Adilah in the travel agency said there was still room on the one p.m. ferry. Did he want a day room or just a seat in the lounge?

"I have some valuable items which I would prefer to have under lock and key, so I'll take a cabin," he replied. "With this weather, I'll probably be out on deck the whole time anyway."

"That's where I would be," Adilah said with a smile. She then arranged all his train tickets and booked him a room at his regular hotels in Madrid and Zurich.

Just-Call-Me-Ishmael paid for everything in cash, adding a generous tip, and put the tickets in his inside jacket pocket, next to the folded yellowed manuscript page he had forgotten about in the course of the long psychedelic night. He thanked Adilah and she wished him a pleasant journey. From the travel agency he walked down the boulevard to the Café de Paris, where he wanted to have breakfast before returning to his apartment to collect the collage and his bag. He looked at his watch. By then it would be time to board the ferry.

He found a table outside and ordered an omelette au fromage and a café au lait. The table on his left was unoccupied, and lying on one of the empty chairs was a folded copy of the *International Herald Tribune*, which he picked up and began to browse in while waiting for his omelette. But instead of the usual articles and advertisements and financial section graphs and charts, there were just garbled words that made no sense at all, a swarming jumble of letters that was constantly rearranging itself but never cohered into any kind of meaning. Just-Call-Me-Ishmael quickly folded the paper and set it back down on the chair. He felt a twinge of nausea which he hoped would pass after he'd eaten breakfast.

At the next table to his right an elderly German-looking tourist was reading *Stern*. Just-Call-Me-Ishmael watched as the man's expression turned from one of bemused bewilderment into one of confusion and then anger. He threw the magazine down with a petulant gesture and turned to Just-Call-Me-Ishmael, saying indignantly, *"Was soll das? Alles durcheinander! Was für ein Scheiss!"* But he was speaking a language Just-Call-Me-Ishmael did not understand.

Tony Mahoney and Ravi Khan were helping the roadies load the gear from the Gran Teatro Cervantes into the luggage hold of the tour bus they had backed up to the side door. Although they'd been up all night and were dead tired, they wanted to be sure that everything was packed correctly for the start of the tour, whose first show would be in a Gibraltar club that evening. They were booked on the one p.m. ferry and had no time to lose. Brian Jones found an empty bunk in the back of the bus, slipped in, and shut the curtain. The members of the Gnawa ensemble were waiting in their own van nearby, packed up and ready to go.

Sayyad, Cheikh, Evangeline, and Piet arrived at the warehouse and turned down the small alley that led to the back. Sayyad removed the boards and climbed in through the window, indicating that Evangeline and Piet should follow him. Sayyad called out for Steetoo but there was no answer.

"He must be out making his rounds," Sayyad said.

"What is this place?" asked Piet.

"Our home away from home. Steetoo lives here more or less, when he's not out on the street."

"So where are the papers?" asked Evangeline. Piet could hear the suppressed impatience in her voice.

"Out here," Sayyad said, opening the door and stepping into the main hall. It smelled like machinery and old oil. Evangeline and Piet followed him around the decrepit old trucks to the opposite corner of the warehouse, where there were old washing machines and refrigerators stacked up almost to the ceiling. Sayyad climbed partway up the mountain of appliances and wrenched open the door of an old Maytag washing machine. He pulled out the rattan basket and made his way down to the cement floor of the warehouse.

With one hand he held out the basket; the other hand was extended palm up. "Here," he said.

Evangeline reached for the basket, which Sayyad quickly retracted. "First the money," he said.

"How do I know they're the right papers? Maybe it's just an old telephone book."

Sayyad set down the basket, took out a handful of pages, and handed them to Evangeline. She scanned them closely, flipping through them one by one, stopping now and then to read a few lines. Piet looked over her shoulder and was immediately reminded of the sheets of paper he'd seen blowing down the street the other day, the ones he'd helped the kids retrieve from the tree in front of the Café de Paris. Could they be the same ones?

"Okay," Evangeline said, placing the papers back in the basket and pulling a wad of notes from her pocket. "A deal is a deal."

Sayyad took the notes, folded them together with the other one, and shoved them deep into his front pocket.

As Evangeline picked up the basket Cheikh realized that the papers were changing hands from Sayyad to the Nasrani couple, although he had promised Bruno that he would look after the manuscript and see that it was returned to the ghosts. There may not be any honor between old white men and Barbary macaques, but there is certainly honor among macaques. Cheikh emitted a blood-curdling screech and from his perch on the mountain of appliances, leaped down and attempted to grab the basket from Evangeline. She quickly turned away, clutching the basket to her chest with both arms, and Cheikh landed on the floor empty-handed. Sayyad reined in Cheikh on his leash.

"Cheikh! What's the matter with you?" yelled Sayyad.

Cheikh chattered and growled, but no one understood him.

"What's his problem?" Piet asked.

"I don't know. Lately he's been acting crazy. I think there are some evil spirits in Tangier who are making life difficult."

"Well, there's certainly something in the air," Evangeline said.

"So what are you going to do with all that money?" Piet asked, hoping to defray the tension.

"I'm going to take the ferry to Algeciras and visit my father. He works as a welder in the shipyard there. I haven't seen him in months."

"Don't you go to school?" Evangeline asked.

"No, but I want to. When I come back I'm going to ask my mother to enroll me in school. I want to learn to read and write."

"That's commendable," Piet said, nodding his head in approval. "Do you know what you want to be when you grow up?"

"A writer. A storyteller, like my grandfather was."

"What will you write about?" Evangeline asked.

"About everything that happens. Every time I look around there is a story happening. You don't even need to make anything up. You just have to write it down. You don't have to go to the story, it will come to you."

When Dr. Microbio arrived at his office at nine, the waiting room was already full, and Abdallah was trying to placate a crowd of impatient and nervous patients. Almost all of them complained of the same symptoms—there was something wrong with their eyes. Every time they looked at a sign or a newspaper it seemed to be swimming about and turning into strange words no one had ever seen before. Was it some sort of eye virus? Were they going to go blind? Were they going crazy?

Dr. Microbio treated each of them with a tincture of cannabis dropped directly into the eyes, so they would at least have some pleasant sensations to accompany their hallucinations, and recommended rest and a blindfold until the symptoms subsided. He told them he was not an eye doctor but that it certainly seemed like a virus or maybe an allergic reaction to something in the air—perhaps pollen, or a pollutant from the harbor. No need to worry though; it was certainly a temporary condition.

But the patients kept coming and soon he was running low on the cannabis tincture. Just before noon, Abdallah stuck his head in the door of the treatment room and said there was an urgent call for him in his office. Dr. Microbio finished with the patient, went into his office and picked up the phone. It was his sister Isabella in Gibraltar; their mother had suddenly taken ill and been rushed to St. Bernard's Hospital. Could he come over as soon as possible? Yes, he said, of course. He would catch the next ferry. Dr. Microbio called the travel agency and got himself booked on the next available ferry to Algeciras, which would be leaving Tangier at one p.m. He closed the office at noon, leaving a sign taped to the front door saying he'd gone to Gibraltar for an emergency, went upstairs to his apartment and quickly packed a bag.

Sayyad, Cheikh, Evangeline, and Piet left the warehouse and walked toward the Avenue Mohammed V. Her mission accomplished,

Evangeline wanted to get on the next ferry to Algeciras, from where she could use her Interrail Pass to take the train back to England. Sayyad said that he knew a good travel agency where she could buy a ferry ticket. It went without saying that he got a kickback for bringing in customers. As they neared the travel agency, Evangeline turned to Piet and asked him what his plans were.

Piet had been waiting for that question, but he was still not prepared. They were just passing the Place du Nations and he stopped and looked out over the plaza at the harbor below, sparkling in the sun. He pushed the fingers of one hand through his hair while he squinted into the bright sunlight, letting his mind consider the various contingencies that had been revolving there over the last few days. In the distance he could see a ferry returning from Spain, making the wide turn into Tangier harbor.

"I'll go with you," he said, turning toward Evangeline. "At least as far as Algeciras. Then we'll see what happens."

Evangeline smiled and they turned and continued along the sidewalk. Cheikh kept his eyes on the basket with the manuscript, which Evangeline clutched tightly under her arm. At the first opportunity, he intended to grab the basket, wrench the leash out of Sayyad's hand, and disappear into a side street. From there he would make his way to St. Andrew's and hide the basket in the cemetery until he could make contact with the ghosts.

The woman at the travel agency said the next ferry to Algeciras was at one p.m. and there were still tickets available. Although it was considerably more expensive, Evangeline booked a cabin for two, since she needed a safe place to store the manuscript and it meant they also could sleep a little in a real bed. Sayyad booked himself a place in the lounge and received a discounted ticket for Cheikh.

They parted ways outside the travel agency. Evangeline and Piet were returning to the Hotel Lutetia to pack and check out, while Sayyad was heading home to tell his mother and sister he was going to Algeciras. Cheikh looked back at Evangeline walking down the sidewalk with the basket under her arm and growled. Sayyad yanked at his leash and they started walking home.

The Apostles of Pandemonium's tour bus clanked up the ferry ramp, and a deckhand in a fluorescent yellow vest and hard hat directed them to a parking place deep in the cavernous hold of the ferry. Directly behind them was the smaller Renault van with the Gnawa ensemble. While Tony Mahoney and Ravi Khan retired to their bunks in the back of the tour bus to get some much-needed sleep, the driver and roadies all went upstairs to the bar. As Tony was getting comfortable in his bunk, he thought he heard snoring in a nearby bunk, although the rest of the crew had all gone topside.

"Hey, Ravi, who's that snoring?"

"I don't know," answered Ravi as he climbed into his bunk. "Maybe it's a ghost."

The Gnawa ensemble took their instruments and baskets of food and went up the stairs and out onto the open rear deck, where they spread out rugs and blankets and began to prepare a late breakfast.

Parked a few trucks ahead of the tour bus in the hold of the ferry was the olive oil truck in which the macaques had settled for the journey across the strait. They'd rearranged the cargo in such a way that they had their own little enclave surrounded by cases of oil, hidden from the view of anyone who looked under the canvas covering. But now they were getting hungry again. They had become accustomed to regular mealtimes during their captivity at Mr. Garland's villa, and it was long past their usual breakfast time. Pancho and Lefty volunteered to go out in search of food. Maybe they could break into one of the nearby produce trucks and get some fruit and vegetables; if not, they would head up to the main deck and steal some food from the galley or even from the buffet.

When the uniformed guard asked to see his ticket at the boarding gate, Just-Call-Me-Ishmael pulled out the envelope Adilah had given him at the travel agency and handed over the ferry ticket. The guard took a look at it and laughed loudly, shaking his head. "What's this?" he asked, his smile revealing several gold teeth.

"It's my ticket for the ferry, what does it look like?"

"You tell me," the guard said, handing the ticket back to him.

Just-Call-Me-Ishmael looked closely at the ticket. Had he handed him one of the train tickets by mistake? No, it was the usual red and white FRS ferry ticket with the familiar dolphin logo—except that all the printed information was now just a jumble of words, symbols, and strange ideograms. He quickly looked at the other tickets in the envelope. They had all undergone the same strange transformation. He patted his jacket pocket and felt the folded yellowed manuscript page. Something was starting to make sense, but there was no time now to think it through. He produced a hundred-dirham note from his wallet, folded it into the ferry ticket, and handed it back to the guard. A flash of gold teeth and a hearty "Bon voyage" and Just-Call-Me-Ishmael passed through the doors onto the long catwalk leading to the ferry.

44

Le Rif cleared the jetty and made the wide turn that put it on course for the crossing to Algeciras. Its departure had been slightly delayed, but that was normal for FRS ferries, and no one seemed bothered. The Gnawa ensemble gathered on the rear deck had finished their improvised breakfast and while one of them brewed mint tea on a portable gas stove, the others got out their instruments and began playing. There were still some rough spots in "Stairway to Hell" they wanted to work out before tonight's gig.

The superb weather had drawn most people on deck. They were standing at the railing watching Tangier recede into the distance or sitting on chairs and benches, eyes shut, soaking up the warm sun and breathing in the sea air. The almost subsonic rumble of the engines and the vibration of the hull, combined with the Gnawa music, acted like a tranquilizer, and many passengers had already dozed off, especially those who had attended the all-night rave.

Dr. Microbio sat on a bench not far from the Gnawa ensemble, his pen and notebook in his lap in case a flash of literary brilliance needed to be jotted down before it disappeared into the ether from whence it came. He was absentmindedly watching a flock of gulls that trailed behind the ship, on the lookout for any scraps tossed over the side by the cooks or handouts offered by the passengers. Suddenly he had what seemed like a brilliant idea. What if there was indeed a lost manuscript by the late William Burroughs that had now surfaced in Tangier? And what if it was the host for a kind of virus, a virus that attacked words, both written and spoken? And what if that virus was actually some kind of evil spirit, whose destruction was the only way to stop the virus? What if the story was to begin in the cemetery of St. Andrew's church, with its ingenuous if well-meaning groundskeeper, Moustapha? Dr. Microbio tapped the tip of his Mont Blanc fountain pen against his lip as he pondered the possibilities, spinning them further in his mind. He uncapped the pen, bent forward, and started writing like a man possessed.

Sayyad and Cheikh were seated not far away. They had both been listening to the music and admiring the view until Sayyad eventually dozed off as well. Cheikh was still wide awake, watching the musicians, watching the passengers, watching the gulls, watching everything. Then he caught sight of Evangeline, standing on the other side of the Gnawa ensemble, listening to the music. Evidently she hadn't noticed him and Sayyad. The man was not with her, and she didn't have the basket with the manuscript, either. Instead she held two bottles of Sidi Ali mineral water, one in each hand. When the musicians stopped to take a break, she turned toward the door that led to the lounge and the cabins below. Cheikh carefully undid the knot in the leash with which Sayyad had tied him to the leg of the wooden bench and, making sure that Sayyad was still asleep, sneaked off in the direction Evangeline had gone.

The ferry's lounge was virtually deserted; everyone seemed to have gone outside for the duration of the crossing. Cheikh followed Evangeline at a distance, so she wouldn't notice him when she went down to the lower deck. She walked along the narrow passageway, stopped at the door of a cabin, unlocked the door and went inside.

"Here, I got us some water," she said. "And guess who I met up on deck—Arturo and Ulises, those vagabond poets. Phew! Open that porthole and let some fresh air in here, would you?"

Cheikh heard her lock the door from the inside. He went back up the stairs and up another flight of stairs to the next deck, then went back outside. He went over to the railing between two lifeboats and from there he looked down and saw one open porthole amid the others two decks below. That's where they must be, he thought, and that's where the manuscript was. He made a mental note of the position and started back down to the lower deck where Sayyad was. Just as he was about to step outside, he heard a noise behind him and turned to see Pancho and Lefty coming down the passageway lugging two large black plastic bags that seemed to be heavy.

"Cheikh! Have you changed your mind? You're coming with us?"

"No, we're going to visit Sayyad's father, who works in the shipyard in Algeciras. What's in the bags?"

"Bottled water. We found plenty of food in the trucks below deck, but nothing to drink. We grabbed these from the pantry."

Cheikh told them what had happened in the hours since the group had left the warehouse—how the manuscript had changed hands again and was now in the possession of the Nasrani couple, who were also on board the ferry. He also told them he knew which room they were in.

"I thought we were through with that shit," Lefty said.

"Let's get this water down to the others, then we'll meet up on the lifeboat deck," Pancho said, hefting the bagful of water bottles over his shoulder.

"What happens then?" Cheikh asked.

"I have an idea," Pancho said. "But we'll need your help."

"Okay, see you there in fifteen minutes."

With the Schwitters collage and his bag locked safely in his cabin, Just-Call-Me-Ishmael decided to go on deck to enjoy the sun and sea air. The rear deck was crowded, but he found an empty chair in the shade of a bulkhead out of the breeze and made himself comfortable. He took the envelope with his various tickets out of his inside jacket pocket, along with the yellowed typewritten page. He went through his tickets one by one and saw that every single line of text had morphed into indecipherable gibberish, then unfolded the yellowed sheet and looked at it. He had hardly memorized the text, but it seemed to be totally different to what he had read the night before, as if it too had fallen victim to some strange process of mutation. Just-Call-Me-Ishmael had read enough Burroughs to be familiar with his crazy theories about word viruses and the Ugly Spirit, but he had never taken any of it seriously. Wasn't it all just the product of paranoid drug fantasies that Burroughs had while he was living in Tangier back then? The crazy scribblings of a junk-addled mind?

Just-Call-Me-Ishmael looked again at the tickets and then at the manuscript page, as if by looking closely enough he might find an answer there. What if it was all true? What if the manuscript page was the real thing, and was infecting every kind of text that came into its immediate proximity? In that case it would have to be destroyed, wouldn't it? But that went against Just-Call-Me-Ishmael's entire way of thinking. He should let the auction house in Zurich authenticate the manuscript page and then sell it for a healthy sum. Let someone else worry about any viral and supernatural consequences. That seemed the smarter—and more profitable—course of action. But if all his train tickets and reservations were now useless—how much baksheesh would it end up costing him to bribe his way to Zurich?

Piet drank only a few sips of water then rolled over and went back to sleep. Evangeline watched him sleeping, wondering what their future was, if there even was one. She was attracted to him, but she was also put off by certain aspects of his personality. He was kind of a wimp, lacking the kind of self-assertiveness that Evangeline expected in men. Or was she just projecting clichéd expectations of her own onto his character?

She sat down on the edge of the opposite bunk and pulled the leather shoulder bag into which she'd transferred the Ultrazone manuscript toward her. She took the huge bundle of paper in her hand, weighing it thoughtfully. So it was true—there really was a trove of previously unknown Burroughs writings. The hour she'd had at the hotel to leaf through the manuscript had been enough time for her to be convinced of that. There were passages that featured familiar Burroughs figures such as Dr. Benway and the Sailor, but also ones she'd never seen before. More excitingly, there were evidently hundreds of pages written in a very different style, in which a cacophony of voices by turns anguished and brutal, pleading and monstrous, clashed with each other. Apparently Burroughs had ventured so deeply into his own subconscious that what he encountered there frightened even himself. Had he come face to face with the Ugly Spirit? Or had he made a discovery that was even more revealing, more terrifying—that where he expected to find the Ugly Spirit, the very incarnation of evil, there was in fact no one other than William Seward Burroughs?

If she handled matters intelligently, which she trusted herself to do, there was a good living to be made curating, editing, and publishing all this. It could become a literary sensation. And she would be the sole beneficiary. She had inherited it; she hadn't stolen it. There might be legal issues to negotiate with greedy heirs and obstinate estate executors, but she could deal with that. It was still very much a man's world, but she had been learning how to navigate it for some time now.

She glanced at a few pages and was immediately reminded of what it was she did *not* like about Burroughs. In his work he had spoken out against control and subjugation, yet for the greater part of his life he had been unable to free his mind and body from the metabolic tyranny of heroin. He had advocated for the expansion and altering of human consciousness, yet his preferred drug was heroin, one of the most mind-numbing drugs available. There were other contradictions—his love for cats coexisting with his abiding fascination with guns, for example—signs of an irreconcilably split personality, especially since he had shot and killed his own wife. But it was his antisemitism and misogyny that bothered her the most. They weren't just provocative elements in his many fictions, intended to stir up emotions—Burroughs expressed similar sentiments over and over in his voluminous correspondence, which Evangeline had read thoroughly prior to leaving for Tangier. And much of what had been written about Burroughs made no reference to his offensive attitudes toward women and Jews. Why all the myopic hero worship, she wondered. Who was afraid of the truth, afraid of kicking the pedestal from under the feet of their idol? Maybe publishing Ultrazone would help set the record straight. First she would have to read it all. Who knew what was waiting there?

Evangeline put the manuscript back in her bag and picked up the battered, sweat-stained fedora, pondering its existence briefly before tossing it back on the bunk. She got up and looked out through the open porthole; blue sky and blue sea, a range of dry brown hills in the distance, a lone seagull executing strange avian acrobatics. She looked at Piet, gently snoring in the opposite bunk, then went over and lay down next to him. Soon she too was fast asleep.

Cheikh was back at the railing between the lifeboats, looking down at the open porthole, when Pancho and Lefty came up the stairs and joined him.

"You see?" said Cheikh, pointing down at the single open porthole. "That one there."

Pancho looked around, then went over to one of the lifeboats, lifted the canvas tarp, and crawled underneath, emerging after a minute or so with a coil of orange polypropylene rope.

"Here," Pancho said to Cheikh, gesturing for him to step closer. "One end of this we'll tie around your waist."

"Wait—why me?"

"Because you're the smallest. You'll fit through the porthole easiest."

After they had improvised a harness and Cheikh was secured to one end of the rope, he climbed onto the railing and looked over the side of the ship. It was a long way down, and the water was deep and going by fast. He was a good swimmer, but if he were to fall, it would be very unlikely he would be rescued, and because of the treacherous currents there was no way he could swim all the way to Spain or back to Morocco.

"You guys, I don't know about this."

"Cheikh, no one is forcing you to do this, of course," Pancho said. "You're free to decide for yourself. As I'm sure you know, that's one of the difficulties inherent in the concept of freedom—you can never escape it. It's not exactly a curse, but the freedom to decide will never leave you alone."

"Okay, okay, but let me down *slowly*."

Gripping the rope firmly in their paws, Pancho and Lefty slowly lowered Cheikh down the side of the hull until he was even with the open porthole. He waved to tell them to hold the rope where it was while he grasped the edges of the porthole. After peering inside, he then clambered into the cabin. Evangeline and Piet were fast asleep together; on the opposite bunk lay their luggage, the fedora, and a leather shoulder bag that must contain the manuscript. As quietly as he could Cheikh crept down onto the bunk, checked the contents of the shoulder bag, then put the strap around his neck. It was much heavier than he remembered. He glanced at the fedora but decided to leave it where it was. He turned and was about to climb back out the porthole when Piet suddenly coughed and stirred. Cheikh froze. After a long moment, Piet began snoring. Evangeline rolled over but did not wake up.

Cheikh crawled through the porthole and waved at Pancho and Lefty, who began to hoist him back up to the upper deck.

"Good work," Lefty said, patting Cheikh on the shoulder when he had climbed over the rail, with the leather bag hanging securely around his neck.

Pancho untied the rope, coiled it, and put it back in the lifeboat.

"Now what?" asked Cheikh.

"Follow us," Pancho said, turning and ascending a steep ladder nearby.

The ghosts of Burroughs, Tweed, Gysin, Bowles, Dean, and Brunhilde, not being in any kind of hurry, had convened on the flying bridge of the ferry just as it was departing Tangier. Access to the flying bridge was permitted only to crew members attending to the radar and other navigational equipment, so the ghosts had it all to themselves. They were glad for an opportunity to just be tourists, albeit elite tourists, and they all laughed at the delay in departure; some things just never changed. As the ferry left the harbor and turned toward Spain, they looked on in silence. The view was breathtaking, and even the breathless ghosts were vastly impressed.

"A beautiful day for a cruise," drawled Burroughs as the cubist sprawl of Tangier receded into the distance.

"What's this all about, Bill?" asked Dean. "Why did we need to take the one p.m. ferry to Algeciras?"

"Because I love English marmalade."

"Cut the crap, Bill," Gysin said. "You act like you know something that we don't."

"I made an entire career out of that," Burroughs answered with a smile.

Strains of Gnawa music from the rear deck came wafting up on the breeze, and a man's voice could be heard calling "Paloma? Paloma?" from somewhere below.

"Man, that was a hell of a party," Gysin said. "I haven't had that much fun since the Master Musicians of Joujouka played in my restaurant."

"What did you make of that Gnawa–rock fusion, Paul?" asked Brunhilde.

"Oh, you know me, Brunhilde. I've always been sort of a purist, whether it's the purely indigenous or the purely avant-garde. To me it seemed a little forced, and not entirely successful. As your people would say, *weder Fisch noch Fleisch.*"

"Reading you loud and clear," said Burroughs. "But the punters didn't seem to mind. All in all, quite a shindig, I'd say."

From out of nowhere a sheet of paper fluttered past them and out to sea, followed by another, then another. Burroughs snatched one out of the air as it flew past and looked at it closely. "I knew it," he said, slowly turning around and looking up. The others turned as well. There, on the uppermost platform at the top of the ferry's communications mast, stood Pancho, Lefty, and Cheikh, flinging handfuls of papers out into the stiff breeze, which carried them out to sea.

"What the hell are they doing?" asked Tweed.

Burroughs handed Tweed the sheet of paper. He took it and after briefly scanning it, looked back up at Burroughs with an astonished expression. "It's the Ultrazone manuscript!" he exclaimed.

"In all its hoary glory," Burroughs confirmed.

The pages flew past them in a blizzard now, and the other ghosts each grabbed one to look at, then released them and watched them blow out into the Mediterranean blue. The pages were so dried out and brittle that no sooner had they landed in the cold, salty water the ink began to dissolve, and within minutes the paper had disintegrated. And the chronic itch that had been pestering Burroughs since he'd picked up a stray page of the manuscript in the cemetery abruptly ceased.

45

The ghosts moved over to the railing of the flying bridge to watch as the last pages of the manuscript decomposed into gelatinous globs bobbing on the surface of the water, then broke apart and disintegrated into nothingness.

"Well, I hope that's the end of that," Dean said.

"I hope so too," Burroughs said. "Although there's no certainty when you're dealing with the Ugly Spirit. Like I said before, even one rogue page could start the whole machinery in motion again."

"Seems to me the apes did a pretty thorough job," said Tweed.

"Thanks to you, Tweed," Burroughs said.

"That's our only hope," said Gysin.

"Just think what might have happened if that young couple had run off with the manuscript," said Bowles.

"I'd rather not," Burroughs said. "A word virus pandemic." He looked up at the macaques again and gave them a military-style salute in recognition of a job well done. The macaques waved back and began to descend from their airy perch.

Burroughs turned around and leaned on the railing, watching Tangier as it receded into the distance. "You know, Heidegger once said that 'language is the house of being.' But when you have the Ugly Spirit for a roommate, you're in deep shit."

"Bill, you knew something like this was going to happen out here, right?" suggested Brunhilde.

"Let's just say I had an inkling."

"But how?" asked Gysin.

"Our avian messenger, that seagull."

"You mean Aicha?" asked Bowles.

"I'm not so sure that was Aicha. I think it may have been Joan."

"Joan? I don't follow you," said Bowles.

"I'm thinking Joan hacked the ghost of Aicha and used her powers to help destroy the manuscript. Thus exorcizing the Ugly Spirit and freeing me from its lifelong curse, a curse that even followed me into the afterlife. Maybe it's Joan's way of showing she's forgiven me."

"Sounds plausible," said Brunhilde. "Forgiving is a form of compassion, after all."

"Yeah, why not?" Dean said thoughtfully.

"Anyway, it looks like I won't be needing this stuff anymore."

They watched as Burroughs removed the various items from his pockets that had accompanied him into his coffin and dropped them over the railing one by one—the Smith & Wesson .38 revolver, the packet of heroin, the Indian-head five-dollar gold piece, the reading glasses and ballpoint pen, each vanished into the water below. He was about to flip the three joints over the rail when Dean put his hand on Burroughs's. "Wait a minute, Bill. That's perfectly good dope. Why waste it?"

"I'm no longer a factor in the formula of desire, Dean. Right now I'm as high as I'll ever need to be."

"Well, maybe you'd consider making a donation to those of us who are not yet entirely freed from the bonds of earthly desire."

Burroughs hesitated, then smiled and handed the joints to Dean. Gysin produced a Zippo and lit one of the joints while Dean inhaled deeply. "You sure you don't want a hit, Bill?" Dean asked through clenched teeth, trying to let as little smoke escape as possible.

"Okay, but just one hit. Last thing I need is another damn habit."

Burroughs took a deep drag then passed the joint to Tweed. A strange sound came from above, like cackling laughter, and they looked up to see a lone mottled-white seagull lift off from the observation post the Barbary macaques had recently left. They watched as it ascended and joined a flock of seagulls flying in the direction of Tangier.

Just-Call-Me-Ishmael was still sitting in a chair on the rear deck, puzzling over his now useless tickets and the yellowed page lying in his lap, weighing the various quandaries inherent in his current dilemma. The Gnawa ensemble had finished their tea and launched into an impromptu jam, loosely based on the "Stairway to Hell" riff but hewing closer to the scales and patterns of traditional Gnawa music.

Cheikh had accompanied the other macaques back to the olive oil truck and bid them farewell. They had asked again if he wanted to join them; again he had declined. He returned to his place next to Sayyad, who was still sprawled out asleep on the bench, and retied the knot in his leash that was attached to the leg of the wooden bench. As Cheikh sat there on the warm steel deck, a strange feeling overcame him, as if the music of the Gnawa ensemble was pulling back a veil and revealing aspects of reality of which he'd previously been unaware. All his senses seemed hyper-acute. The evil energy he had sensed in the apartment when the manuscript had been there in the basket on the floor—it seemed to be present again. But how could that be? Had he and his brethren not just overseen the manuscript's destruction? He looked around at the other passengers, nostrils widening and contracting, eyes alert and glinting.

Just-Call-Me-Ishmael was not one to tarry when it came time to make a decision. He would continue to Zurich and sell the Burroughs manuscript page at the auction house. He no longer had any doubt about its authenticity. How else to explain all the textual madness that had been unleashed since he first picked up that stray page in the street? It wasn't coincidence; it was some kind of malign magic. He was certain the manuscript page would bring a healthy sum, easily enough to cover the baksheesh he would have to lay out on the rest of his journey. Before folding up the manuscript page and returning it to his pocket, he picked it up to study it a little more closely, to see if he could possibly discern anything meaningful. How did an evil spirit occupy a text if the text wasn't even aware of it?

From over his right shoulder a furry arm suddenly shot into view and a small hand grabbed the page and just as quickly vanished with it. Just-Call-Me-Ishmael turned and saw a macaque scurry away between the legs of a crowd of passengers. Not *again*, he thought. He jumped up and went after the macaque but could not keep up with him and soon lost sight of him altogether. Cheikh reached the stern of the ferry and gracefully jumped up and landed on the railing, which he then gripped firmly with his feet. He wadded up the manuscript page into a tight ball and tossed it out over the water, so that it landed in the swirling white foam of the ferry's wake.

As though some invisible hand had pressed a huge reset button, every corrupted text, letter, magazine, ticket, notebook entry, and street sign in Tangier and on the ferry at once reverted to its original state. People rubbed their eyes in astonishment but soon turned their attention back to everyday events as if nothing unusual had happened. This was Tangier, after all, where mysterious, inexplicable things were known to happen from time to time.

The six ghosts were looking ahead at the port of Algeciras and the Rock of Gibraltar looming up to their right.

"So now what?" Dean asked.

"My business here is settled," Burroughs said. "I'm thinking of heading to Madrid to see if I can find the ghost of my old Tangier boyfriend, Kiki. The one who was murdered there by an insanely jealous Cuban bandleader in 1957. He was the sweetest of kids, one of the true loves of my life, and I would like nothing more than to rekindle that romance. If I can't find Kiki, maybe I'll head to China. I hear the Wuhan Institute of Virology will soon become mainland China's first biosafety level four laboratory. SARS, influenza, encephalitis, dengue fever, anthrax—you name it, they're working on it. They might be on the threshold of some kind of breakthrough. And you know me, I love breakthroughs. What about you, Dean?"

"Brunhilde and I are going back to Tangier. There's still the issue of her unsolved murder, and I've volunteered to help her get to the bottom of that. With my old connections and knowledge of the seamy underside of Tangier, I'm sure I can be of assistance."

"You're certainly the right man for the job," Burroughs said. "But if you need any help, don't hesitate to give me a call on the ghost grapevine. How about you Brion, where to and what to do there in the netherworld?"

"Paul and I have talked about revisiting the southern Sahara. After all this malevolence and treachery, we both felt we'd like nothing more than to bask in the vast silence of the sand dunes. No better way to clear your head. And maybe see if there's still any indigenous music to be heard, although the chances are slim these days."

"And you, Mr. Tweed?"

Tweed looked a little surprised, as if he'd been caught off guard, though it must have been obvious the question was coming.

"I don't know! I hadn't really given it any thought. I'm still quite new to all this afterlife stuff. But I quite enjoyed revitalizing my psychic powers and hypnotizing those apes."

Tweed turned and looked at the Rock of Gibraltar, steadily

growing in size as they approached the harbor of Algeciras. "Maybe there's a future for me there with the rock apes. Spiritual trainer; psychic coach for the team; who knows? Maybe we can work up an act and freak out the tourists. That would be fun. At any rate, I've had enough of human nature to last me several lifetimes. What I like about dealing with animals is that deceit doesn't seem to be a part of their behavioral vocabulary."

"Amen to that," said Burroughs. "You know, I spent most of my life working on a project that was intended to free the human mind from its various social-culture strictures, an ongoing deconditioning, if you will. But maybe that was just too tall of an order. The human species has undergone many changes in the course of its evolution, but not all of them were for the better. On the contrary, the way it looks now, mankind may eventually snuff itself out altogether. But look, the dinosaurs didn't survive, and the human race may not survive, but the apes are still going strong. You know that DEVO song, 'Jocko Homo'? 'God made man, but he used a monkey to do it.' I think they might have been on to something there. Maybe it's time to climb back down the ladder of evolution, take a good long look around, and consider what went wrong. A little de-evolution might be just the thing."

The ghosts all turned toward the Rock of Gibraltar and looked at it with reverence as they contemplated the metaphysical implications of this last bit of Burroughs wisdom.

A change in the sound of the ferry's engines and an increase in the frequency of the hull's vibrations caused Dr. Microbio to look up with a start. The Rock of Gibraltar loomed across the bay in all its bleak majestic glory, while to his left the container cranes of Algeciras harbor were silhouetted like great spidery creatures against the bright sky. He stood up and stretched. He had a cramp in his neck and his shoulders hurt. He realized now that he had not looked up once during the entire crossing, not since he'd started writing. He looked down at the notebook in his hands and smiled. Finally he had been blessed with the lightning bolt of genius that he had been yearning for all these years. Something about the combination of the Gnawa music, the warmth of the sun on the rear deck, and the steady drone of the ship's engines had produced the appropriate setting for his creative powers to be unleashed in a rush of literary brilliance. Now he had it, the ultimate concept, the great tale of the lost William

Burroughs manuscript with all its inherent contingencies. His entry into the pantheon of literary greats would soon be secured.

Wondering how much he had actually written, Dr. Microbio opened his notebook and began flipping through the pages. Where he expected to find page after page covered with a frenetic script that might have seemed foreign even to him, as if some unknown madman had feverishly scrawled across the pages, crossing out words, adding new ones, smearing blots of ink in some demonic rush, there was nothing. The entire notebook contained not a single word. He was certain he had been writing, but it was as if it had all been erased by some mysterious force. All he had to show for his inspiration were a few ink stains on his fingers and an empty Mont Blanc fountain pen.

In the cemetery at the Church of St. Andrew Moustapha stood waist-deep in a grave he had started digging earlier that morning. Other than the repetitive sound of the shovel's blade biting into the earth and the droning buzz of the cicadas it was quiet and peaceful. The funeral service for Mrs. Walcott, who had died suddenly the day before, was scheduled for later that afternoon. Mrs. Walcott's death was not something Moustapha saw as a loss; her proximity to the cemetery, her nosiness and gossiping had been the source of much annoyance over the years. For Moustapha, her passing was just another of the many recent improvements in his situation, a further indication that the baraka was flowing properly again.

He continued digging with the steady rhythm he had learned over the years, a plodding, persistent motion that enabled him to dig for hours without getting tired. He didn't even have to think about it, allowing him to conserve his energies, freeing his mind to consider entirely different matters while the grave gradually grew deeper, almost on its own.

He heard a familiar meow and saw Zora padding out of the shadows, looking for a suitable patch of sunlight between the trees in which she could stretch out for a few lazy hours until the first mourners arrived for the funeral. Moustapha leaned the shovel against the wall of the grave and stood up. He bent over backwards to get the crook out of his spine then stood upright again. Removing his straw hat, he mopped the sweat from his forehead with his handkerchief. The cat had found a sun-warmed spot and set about some serious pre-nap preening and cleaning.

Then Moustapha heard Zora growl and looked over to see what the problem was. She was staring up through a wide opening between the trees and growled again, a low guttural growl Moustapha had heard before that usually did not bode well. Moustapha looked up too and saw a ragged V-shaped formation of seagulls flying in from the direction of the harbor. One mottled-white bird was out of line, a little off to one side. Suddenly this gull made a 180-degree turn yet continued flying forward while facing backward. A minute later it swiveled around again without missing a wing beat and continued with the others.

Moustapha felt a shadow passing over his soul and a chill ran down his spine. The cicadas had lapsed into silence. He stuffed the handkerchief back in his pocket, pulled the straw hat firmly down on his head, spat into the palms of his hands and rubbed them together, then resumed digging with forceful yet measured strokes. He dug at the same pertinacious pace he had dug all his life, as though the continuation of that very life depended on it. He dug as if he were planning to dig down into the earth and eventually disappear in its depths, down past the worms and grubs and shards of Phoenician pottery, down through the arm of the tunnel connecting the crypt and the warehouse, where at that very moment, unknown to Moustapha or Zora or anyone else in the world, a single page of the Ultrazone manuscript that had fallen out of the basket as the macaques were carrying it to the warehouse was undergoing a strange transformation.

That page bore only a few hand-scribbled words—mere fragments, barely legible, and hardly enough to host even a sinus infection, much less a bona fide word virus. But the Ugly Spirit's will to power, still latent in even the faintest smear of microscopic DNA, knew no limitations and was forever anticipating its next manifestation. There in the dank, dark tunnel the page rustled and quivered, crackling and flexing, about to execute an act of amoeba-like mutational self-reproduction which would not be without certain dire consequences for all and sundry.

DEAN
MISSED BY ALL
AND SUNDRY
DIED
FEBRUARY, 196

About the Authors

MARK TERRILL was born in Berkeley, California, shipped out as a merchant seaman, and has traveled extensively as a tour manager for various bands (American Music Club, Mekons, etc.). He participated in the School of Visual Arts writing workshop taught by Paul Bowles in Tangier in 1982, and has returned to the city many times. His 2002 memoir, *Here to Learn: Remembering Paul Bowles*, was recently republished by Moloko Print. His collections of poems and prose poems include *Bread & Fish* (The Figures, 2001), *Great Balls of Doubt* (Verse Chorus Press, 2020), *The Undying Guest* (Spuyten Duyvil, 2023), and numerous chapbooks. He has lived in Germany since 1984.

FRANCIS POOLE taught for some years in the 1980s at the American School of Tangier, where he became friends with Paul Bowles. He has also lived and taught English in Portugal. His publications include *Lisbon: Poor Man's Paris* (Exquisite Corpse), *Tangier and the Beats: Sanctuary of Noninterference* (International Quarterly), *Hotel Nassin* (New Feral Press), and *Everybody Comes to Dean's: Dean's Bar, Tangier*. His poetry has appeared in *Bukowski Review*, *New York Quarterly*, *Poetry East*, *Rolling Stone*, and elsewhere. A collection of his poems, *Snakeskin Raincoat*, was published in 2011 by Poporo Press. He lives in Delaware and edits *BLADES Ze Magazene*.

In addition to co-authoring *Ultrazone*, Mark Terrill and Francis Poole have published two collaborative chapbooks of poetry, *The Spleen of Madrid* and *A Pair of Darts* (Feral Press).

Acknowledgments

An excerpt from *Ultrazone* first appeared in *BODY*. Mark Terrill's story "The Travelers" was first published in *Urban Graffiti* and subsequently as a chapbook by Feral Press. Francis Poole's poems "West of Ceuta," "The Big Feast," and "His Own Two Feet" are taken from his collection *Snakeskin Raincoat*, published by Poporo Press. Special thanks to Steve Connell for his editorial savvy and commitment above and beyond the call of duty.

www.ingramcontent.com/pod-product-compliance
Lightning Source LLC
Chambersburg PA
CBHW030120010826
48973CB00002B/356